TOO MUCH TIME TO KILL

TOM MACKINNON

Paperback edition:
Also available in multiple e-book formats.

Published by:
The Endless Bookcase Ltd,
Suite 14 STANTA Business Centre, 3 Soothouse Spring,
St Albans, Hertfordshire, AL3 6PF, UK.

More information can be found at:
www.theendlessbookcase.com

ISBN: 978-1-914151-98-9

For Lil

ABOUT THE AUTHOR

This is the first book in the three book *"Bremner"* series. The author, having completed thirty-six years military service, spent three fulfilling years in Afghanistan attempting to disarm warlords. This led him to set up his own company specialising in crisis management. In quieter moments, free from the remorseless tyranny of demanding deadlines, he once again picked up the pen.

Influenced by Cornwell, Clancy, Archer and Forsyth – and a devoted fan of Ian Rankin and James Grant writing as Lee Child - it was actually reading Frank Gardner's *Crisis* and immediately thereafter, *Ultimatum*, which provided the inspiration to attempt his own book. Sharing a similar background to Gardner's principal character – Luke Carlton – explains why he chooses to write under a pseudonym.

Helpfully, having spent much of his professional life advising ministers, ambassadors and heads of foreign governments, colouring-in the storyline's political backdrop proved to be fun and comparatively stress-free.

Quite deliberately, the Book's narrative only involves countries, cities and streets of which the Author has personal knowledge; the corridors, alleyways, cafes and exotic locations are all, or once were, familiar haunts. The exception, which he invented, is an open prison in the English county of Shropshire, near to home on the banks of his beloved River Severn.

1

THE AUTUMNAL weather was awful; clouds rushing across the dark, overcast sky, swirling winds and torrential rain lashing the windows. At best described as tacky and long past its heyday, the hotel suite was equally depressing and, in a word, tired. Not that their surroundings mattered to the three men sitting around the small conference table littered with abandoned coffee cups and remnants of a sandwich lunch.

They had been there most of the day. The youngest of the three was the first to break what was becoming an embarrassingly protracted and uncomfortable silence. "Let me be sure I've understood correctly," he began. "You are asking if I'm okay with the idea of being shot. Have I got that right?"

Exchanging a look with his associate before answering, one of the other two said, "Yes, that's the essence of it."

"And you've got someone in mind have you to... you know... do it?"

"Yes, we don't envisage that being an issue."

"And I'll be on my own, will I?"

"Yes and no: there will be others in the vicinity and, if needed, medical assistance won't be far away."

"If bloody needed?" the younger man, Callum, said with increasing incredulity. "You're telling me I'm going to be shot! Of course I'm going to want medical bloody backup."

"Quite understood. We'll have to have your blood group… you know… just in case."

1

"In case of what, exactly? And whilst we're on the subject, where is it you have in mind for me to be shot?"

"Do you mean geographic location or specific part of your anatomy?"

"Both?"

The other man intervened. "Ah, well… we're still working on location but, in answer to the second question, most likely the lower abdomen – avoiding major organs, of course." A further silence ensued.

"You're serious about this, aren't you?"

"Oh absolutely," came the reply.

"Bit of an ask, don't you think?"

"Trust: it ultimately comes down to trust."

"Trust in who, precisely? The person who's going to shoot me?"

Turning to his colleague, "Perhaps this might be an opportune moment to take a short break?"

****

"Sod off," the figure mouthed silently at the brown rat staring defiantly from above. He'd heard them scurrying about during the night – one brushing against his leg – but this was the first face-to-face encounter. Devoid of cobwebs, the old wooden beams reminded him of airport runways and looked to be in regular use. "Go and annoy someone else; I'm busy – well, I will be soon."

It was April in the English county of Shropshire. Prompted by a demented neighbourhood cockerel with serious time management issues, birdsong had started horribly early and was ratchetting-up by the minute. Only to be expected in early spring, he surmised, what with mates to find, nests to build and territory to defend. There was a chill in the air but it promised to be a fine, cloudless day. The sun was starting to warm the small, long-abandoned farm building where he now sat.

Standing on rising ground, the dilapidated structure was ideally suited for his purpose. Partially clad in ivy and surrounded by ever-encroaching brambles interspersed with gorse, the old barn was conveniently flanked by scattered woodland. Crucially, it commanded an uninterrupted view of what could easily be mistaken for some sort of industrial complex a short distance away, where the ground flattened at the bottom of the slope. It was the reason he was here.

Stretching his shoulders and strenuously massaging aching knees, he refilled a cup of tepid coffee from his flask and reached into a bag for a handful of broken-up biscuits, mixed with chocolate and raisins.

Approaching eight o'clock in the morning, thus far everything had gone to plan. Confirming the barn's suitability the previous month – approaching then, as now, in darkness and reliant on night vision goggles – he was acutely aware of its precarious state and had exercised inordinate care negotiating the deeply rotted wooden stairs leading up to the small loft. As before, he'd heard the owls and, on entering, seen copious rat droppings littering the creaking floorboards. It smelt and felt old.

Positioning mattered. He wanted the sun behind him – preferably with any shadow falling forward off the building. Conveniently, natural gaps already existed where old masonry had come away from some of the walls. The couple of small pieces he'd removed at one of the gable ends during the recce didn't look out of place.

Resuming the uncomfortable prone position on the floor and munching the last of his meagre breakfast, he returned to his observation post. The cluster of buildings he saw before him was already showing signs of activity – sights and sounds conforming to patterns he had noted previously. Adrenalin was fighting off tiredness, but he knew he'd closed his eyes for an involuntary catnap once

3

or twice during the night. Dismissive of pills to stay awake and equally the use of a sleeping bag, there was a reassuring familiarity about the circumstances in which he found himself. Success was all about getting the small things right and the long hours spent poring over large-scale maps and photographs were now repaying in spades.

In the event, the stealthy approach to the barn had been circuitous but incident-free. Carefully avoiding boggy ground, he had taken great care to reduce discernible ground sign as much as possible and, other than a solitary dog-fox padding purposefully along a hedge line beneath him, there had been nothing of note. Even the sheep, huddled for warmth with young lambs in the shelter of low stone walls, had been disinterested. *No thermals for you*, he'd mused passing silently by.

The importance of the assignment left no room for misunderstanding. "There will be one chance," they'd said. "Once you're done, don't hang about because the reaction will be fast and thorough: you won't be able to move for flashing blue lights." He had felt the lecture unwarranted but chose to let it go. There had been other jobs in different parts of the world but none quite so technically challenging. This would be a first. Any private misgivings were confined to what he regarded as Phase 3 – the tricky part, his exit plan – in which, like the approach, he had invested hours and hours of painstaking research. Unusually – which did not sit at all comfortably with him – this time he would be reliant upon others.

The final hours were always the most trying: self-doubt battling to assert itself and playing games with the subconscious – a distraction he could do without as the clock ran down. Affectionately stroking the bipod-mounted rifle in front of him, he once again checked the graduation settings on the telescopic scope. Intimately familiar with its renowned idiosyncrasies, there was something very reassuring about the Remington 700. A thing of beauty and exquisite craftsmanship, the rifle was self-selected as his weapon of choice. Thankfully, someone else was footing the bill for the expensive modifications: an extended floating barrel, bipod to aid stability, a lightened trigger and re-engineered bolt. He had no regrets about insisting on the noise-reducing suppressor or external ten-round magazine since it – or rather he – needed to deliver the intended effect, at the required range – accuracy guaranteed. Personally having hand-loaded the Match-quality bullets, coupled to the hours spent patiently zeroing the rifle on the Isle of Lewis – a familiar and essential ritual that could not be rushed or ignored – they had bonded.

In technical terms, the distance to the target was not especially challenging. He could dispense with laser sights – the associated red dots of which he knew were guaranteed to strike fear into mortal souls. Alas, this assignment would have to be handled the traditional way and, with only ten rounds available, he did not want to be messing about changing magazines. Shots would be fired in quick succession; the final one or two ultimately defining success or failure.

Once its job was done, the rifle would be returned to the fishing rod case. In due course, should for any reason his extraction plan unravel, the fisherman cover made sense – at least initially because trout and grayling inhabited the brooks, streams and rivers of Shropshire. If necessary, as a fallback, the rifle, rucksack and all clothing could all be dumped in the deep contingency hide he'd prepared during his recce. Nothing of forensic use would be found in the barn and he would take with him all spent ammunition cases and the polythene bag full of his piss and crap.

There would be no more coffee now; his heart rate and breathing needed to be nice and steady. Looking through the scope's aperture and once again checking the rifle's bipod, there was nothing more to do. Time to kill. Almost too much. He felt calm; his resting pulse of sixty exactly where it should be. Now it was all about experience, recalling lessons never forgotten:

"Take your time in the approach; align your body correctly when in the prone position; properly assess the range, altitude and wind before finalising the settings on the scope; establish good breathing control, commit to the shot and under no circumstances snatch the trigger."

He stared at the rat and the rat stared back – holding his gaze a little longer before cautiously scuttling off along the beam on more urgent business.

2

CALLUM BREMNER was becoming increasingly worried about losing focus. They said it would happen over time. Being honest with himself, he was feeling the stress, not helped by having badly underestimated the unrelenting mind-numbing monotony of prison life. Not so much the confinement and restrictive regime, but rather the lack of what he felt was any serious effort by the authorities to rehabilitate those in their charge. It had been an eye-opener. The only saving grace – deliberately arranged in his case because it would have added an unnecessary complication – was not having to share a cell.

With only days left to serve, he was determined to avoid mistakes. He had to remain vigilant: putting as much space as possible between himself and the other cons – many of whom were a lot older and, judging by their demeanour, *"institutionalised"*. He found it perplexing that not everyone relished the prospect of release and, what troubled him the most, some would unquestionably contrive to find ways to prolong their stay. And that made them a threat.

Of necessity, and despite the minimal security regime associated with *"open prisons"*, set routines were observed and enforced, Sundays providing the only respite. Most mornings, Bremner would be busying himself in the vegetable allotment where, to his surprise, he had rediscovered a childhood interest in growing things. Last year's courgettes, runner beans and beetroots had been a triumph, less so the potatoes and marrows. Working the soil to prepare for early planting kept him busy and he thrived on the manual labour. Impervious to the weather, and well accustomed to the daily ritual, he never found the work onerous. There was something hugely satisfying about seeing the first green shoots appear. Happy in his own company, solitude rarely troubled him and his natural curiosity and propensity for physical work combined to fill the day.

As a young man he had been taught to fish by those skilled in the dark arts of pursuing trout and salmon. It taught him patience. Fishermen are naturally inquisitive: they see and remember things. In that sense, the allotment was rarely dull. Listening and watching.

Callum Bremner's official prison record spanned four years. Her Majesty's Prison Maxwell was his first open prison and, if the Review Board was to be believed, the final staging post before release on parole. As his *"Personal File"* succinctly summarised, the transfer to HMP Maxwell was the fourth in a series of *"relocations"*. There being few secrets *"inside"*, it had quickly become known he was doing time for fraud. White collar crime being a traditionally low-scoring offence amongst cons, hitherto it had provoked little interest or comment. Therefore, in theory, he did not represent a threat or, for that matter, opportunity. As instructed, he had studiously kept himself to himself; the quintessential *"grey man"*, avoiding eye contact and any form of confrontation. It was accepted behaviour necessary to survive and thus far – with one exception – he had managed to achieve it.

The exception had been a significant altercation at his first prison resulting in temporary loss of privileges and, soon after in accordance with established procedure, relocation. He knew he would be tested by inmates at some point and, alert to the threat, was ready when it happened. At forty-two years of age, just over six feet in height, broad-shouldered and of lean build, he was not – at least so he thought – an obvious target: others saw it differently.

And so it proved in a short, vicious encounter in the shower block on his fourth night as a con. The cuts had healed in time, leaving only minor scarring on his arms and chest. His attackers both suffered a heavy beating, one forfeiting an eye. Appearances can be deceptive and within prison communities invariably are. Nobody bothered him after that.

According to his file, the only regular mail he received was from a relation in Northumberland where, it said, he was raised following the loss of both parents in a traffic accident. There was no reference to brothers or sisters. On academic qualifications, his file recorded attendance at university in Aberdeen – long recognised for its technical proficiency in the offshore industry and related disciplines – which had set him up nicely for a career in the lucrative oil and gas sector.

The fraud that landed him in prison, his first reported offence, was purportedly to do with falsifying a geological survey carried out in the deep waters off the Shetland Islands. It related to a multi-million-pound sales contract being pursued by a multinational offshore operator.

Psychiatric assessment notes described a *"normal upbringing within a loving environment by a spinster aunt"*. Specific interests were listed as *"field sports – mainly fishing and shooting"* and, as a young man, he had been a *"competitive distance runner and shown promise as a boxer."* There was reference to a *"proficiency in languages and considerable time spent abroad in geological work within the oil and gas industry"*. Single and currently unattached, there was nothing recorded about property ownership in the UK. He paid his taxes and possessed a good credit rating. Under *"religion"* he was listed as *"agnostic"*.

Successive file notes flagged up Review Boards frequently asking why Callum Bremner had fallen foul of the law and ended up in prison: a question equally unfathomable to his legal team – according to the case notes. However, as they also highlighted, he appeared to have learned the early lessons during his sentence and was now regarded as a *"reformed and a model prisoner quietly serving out his time".*

It was HMP Maxwell's large allotment that kept him busy. There every day except Sundays when it was officially closed, working outside was a keenly sought-after privilege and a reward for sustained good behaviour. That said, most things in prison were attainable if one had sufficient money and influence.

Money, influence and a reputation for violence explained the presence on the allotment of another senior inmate. One who, despite no apparent interest whatsoever in growing things, spent all day, every day – except Sundays – secluded in one of the sheds. Having assumed ownership and rumoured to possess at least one unauthorised mobile phone – in almost constant use – it was widely believed that the six by ten wooden structure was effectively an office. Privacy and personal security were the responsibility of a large, powerfully built, nasty-looking man – most observers took to be the chief *"minder".*

Fourteen years into a twenty-year sentence for racketeering, Guzim Shala was seventy-two years old and a type 2 diabetic. Just under six feet in height and a physically imposing figure, his bald head, jaundiced skin and dark intimidating eyes all contributed to the impression of menace. Like his two younger brothers, and although born in England, he took pride in his heritage and saw himself as Albanian. The brothers maintained strong links with what they affectionately referred to as the *"old country".*

Always protected by carefully selected and well-paid cons, Guzim had astutely avoided trouble in a succession of institutions. Fully expecting to be paroled within the next year or two, the day could not come soon enough. Having learned the virtue of patience during his years inside and only occasionally required to impose his authority within prison hierarchies in the early days of his confinement, all things considered it had been a tiresome but not unduly stressful period of his life.

The family businesses thrived and his brothers made sure he received whatever creature comforts could be arranged. Like them, he had never married, which, in hindsight, was a source of regret. No particular reason, it was just the way it was.

****

Of Albanian descent, the Shala family arrived in London at the end of the Second World War. Christians, hard-working and determined to carve out a new life, they opened the first of many successful bakeries in London's East End – later diversifying into market stalls, property, betting shops and money lending.

Guzim was the eldest of the three brothers, all of whom worked for the family businesses. For his part, the middle brother – Saban – was perfectly equipped for the role of "*enforcer*" and, some would say, derived inordinate pleasure from his work. Only the youngest brother, Erjon, had bothered with university education – successfully completing a law degree and later qualifying in accountancy.

As a unit – "*team*" would be stretching it given Guzim's dictatorial style of management – the brothers had achieved considerable financial success. Whilst enjoying the trappings of their wealth, they chose not to flaunt it – at least on their home patch in London. Revered within the Albanian community and respected for their charitable works and preparedness to support those in need, the Shala brothers prospered.

Less widely known was the expansive illegal network

they ran in the UK. Principal income streams involved prostitution, money laundering and protection rackets. Having stepped up to lead the family business after the death of his parents, and to the dismay of the other brothers, Guzim had always steadfastly refused to get involved in such lucrative activities as people and human organ trafficking. Why he chose to draw the line where he did was never clear.

As with all their undertakings, legal and illegal, only those of Albanian lineage were employed. In the sort of high-risk, high-reward business world the brothers inhabited, security was a constant concern. Woe betide anyone who chose to transgress the rules, protocols or expected behaviours.

The Albanian mafia, or *"Mafia Shqiptarei"* is, first and foremost, in the business of making money. Continually seeking to further its interests, often at the expense of others, they play to their own rules and represent a major challenge to international law enforcement agencies. When interests align, Mafia networks can and do cooperate in the pursuit of shared objectives and, despite his long years in prison, Guzim remained well connected within the European families and, it was rumoured, headed the organisation's operational activity in the UK. Similar to its Sicilian counterparts, the Albanian mafia embraces the concept of *"bese"* (trust) as the name for their code of honour. The word itself is culturally significant – a verbal contract – when someone pledges their *"bese"*, they have in effect pledged their life.

The name Guzim Shala was well known within the Albanian community in the UK and, despite being locked away for many years, his influence extended far and wide. Things happened when Shala interests were threatened; scores were promptly settled. The Code of Bese was woven into the prevailing culture and reflected in the cell-like business sub-structures – all tightly integrated and focused exclusively on the particular activity in question. It continued to be remarkably resilient.

Great care was taken in all forms of communication and, for sensitive matters, established practice was to restrict critical messaging to face-to-face exchanges, predicated upon the working assumption that all electronic networks were vulnerable. International law enforcement agencies were credited with sophisticated technical surveillance capabilities and were not to be underestimated. It made them a threat.

3

LONDON'S MORNING rush hour had virtually subsided. It was overcast but dry. Colour was absent: nature's palette uniformly grey. From a corner bench of the coffee shop, Hugh Everard had a good view of the street and patiently awaited the arrival of a bacon sandwich, lightly enhanced with brown sauce and accompanied by an espresso. The place felt reassuringly familiar, and snug.

Out of habit, he had arrived thirty minutes early and, riding the Tube's Victoria Line up from Pimlico, only needed to swap to the Piccadilly Line for the one-stop leg to Hyde Park Corner. He would normally have been driven but fancied some fresh air. Walking south along Grosvenor Place from the Tube Station, he turned right into Halkin Street and then took a left into Montrose Place. Nobody had showed any undue interest. Only his Personal Assistant, Marjorie, knew the details of his work commitments – none of which were publicised on any schedule. As a point of principle, he steadfastly refused to justify how he apportioned his time – even to his boss.

For those in the know, the Old Coffee Shop in Montrose Place just off Chapel Street serves what are arguably the best bacon sandwiches in Mayfair – if not the whole of London. Unimposing and unpretentious, the cramped split-level establishment retains loyal and appreciative customers. Everard had been a patron for more years than he chose to remember, but visits in recent times had become less frequent. In his line of work, it was not good practice to be predictable. Only last month, a missive was circulated reminding staff of the risks associated with *"pattern-setting"* and exhorting *"senior colleagues"* to *"set an example"*. God bless Human Resources – they tried their best – but he despaired at the political correctness now endemic in most of the great ministries of State. The Foreign Office was no exception.

Hugh Everard or, to give him his full appointment title, Director of Operations Secret Intelligence Service, was a senior civil servant. SIS, or MI6 as it is often called, is the UK's foreign intelligence service – the key word being *"foreign"*. Its sister organisation, the Security Service – referred to as MI5 – is responsible for dealing with threats to *"national"* security at home.

A history degree at Oxford had preceded a Short Service Commission in the Army which, not only had he enjoyed enormously, but which had shaped many of his personal values and beliefs. On return to civilian life he successfully applied to the Foreign Office, subsequently moving through a number of diplomatic postings in Europe and the Middle East. It was after his second such appointment that he applied to SIS to which, as time would tell, he was particularly well-suited.

There had been several secondments to Washington DC, where he built up a good network spanning most of the national agencies straddling the City's infamous ring road – the Beltway. Now mainly London-based, with a family home and his beloved dogs in Norfolk, Everard owned a modest flat in Pimlico. When not abroad on business, he joined the ranks of weekend commuters, albeit in his case using the services of a personal driver.

A devotee of field sports and an accomplished fly-fisherman, he was already looking forward to retirement when, once again, his time would become his own.

Hugh Everard was a *"people person"*. Nurturing and carefully mentoring subordinates was always a priority and, in consequence, he was able to delegate much of the day-to-day operational decision-making, allowing him to concentrate on longer term strategy; putting out political fires and, if required, setting a few himself. There were always internal battles to be fought and protecting the freedom of action of his subordinates and ensuring they had the resources needed for their purposes was emphatically one of them. The approach had served him well. His people completely got the point that *"empowerment through effective delegation"* gave him the absolute right to periodically cast an eye over tactical level detail. This was what brought him to the Old Coffee Shop, looking for reassurance that the pieces were all in place: no loose ends.

At the appointed hour, his guest entered and, smiling, extended a hand before taking a seat opposite with her back to the window.

"Is that the bacon sandwich you're always going on about?" she asked.

"It most assuredly is," he replied and, turning to the counter, said, "another of the same please, Linda, and with brown sauce if you would. I imagine it'll be herbal tea, too?"

His guest nodded. Tall, slim and with shoulder length auburn hair, Everard had known Mary Stewart – his opposite number in MI5 – a long time. Still only in her early fifties, attractive, single, ambitious and with a reputation for getting things done with minimum of fuss or drama, she was a proven field operator. Not one to take herself too seriously, Everard had always valued her instincts and judgement. It was widely accepted in Whitehall that she was destined for the top.

"It's been a while, Hugh. How are Penny and the girls?"

"All good thank you, Mary. We've got our third grandchild due in two months and Penny is in full planning mode. It's been made abundantly clear to me that we'll be deploying to France for the birth – which, although I haven't summoned up the courage to tell her, for me is frankly a non-starter; too much going on. How about you?" he asked, looking across the table.

"I reckon our new boss man is on manoeuvres," she said. "There have already been some early retirements, sideways moves and unexplained departures. The troops are unsettled!"

Everard was aware of the active new broom at the top of MI5, rumoured to be pursuing a private agenda. His own Service was no stranger to *"good ideas"* and had undergone repeated restructuring – currently configured with one *"Chief"* sitting above three Director Generals and, below them, a series of departmental directors. The next organisational restructuring tsunami was building over the horizon and, according to his sources, could be expected shortly – preferably after he'd left.

"Conscious of the time," he said. "Perhaps we might take a stroll when you've finished your tea?" Ten minutes later, having paid the bill, thanked Linda and pocketed another tin-foiled bacon sandwich, he led the way outside. Not the weather or time of year to be conspicuously sitting on park benches, they headed off towards Belgravia Square. "So," he said, as they walked, "how's it looking?"

"Good," she said, "I'm comfortable with everything... probably best we leave it to the teams on the ground from now on."

"Agreed," he said without looking up but fully grasping the obvious message.

"Usual routine," she said. "They'll only break comms if there's a problem."

His Service used similar tradecraft and protocols – something both sides recognised as essential for *"joint"* operations. An approaching woman with a pram prompted a pause in conversation. Everard knew Mary would have people providing covert security in the area and it was reasonable to presume the not-unattractive woman pushing the pram was one of them. "Can we assume your guys will be on hand once it's done?" he asked.

"Absolutely," she said. "If there's no show by the agreed time, they'll return to the same spot every hour, on the hour, until 2000."

"So, we're all good, then?" he asked, still keeping half an eye on the woman and the pram.

"Yep," she replied. "We're good and my team are well capable of handling anything unexpected."

"Okay, fine," he said. "Could I ask that you keep Brian Finlay fully in the loop and perhaps we can meet for a catch-up next week?"

"Absolutely."

Glancing at his watch, Everard indicated their business was concluded and, after quickly shaking hands, they headed off in different directions. Noting the departure of the blue Ford Mondeo with two occupants originally parked on Chapel Street, and then again across from Belgravia Square Garden, he smiled to himself. As a graduate of the Royal College of Defence Studies – a superb sabbatical many years earlier – he was intimately familiar with this part of the city. It was how he first happened across the Old Coffee Shop.

A dark BMW saloon pulled up alongside as he approached the junction of Eaton Place and Lyall Street. Everard slipped into the front passenger seat before the vehicle eased into the traffic and headed off to Vauxhall Cross – SIS headquarters on the south bank of the River Thames.

Unusually within the organisation, Randell – he was rarely referred to as *"Steve"* – had been Everard's personal driver for eight years. The arrangement suited them both very well. A former Royal Marine, Randell's second career was in private security looking after high net-worth individuals. It had somehow led to Diplomatic Protection within the Specialist Operations Directorate of London's Metropolitan Police Service. Single, but with an active social life in London – including within the HR Department at Vauxhall Cross – he was discreet, unfailingly loyal and enjoyed the complete trust of his boss. It helped that he could scrub up well in sharp suits when the situation called for it, didn't drink and was an acknowledged expert behind the wheel of fast cars. Like his boss, Randell was a keen fly-fisherman, with a weak spot for bacon sandwiches.

Sitting in the back of the blue Mondeo on her way back to the office, Mary Stewart thought about the conversation with Everard – mentally ticking-off the names of the few senior colleagues she had felt obliged to consult before agreeing to run the joint operation.

There was precedent for such things, albeit in the minds of some of her MI5 colleagues, they were not to be encouraged: *"too risky"* and *"an intrusion on our turf"*. In mitigation and to silence any dissenting small minds, which she tried to make clear in her in initial submission, the Service didn't have much to lose and potentially a lot to gain. Political exposure was minimal and within risk tolerances. It was not lost on those at the top that "*joint*" operations with their sister Service was always useful before the Annual Comprehensive Spending Review.

Reaching for her mobile phone she called a number recently put on speed dial. Pick up was immediate. "It's on," she said. "Only text me when it's done or there's a problem."

"Understood," came the terse reply and the line went dead.

****

After confirming there was nothing else on the schedule

until early evening, Randell dropped Everard inside the underground carpark at Vauxhall Cross. Reading his boss as well as he did, there was clearly something significant about to happen somewhere in the world and, watching until Everard had entered the lift, he reached across for the still warm, tin-foiled package left by the gear stick.

Like Randell, Marjorie was inordinately protective of Hugh Everard and had been with him a long time. The consummate Personal Assistant – the word *"secretary"* being long gone from the Civil Service lexicon – she loved her job and, like others on his team, was accorded enviable freedom of action. All calls came via her office, together with most emails. Often extending beyond the parameters of her Terms of Reference, she prided herself on solving what at times seemed intractable problems within the offices and corridors of the headquarters.

A widow of nearly fifteen years, into her early sixties and previously married to a stockbroker in the City, there had sadly been no children. SIS was her life. Adroit at maintaining her own extensive network of contacts across Whitehall, she kept a close finger on the corporate pulse in Vauxhall Cross – diplomatically resolving issues before they reached her boss. Always first into the office and routinely last to leave, she both liked and trusted Hugh Everard. He was, first and foremost, a lovely man, and whilst manifestly possessing a formidably sharp mind, he rarely if ever lost his temper, and never with her. Penny Everard was a different proposition – monied, county and of forthright opinion, she was not the easiest person to deal with and, thankfully, rarely came to London.

"Morning Marjorie," Everard said, entering the Outer Office. "Can you get me in to see 'C' at his earliest convenience this morning, please?"

"C", abbreviation for *"Chief of SIS"*, was Sir Andrew Summers and he, too, was a career civil servant.

Immediately grasping the urgency from Everard's look, she picked up the phone whilst he continued into his office. A couple of minutes later she walked in with an espresso from a top-of-the range machine bought for them at his own expense. "He's tied up with a secure video conference call until 1100 but free from then until lunch," she said, setting the coffee on Everard's desk. "I'm bound to be asked, is there anything he needs to read before the call?" she enquired, wondering why he always insisted on such austere surroundings in the office. The uniformly white walls were entirely devoid of pictures, so, too, the miscellany of professional memorabilia of which most people are so fond of carting around with them. Not so in this case. The furniture was plain but functional and the only thing the office really had going for it was the view. Pausing in case he hadn't caught her question, she gently repeated, "Nothing for him to read, then?"

"No, I don't think so – thank you – but could you ask Brian to pop in."

Brian Finlay was Everard's right-hand man and, having worked together for nearly six years, there were few secrets between them. Like his boss, he was a skilful and experienced intelligence practitioner who commanded an enviable reputation for getting results. Gifted with a sharp eye for operational detail, he took little at face value. Raised in Cornwall and, like many of his forebears, commissioned into the Royal Navy, the Finlay marriage had not worked out and, wanting a change of direction in his life, he successfully sat and passed the Civil Service Exam and joined SIS.

"How's Mary?" Finlay asked upon entering the office. Everard smiled – long suspecting that his colleague burned a candle for Ms Stewart, although he had never declared his hand. It was more than coincidental that Brian was always available to attend meetings with MI5 if for any reason Everard was busy.

"I'd like to say she asked after you, Brian, but I'd be lying," Everard said, doing his best to keep a straight face. "However, she confirmed that her lot are primed, in place and in all respects ready to go. She also mentioned that the top man over there is being a pain in the arse and, in her words, *'unsettling the troops'.*"

"Heard that," said Finlay. "Wouldn't be the first, would he?"

"Take a seat, Brian," Everard said as he turned to gaze out at the superb view across the river. "It might be sensible to recap on the next stage before I see Summers at 1100." Pausing as a pigeon landed on the windowsill, he went on, "He'll quite rightly want to feel in charge of his brief before he sees the Foreign Secretary."

Both *"C"* and his boss knew from experience that, when it came to sensitive intelligence operations, both the Foreign Secretary and Prime Minister could be guaranteed to irritate everyone by bypassing chains of command in order to seek reassurance directly from the person responsible which, for SIS, meant Everard. It was all very predictable; circumventing established procedure most often ended up being summoned to the eighth floor for an interview without coffee and a verbal spanking. Irrespective of having been pals at Cambridge, Everard was all-too-aware that Summers had lost confidence in his boss – the Foreign Secretary – who, it was widely believed, was incapable of respecting confidential information. That aside, political commentators were convinced the man had his eye on the top job across the river in Downing Street. Following a soft knock just as Finlay was unfolding a map, Marjorie entered and, handing him an espresso, slipped out and shut the door.

4

THE HEADQUARTERS of Shala Holdings Limited was situated on the top floor of a modern, glass-sided, multi-storey building in Limehouse, East London. The décor, fixtures and fittings were inescapably the work of an interior designer and conveyed the feeling of under-stated affluence, style and good taste. Served by its own lift, security staff kept a tight grip on access. It was the hub through which all the family's legitimate business was conducted. The largest office, unoccupied since the day of Guzim's arrest, unquestionably commanded the best view. All rooms, including the lift, kitchen, corridors and bathrooms were regularly electronically *"swept"* for implanted listening devices. Windows were double-glazed with a vacuum inner seal to reduce the risk of technical eavesdropping.

When they needed to talk about more sensitive matters, Saban and Erjon adjourned to a separate facility on the first floor of a bakery across the River Thames in Streatham. Counter-surveillance precautions extended not just to offices, including the bakery, but also their respective homes – all routinely *"swept"*. Vehicles were changed monthly. The security arrangements gave them peace of mind and were seen as a legitimate business expense.

Saban and Erjon were markedly different men: not only in character and temperament but also ambition. Saban chose to restrict his business and social activities to the company of fellow Albanians. Tall, muscular, dark-haired and with an unforgettably pock-marked face, his physical appearance alone was enough to intimidate. Brooding, insular, petulant, excessively suspicious, easily bored and used to having the last word, he possessed an explosive temper. Like his brothers, he was obsessive about security which – boasting an impressive number of enemies outside the Albanian community – was entirely understandable. Saban traded on his reputation as an unprincipled thug, the family *"fixer"*; a bully whose presence made people nervous. That said, within his own circle of friends he was approachable and never slow to proffer a helping hand.

By contrast, being better educated and altogether much sharper, it was Erjon who traditionally came up with innovative business ideas. Of medium height, well-built and handsome, he had a penchant for anything expensive – clothes, cars, restaurants and women. Not short of confidence or self-belief, he privately resented the lack of fraternal recognition for his business acumen and creativity. Politically astute, he kept the private phone numbers of a diverse network of national and international contacts and went to great lengths to reward *"favours"*.

Erjon Shala was by instinct a risk-taker and entrepreneur. It was all about making money and, as he frequently reminded everyone, the *"bottom line"* was what mattered. How he made money was largely irrelevant; such things as morality and ethics were for others to worry about. The considerable income accrued from his separate international businesses was channelled through a complicated patchwork of offshore accounts and holding companies. The substantial sums involved financed the development of a large and ever-expanding international property portfolio, operated by a management company in the Cayman Islands. Although fully conscious of the risks he was running with his brothers – who remained ignorant of his private enterprises – he revelled in the freedom to make his own deals and decisions.

Erjon's private business hub was in Cyprus. No office,

no Board meetings, no records, paper-free or otherwise, no reporting other than financial results linked by dashboard to a set of *"Key Performance Indicators"*, it had proved an exceptionally efficient arrangement. Organisational architecture and connectivity were as secure and sophisticated as money could buy, and he paid clever people big salaries to make it work. He had never met any of his multi-national employees in person – indeed, none of them even knew what he looked like. Working assiduously to protect his anonymity, his legal training and ability with numbers served him well.

The biggest risk for Erjon – rarely out of his mind – was Guzim discovering his *"other life"*. It was, inescapably, something to be carefully managed and, given the unfortunate circumstance of his brother's pending release, even greater care was going to be needed. Erjon did not see Saban as a threat, but neither did he underestimate him or, which could still send a chill through him, his liking for dispensing violence.

Sitting alone at the large, polished mahogany desk in the top floor office in Limehouse – surrounded by expensive original artwork, each picture individually lit and combining nicely with the lush dark blue fitted carpet and subtle lighting, Erjon stared at the towering new buildings continually going up across the Thames. Smiling to himself, he reaffirmed a longstanding promise made on the day of Guzim's conviction: *"one day, this will be my desk."*

It was at that moment his mobile rang and, after checking the caller ID, he pressed to answer: "Hi, Saban… where are you? I thought we might have lunch."

After a pause his brother replied with barely concealed irritation, "You have clearly forgotten that tomorrow is my monthly visit to Shropshire."

"Ah, of course, how forgetful of me. I'm doing the next one, aren't I? It must be the jetlag. What time's your visit?"

"Usual time," came the terse response. "I shall pass on your warmest regards to our brother," he said with undisguised sarcasm.

"Don't forget to say I'll be up there to see him myself next month," Erjon said before realising Saban had already ended the call.

****

One hundred and thirty miles away in the Midlands, three men and a woman approached the reception desk at the West Mercia Police Headquarters at Hindlip Hall, just off the M5 motorway north of Worcester. Responsible for policing the counties of Shropshire and Herefordshire as well as Worcestershire, it employed just over 4,000 people, including intelligence elements involved in the fight against serious crime and terrorism.

"Morning," said one of the group breezily to the uniformed officer behind the counter, slipping his and his colleagues' identity cards beneath the plastic screen as he did so. Having clocked them on the CCTV camera when they pulled up in a black Mercedes, the officer on reception prided himself in being able to recognise Special Branch when he met it, and the ID cards proved him right.

"No need to sign in – you're expected upstairs – Room 24. They'll meet you by the lift," they were told.

Room 24 was the Special Branch office at Hindlip and, on entry, the four visitors gratefully accepted the offer of coffee whilst taking in their surroundings. Maps and aerial photographs covered the walls – all *"gridded"* for ease of precisely referencing key points. After exchanging quick introductions, the senior member of the visiting team briefed the eight officers present, frequently emphasising and repeating key aspects – especially critical timings. Subsequent discussion – mainly for the benefit of local Branch members – provided ample opportunity to clarify the finer points of the operation. It was axiomatic that the detail had to be absolutely nailed: locations, timings and sequencing. All arrangements – especially contingency plans – were covered and, in some instances, resulting in minor tweaks and refinements. The session lasted over two hours and, business concluded and having signed for two sets of vehicle keys, the visitors took their leave – receiving a cursory nod from the officer at reception on the way out.

****

Further north in Shropshire, the sun had reached the expansive allotment on the east side of HMP Maxwell. Modern by conventional standards, the prison having been built in the 1970s, it was located some seventeen miles west of the M6 motorway which, whilst convenient for Her Majesty's Prison Service's administrative purposes, was distinctly less so for family visits – the policy for which was no more than twice monthly, booked in advance, and capped at one hour. The absence of a regular bus service was a further irritant for visiting family members but a bonus for local taxi firms.

The Shropshire Union Canal bordered the prison estate to the south west, but planted woodlands effectively screened the facility from nosy tourist folk on passing narrow boats during the boating season. To the east, the ground climbed gently through further woods and then into open fields. Unashamedly rural – other than prison staff, deliveries and visitors – agricultural vehicles were the main users of the surrounding country lanes. Signs giving directions for Maxwell were conspicuously few and far between.

5

A CREATURE OF habit, Callum Bremner wasted no time going out to the allotment and sat contentedly in his shed making short work of an egg roll hastily made up in the canteen – well ahead of the morning scramble for the breakfast hotplate.

Today was going to be different and explained his even earlier than normal start. A key milestone – more than a year in the making – he'd need his wits about him. Behind the shed stood a collection of black bins. After finishing the roll and lukewarm tea, he walked outside and surreptitiously removed a bag from one of the bins before casually returning to the shed. Quickly taking off his prison jacket, he replaced it with an identical one in the bag – suitably stained and aged. Reassuringly, he saw the small sachet sown into the lining material inside the front left side. Rolling up his original jacket in a discarded bin liner, he slipped out to the compost heap and pressed it deep into a pre-dug hole. That done, he raked over the soil before going over to inspect the neat lines of what he rather hoped would become sensational early potatoes within the next week or so – not that he envisaged being around to harvest the fruits of his labour.

Sometime later, a full fried breakfast hardening the arteries, other members of the allotment community began turning up in drips and drabs. A forlorn lot they looked, too, shuffling along in the half-light resembling soldiers returning from an all-night patrol. Pausing to collect rakes and spades of all shapes and sizes – carried in rusting but ever-faithful wheelbarrows – they moved out to begin the day. True to form, engrossed in conversation with the equally familiar chap who everyone presumed to be his minder, the Albanian was last to arrive.

Bremner had never made any effort to speak to the old guy, either inside the prison or on the allotment. But, with their respective sheds being only five metres apart, neither of which had a door, some form of acknowledgement seemed appropriate. A *"greeting"* would be stretching it but they had fallen into the habit of exchanging cursory nods. Like Bremner, the Albanian and his associate wore prison jackets and standard issue black woollen hats.

Soon after disappearing into his shed – an established routine for his neighbour – clouds of cigarette smoke drifted upwards into the morning air – further attesting to the absence of wind. In between raking what would eventually be home to a row of bamboo canes supporting runner bean plants, Bremner casually looked across at the sun climbing slowly above the higher ground to the east and saw that the lingering valley mist was beginning to disperse. Sheep could be heard in the distance and somewhere a tractor engine was stubbornly refusing to start. To his right, he heard the familiar chugging sound of a narrow boat gently making its way along the canal at a stately four miles an hour.

The thought of a sedate few weeks cruising the canals of England and Wales had grown in appeal since taking up residency in Shropshire. Something he had never done, or even considered, he was beginning to see the attraction. Maybe take a dog for company if – always a strong possibility – he failed in persuading a female companion to join him and operate the locks. A bike for exercise would be good, too. Then of course, he would need a fishing rod and a supply of good books. And, which was the real appeal, there would be no pressure of time: no fixed routines, free to talk to whomsoever he liked, whenever he liked. It was definitely a thought for the future.

Returning to the present, he started walking back to the shed. No need to look at his watch to know that Maxwell's public address system would be announcing lunch. Times never varied. A ten second blast of the hooter at precisely 12 noon was how most inmates and staff measured time. The sound of the narrowboat was now long gone and, given the absence of noise, he assumed efforts to turn over the tractor had been abandoned.

****

Earlier in the day, a West Mercia Police Range Rover, followed by an ambulance of the West Midlands Ambulance Service, had pulled out from behind a building off to the side of the Main Car Park at Hindlip Hall. Joining the M5 at Junction 6 by the Worcester Warriors Rugby Stadium, the two-vehicle convoy headed north. Rush hour having ended, there was no requirement to use flashing blue lights to expedite progress to the M6 and, soon thereafter, exit at the M54 turnoff at Junction 10a. After a brief exchange over the radio, the two vehicles separated and proceeded independently to their respective predetermined positions in Northern Shropshire.

****

In the disused barn, precisely 542 metres away on the rising ground to the east of Maxwell's prized vegetable allotment, the prone figure lay completely still. Relaxed but with his breathing nicely controlled, it was now all about delivering the result. Smiling to himself, he thought about the rat purposefully going about its business. He would very shortly be doing the same.

6

ANDREW SUMMERS was getting scratchy. Everard was already two minutes late for their scheduled meeting. It was becoming an irritating trait and one which, knowing the Director of Operations, he suspected might well be deliberate. Lateness was inexcusable and to his mind showed a lack of respect and set a bad example. A word or two in the next Annual Appraisal Report might not go amiss, although he doubted if Hugh Everard bothered with such things.

Everard unsettled Summers. He had never managed to get the full measure of him. The classic *"grey man"* so typical of the Service; average height, no distinguishing features, fair-haired but silvered at the edges and a handsome but unremarkable face. Certainly shrewd, no question about that and, in Everard's favour, he rarely failed to deliver the required result. Hugh Everard was an inordinately patient listener in whom people confided. He was emphatically his own man, always had been, and possessed the *"street cred"* Summers so patently lacked. It was what differentiated the two of them.

When it came to operational matters, Summers was always reluctant to question his subordinate's judgement on fine points of detail. Unfortunately, this put him at a distinct disadvantage in dealings with the Foreign Secretary and PM, both of whom – without any encouragement whatsoever – could be relied on to climb into the metaphorical *"front trench"*, fix bayonets and lead the charge. And why not, from a political perspective it generated strong good images – like riding on the top of a tank. The warrior class: forceful, decisive and embarking upon a just cause. Worryingly, as a key link in the chain of command, neither of them would have a second thought about bypassing him and calling subordinates like Everard direct. And, as his wife frequently pointed out – lest it be forgotten – there was the added complication that Lady Penelope Everard was a distant relation of the PM and, unhelpfully, they had mutual friends in Norfolk.

A sharp rap on the door announced Everard's arrival and, without waiting to be invited, he walked in and took his customary seat opposite Summers' impressively large desk facing the window. Commanding an even grander view than his own, the large office conveyed an unmistakable – some might say exaggerated and contrived – sense of status. It exuded *power*. Even the silver-framed family pictures were correctly sized and neatly aligned – a bit like the neat row of pens to the side of the jotter. A place for everything and everything in its place.

"Thanks for coming up Hugh," Summers said reaching for a file. "I'm due with the Foreign Secretary at two o'clock and he's specifically asked for an update on our activities in the Balkans and Eastern Med." Looking over Everard's shoulder at the array of clocks on the wall, each displaying different time zones for various important international capital cities, he added, "How's that business with the Albanians coming along – a London-based family if I remember correctly?"

Alarm bells triggered in Everard's head. Where on earth had he got that from? There was deliberately nothing on paper beyond referring to *"an Albanian faction possibly based in the UK with expanding influence in organised crime and potentially including terrorist and subversive organisations"*. Whilst aware that Summers had his own contacts within the Security Service, he doubted Mary Stewart would have briefed her own Director General to such a level of detail.

"Well," said Everard, looking at the thin file on Summers' desk and wondering what else it contained. "We have, as you know, been examining ways to improve our intelligence-gathering effort regarding Albanian criminal gangs. And, as you will recall, the Foreign Secretary gave an undertaking to that effect late last year to our *'cousins'* in Washington at the bilateral security conference. I am reasonably confident there will be some positive progress to report within the next couple of months; if there is, I shall of course immediately share it with you." Sensing a question was forming across the desk, "What I can say," Everard quickly continued, "is that we are currently working on something with our sister Service which, if it comes off – as I'm sure will be the case – you'll be able to cite as an example of the splendid progress being achieved in joint operations."

Summers understood the game all too well. If an operation was being planned – by the sound of it possibly in the UK – it was in the first instance a matter for MI5 to lead. Better not to press too hard just in case lines of authority were being circumvented or blurred. His job, as he so often sought to remind himself, was to protect his own reputation first, and the Service's second. If whatever operation being run went wrong, he would resort to the classic defence – *"operational information relating to this matter was unfortunately not fully disclosed to me".* He would leave it at that for now. Moving on, Everard spent the next half hour describing the status of ongoing operations around the world – fielding questions as they arose – and, on completion, took his leave. Back at his desk in the office, he stared at the sole clock on the wall for several minutes before picking up the phone. "Fancy grabbing a bite to eat, Brian?"

****

At that precise moment, one hundred and fifty miles to the

north west of London and bang on time, the twelve o'clock hooter sounded at HMP Maxwell. Bremner emerged from his shed and, turning right, started walking briskly along the path.

Travelling at approximately 1,790 feet per second and taking 0.74 seconds to reach its intended target, the first 30-06 match bullet exploded into the watering can on the left of the Albanian's shed just as he was following his minder out onto the pathway. Startled, the old man turned to his left and froze. The next shot ripped into the right side of the shed's entrance barely nine inches from his shoulder, shattering the wood and throwing up splinters and dust in every direction. Instinctively, the minder – now some ten feet further down the pathway – threw himself onto the concrete and crawled towards a low wall, desperate to find cover.

Having sprinted towards him on seeing the first two shots explode, Bremner hit the old man with considerable force, knocking him to the ground. The next round slammed into the brick wall at the side of the walkway. Slumped across the Albanian and now with some protection from the wall, the surrounding ground erupted as more shots tore apart an adjacent water butt literally inches above their heads, soaking them in a torrent of water. Lying across the old man now shaking uncontrollably, Bremner began groaning, clutching his lower chest. Seemingly disorientated, he tried to sit up and was dragged back down by the Albanian who, on taking his hand away saw it was covered in blood. Panicking, just as another round smashed into concrete close to where they lay, he rolled Bremner off and tried to see which of them was wounded. Frantic cries to his minder went unanswered – there would be no help coming from the terrified man further along the path, now curled into a foetal position, hands over his ears and whimpering incoherently.

No sooner had it started, the onslaught abruptly stopped. The scene went into freeze-frame. Even the birdsong was silent. All the other cons in the immediate area sensibly kept their faces pressed into wet soil. Some, unsure of what was happening, had sprinted towards the allotment entrance.

Guzim Shala was in deep shock. Still trembling uncontrollably, "Bastard, Bastard!" he cried intermittently… "Bastard, Bastard…" Lying next to him was the semi-conscious man whose name he had never known but who had obviously been hit. The prison's alarm system, now at maximum decibel level, was deafening. Duty personnel in the Security Control Room were quick to react and, in keeping with established procedure for a Major Incident Response, put out calls to emergency services – police, fire and ambulance.

Nervous prison officers moved sheepishly onto the allotment and started calling for petrified inmates to evacuate. CCTV monitors in the Control Room proved ineffective and, as later investigations concluded, left much of the inner allotment out of sight. Eventually – subsequent investigation assessed it to be in excess of twenty minutes – officers with First Aid training reluctantly began edging their way towards where Guzim and Bremner lay on the concrete path. Being shot at was not in their terms and conditions of service.

The wailing of an incoming ambulance could be heard in the distance and, in what seemed like no time at all, and having inserted a drip into him, paramedics lifted Bremner onto a stretcher – efficiently transferring him to the ambulance that had reversed up to the allotment entrance. Slightly embarrassed at the paramedic's lack of self-regard for their own safety, prison officers were making a more determined effort to assert themselves and take charge. The arrival soon after of a West Mercia Range Rover and an offer to escort the ambulance to Stoke Hospital negated the need for an accompanying prison officer.

Guzim was examined where he sat on the path, an irregular heartbeat and high pulse cause for concern. But, on closer investigation, other than clearly being in shock and having sustained a few scratches from his fall, there were no major injuries. Still hunched over, he had watched closely as the stretcher passed without uttering a word. When his so-called minder reappeared, he completely ignored him.

Bremner had lain motionless with eyes closed when lifted into the West Midlands Ambulance, immediately plugged in to onboard oxygen and heart monitoring systems. The female paramedic stayed with him while her companion closed the rear doors and climbed into the driving seat. The West Mercia Police officer jumped into the cab alongside and began talking into his radio. As the ambulance pulled away under its wailing siren and flashing blue lights, it passed two others racing at full pelt towards the prison – sirens blaring and lights flashing. Stationary police patrol cars were beginning to take up positions at road junctions and waved the blue light convoy straight through.

Not long after, the two vehicles – now with blue lights switched off and moving at normal speed – were heading west on the M54 – away from the M6 – exiting at Junction 3. Stopping on a quiet side road, the passenger in the front seat of the ambulance rejoined his partner in the police Range Rover which then drove off, leaving the ambulance to continue to its next destination alone. Both vehicles would be returned to Hindlip Hall later that evening, keys left in ignitions and borrowed uniforms dumped in the back of the ambulance.

7

STRUGGLING TO recover his breath and sweating profusely, the lone figure sat huddled in a deep culvert close to a narrow bridge over the Shropshire Union Canal. Reaching into the bulging pack by his side, he grabbed the remnants of broken biscuits and raisins and wolfed them down. No coffee left, unfortunately – he would have to make do with water.

It had taken less than thirty minutes to reach the culvert – the route having been carefully committed to memory in advance. Half-stooped as he ran, the climb to higher ground had been brutal. Now, too soon to relax, came the part that had prompted so many sleepless nights. The sound of police sirens was intensifying and he hated to think what his pulse was registering.

He was now entirely reliant upon others and there was no point getting unnecessarily wound up. Still munching away under the net, he was briefly surprised by loud flapping in an adjacent tree and looked up to see a buzzard glide gracefully past.

Counting down the minutes, he mentally replayed what had just taken place and, on balance, reckoned it had gone pretty well. A novel experience for sure and mildly irritating that the magazine had jammed, denying him the last three shots. It had all happened very fast and, under pressure to get going, he had simply removed the magazine, made the weapon *"safe"* and slid it back into the rod case. Then, after quickly collecting up the spent ammunition cases and stashing the crap bag in his rucksack, he picked up his pack and the rod case and cautiously descended the rotten stairs and was away into the woods at a jog. All in less than two minutes from the first round going down.

At the sound of a vehicle approaching he froze. Obviously slowing down, it finally came to a stop nearby. Looking at his watch, after a short wait, he was reassured to hear its siren briefly crank up and, three seconds later, stop. Quickly shouldering his pack, he clasped the rod case and climbed up to the road. Walking briskly up to the parked police Range Rover – the boot and rear offside passenger door of which were already open – he dumped everything in the back, covered it with a tarpaulin and climbed into a rear seat. Swiftly donning the West Mercia Police jacket lying on the seat next to him, he gave a thumbs up and the vehicle drove off under flashing blue lights.

Smiling at the driver looking back at him in the mirror, he at last felt able to relax – his thoughts switching to the comforting prospect of being dropped off by his narrowboat on the Llangollen Canal near the Welsh Border close to Chirk – the immediate priorities being a cigarette, shower, food and sleep. Everything else would be disposed of in slower time.

****

Media platforms were quickly onto the reported shooting at HMP Maxwell. West Mercia Police issued a short and characteristically bland statement later the same day, simply reporting that shots had been fired by a person or persons unknown, with one inmate – now in protective custody – undergoing urgent medical treatment. It would be left for the media to speculate on motive. In a subsequent statement put out by the CEO of Her Majesty's Prison Service, the Governor and Staff of HMP Maxwell were praised for their thorough handling of the incident, and also the speed of reaction by emergency services. Formal internal investigations would take place in due course, the follow-up press release stating, *"lessons would be learned and procedures amended as necessary."*

****

Back in London, Hugh Everard and Brian Finlay were in no rush to finish their late lunch. When the subject was raised about *"C"* being so remarkably well informed on the current joint operation possibly involving Albanians, there had been an exaggerated shrug of the shoulders and a quizzical look. Everard was formulating a follow up question when he received a brief text message. Replacing the mobile in his pocket, he asked the waitress for another expresso. Finlay looked at him as if to say "And?"

Putting him out of his misery, Everard said, "That was Mary to say we've had a positive result, everything went to plan, no loose ends. She'll call me tomorrow once things have calmed down a bit."

"I could pop over and see her if it would be easier?" Finlay offered.

"Okay, Brian, why don't you do that."

****

Guzim Shala sat alone in his unlocked cell. Kept in the Sick Bay for observation overnight and informed that all prison visits were cancelled until further notice, he assumed that Saban had seen the media reports and sensibly returned to London. He needed to contact him but, without recourse to the mobile secreted away in the shed, he would be obliged to use the phone in the Canteen – something he never did under normal circumstances. Walking into the canteen and having given the inmate using the phone a stern look, he moved into the hastily vacated booth.

The pick-up by Saban was immediate. Greatly relieved to hear his brother's voice, he quickly confirmed he knew all about the shooting and asked if everything was okay. Guzim said it was but they needed to talk as soon as possible. That told Saban he could expect to receive a call from the untraceable mobile. "I understand," he said, "and will let Erjon know you're okay."

After a short pause, Guzim ended the conversation with, "I will call you again as soon as I can. There are things to be done... without delay."

Sleep eluded the old man that night as he tossed and turned on his bunk, brain on over-load and an unshakeable sense of foreboding. Too many questions and too few answers. Was he the intended target or the other guy – whose name he now understood to be Bremner? Accepting the reality that there were people who would happily see him dead, he found it hard to believe anyone would seriously go to all the risk and expense of putting out a contract. Reminding himself of the long list of those bearing a grudge, or were in his debt, none immediately stood out. And yet, and yet... he knew enough about contract killings to realise that whoever did the shooting was a professional – and professionals tend not to miss. Moreover, had he not been pushed to the ground by Bremner, he would most likely be dead. On the other hand, he reasoned, could it be that Bremner was the intended target? Who was this man?

Forensic investigations were completed in the allotment by early afternoon the next day. Removal of fluorescent crime scene tapes signalled a return to business as usual and the gardening brigade were allowed to resume their activities. Not all chose to do so. Somewhat out of character, Guzim was amongst the first to arrive, moving cautiously to his rather decimated shed.

Shuddering at the sight of the smashed woodwork and strike marks scoring the concrete, he looked distinctly unsteady on his feet. Once inside and grateful to be sitting down, he recovered the mobile concealed beneath a brick in the floor. Saban answered the call immediately and, over the course of the next few minutes, listened intently to his brother's version of events.

At the end of the call, Guzim said, "There are four things I want you to do. Are you paying attention – you might want to write this down."

"Go ahead."

"First: you and Erjon are to sound-out all known contacts to see if anyone has picked up word of any contract being put out. Second: I want everything you can get on this man Bremner. And I mean everything. Third: we need to find him – presumably he's in a hospital somewhere. Did you get that?"

"I did," Saban said, re-licking the end of the pencil. "What's the fourth thing?"

"You will find a replacement for that coward of a minder and, in due course, arrange for him to receive a lesson he's unlikely to forget. Do you understand?"

"I do."

With the call concluded, Guzim felt in need of a lie-down and walked slowly back to his cell.

****

When the initial report of the shooting at Maxwell crossed the desk of the Prison's Minister, a junior ministerial post within the Ministry of Justice, there was widespread disbelief and considerable anxiety in outer offices – not helped by wild speculation in the morning papers and rampant conspiracy theories on social media. Civil servants and Private Secretaries were struggling to hold to the defensive line drafted in haste by the Communications Team. The Secretary of State for Justice was sensibly declining to make a statement.

Andrew Summers, recognising a developing shit storm when he saw it, and having already fended-off several calls from the Foreign Secretary, cut short his breakfast and instructed his PA to tell Everard to meet him on arrival at the office.

Less than an hour later and thinking it prudent to remain on his feet, Everard stood before the familiar and impressively large desk on the eighth floor. Summers, also standing, red faced and clearly struggling to control his anger eventually spoke: "Do you have any idea of the seriousness of what you've done? How on earth could you possibly have signed up for such a high-risk – some might say *'cowboy'* – operation and even begin to think it wouldn't backfire on the Service? Firing live rounds into a bloody prison for Christ's sake… have you entirely lost your mind?"

Everard remained expressionless.

"I'm at a loss for words…" Summers continued. "God knows what the fallout will be."

Now staring out of the window, Everard was rehearsing what he would say if and when he got the chance to speak but was saved temporarily by a short buzz on the intercom. Summers reached down and pressed a button. "What?" he shouted.

"The Foreign Secretary is on the other line and insists you take the call."

Summers went momentarily quiet and turning to the window said, "Tell him I'm debriefing the Director of Operations on the business at Maxwell and will be over to see him in the next forty minutes." Turning once again to Everard, he said, "You'd better make this quick: I want facts, and I also want a written report from you by 1100."

Everard succinctly summarised the background to the joint Security Service/SIS operation, choosing his words with inordinate care. "The operation is specifically designed for the purpose of penetrating an international network posing a significant threat to the security interests of this country." Without naming any individuals, he then went on to make clear that the Security Service was the lead agency and, together with SIS, would directly benefit from its success. The list of those *"in the know"* had, for reasons of security, deliberately been kept to an absolute minimum and all classified briefings handled on a one-to-one basis, and unrecorded. CEO HMPS and Governor HMP Maxwell were fully briefed on the operation – which, as things turned out, together with the Emergency Services, had earned wide praise for their prompt and comprehensive response. In short, there were no losers and potentially lots of winners – including SIS.

Summers listened carefully without interrupting and asked only one question. "What about the inmate who was taken to hospital?"

Everard looked at the man standing opposite and said calmly, "He's a Secret Service operative in deep cover, unharmed and now secure in a safe house." He stared at Summers for several seconds, almost daring him to press for further information – which he did not.

Back in his own office Hugh Everard put the final touches to the report he had drafted after lunching with Finlay the previous afternoon. It ran to a single page of A4 paper and omitted the names of everyone involved in the events in Shropshire. Once signed and dated, Marjorie walked it upstairs together with a second envelope – his formal letter of resignation. "Stuff 'em," he said. "I'll quite miss this view, though." He then reached for his phone and asked Brian to join him for an espresso – assuming that he was capable of operating the machine in Marjorie's absence. The next call would be to Mary Stewart and, thinking about it, he would pass her a private copy of his report to Summers. At some point he would also have to arrange for Randell's career to be taken care of – making a note to talk to Brian.

Having received his text, Mary was already sitting in a

corner of the Red Lion pub opposite Old Admiralty Building as he walked in. Seeing she was nursing a drink of some sort he ordered a bottle of lager at the bar. Watching him standing there, she was reminded of their days together in Washington DC: she serving as the British Embassy's Liaison Officer with the FBI and he on secondment to the Central Intelligence Agency at Langley.

Their relationship had remained entirely platonic – which, in hindsight, she'd rather regretted since they were both single at the time. Occasional lunches and dinners in Georgetown or Old Town Alexandria were always fun. She vividly recalled his diplomatic but forensic questioning of senior leaders at the FBI Hostage Rescue Team in Quantico after the tragic resolution of the Branch Davidian's siege at Waco in Texas in April 1993. The dreadful and unnecessary loss of life had shocked the nation. Resolving to stay in touch, they'd regularly bumped into one another in later years. Hugh Everard was a keeper of secrets and delightfully *"old school"*. Not everything had a cost, but favours were expected to be returned. "Bit of a shit storm don't you think?" she said with a grin as he sat down.

"My thoughts exactly. The great men are caving in all about us, Mary. Frankly, it's a disappointment and I struggle to understand why," he said, reaching into his jacket pocket and handing her a single page of A4. Allowing her a moment to read the document, he continued, "I think this accords with what you and I agreed as an appropriate line to take."

Lifting her eyes from the page, which she read twice, she said, "Yes, Hugh, it captures the key points… I presume *'C'* went predictably ballistic?"

Thinking back to the tense conversation on the eighth floor, Everard replied, "Mary, I kid you not, he went completely ape shit… incandescent doesn't do justice to it… I have never seen the man so upset, although, in his defence he did calm down after I gave him the bones of what's on that paper."

Mary took a sip from her glass. "My lot are actually okay with it," she said, "at least the ones in the know… it's those I didn't brief who could make mischief. What was that about never letting a good crisis go to waste?" As she scanned other drinkers in the bar she added, "We can ride it out. Besides, I hear that Number Ten is announcing a new policy initiative tomorrow: bound to relegate Maxwell to the *'old news'* box."

Continuing the discussion outside as they walked along Horse Guards, Mary said, "Hugh, you need to know we've deliberately leaked a story that the shooter was a former inmate, recently released from a psychiatric hospital. We felt the need to feed the beast – you know. Bottom line, my Service is content to weather any political backlash and, in this particular case, the boss has accepted my line that the potential ends will more than justifying the means."

"How's Bremner doing?" asked Everard.

"He's fine," she replied, "the effect of releasing the blood capsule sown into the replacement jacket appears to have fooled our Albanian friend and, as it turned out, thankfully the prison's first-aiders never got a chance to get a close look at him before the paramedics arrived. According to the Special Branch team in the ambulance, the gunshot wound looked incredibly realistic. Blood everywhere. As you stated in your report, Bremner's now gone to ground and will stay there until instructed otherwise."

"Where?"

"We've got a place in Kent. Debriefing will begin within the next day or two."

Everard sensed she wasn't quite finished.

"I don't want his cover blown, Hugh. We've invested

too much effort creating the backstory – not to mention the time he's spent living it in various prisons."

"Mary," he said, "how many people actually know his real identity?"

She looked across at him before replying. "He falls within a special *'asset pool'* – so probably only two or three people currently serving, and I'm not one of them. There's also a couple of others in our retired community. I imagine you work a similar policy?"

To which Everard slowly nodded. "We do – compartmented – but the circle of knowledge is normally quite a bit larger. For what it's worth, I think you've got it right. Anyway, back on the issue of making sure your asset doesn't get blown, how do you want to handle it?" he asked, at the same time wondering whether he should mention his resignation.

"Let me talk to some people over the next couple of days and I'll get back to you," she replied.

Everard was thinking about how much Mary Stewart impressed him during the ride back to the office. Calm, pragmatic and seemingly unfazed by the risk of things going pear-shaped, he liked the way she processed information without rushing to judgement. Her connections across the Whitehall corridors of power were impressive – especially the close relationships she enjoyed with prominent figures in both Houses of Parliament and, in particular, several influential members of the Intelligence Select Committee. She, too, knew the rules of the game and how to play them. Turning to Randell he said, "We can't be delayed getting away this afternoon, Penny's organised a dinner party and will kill me – and you – if I'm late."

8

ANDREW SUMMERS sat uncomfortably while the Foreign Secretary carefully read Hugh Everard's one-page report. "Bit thin, isn't it?" he said without looking up. "Anything to add?"

"Everard has submitted his resignation," came the reply, "which I shall of course accept. We're clearly into damage limitation; trouble-makers are having a field day – especially the Opposition Party. We need to serve up a head. Everard's pre-emptive move is regrettable but serves the wider interest."

"Whose interest?"

"Ours."

"Are you sure about that... bit of an overreaction isn't it?"

"Not in my opinion, Foreign Secretary."

"Okay, leave it with me, Andrew… I've had an informal chat with the PM who, as far as I can make out, has been briefed by the Security Service Director General and is happy to let things soak over the weekend. He wants to review it early next week and is more focused on the statement he'll be giving Parliament on the new security initiative."

Having watched *"C"* close the door as he left, John Pelham got up and walked over to the stone fireplace. "Dear oh dear…" he said quietly to himself. "The Nation deserves better, and so do the men and women in SIS." He had been Foreign Secretary for just over two years. Contrary to popular belief, he had no ambition – or expectation – to lead his party. Nor did he particularly wish to. Be that as it may, as one of the three Great Offices of State, his prestigious appointment put him at the epicentre of power where, like so many of his contemporaries, he was seized by the cut and thrust of government.

As the PM had sought to remind him, this was not the first time SIS had dropped the ball on Summers' watch and it was becoming embarrassing. Although Pelham knew all about the fractious relationship between Summers and Everard, the latter was regarded as highly competent: the proverbial *"safe pair of hands"* when it came to running sensitive and politically high-risk intelligence operations overseas. The Americans trusted him. Summers, on the other hand, had done minimal operational time on the *"front line"* – if indeed such a thing existed in the murky world in which SIS operated. He was a bureaucrat: a rule-taker who thrived on policy, budgets and battles with the Treasury. Widely regarded as wearing both his intellect and ambition on his sleeve – Summers was not his preferred choice of company and they had little social contact. The man had a reputation for overreacting and a strong instinct for self-preservation: invariably first into the lifeboat if there was any risk of the ship sinking. Reaching to the intercom, he said, "Susan, could you see if the PM's Chief of Staff can spare me a few minutes after the Cabinet Meeting, please."

****

Erjon Shala was deep in thought as he sat alone in the well-appointed drawing room on the first of the three-storey house he owned in Chelsea. Still weary from a lively, sustained and expensive encounter with one of his favourite Croatian ladies provided at exorbitant cost by the upmarket escort agency, which for many years had enjoyed his lucrative patronage, he began reviewing recent events and had listened with disbelief when his brother related Guzim's version of the shooting.

Could it really be, he thought to himself, *that Guzim was the intended target and, if so, who on earth was responsible and, of equal importance, why?* That apart, paid marksmen rarely missed and, dismissing the media speculation about "*nutters with a grudge*", the thing bore all the hallmarks of a professional assassination. No stranger to the expedient of permanently disposing of adversaries, like his brothers he too was acutely aware of the attendant risks to the person placing the contract.

In accordance with his brother's instructions, Saban and he had already put out word on the streets and were cautiously optimistic that a lead would surface before too long. Favours were being asked, threats made, and markers called in. The Albanian mafia in the UK was in overdrive. No one in any doubt about the consequences of failing to forward titbits of information, rumour or gossip.

What surprised Erjon most was this man Bremner. Whilst understanding the urgency to establish who the hell he was, he did not altogether buy the line that Bremner was the intended target. It simply didn't square with what happened – at least as far as he was concerned. These sorts of enquiries always fuelled rumour and attracted unwelcome interest from other parties – the unintended consequences of which could be hugely damaging for him personally. No choice, he concluded, it was far too risky; he would have to commission his own discreet investigation. It would not be shared with his brothers. He had come too far to risk anyone stumbling across his private business affairs and was resolved to do everything necessary to avert such a disastrous outcome.

****

Everard's eyes were shut as Randell skilfully negotiated the Friday afternoon exodus from London. Having read the signs almost as soon as they left the underground car park at Vauxhall Cross – it was written all his boss's face – the man was mentally exhausted. Once clear of the City, their trip to the family home in Norfolk was incident-free and they made good time. A regular visitor to the Everard estate, he enjoyed unrestricted use of a cottage at the weekends and regularly chose to stay. Before leaving the office, Marjorie had mentioned something about a dinner party and a day's shooting, but without disclosing the list of guests.

Ten miles north of Thetford, Randell turned through an ornate set of iron gates and made his way down the long tree-lined drive leading to a wide gravel forecourt at the front of a large Georgian manor house. Penny Everard awaited – three working cocker spaniels busying themselves on the steps – all racing to the car as their master got out. Collecting his case from Randell, Hugh Everard fondly embraced his wife whilst at the same time tweaking the ear of Bess, his favourite spaniel and the mother of Rambo and Reg. At Marjorie's suggestion, Randell planned to stay at the cottage that evening in order to acquaint the guests' protection teams with the inside of the house and overall security plan. His briefing would also include out-buildings, their accommodation in the second cottage, surrounding grounds, location of panic buttons to connect with local law enforcement as well as the discreet security camera arrangements and ground sensor system.

A well-practiced routine, once all the house guests had retired to their assigned bedroom suites in the two wings of the main house, he could relax and let the protection officers do the worrying. Still only in his late thirties, single and solvent, Randell's quiet confidence and easy manner ensured no shortage of female company. The only pressure on him was from his mother constantly asking if there was any likelihood of grandchildren.

****

Having changed out of his suit, Hugh joined Penny in the

drawing room for tea. One of his favourite places, the high ceiling with its elaborate cornicing, oak panelling and huge stone fireplace beneath a large gold frame mirror created the perfect setting for the paintings of ancestors and hunting scenes – all individually lit. Clusters of photographs in silver frames – lots of them – were proudly displayed on Penny's piano and most other flat surfaces. The original Georgian features had all been carefully preserved and conveyed a sense of history. It was a bright and airy room: uninterrupted views of the garden visible through tall French windows opening onto a patio. Deep settees and armchairs in rich colourful fabrics picked up the colour of oriental handmade rugs covering polished wooden floorboards. In a corner, in strict order of seniority, sat the dogs' wicker baskets.

After bringing him up to date on the imminent arrival of their next grandchild – without pausing for questions – or breath – Penny reminded her husband of the names of those coming for the weekend. Marjorie had done the same thing, but he hadn't been paying attention. "Did you say James Wadsworth?" he asked.

"Yes, darling, Daddy suggested it – they're staying with him and Mummy and he asked if they could come for dinner."

Everard was intrigued. "Are we talking about James Wadsworth – the PM's Chief of Staff?" he enquired.

"Not sure what he does darling but that sounds familiar… shall I ring Daddy?"

After reflecting for a moment, Everard said, "No need."

Penny Everard was the second daughter of Lord and Lady Brigstock – long-established in the county and owning several estates, the Brigstocks were on first name terms with prominent politicians at local and national level. An elegant and attractive woman with fine cheekbones, grey turning to slate eyes and shoulder length auburn hair, regularly exercising the horses had helped her to keep her figure. Beneath what was often mistaken for an austere and rather intimidating manner, Penny Everard had a more sensitive nature than most gave her credit for.

She and her husband differed in a lot of things but were a formidably tight unit when it came to their three children and grandchildren. She was inordinately proud of him and took care of all the domestic stuff. She, too, was ready for Hugh to give up his career and come home permanently. For her part, it could not come soon enough. The attraction of London had worn off years ago but she would still make the effort for the big social gatherings... the "*duty attends*". Until Hugh drew stumps and closed the innings with the Service – or more likely got pensioned off – she would continue as now: playing her part in the local community, running the house and estate and making sure the Norfolk home was emphatically a home not a museum.

Looking across at her husband with obvious concern, she said, "You seem even more tired than normal, is everything alright, Hugh?"

"It's fine, Penny, thank you – just got a lot going on at the moment."

"Why don't you take the dogs for a walk before dinner?"

Hugh looked at her and smiled. "Yes, poppet, good idea – I'll do that." He saw no reason to ruin her weekend with such trivial matters as his very recently tendered letter of resignation.

Hugh Everard was never happier than when walking the grounds with the dogs. The property, a wedding gift from Penny's parents, and more especially the extensive gardens surrounding it were her pride and joy. An accomplished horsewoman, they kept two thoroughbreds; she still rode out most days but had long given up hunting after country folk lost the argument and the law changed.

Situated in two hundred acres of arable land, most of which was sublet to local farmers, the jewel for him was the ten-acre lake fed by two streams and stocked annually with a thousand trout. Whenever at home in the early mornings between April and September, Hugh pursued his lifetime passion – fly-fishing – usually from the ten-foot, clinker-built wooden boat he had painstakingly restored. Bess, the most frequent companion, would quickly lose interest and curl up on an old rug.

When the children were young, the lake had doubled as a place of adventure: to swim as well as fish. He recalled the summer picnics and treasure hunts with great fondness. Randell kept his own rod at the cottage and was a willing worker with the Estate Manager's team, happy to help with whatever jobs needed doing. Shooting weekends were less frequent these days – just sufficient to offer hospitality to friends.

Assembling for pre-dinner drinks in the drawing room, whilst Penny was busy at the other end of the room, Hugh's father-in-law came over to introduce James and Judy Wadsworth. Sixteen sat down for dinner and conversation became increasingly lively as the wine flowed. In keeping with the rest of the house, the dining room exuded history. The long, oak table reflected flickering candlelight from ornate period candelabra. Elegant silver figurines – mainly huntsmen, horses or hounds – featured prominently. Thick curtains covered oak shutters and the enormous log fire gave it a cosy feeling. In keeping with habit, Hugh and Penny sat at opposite ends of the table.

Despite never having been formally introduced, Everard recognised Wadsworth as soon as he saw him. Comparatively new in post, he was a constituency Member of Parliament in Oxfordshire and had previously served on a number of Parliamentary Select Committees, including

Defence. SIS had identified him as a rising talent and *"one to watch"*.

Everyone returned to the drawing room for coffee and liqueurs after dinner: port and madeira having been offered at the table. Everard invited any smokers to make use of the adjoining orangery and, partial to cigars himself, led the way.

Wadsworth joined him shortly after and accepted a Cohiba. "Thank you so much for a lovely evening, Hugh: what a gorgeous home… I imagine you've got a lake tucked away in the grounds… full of fish?" he said, lighting his cigar.

"Yes, James, we're very fond of this part of Norfolk and yes, I do fish… and I'm getting the feeling you do, too."

Wadsworth broke into a wide grin. "Absolutely," he said. "What is it they say about fishing: *'incessant expectation, and perpetual disappointment'*. Bit like Prime Ministers," he said laughing at his own joke and prompting a big smile from his host. "I'm in a couple of syndicates at home – mainly trout – but I also get up to Scotland to chase salmon whenever I have the time."

Much as he'd suspected, this was a man after his own heart. "You know, James, I do, too. Matter of fact, Penny's no slouch with a salmon rod either… or a shotgun come to that. Keeps me on my toes."

Drawing on his cigar, Wadsworth was getting the distinct feeling that Everard was sizing him up. "How's the new job going?" Hugh asked. "I imagine your opportunities to cast a fly are few and far between these days?"

"We're certainly not short of excitement," Wadsworth replied, "but no need to tell you that, Hugh."

Here we go then, thought Everard and asked, "Is there anything in particular I can help you with James?"

His guest took another long draw on his cigar before responding. "That business in Shropshire, Hugh; I've seen your report and so has the PM who, by the way, discussed it with John Pelham and the Security Service Director General. You would wish to know that Andrew Summers is going to be offered the EU Ambassadorship and, should he accept – and doesn't cock it up – thereafter a position as Master of one of the Cambridge colleges – not Trinity. There will of course have to be an interim boss at Vauxhall."

Everard watched Meg enter and, sniffing him, curl up on the floor by his feet. "I'm instructed to tell you – informally, Hugh – the job's yours if you want it. The Foreign Secretary is fully onboard: indeed, he proposed you. Perhaps you might like to have a think about it and give me a call in the office sometime after lunch on Monday."

Everard, struggling to mask his surprise, said, "Thank you James, I appreciate you sharing this with me and I'll most certainly give you a call on Monday. Shall we join the others…? I'm sure Penny will forgive our cigars. Come on, Meg."

9

"WORSE PLACES to be miserable," Bremner said to himself as he stood in the garden of a cottage in Kent. It was a beautiful morning, warm and without a cloud in the sky. The contrast to his last surroundings was stark, and he found it remarkable that only six days ago he was being whisked away from Shropshire under flashing blue lights in the back of an ambulance under police escort. Nursing a mug of coffee, he sat down on a rusting metal bench and, replaying the sequence of events, tried to make sense of it all.

The incident on the prison allotment had played out more or less as he'd expected. That said, there were still gaps in his knowledge, including how everything had been so meticulously arranged. As an example, he had absolutely no idea who or when the prison jacket was substituted and put in the bin by his shed. There must have been someone else on the team inside Maxwell. His biggest worry had always been about the weather and, specifically, its potential implications for the shooter. Thankfully, it had cooperated and so, too, unwittingly, had his Albanian neighbour. Basing the timing on the lunch hooter was a masterstroke. Crashing into the old guy had left him badly winded and thank Christ he'd remembered to smash the outside of his jacket and release the blood capsule. The effect had been immediate, dramatic and incredibly realistic.

As the bullets had reined in, he vaguely remembered the Albanian pulling him down behind the brick wall – presumably for the old guy to better protect himself. Fake or not, it was a frightening experience, and he gave credit to the skill of the marksman whose accuracy was little short of miraculous. What he would remember most, however, apart from the noise and dust, was the look of abject fear on the face of the old man: unmitigated terror and total disbelief. Also, the stunned silence as he was carried by him on the stretcher before being transferred to the ambulance. No question about it, the whole thing was utterly convincing. That said, he had no wish to repeat the experience of being shot at.

Once out of Shropshire, he recalled the female paramedic whispering in his ear. "Wakey-wakey," she'd said, assuming he really was asleep before handing him a drink and systematically removing the wires stuck to his body. "Oh no, all that blood has made a real mess of your shirt," she'd remarked, laughing. "But I guess you won't be needing it anyway." Having unbuckled the retaining straps on the stretcher, he'd gently swung his legs over the side and sat up. "There's a set of clean clothes and a pair of shoes in that duffle bag," she'd said, pointing it out at the back of the vehicle. "If you're not shy, why don't you clean yourself up with this cloth and put them on – we have another hour or so until the drop off. Put all your old stuff in the plastic bag."

Taking in his surroundings whilst sipping the tea, "What happens next?" he had asked.

Turning towards him with the duffle bag, she'd said, "You'll be dropped off and I'll be signing you over to other colleagues. Job done as far as we're concerned."

Small talk not being one of his notable strengths, he'd resisted the urge to engage in further conversation, despite having registered the presence of the gorgeous, thirty-something year old woman in uniform sitting next to him. Doing as he was told and having to rub hard at the congealed blood stains, he slowly changed into his new clothes – the first time he had been out of prison uniform in seven months. It had all felt very strange.

What happened next had, he remembered thinking at the time, been carefully choreographed. After what seemed like no time at all, the ambulance had drawn to a stop; the scraping of metal doors announcing their arrival at their destination. Pulling forward a short distance and then stopping again, the ambulance's rear doors opened and he was asked to get out. It was some sort of hangar, lit by an array of ceiling lights. On closer inspection, there was a dark saloon parked at the far end – standing by it, a man and woman in casual clothes. Their task apparently completed, the female paramedic pointed in the direction of the car and indicated he was to walk over to it. Just before doing so, he had turned to her and her colleagues, one of whom was in police uniform and said, "Thank you."

"You mind how you go," she'd replied.

The woman at the far end of the hangar had opened a rear door of the saloon and he'd gotten in. The hangar doors had slid apart and the car headed back out. Not long after, they'd been on a motorway, but he would have been pushed to say which one.

The woman in the passenger seat had turned to face him. "My name's Jo," she'd said. Glancing at the driver, "This is Rob. I appreciate you'll have lots of questions, but right now the priority is to get you to a safe house. A proper debrief and discussion about the future will begin in a day or two. How are you feeling?"

Bremner had been hungry and more than ready for a long shower. "Okay," he'd answered, "just a little disorientated. Where are we going?"

"Kent," she'd replied. And, looking across at the driver, "How long, Rob?"

"Couple of hours," had come the reply.

Jo had taken out her mobile phone and tapped in what

Bremner presumed to be a short message to higher authority. That done, "There's some sandwiches in the bag," she'd said. "We can't risk stopping for proper food, but a meal will be waiting when we get to the house."

After devouring the sandwiches and accompanying packet of biscuits, he'd fallen into a deep sleep.

****

The pheasant shoot at the estate in Norfolk was great fun and, reassuringly, Everard had not disgraced himself with his personal tally of birds. The guests left after a leisurely lunch and only then was he properly able to reflect on the conversation with Wadsworth in the orangery. It had definitely left him with a lot to think about and, rising early on Sunday morning, Penny still fast asleep, he slipped into his dressing room, washed, shaved and went downstairs to let the dogs out. Putting on a coat over his pyjamas and donning his wellies, armed with a mug of tea, he made his way through the gardens to the lake. Even though overcast with rain expected within the next couple of hours, he noted the dew-soaked grass and the flurry of ducks taking flight at the approach of the dogs. Like the spaniels – now closing fast – they, too, knew the rules of the game and noisily sought sanctuary in the middle of the lake. Young Reg gave token chase with Bess and Rambo watching on. A solitary surviving pheasant poked its head out of a hedge wondering what the excitement was about.

Everard sat down on his favourite bench under the expansive shelter of a stately cedar tree. In hindsight, he was so glad he chose not to tell Penny about resigning. Apart from anything else, it would have seriously scuppered the dinner party and, more importantly, the conversation with James Wadsworth.

The question now, he realized, was what to do about the offer. All his instincts were telling him the wisest course of action was to leave things be. After all, in career terms, he'd enjoyed a good run; there were no underlying health issues he knew about and, with a tidy pension, the thought of retirement was rather appealing.

Distracted by a trout rising twenty yards away, he remembered that Wadsworth was a fisherman – a fraternity in whose company he always felt comfortable. Not for the first time, he reflected on the truism that fishermen were by nature curious and keen observers. They noticed and remembered things – in his case, the first fish he ever landed and, perversely in the case of salmon, the ones he'd lost.

What would Penny want? Could she really handle him being around permanently or might it upset her routine? She always maintained that she wanted him home, permanently. But he couldn't be sure. Would he want to be and would it actually suit him? A man could only fish for so many hours in a day. Still short of State Pension age by three years, it wasn't as though he was anywhere near his sell-by date. Anyway, he'd always believed that one would know when it was time to call an end to the innings.

First and foremost, as far as he was concerned it all turned on the central question of *"relevance"*: relevance within the Service of which he was so proud; relevance to the colleagues in whose futures he was a major stakeholder. If and when his opinion or advice was no longer sought, the question of relevance would be settled. The telltale signs were well known: instead of being asked his opinion, the question would be whether he had *'anything to add'*.

The message conveyed by James Wadsworth was unequivocal: those in a position to judge such things believed him more than capable of stepping into the shoes of Andrew Summers. Reassuringly, he interpreted this to mean that he was not yet to be put under wraps or, as the ghastly phase had it, *"let go"* for fear of him spontaneously uttering something of interest or alarm. On that basis, he reasoned, coupled to the fact that he had fingers in all sorts of operational pies, it would be crazy to turn down the offer. Decision taken, he saw no reason to trouble Penny with it and, gazing affectionately at Bess, said, "Another month and that trout over there will need its wits about it." With the now empty mug to hand, he returned to the house with the dogs, all equally excited at the prospect of breakfast.

****

South of the river in Streatham, Saban Shala had company in the first-floor office of the bakery. Sparsely furnished but equipped with the basics, the pervading smell left no doubts about what went on downstairs. Indeed, on close inspection, a fine layer of white flour coated most surfaces. Two desks faced one another, each with a computer screen and several telephones under Anglepoise lamps. The furniture was past its prime but functional. The only concession to luxury was a state-of-the-art coffee machine. Half drawn blinds covered the two windows. The impression was of a well-used but unloved space, and the contrast with the office suite in Limehouse could not be more marked.

Staring at the anxious young man sitting opposite, Saban was the first to speak. "Do you know why you're here?" And, after an uncomfortable silence, "Look at me, I want to remember your face... And I also want you to remember mine."

The pale-faced, slightly under-nourished youth with long unkempt hair and thick glasses was feeling way outside his comfort zone – bitterly regretting finding himself in such close proximity to such a frightening person. "I believe you want information," he said, struggling to hold the big man's eye.

"That's exactly right, son," said Saban. "Do you know who I am?"

To which his young visitor said, "I do – yes."

Pausing for what in other circumstances might be misconstrued as dramatic effect – but in this instance was emphatically not – Saban said, "Can I trust you son? Have you any idea what will happen if you fail me?"

The youth looked up and said, "Yes... you can, and yes... I do."

"Good… we have an understanding then. Now, I want you to listen very carefully to what I'm going to say. When I'm finished, we'll talk about money and, as you will see, I pay well. Just to be clear, you will not record or write down this conversation; you will not discuss it with anyone – and I mean anyone – and you will only report your findings to me. Is that understood?"

The young man nodded.

"I asked you if that was clear?" Saban repeated, raising his voice – his cheeks beginning to colour.

"Yes," came the reply.

Getting up from his chair, he walked over to refill his coffee cup before returning to sit on the edge of the desk. "Okay, so this is what you're going to do," Saban said. "You're going to find out everything you can about a man: an ex-con by the name of Bremner who, until recently, was an inmate at Maxwell prison up in the Midlands. No first name. He might be from up north – maybe Scottish. I have no idea what he was inside for – something you're going to tell me. In fact, I want everything you can get, including, where I can find him. Do you have a problem with any of that? Is it feasible and how long will it take?"

The young man took a few moments to process what he was being asked to do, at the same time trying hard to ignore the fact that his hands were sweating. "Yes, it's possible but I can't tell you how long it will take."

"And why is that?"

"Because, if the man was in prison, I'll have to try and breach what are normally very tight security systems: sophisticated protective software."

None of what he was hearing surprised Saban. It was obvious that the UK Government ministries and agencies would take their cybersecurity seriously. After all, he did. He also knew from Erjon – who had found him – that the young man was an acknowledged hacker with a formidable reputation on the so-called *"dark web"*. "Okay," he said. "Come back to me when you've got anything significant to report." Then, unwrapping and passing over a new mobile phone, he added, "You will only use this burner to talk to me and for no other purpose… is that understood?" To which the youth said it was. "Okay. Now let's talk about money…"

Sitting in the smaller office next door, Erjon had listened-in on the conversation. Others had been paid to track down the young hacker and, which had been the hard part, persuade him to come to the bakery. After the young man left, Erjon walked next door to join Saban and poured himself a coffee.

"Do you think he'll come up with the goods?" Saban asked as he watched their new associate disappear down the street.

"Time will tell," Erjon replied. "He's certainly got a big reputation, but we'll have to see. If and when he's given us what we want, we'll have to think about what we do with him."

"Understood."

"Just so you know," Erjon said, "I've arranged an insurance policy – call it independent verification. We can expect to be told how things are going from another member of the hacker fraternity who, I understand, is equally proficient."

This was confusing Saban. "I don't understand. Are you

saying we'll be hacking our own hacker?"

Erjon grinned, "Precisely. Neat eh? It's like a game to these people; they inhabit what I'm told is an ego-rich environment. We'll have to pay extra but it'll give us peace of mind." Then, turning to his brother before going out of the door he added, "I'll leave it to you to speak to Guzim."

****

Across the river, Mary Stewart was in her office working through an intimidating inbox on the computer. The meeting with Brian Finlay on Friday had turned into dinner and she'd enjoyed herself immensely. Brian was a nice man, a little older but like herself, single. Everard had mentioned a sticky divorce but there were no children. She was beginning to appreciate the man's company; yes he was quirky, but he made her laugh. For a senior SIS executive he was surprisingly uncomplicated and, whilst clearly a shrewd and hard-nosed intelligence professional, she was slowly unlocking his softer side. Despite the gruff exterior so often associated with ex-service types, he was an attentive listener. Not much cultural depth, but that didn't matter. He made her relax and, more important, laugh.

It was a nice meal – the Rioja alone had been worth crossing the river for. *Yes*, she thought to herself in the taxi home, he was definitely fun to be with and, according to her sources, a bit lonely. It might be sensible to see what else they shared in common before making any commitment.

Mary had been relieved to get the text confirming Bremner's successful extraction. It was also gratifying that her own Director General had somehow managed to hold his nerve despite being bombarded from all quarters when the story broke in the media. Such a predictably frenzied response was foreseen and, for that reason, creating and leaking various anonymous bits of information had helped

– including, in this instance, fabricating the story about the *"ex-con nutter with a gun and a grudge"*.

Never having actually met Bremner or, for that matter, seen a photograph, she was nonetheless very conscious of the huge effort invested into painstakingly stitching together his fabricated personal history – commonly referred to as a *"legend"*. Inventing a comprehensive and credible prison record represented hours of specialist work. In some ways, she felt she knew him and was curious to meet the man in person. However, she was sufficiently realistic to understand that one rarely got to know individuals like Callum Bremner – or whatever his real name was – one of the truly remarkable people who somehow manage to live a lie and, against formidable odds, function indefinitely in the most frightening circumstances. It took a very special personality type to endure deep cover – a rare breed indeed. Prized assets.

On instinct, she re-read the short briefing note she'd sent the previous year to her immediate superior describing the man known as Callum Bremner. *"He has an organised mind,"* it said, *"with good powers of observation and an enviable memory. His personal risk tolerance is assessed to be distinctly above average. Fair-haired and without any facial distinguishing features or physical characteristics, he has blue eyes and maintains a good standard of fitness. Well able to look after himself, he does not lack physical or morale courage."* She was amused to note her comment about relationships: *"Women find him difficult to read, introverted and not given to displays of affection. He can appear socially ill-at-ease and often comes across as disinterested, detached and uncommunicative (the latter personality traits are not regarded as a significant threat to maintaining assigned cover)."*

Turning her mind to the operation against the Shala Family, she brought up on screen the planning file and revisited the operation's underpinning assumptions. First, if things ran to plan – as they had – an intense follow-up could be expected from the Albanian mafia in general, and the Shala's in particular. As a deduction, therefore, it was imperative that the *"legend"* created for Bremner be able to withstand the closest scrutiny. A related assumption was that Prison Service computer files were vulnerable to hacking – an opinion reinforced by subject matter experts at the Government Communications Headquarters (GCHQ) in Cheltenham. *"Less than fully robust"* was the expression they had used. It had therefore been agreed that, once fully constructed, the legend for Bremner would be tested by GCHQ experts in order to find and close any gaps and eradicate inconsistencies. The cooperation to date had been first class and she was now more reassured. Bremner could be, too.

Convincing as it was, she reminded herself that the description in his record was largely a work of fiction and bore no reality to real life. That said, yes – the vicious assault in his first prison had indeed occurred and the outcome was as described – he would bear the physical scars for quite a while the medics had said. However, there had been a *"time out"* during the period of his incarceration when he was spirited away for a while before, months later, discreetly re-entering prison prior to transferring to Maxwell. The narrative had to be seamless. No unexplained breaks. Mary remembered being told that Bremner had spent the intervening months at a safe house in Northumberland, not a million miles from the River Tweed in the Scottish Borders.

Easy to forget, she reminded herself, the staged shooting at Maxwell was solely a means to an end; a phase, specifically seeking to implant and exploit the sense of indebtedness inherent within the Albanian mafia culture. The outcome was far from certain. If successful, it potentially opened up all sorts of opportunities and, in a word, leverage. Thankfully, GCHQ had also agreed to be a partner in the next phase of the operation and stood up a dedicated specialist team – initially for the purpose of monitoring all potential cyber-attacks directed at Her Majesty's Prison Service computer systems – specifically those directed at HR record departments.

It had been made clear to her that any potential hacker bent on mischief would have to be at the top of their game: first division players. In her own mind she had accepted that it was not a question of whether there would be an attack, but rather when, by whom and with what level of success. The objective was to stay ahead of any adversaries. Bremner's life depended on it.

****

Andrew Summers' life was unexpectedly upended when he was formally offered the EU Ambassadorship. Whilst he might have preferred Washington or Paris, it was nonetheless a fantastic posting opportunity and he was exceedingly chuffed. The icing on the cake was the hint of a sinecure as Master of a college at Oxford or Cambridge. His wife was over the moon. Accepting the position without even bothering to question the rather short notice, he was to be placed on administrative leave with effect from the end of the week. Surprisingly, the subject of his successor never arose.

And so it was, one week later, Hugh Everard found himself sitting behind the mahogany desk in the big office with the spectacular view on the eighth floor of the SIS Headquarters in Vauxhall Cross. Penny and her parents were delighted, "But not in the least surprised, darling." Marjorie was lost for words when he told her about his promotion and became uncharacteristically emotional when he said that she, too, would be moving upstairs. For his part, Randell was happy to continue as before because he was becoming increasingly fond of Lucy in Human Resources. Everard would love to have been a fly on the wall when Summers learned the name of his successor – a question which, according to his sources, had never arisen.

In keeping with habit, the new office would be just as austere as the last one. There would be a fresh coat of white paint with, at Marjorie's insistence, new furniture, carpet and curtains – all of which she personally chose without reference to him or anyone else.

Mary Stewart wrote Everard a congratulatory note and received a prompt response by text proposing a meeting at her earliest convenience. Brian Finlay continued in his appointment, never having expected to step into Everard's shoes. His workload just became considerably heavier.

****

Having run out of things to say about the incident at Maxwell, the media were lining up other victims in their crosshairs. As far as senior politicians and civil servants in Whitehall were concerned, they would await the findings of an internal investigation by the Prison's Minister in due course. It was unlikely to command a high priority on the Minister's agenda, or that of his boss in the Justice Department, and no one was holding their breath.

Having responded to his invitation, Mary joined Everard at a quiet table in the Red Lion and watched Brian order drinks.

"Okay," said Everard after Brian sat down, "we need to talk about the next steps concerning the brothers at the bakery."

Anticipating this, Mary had rehearsed the Security Service position with her boss. "We think," she began, "it's on track. I have not personally seen our guy. He remains in protective custody and, I'm reliably informed is happy to carry on." She then talked about the updated risk assessment and, which she enthused about, the partnership brokered with the technical wizards in Cheltenham.

Everard and Finlay exchanged occasional glances but listened without interruption.

"However," Mary went on, "in view of the likelihood that the focus will at some point shift abroad, we think there's a good case for amending the command-and-control arrangements." Which prompted another exchange of looks between the two men. "In short," she continued, "we propose that our man is formally transferred across to your Service with immediate effect. Without getting too far ahead of ourselves, this, too, has been run past our asset and he has no issue with it."

Everard and Finlay had privately discussed this idea of a secondment and Hugh had run it past both the Foreign Secretary and his new chum in Downing Street, James Wadsworth. Neither had objected. "Mary," he said, "I think that makes absolute sense, so let's make it happen as soon as possible. Perhaps you and Brian can sort out the necessary paperwork and anything your man needs to sign which, at risk of stating the obvious, should of course be done under his alias." Looking across at Brian Finlay, he added, "Brian, please personally walk this by HR – I'll want to be assured that all pension provisions are properly squared away. Can we tempt you to lunch, Mary?" asked Everard.

10

OWN IN KENT, a string of unfamiliar people had been to visit the man answering to the name Callum Bremner. It was starting to try his patience. He was beginning to feel he was back in jail. What he found particularly galling, was the tedious repetition – all intended to assess his mental health. He had played along; telling them what he suspected they wanted to hear… adding colour as necessary to enhance dramatic effect. In other circumstances it might have been fun.

The safe house was a comfortable four-bedroom gatehouse cottage with convenient access to expansive adjacent grounds at the entrance to a disused retirement home. Jo and Rob, who were rarely far away – except during the interviews – sought to make his stay as comfortable as possible. The housekeeper, Mrs Grant, was a retired member of the intelligence community. An accomplished cook, she produced fantastic meals and kept them all tidy. A wise and bubbly character, with a wicked sense of humour, Bremner was spending a lot of time in her kitchen.

"House rules" had been briefed on arrival and, lest there be any misunderstanding, he would not be left alone except in the privacy of his bedroom. If and when he wanted to take any form of exercise, most often a run, Rob or Jo would accompany him. There was no internet access, mobile phone or landline but he had use of a TV in his room. Conversation at meals omitted any reference to the past, present or future. If he wanted anything, it was bought locally. He had no passport, money, credit cards or

any such life essentials and was thus entirely reliant on his colleagues. He did, however, have some new clothes and full running gear. Jo said that he was likely to remain at the cottage for a minimum of three weeks.

More out of habit than anything else, and with encouragement from Mrs Grant, Bremner began spending time in the cottage's small garden. Unloved for months if not years, there was a lot of clearing to be done and he once again found himself with a pick in his hand. Jo, it transpired, was also a lapsed gardener and seemed happy to use a shovel and rake. Estimating her to be in her mid to late thirties, demonstrably fit and unsettlingly well organised, he was becoming accustomed to her company and beginning to appreciate their time together. It was not lost on him that she seemed totally unaffected by her beauty. Knowing nothing of her background, or Rob's, he naturally assumed they were either Security Service or Special Branch.

"You have a visitor," Jo called out to him in the garden. He washed his hands at the outside tap and entered the kitchen.

"My name's Mary," said the tall, smartly dressed, attractive woman leaning against the Aga in a grey trouser suit, white shirt, medium heels and no jewellery. "I've come to talk about the future."

As if on cue, Jo said, "I'll make some tea, would you like to go through to the Sitting Room… I won't be a minute."

Bremner led the way and Mary watched him duck below the wooden beams. He was not at all as she had imagined. There was an unmistakable intensity about him and she got the impression he was trying to work out who she was. It seemed like he was choosing to avoid eye contact – which she attributed to his time in prison. Feigning subservience as a con was habit-forming, she remembered being told during training… someone said it had been the same with defectors in the days of the Cold War.

Taking an armchair to the right of the fireplace she sat down opposite Bremner who had opted for the sofa. The room was cosy but thinly furnished with few pictures and no framed photographs to make it homely. Mary saw the camera lens high on the wall facing the window. There would be extensive coverage, all feeding back to a central control hub in one of the upstairs rooms and automatically relayed to her building in London. She was aware that all conversations were being recorded. "So, how are you doing?" she asked.

"Everyone starts with that," came the reply. "I feel fine; putting on weight thanks to Mrs Grant's marvellous cooking: the exercise regime and garden help to pass the time. Jo and Rob are good people: never far away and, as you know, I've been in far worse places lately."

She was studying him closely and, as others had observed, he looked and sounded in control. "I understand," she said as Jo came in and started pouring the tea, "that you are happy to continue this assignment. If that's not correct, you need to tell me."

As he stared into the unlit fire she heard him say, "I'm prepared to carry on."

"Good," she said, which Jo took as a signal and quietly left the room closing the door behind her. Mary noticed Bremner watching as she walked out and, remembering he hadn't seen many women whilst in prison, thought it would be unnatural if he didn't find Jo attractive. Her involvement was no accident because they wanted reassurance that Bremner didn't have a problem with women – especially women in positions of authority. She would talk to Jo, and Mrs Grant, but on the evidence thus far it seemed unlikely.

Mary sipped her tea and putting it on the side table, said,

"We're picking up that the events at Maxwell delivered the intended effect."

"From where?"

"As we suspected, old man Shala uses a mobile phone stashed somewhere in his shed. Rather than try and find it, our man – the same one who dropped off your replacement prison jacket – left a device and that's how we're getting our information." She could tell that Bremner was listening intently. "Word is," she continued, "Guzim's going to be transferred to another prison unless the authorities intervene and decide to grant early release – probably on medical grounds."

"Are you able to influence that decision," Bremner asked, now looking at her very directly.

"We're working on it. Anyway, no dates yet but we think it's likely to be within the next week or so. What we do know is that, in the aftermath of the shooting, he told his brothers to get on the case: find out who you are and, which we guessed might happen, to find you."

"Presumably, early release is a good thing?" Bremner asked, now seemingly happier to join the conversation.

"Yes, it will throw up all sorts of opportunities and we can start to move things forward." Mary let Bremner absorb what she had said before continuing, "Our assessment is that they will pay a specialist to hack the Prison Service databases and get at your record.

"That doesn't sound good," he said reaching for a sugar cube.

"Quite the opposite," she said. "It's exactly what we want them to do. There are contingency arrangements in place for just such a scenario."

"So I'm watertight, am I?"

"Yes. Your legend is robust enough to withstand the closest scrutiny. The important thing is that, if and when they attempt the hack, not only will we know about it but there's also a reasonable chance we'll get their identity."

"That's impressive," he said.

Mary paused again. "Is there anything you want to ask me about what I've said?" to which Bremner shook his head. "So," she continued, "the safest course of action for the time being is to let the bad guys make the play. We want you to stay here where it's secure."

Bremner reached for a biscuit.

"There's one more thing I need to talk to you about," she said. "In the likelihood this operation goes international – which it almost certainly will – we want to place you on formal attachment to MI6. Are you okay with that?"

"Yes..." he replied. "With effect from when?"

Mary looked at him directly and said, "Within the next few days." And with that she rose from her chair. "Thank you for your cooperation. My colleague, Brian, will pop down in a day or two. If there's anything you need, anything at all, please ask Jo."

Heading back to London in her car, Mary was now more confident that Bremner fully understood what he'd signed up for – the detail of which would be extensively briefed in due course. Furthermore, having read all the psychiatric assessments done at the cottage, she was reassured that he was in good physical and mental shape.

On the separate but pivotal issue of the Shala brothers, she was becoming increasingly suspicious that all was not necessarily as it appeared. She was getting the clear impression that Hugh Everard was of similar opinion and his interest was switching to the youngest brother. Time would tell.

****

Two days later, Brian Finlay drove down to Kent and

introduced himself to Bremner as his new *"controller"*. He went through the paperwork provided by HR and got the required signatures. Bremner was now an SIS operative – not that it made a material difference from his perspective until, that was, Finlay handed over a new passport, set of credit cards, replacement driving licence, international insurance cover and details of two bank accounts – one in London and the other in Palma on the Spanish island of Mallorca.

"Well," Bremner said smiling, "this rather suggests I'm going on a trip. Am I right?"

Finlay was prepared for this. "Yes, you are but there's no move from here for at least two weeks. I'll be in touch. Don't use any credit cards until I've personally authorised it. In fact, once you start travelling stick to cash. No point making it too easy for your pursuers," he said.

Jo re-entered the room and showed Finlay out. Before getting into his car, he asked her to join him for an *"off-the-record chat"*. Twenty minutes later he left for London having first made a quick call to Mary Stewart and, immediately after, Hugh Everard.

Finlay was experienced in the intricacies of agent-handling and had studied the impressively comprehensive legend Mary's team had created for Bremner. Meeting the man in person reinforced his opinion that he was well up to the job. He liked what he had seen and heard and Jo said the same. The impression was of a man in complete control of his emotions; the guy chose his words carefully and seemed very matter of fact when it came to risk. It was hard not to admire the man's courage and resolve. Unquestionably the biggest risk, as everyone understood, was whether the fabricated prison file was good enough to fool clever people.

He decided there and then that a visit to GCHQ might be timely.

11

VINNY BITTERLY regretted his frightening encounter with the scary man in the bakery but knew he was now committed. It had been made very clear that failure was not an option. Perversely, whilst on the one hand frightened; on the other he was intrigued. The money on offer was amazing – far exceeding anything he'd earned for a single job. Reasonably confident in his technical proficiency, he was under no misapprehension about the time and effort it would demand: literally, hours and hours. Disguising the attack would have to be handled with inordinate care. It could not be rushed.

****

In the bakery, Saban poured himself another cup of coffee before reaching into his desk and removing a mobile phone. A call was expected within the next five minutes and he needed to get his act together because his elder brother would demand answers. Ringing bang on schedule, in the short conversation that followed he was able to reassure Guzim that action was in hand to get the information he wanted. Granted, it might take a little longer than originally anticipated, but their *"expert"* was on the case – payment on results – and had been left in no doubt about the consequences if anything leaked.

Pronouncing himself satisfied, Guzim said that he wanted to see *"substantial progress"* by the time they next met. He then talked about being summoned to appear before the Parole Review Committee the following week, allegedly on medical staff recommendation because they had concerns for his physical and mental wellbeing. His diabetes was not getting any better and specialist care was strongly recommended. "It might well be that I get out of here much earlier than expected," Guzim said, and ended the call.

Later that evening the Duty Operations Controller at GCHQ dispatched a message to Vauxhall Cross via a fully encrypted communications circuit. It repeated word for word what Guzim Shala had said from his shed at Maxwell, but not for obvious reasons what was said by the other party. The assessment was that an *"expert"* of some sort had been recruited which, in all likelihood, was a hacker. It talked about a forthcoming appearance before the Parole Review Committee. Brian Finlay forwarded the report to Mary Stewart and copied it to Everard. The final part assessed a cyber-attack was highly likely – time unspecified but probably within the next seven to ten days – maybe sooner.

Finlay went to Cheltenham by appointment the following afternoon and was met on arrival by Mike and a member of the operations research team. They spent the next two hours talking about the complex world of computer hacking. "There are three sorts of hacker," Mike explained. "The so-called White, Black and Grey Hats. The easiest way to think about it is that White Hats are often employed as *'penetration-testers'*. In other words, they operate ethically, with permission, to try to compromise security systems so that any gaps or points of vulnerability can be closed."

"Good guys?"

"More or less," said Mike, smiling. "Black Hats, on the other hand, operate illegally and are motivated by personal gain – often fuelled by ego. Grey Hats are *'swingers'* who, circumstance dependant, can work ethically or for profit."

"Which ones pose the biggest threat?" Brian asked, struggling to keep up.

"The really dangerous hackers – the Black Hats – are the most technically sophisticated. They devise and employ their own codes rather than buy them on the dark web."

"So, how will we know when a computer network has been penetrated if the perpetrator is not using commercially available software?" This led into a long and very detailed explanation, at the end of which Finlay said, "You guys live in a different world, don't you? But then, I guess you have to with all the threats out there."

"We do," Mike said grinning. "The most difficult thing we have to deal with is confronting opponents in the pay of foreign governments. Ultimately, it comes down to resources – money, people, technical innovation and time. For this operation, we have taken the precaution of deploying assets forward in order to improve our chances of early detection."

Finlay knew better than to ask for details and, thanking his GCHQ colleagues for their time, returned to London. The following day he went to see Everard. Marjorie had a coffee waiting and he smiled when he saw that the fancy espresso machine had also been relocated to the eighth floor. Randell sat in the outer office reading a newspaper and stood up as Finlay entered. "I hear you're keeping yourself busy," he said. "How's the social life?"

Randell was just about to mention the new love of his life from HR when Everard opened the door. "Brian, come in."

Finlay gave a quick summary of his visit to Cheltenham and quoted Mike's remark about *"taking the precaution of deploying assets forward"*, which he took to mean to wherever the Prison Service kept their servers. The challenge was the sheer number of access points within the nation's geographically dispersed matrix of prisons. Both men were fully seized of two things; first, the working assumption was that a *"Black Hatter"* would eventually defeat any in-place network security system and second, that was precisely what they wanted to happen – which is why so much effort had been put into crafting such a resilient legend. The other challenge was to establish the identity of the perpetrator and, by association, his or her employer.

"On timing," Everard said, "when are we seeing the next stage happen?"

Brian was ready with the answer. "Within 48 hours," he replied and then talked through the details of the plan.

"Mary happy?" Everard asked, which appeared to fluster Finlay.

"Early days but she seems to be."

****

In another part of London, Vinny sat facing a bank of computer screens. His bedroom at the back of the first-floor tenement flat resembled something out of a Star Wars movie. A cluster of supporting processors, cooled by fans and dehumidifiers, hummed contentedly. The curtains were drawn and a single lamp lit the desk. Empty drinks cans and discarded sandwich wrappings were strewn across the floor which, as his mother was at pains to remind him, was his space to clean, not hers. This was his world, his life, and had been since a young boy – fascinated by computers and able to write elementary codes before he was twelve years old. This is what he did – it all came naturally. Disinterested in sport and pretty much everything other than computer games, he was nonetheless intensely curious and exceedingly clever. Rejecting university despite a formidable set of exam results in the Sixth Form of his local grammar school, he had opted for technical college and studied computer applications and coding. His so-called friends were faceless: many living in different time zones around the world. Never lonely, he was rarely intimidated by a technical challenge.

The state-of-the-art computing equipment in his room

was financed through illegal activity, including writing and selling software. Having already mapped the electronic footprint of Her Majesty's Prison Service, it was now a question of choosing the most vulnerable point of entry or, in the language of what he considered his craft, attack. He loved this stuff but could not quite erase the memory of his encounter at the bakery south of the river in Streatham. At some stage he would have to file an insurance policy, and the only way to do that was to learn more about what his new employer's business actually involved. He doubted it would prove to be legitimate.

Where to start, that was the question. He needed early results to reassure the client and, at the same time, allow himself time to work up the insurance policy. As his fingers flew over the central keyboard, he sensed his anxiety receding. He was in control. They would be ill-advised to doubt his innate ability to wreak havoc if provoked. No doubt about it: this was unquestionably the biggest project he'd ever taken undertaken. Thinking about his security, he knew he ought to find an alternative place to live because it was entirely possible the client already knew his current address. Moving all his stuff would take time but he had an alternative in mind.

*****

Back in the family's grand office north of the river in Limehouse, Saban and his younger brother were talking about the implications of Guzim securing early release which, they agreed, looked increasingly likely. As a statement of fact, life would not be as it was: their brother's resettlement would almost certainly prove a bumpy ride. Saban candidly admitted that he fully expected to have less freedom of action when it came to day-to-day business matters and decision making, grudgingly acknowledging they would be kept on a tight rein. There would be much greater accountability, more checking and less *"creative"* accounting. It was not going to be fun.

Erjon had his own reasons to be worried. "Why don't we suggest a holiday in the sun, time to regain his health without having to fuss about the business?" he asked, watching his brother demolish a stack of pancakes.

"Now that's a good idea," came the mumbled reply. "Where do you have in mind?"

Erjon sat up abruptly as though the idea had just come to him, "It would need to be a safe location," he said, "somewhere warm – ideally with medical support immediately available. What about chartering a yacht? I know some people who could make the arrangements. We could fly Guzim out by private jet."

"To where?" asked Saban.

"The Mediterranean – Italy, the Adriatic – Albania?"

Saban thought about the suggestion for a few minutes before answering. "I like the sound of that. Let me run it by him when I go up next week."

Erjon got up to leave. "Okay, let me know what he says, and I'll make some preliminary enquiries."

****

On learning about the possibility of Guzim's early release Mary Stewart arranged a meeting with a civil service colleague intimately familiar with the UK's penal system and relevant administrative procedures. The conversation left her in no doubt whatsoever that early release was virtually guaranteed. Apart from anything else, it would save the State money on expensive medical bills. The downside, which she had discussed with Finlay, was the cost of keeping tabs on the senior Shala brother after he left prison. Timings were ridiculously tight to put together a credible surveillance operation. That apart, as Mary had reminded Finlay, all they had to go on so far was rumour. There was a great deal they still didn't know about the brothers other than the flash office in Limehouse and

Saban's home address. Their knowledge of Erjon was at best patchy and, since he was probably the brains in the family, he self-selected as the focus for further investigation. With that in mind, she had begun scoping options with her colleagues and, as the first priority, worked-up a surveillance *"concept of operations"*. Finlay's offer to contribute some of his people to the planning team was readily accepted.

****

Guzim leapt at the idea of a holiday on a yacht in the sun, which was a surprise. *"The sooner the better."* The enthusiastic response made Saban smile as he drove back to London – it had gone a lot better than expected. "Nurses," Guzim had said. "Lots of them: the prettier the better." Having forgotten to ask, he wondered whether he, too, would be invited to go.

****

Mary Stewart sat at a table with the planning team she'd summoned at short notice. Opening the meeting by giving the overall aim of the operation, she then listed the planning assumptions together with any caveats and constraints.

"The main effort will be a 24 hour, 7 days a week surveillance operation on Guzim Shala from the moment he leaves prison. In parallel, we will mount a secondary operation against the youngest brother – Erjon Shala."

"What about the middle brother – Saban?"

"He's of secondary importance, but I want us to be ready to exploit any emerging leads."

"Presumably SIS will take the lead if it goes overseas?"

"Correct, which means that the contingency command and control arrangements will have to be agile."

"Special Branch is responsible for all mobile and static surveillance," she said, "but if we decide on covert entry it will he handled by our technical people."

"Where are we on the legal side?" someone asked.

"Legal Department have been warned off for any short notice requests – wire intercepts, search warrants and covert building entry."

"Has the operation been assigned a codeword?"

"It has," Mary said trying to keep a straight face but failing. "*Mildred*."

After the laughter subsided she added, "We're dealing with some nasty people and I want tight security and strict adherence of '*need-to-know*'."

****

Finlay and Everard were nursing their pints in the private back room of a favourite pub just off Wandsworth Bridge Road. It was early evening; rowers were punishing themselves on the river. Ashore, the place was bustling with commuters fortifying themselves with a few quick *"stiffeners"* before returning to loved ones. Sufficiently noisy for their purpose, and without naming names, places or dates, they had both sensed a need to review the status of planning against the Shala brothers. Everard never ceased to be amazed at the names the computer threw up. "'*Mildred*', for Christ's sake," he said lifting his glass and slowly shaking his head.

Finlay played-back the key points from Mary Stewart's team briefing. He wanted to be sure that Everard was comfortable with the command-and-control arrangements… which he was.

"I'd be keen to know if our people in Washington can find out what, if anything, the Americans have on the Shala's," Everard said.

"You're particularly interested in Erjon, aren't you?"

"I am, but let's keep the old man in the mix."

"When do you intend going over there?" Brian asked.

"Within the next couple of weeks," Everard replied.

Randell dropped Finlay near his flat before delivering his boss to Pimlico where, having caught up with the evening news on TV and in Norfolk, Everard poured himself a glass of wine and thought about the meeting with the Foreign Secretary.

Next morning, on his way to John Pelham's office, he couldn't help noticing the smart new brass plate, *"Foreign, Commonwealth and Development Office". Why*, he mused as he climbed the stairs to the grand office, *do people insist on meddling with things that aren't broken*. Relieved of his coat and accepting the offer of coffee, he was met by Pelham and invited to take a seat. Quickly sensing his boss was in listening mode, he summarised the current status of Operation Mildred. Pelham did not interrupt and neither did he make notes. Inevitably, the question arose about contingency arrangements if – which seemed a foregone conclusion – the lead switched to SIS. In responding, Everard cited historical precedent as well as referring to successful recent joint exercises with the Security Service.

Pelham appeared suitably reassured. Touching on his forthcoming visit to Washington, Everard said he intended asking US colleagues to run some names through their databases. John Pelham already knew that Everard was particularly interested in the youngest of the Shala brothers but not yet why. Pre-empting the question, Everard made clear his belief that Erjon was the real player in the game rather than Guzim. The *"effect"* he sought was to sow seeds of doubt and mistrust within the family and, in so doing, provoke Erjon into over-reacting and thereby opening wider opportunities. "Put simply, we want to provoke a family punch-up," he said, adding, "and as ever, timing is everything."

****

Down in Kent, Bremner was packing a bag. Jo had relayed

a message from Brian Finlay that transport would arrive within the next hour for a road move to Plymouth. He'd be travelling alone. From there, the plan was for him to embark on a twenty-two-hour crossing to Santander in northern Spain. "You will not be coming back here so give me anything you want us to keep hold of," she said.

"You're not coming then?"

"Sadly not," she said with a grin.

"Pity," he said. "I reckon it's going to be a brilliant road trip."

"Know how to do the tourist thing do you?" she asked.

"Absolutely."

****

Later that morning, sitting on a bench in the garden enjoying one of Mrs Grant's sensational lemon drizzle cakes, Bremner revisited the conversation he'd had with Finlay some days earlier. "We think it's only a matter of time before the hacker they've hired cracks the prison system and recovers your file," he'd been told.

"But that's what we want though, isn't it?" he'd asked.

"Absolutely. We're laying a trail for them," Finlay had said. "You need to be absolutely clear about what it is we want you to do when... as they will... they find you. Of course what we don't know, is precisely when and where that will be. The key point, Callum, is the objective: namely, for you to get close to Guzim; gain his trust. Mindful of the Albanian culture, it's reasonable to assume that he feels some level of indebtedness to you. It gives us leverage. However, we cannot be certain that the other brothers will see it the same way – especially the one who interests us the most."

"Erjon?"

"Correct. Not teaching you to suck eggs, but these are seriously nasty people."

"Will I be armed?"

"No, but we'll keep it under review. If you need a gun we'll get one to you. Any preference?"

"Glock 17 if I get a choice – the Generation 5 model. Failing that, Sig Sauer 38."

Before leaving, Finlay had given him an emergency contact number in Monaco – to be committed to memory – and only used in an emergency or when conveying important information.

12

RANDELL MET his boss in the arrival hall of Washington's Dulles International Airport on a frosty Saturday morning. Although unorthodox, on overseas trips he routinely flew ahead. It was their preferred way to handle logistics, rather than rely on the local embassy's arrangements. Hire cars were less conspicuous. He would arrange vehicles and, being familiar with the geography of most national capitals on *"C's"* circuit, could be relied upon to get them to where they needed to be.

Everard rarely accepted the offer of accommodation at British Ambassadors' residences, preferring to stay – security circumstances permitting – in central hotels. Besides, if timings and the season allowed – especially in America – there was always the chance of some fishing. The Rappahannock River in Eastern Virginia and the lakes close to the FBI Academy at Quantico were firm favourites and only a short hop south on Interstate 95.

Rarely using the same hotel twice, on this occasion they opted for the Ritz-Carlton in Georgetown – close to where Everard had enjoyed so many nice meals with Mary Stewart all those years ago.

Having settled into the hotel, Everard took a nap before walking the short distance along M Street NW for a relaxed lunch at a local restaurant with the British Ambassador and his SIS Head of Station. Meanwhile, having seen him into the restaurant, Randell got on with sorting out the *"travel"* fly rods and assorted kit he'd brought with him for their pursuit of Largemouth Bass at Quantico the next day – for which he had already bought Virginia Fishing Licences.

They would head off early Sunday morning, stopping for breakfast at a favoured diner on the way.

The Ambassador returned to his residence after lunch, leaving Everard free for a walk along the adjacent canal with his SIS colleague. A series of office calls were arranged for Monday: the Defence Intelligence Agency; CIA Headquarters in Langley; National Security Agency – the largest and reputedly most technologically sophisticated of all the intelligence agencies – and, at Department of State, the Bureau of Intelligence and Research. Everard was updated on current dealings with the respective organisations and as he'd asked, a request had been submitted for information on, amongst others, the Shalas.

****

Sunday at Quantico chasing bass was great fun and suitably rewarding. It was beginning to warm up and they had been thankful for a breeze. Untroubled by mosquitoes or midges, Randell had obtained a boat from somewhere and also a cool box stocked with lagers and soft drinks. The sandwiches were splendid and so, too, the flask of better-than-average coffee. Like his boss, he loved American diners and had come to appreciate the customary cheerful service. As usual, after the initial stop for breakfast, Everard slept most of the way; doing exactly the same after supper on the way back to Washington.

The very full programme of office calls in and around the Metropolis on Monday, to which he was accompanied by the Head of Station, proved equally productive. Before departing for Dulles for the return overnight flight to London that evening, Everard made a routine office call on the Ambassador to give him a summary of his various discussions, but without going into specifics.

****

He came away from Washington with much to think

about. Erjon Shala was a known name – seemingly for questionable business dealings in the Caribbean where, purportedly, he was linked to several companies involved in money laundering. Some sort of link was believed to exist with Cyprus and, confirming what he already suspected, the man was involved with organised criminal gangs directly engaged in trafficking. However, the jewel in the crown was being told of a connection to several Middle Eastern business organisations with funding links to known terrorist groups. This was what had brought him to Washington, and it was what troubled him the most.

As he reflected at length on the plane when sleep was proving elusive, there was considerably more to the youngest Shala than met the eye. Private enterprise was clearly alive and well and not being shared with the rest of his family. By any measure, it was a high-risk strategy. There was also the strange fact that, for whatever reason, Erjon had chosen not to divulge his conversion from Christianity to Islam and the Sunni faith which, he vaguely remembered, was shared with more than forty per cent of native Albanians. This last piece of information had been another real surprise, leaving Everard to conclude that the man must only practise his religion when abroad and well out of sight of his brothers.

Lying stretched out on the flat bed in the Business Class section of British Airways 747 as it sped eastwards through the night, Everard regretted not arranging to meet up with more of his old friends in Virginia. Most were now enjoying retirement – the thought of which made him smile as he remembered his early morning deliberations under a tree by his lake a few weeks ago.

There was so much to like about America: the people; their inherent optimism; an independent streak which valued self-starters and those with a preparedness to innovate, try fresh ideas, work hard and take risks. In earlier years he had travelled the country extensively and, in different circumstances, could easily see himself on a small farm in the Pacific North West – maybe Oregon or Montana. That said, Penny was like a limpet stuck to an immovable rock in Norfolk. But that was okay, too. She was happy and her happiness mattered a great deal to him.

In what seemed like no time at all, he was being gently woken and offered breakfast with an hour to landing at Heathrow's Terminal 5. Randell had arranged for them to be met by another of the Service's drivers and taken directly to the office.

****

Having relieved him of her present of chocolates on his arrival, Marjorie walked in with an espresso and said that Brian Finlay was standing by as requested. For the next hour they discussed the main points from his trip and, like him, Finlay was intrigued by what had been learned about Erjon Shala – especially his *"double life"*. Curiouser and curiouser.

"Breaking news," Brian said. "Guzim has been granted early release… he's likely to be out in the next seven to ten days."

"Are Mary's lot all set?"

"Yes."

"Where's Bremner?"

"On his way to Santander by ferry."

"Are we squared away with all the command-and-control stuff – the Foreign Secretary's bound to ask me?"

"Yes, we're good and our respective teams have been running through a range of different scenarios. The GCHQ forward elements are in place… nothing heard so far."

"Good. That all sounds very positive," Everard said. "I'm going to talk to our Israeli contacts in Mossad –

they're bound to know what's going on if it relates to somebody being involved in funding terrorists."

"And if they don't they'll make a point of finding out," Brian said.

"Indeed."

****

John Pelham paid close attention to Everard's backbrief on his Washington trip and, not surprisingly, picked up on the possible connection between Erjon Shala and businesses in the Middle East. "Have our US cousins established his connections to terrorist groups as fact?" he asked.

"No," Everard replied, "but they will now make it a priority." Pelham was staring at a painting on the wall of one of his predecessors and seemed completely transfixed by it. Clearly having big thoughts, Everard privately concluded, before saying, "I intend on contacting our Mossad friends to see what they know about our man and, if necessary, we'll send Brian Finlay over to Tel Aviv."

Pelham was patently unsettled by the emerging picture of Erjon Shala. "You see him as a significant threat, don't you, Hugh?"

Taking time to muster his thoughts before responding, Everard said, "The short answer is, yes, Foreign Secretary, I do. But we need to learn much more about him and, in particular, his supposed connections in the Middle East. As you know, surveillance operations are lined up for when the older Shala brother is released from prison. GCHQ is fully engaged and with luck we should start to get some useful feedback on the brothers in general, and Erjon in particular. What we still don't have a feel for is whether Guzim believes he was the target of the shooting rather than Bremner. Once we get closer to him this should become much clearer. That said, as you have already deduced, our principal interest is increasingly switching to the youngest brother. The big unknown is why Erjon appears to lead a double life: why on earth would he conceal his faith from his brothers?"

Turning to a file on his desk, Pelham said, "Okay Hugh, thank you, and please continue to keep me posted. I'll give the PM a brief summary of where we are with Mildred after Cabinet tomorrow – who came up with that name, for Christ's sake? Is there anything else you need from me?"

Everard paused before answering, "It would be helpful if you could have a chat with the Israeli Ambassador and mention that I'll be popping over to talk to some of his people on the specific subject of a British national whom we have reason to believe might have information of interest relating to connections in the Middle East." As he got up to leave Everard looked at the dashing portrait of a military officer which Pelham had been staring at – Sir Austen Chamberlain (1924-1929). Those were the days, cometh the hour cometh the man.

Everard was definitely warming to John Pelham. Contrary to his predecessor's assessment, he felt the man could be trusted with privileged information; but, just to be sure, he had deliberately tested him with a few snippets of low-grade intelligence in order to see whether they found their way to Downing Street. James Wadsworth subsequently confirmed they had not.

Unquestionably clever and comfortable with his responsibilities, unlike so many of his fellow Cabinet colleagues, Pelham did not engage in point-scoring. Moreover, he was inordinately careful about which battles he chose to fight and, said the corridor chat, only engaged in those he could win. Everard was familiar with Pelham's career having previously read his personal file – which was probably inappropriate, but he preferred to know with whom he was dealing. The Foreign Secretary was an accomplished politician and diplomat. Married, with a young family, his home was in Wiltshire where, his file noted, he liked to ride and kept several horses. Reassuringly, at least on the face of it, the Pelham cupboard seemed devoid of skeletons.

****

Vinny stared at his screen and grinned. His three days hard work – including painstakingly trawling the dark web – paid off when he finally managed to access the Prison Service Records Department at the Ministry of Justice. It should now be relatively simple to find the correct file of a man called *"Bremner"* – something he would pursue at leisure tomorrow because the immediate priority was to relocate to the fifth floor, two bed apartment he had rented in an adjacent neighbourhood.

Moving his equipment, all of which had to be boxed up in the event of nosy new neighbours, would take the rest of the day. Reassembling it all could not be rushed and, which was a crucial factor in location, the new place had a strong broadband connection. Thinking about his client, and repressing an involuntary shudder, he decided it might be smart to provide an initial progress report. The expression *"feeding the beast"* came to mind as he reached for the as yet unused burner phone handed to him in the bakery.

Saban was quick to answer.

"We have a point of entry," Vinny said, without giving his name. "It'll take a few more days to get my hands on what you want but I'm pretty sure I can do it."

Saban nodded to himself as he received the welcome information. "Excellent, come back to me when you have further news," he said and hung up.

"Really… you arrogant bastard," Vinny said aloud as he turned off his screens and began dismantling and boxing up his stuff.

****

The GCHQ forward-deployed technical team was remarkably quick to pick up unusual out-of-hours activity on the Prison Service computer network. The hard part, which they knew, was establishing the identity of the perpetrator and, for that reason, they decided to make things harder in an attempt to trap their opponent into making a mistake. Mike forwarded a progress report, summarising the team's initial findings. "We can draw two conclusions," it began. "First, the code used in the hack confirms we're dealing with a *'Black Hatter'*. Second, since it's unique, the code might be impossible to crack – depending, that is, on how often it's used." Further down the report he added, "There is no doubt, whatsoever, that we are dealing with someone at the top of their game. We will need to proceed with caution in order not to reveal our presence."

****

Early next morning, Randell dropped Everard and Finlay just round the corner from the Old Coffee Shop in Montrose Place. It was going to be another nice day and early commuters had abandoned coats and scarves. This was unfamiliar territory to Brian as he followed Everard to a table with a view overlooking the street. Sliding onto the upholstered red bench seat, he could sense the growing expectation of his boss across the table who, he noticed, was taking personal charge of ordering bacon sandwiches and espresso coffee.

Mary Stewart entered the café two minutes later and, pausing to order at the counter, smiled as she walked over to them – both men standing up as she approached the table and eased in next to Finlay. Their food all arrived at once and Everard, reaching for the brown sauce, noted how relaxed his companions appeared in each other's company. Finlay definitely perked-up on seeing Mary, which Everard took to be further evidence of a developing relationship.

Chatting quietly about things in general over their meal, they studiously avoided anything to do with Mildred. Back outside, they walked slowly in the general direction of the Royal College of Defence Studies.

After confirming that they had all read the previous night's report from GCHQ, Mary summarised what she had gleaned from a follow up chat with her team who, reassuringly, shared her assessment that things were falling nicely into place. "I've emphasised to my lot," she began, "that we need to be super quick responding to anything the surveillance op throws up – people, places or activity. I've stressed that everyone has to stay flexible: priorities could well change at short notice."

"Yes," Everard said. "Anything you pick up from the US would be gratefully received."

Anticipating this, Mary said, "I've asked our FBI contacts in Washington to put feelers out amongst the US Albanian community."

Typically one step ahead, Hugh thought. Approaching the College, he bade farewell to them both in the knowledge that they would go on to discuss the surveillance arrangements in more depth. As Everard climbed into the front seat of his car, Randell couldn't help noticing the tin foiled package dropped on the dashboard.

****

Saban called his younger brother from the comfort of the Limehouse office. "Where are you?" he asked.

"Out of the country," came the reply, without offering any clues.

This did not entirely surprise Saban, who had known for a long time that Erjon was fond of spending time in warm climates. It was no secret that he owned at least one property in the Caribbean and liked to go there whenever possible – whereas his preference was for the holiday apartment he kept closer to home in Jersey. "Okay," he said, "Guzim is being released in five days. I will go up there and bring him directly to London. The housekeeper assures me everything's ready at the town house. She's quite nervous at the thought of seeing him after all these years. Anyway, once he's home we can talk about the holiday."

Erjon was listening attentively whilst slowly pacing the veranda of his expansive single-storey house overlooking the lush fairways of the exclusive Hampton Grange Country Club in Barbados. "Understood," he said. "I'll be back at the weekend. What about a party of some sort to celebrate his homecoming?"

"I'll ask him."

"Maybe we could arrange some female company? You could ask him that, too."

After ending the call, Erjon made himself a cold drink and went back out to the veranda. Still dark, the constant chatter of the cicadas was strangely comforting. He adored the mixed scent from the flower beds: pink and white begonias, blue vine, blue lotus and plumbago and, draped across his roof and walls, his favourite – bougainvillea. In hindsight, he should probably have bought a property on the beach but it would have introduced additional security risks and, on balance, he felt more secure within his current gated community. The house was run by an elderly local couple: she managed the housekeeping and her husband took care of the garden, pool and any driving. Like himself, they were Sunni Muslims and, like him, observed prayers five times every day. Having owned the house for over ten years, investing significant money furnishing it, he felt more at home there than he did at his place in London. The housekeeper and her husband lived in an adjoining annex and kept everything ready for his visits. A BMW X5 sufficed for transport.

Barbados suited him. Twice-daily direct flights from

London made it easy. So, too, being in the same time zone as Grand Cayman, from where several of his holding companies operated. He loved the warm water, absence of nosy neighbours and the abundance of good restaurants – The Cliff in St James being a particular favourite. A regular haunt, it reminded him of the outside of a Spanish Galleon; large tarpon constantly circling, drawn by spotlights and offerings of bits of bread roll thrown by amused clients. The only disadvantage of the island was its popularity with Brits. But, keeping to himself and always flying First or Business Class, this was rarely an issue. He had even begun taking golf lessons.

What was increasingly becoming a key issue for him, rarely far from his mind, was the imminent release of his soon-to-be-ex-con older brother. Analysing the situation was comparatively easy, the problem was deciding what to do about it. Even with the onset of old age and worsening health, Guzim was still a force to be reckoned with. Demonstrably sharper and less of a blunt instrument than Saban – with a similar propensity for violence – he was still the head of the family and highly ranked within their particular Albanian tribe. Respected for the resilience he had shown throughout his imprisonment, and his steadfast refusal to relinquish the reins, he retained respect, loyalty and trust: not just amongst the Albanian community in the UK, but far beyond. The big unknown, which frightened Erjon the most, was how his brothers would react when they discovered the full extent of his private business dealings – most especially the trafficking. The policy was always abundantly clear, as far as Guzim was concerned, it was emphatically a *"no go"* area.

There was also the more delicate but equally significant issue of his undeclared conversion to Sunni Islam and, through it, his continuing commitment to pay substantial amounts of money to Middle Eastern groups resolved to oppose the West and everything it stood for. His views were strongly held and originated in his fervent opposition to what he saw as the subjugation of fellow Sunni Muslims in Afghanistan and subsequently Iraq. The devastating attack on 9/11 as a direct consequence of military occupation was, at least to his mind, entirely justified. The ideology of Jihad sat comfortably with him. He sided with those who believed there could be no end date until such time as all Western forces had gone. This was a cause, a holy war, about which he cared deeply. It was also something that his family could never begin to understand or, by association, the money he provided to perpetuate it.

Ever the pragmatist, the first priority was to welcome his older brother back into the fold where, over time, he could better assess how much of a threat he posed. Staring into the darkness, he came to an inescapable realisation: the risks now significantly outweighed the benefits: it was only a question of time before Guzim uncovered the truth. Nothing else for it, his brothers would have to be sacrificed in the pursuit of a higher cause; their continued existence put at risk his wider strategic objectives. Sad, but they were expendable… what was that expression… "*collateral damage*". The paradox did not escape him: it wasn't personal and yet it absolutely was. Sunrise was approaching and it was time for his first call to prayer. He would be seeking enlightenment.

****

Back in London, having moved into his new apartment, Vinny sat in front of his three-screen array. Living on the fifth floor and conveniently not overlooked, blinds had replaced curtains and he liked seeing daylight. Soon after taking up occupancy, all locks had been replaced and a sophisticated alarm system installed. He felt secure. Conveniently, a local café offered ample menu choices and the local corner shop provided whatever else he needed. With fingers tapping on the keyboard, he returned to his task at the Ministry of Justice and began the careful penetration of the database containing individual records of convicted criminals, past and present.

Unpicking the anticipated protective software, it became obvious that the job was going to pose more of a technical challenge than anticipated. "Slow down," he said aloud, cautioning himself, "this isn't a sprint." As the hours sped past, he became oblivious to everything other than the sequences of rapidly changing data on the screens before him – numbers cascading endlessly. Transported to another world – his world – he was utterly gripped and, in truth, in every sense of the word, addicted.

After making himself a cup of tea and dispatching a packet of chocolate biscuits with indecent haste, he sat back in his high-backed leather chair and reassessed his new surroundings. His mother had been on the phone several times asking if he was eating properly and whether someone was doing his washing. This new place was definitely more spacious and, for some reason, he was becoming more conscious of time.

Having fired off an initial report to the client, he judged it appropriate to switch roles and send a related message through a separate channel. Grinning as he tapped out an email message to an address given to him for a different purpose and, unbeknown to the Shala's, he was in fact also the "*insurance policy*". In other words, he was pretending to hack himself. It was his personal insurance policy and, if necessary, a means to defend his interests and, potentially, the way to plunder their ill-gotten wealth. Thinking back to the man in the bakery, he said, "You have no idea who you're dealing with and cannot possibly begin to understand what will happen if you try to mess with me."

And with that he loaded a fresh code into the computer and began probing the Shala businesses. Before beginning this parallel line of activity, he sent a short message to the

Client to say everything was as it appeared regarding *"Hacker Number One's investigations"* and, importantly, that said Hacker had indeed breached the first-tier defences inside the Ministry of Justice.

That would do for now. Feeling more confident and in control, it should satisfy the *"beast's"* insatiable appetite for information – at least in the short term – and, which was the main objective, reassure his employers that everything was on track. There was, he remembered, the question of a separate fee to be negotiated for his secondary role – something for later. Alert to the risk of inadvertently compromising his two identities, he opened a logbook to record the developing parallel narratives. "This is such fun," he mused, "and being handsomely paid for it too – twice!"

13

BREMNER WAS sorry to say goodbye to Jo, Rob and Mrs Grant but not sad to be leaving Kent. Dumping his unwanted clothes after another exemplary breakfast on the final morning and bidding farewell to his vegetable patch, he relieved Rob of the keys to a distinctly scruffy Land Rover Discovery. The logbook and insurance details bore his name. "It's been fully tested and serviced," Rob said. "She's not pretty but runs like a dream." There was a comprehensive tool kit, first aid stuff and road atlases for Spain, France and Italy.

"I loved these beauties," Bremner said, affectionately stroking the bonnet. "The one I've got has never let me down."

Finlay had told him that his whereabouts would be tracked through the new iPhone – currently devoid of contact numbers in the address book; the internet usage history showed only ferry timetable enquiries.

Jo was noticeably quiet and by no means her usual bubbly self. Much of their time in past weeks had been spent in the garden. He had not felt so relaxed in someone else's company for a long time. Daily runs with Rob, and occasionally her, had restored his fitness. Emotionally, though, things were not quite so positive. To his surprise, he'd developed a serious fondness for Jo and, which didn't help, he had a feeling she felt the same. Despite there being ample opportunity in the evenings, nothing had happened between them.

He'd never met anyone like her. Although unquestionably attractive, it wasn't just about looks.

Quietly self-confident, considerate and strong in the emotional intelligence department, her laugh was infectious. Like him, she had studiously avoided anything to do with their respective backgrounds or the Security Service. The reality, which he felt she understood, was that forming any sort of relationship would not be smart. It was an additional burden he couldn't afford.

Having said goodbye to Rob and an emotional Mrs Grant, he and Jo walked out to Discovery. "Jo," he said with more difficulty than he had expected. "Thanks for everything you've done for me. You've made my time here so much easier than it might have been and I want you to know I appreciate it. Pity you can't sow a straight line of runner beans but nobody's perfect."

She laughed, sensing he hadn't finished.

"One day," he said, "when this is all over, I really hope we get to meet again."

Jo, watching intently and looking directly at him as he spoke, had not uttered a word.

Stretching up to kiss his cheek she said, "Me too – please take good care of yourself, Callum." And walked back to the cottage.

Looking into the rear-view mirror as he drove away, he saw her standing at the kitchen window: an image he would carry with him in the days and weeks ahead. Six hours later he was in Plymouth studying the Spanish road atlas and waiting in a queue to board the ferry to Santander.

****

Jo made coffee and sat at the kitchen table after he left. Their time together had been uncomplicated and she had become very fond of him. Unmistakably shy, she found his easy-going and unpretentious manner incredibly attractive. He had a lovely smile and she loved hearing him singing when working on his own in the garden. But it was not lost on her that outward appearances can and do deceive –

which is why he's so good at his job, she reasoned. She'd fallen for him. No question about it whatsoever and, not for the first time, she was left to wonder who he was. One day she rather hoped she'd get to find out.

Finishing the coffee, she had reached for her mobile and sent a brief text. The cottage would be sanitised over the next 24 hours. Mrs Grant assured her that their work in the vegetable garden would not be wasted.

****

Up in Shropshire, Guzim stood in a queue of two waiting to recover his personal possessions at HMP Maxwell. Hard to believe the idiots were letting him out early. Annoyingly, his personal contacts had failed to shed light on the shooting and, in short, he was none the wiser on the central question of whether they were after him, or Bremner – something he would grip later. The last two things to be done before leaving Maxwell had been dealt with, namely destroying the sim card on the burner phone – burying it even deeper in the shed – and arranging for the severe scolding of his former minder in the prison kitchen in the week after his release. "*Bastard!*" he said to himself.

Formalities duly completed and dressed in his tight but still presentable fifteen-year-old suit, he strolled across to the parked Mercedes saloon and hugged his brother. On their way to London, he quickly relaxed in the comfort of the leather seat and, staring ahead said, "Talk to me about the shooting."

Saban had rehearsed his answer. "Our young hacker is on the case. Matter of fact, he's already cracked the Ministry of Justice's computer security system and is close to getting his hands on Bremner's personal file."

"How do you know apart from him telling you?"

"It's been independently verified by our second hacker who, as I told you, we've hired by way of an insurance policy."

"When will we see something?"

"We can expect a copy of the file within the next few days. After that, the priority will be to find him."

Guzim mulled this over. "Excellent," he said. "Where's Erjon?"

"On his way back from the Caribbean. We thought we'd have a few drinks tomorrow night – maybe invite some ladies."

"Too early for that… the ladies I mean… all in good time," Guzim said as he closed his eyes and switched his thoughts to his youngest brother. Being honest with himself, he had never entirely worked Erjon out. Clever, certainly, and blessed with a sharp business mind, he was nonetheless a very private person who tended to keep his opinions to himself.

"We're going directly to your place," Saban said an hour later on seeing his brother's eyes open. "The housekeeper has kept everything in order and is very excited about seeing you. I have arranged a visit to a Harley Street medical specialist for tomorrow and Erjon suggested putting your old Saville Row tailor on standby."

"I thought he'd retired?"

"He did but will make an exception in your case."

Guzim listened without interruption. "I'm disappointed we've heard nothing from our own people about the shooting," he said. "We will arrange a meeting – someone out there knows more than they're choosing to share with us."

****

Despite being reasonably *"surveillance aware"*, Saban failed to notice the grey saloon parked in the prison carpark or, for that matter, the black van with a man and woman that was keeping pace three cars behind as they turned onto the M54 – alternating with a blue estate car with two male occupants once on the M5. The mobile surveillance team comprised the same three men and a woman who had handled Bremner's extraction from Maxwell. The two additional colleagues were also from Special Branch. Foot surveillance teams were at notice to deploy in London once the destination was confirmed. In anticipation, a static covert observation post was already in place overlooking the town house.

Judges had approved requests for phone taps on the brothers' respective landlines and, should it be decided to conduct covert placement of listening devices, a technical team was putting together a detailed pack on the building layouts. At Mary Stewart's instigation, a discussion was underway with the provider of the property's security alarm system and, as a contingency, her people were toying with the idea of a local power cut to facilitate covert entry.

Needing time to think, Mary was alone in her office and had asked not to be disturbed. Happy with the surveillance plan, she'd heard about Guzim's departure. Now convinced that the operational lead would switch to SIS, she was keen to explore what more her Service could provide in support. It was for this reason she called for the personal file of one of the "*cleared*" operational staff.

Jo Williams had been marked as "*definite potential*" by Security Service recruiters when a student at Manchester University working towards an eventual 2:1 in modern languages. Thereafter, she took a late gap year travelling in North and South America. On return home, for lack of anything better and mainly to be with her friends, she found employment with an advertising agency in London. It didn't last. After a short stint as a waitress, friends stepped in and suggested she should try for a position in the yachting industry. At the time something of a boy's club as far as the deck side went, it meant starting down below as a stewardess. In addition to polishing, scrubbing, making beds and endlessly hoovering, the laundry became her domain: a dab hand at ironing – everything.

Two years later, having saved sufficient cash for a deposit on a small flat in Hackney, she successfully passed the Civil Service entrance exam and entered the Home Office. Three years after that, she decided to apply for the Security Service and, on completion of training, took up her first field assignment undercover as a translator with a company in the city.

Described as an *"innovative and independently minded self-starter"*, the file referred to a *"somewhat reserved character but justifiably confident in her own abilities"*. The training report was impressive. She was credited with loads of initiative and capable of *"thinking her way out of trouble"*. According to her file, there had been a string of boyfriends but nobody special and she was currently *"unattached".*

Jo impressed Mary when they'd met at the cottage and was already aware that she'd spent several stints working under alias – including one which had turned particularly nasty and landed her in hospital. Mary made a note on the file. "Talented woman," she said aloud, before ringing Brian Finlay and inviting him to lunch.

****

Flying back to London overnight, Erjon was at the Chelsea town house to greet Guzim on arrival. The brothers chatted amiably for the next couple of hours over lunch before leaving Guzim to retire for a nap. Saban did most of the talking, basically updating various legitimate business issues. A separate session in the privacy of the bakery would follow in slower time. There was no discussion about the shooting but it was obviously weighing on everyone's mind.

Erjon thought his older brother looked old and sounded frail; he seemed to lack his usual sharpness – asking for words to be repeated. But, he reasoned, it was hardly surprising and couldn't have been much fun being shot at – thankfully something neither he nor Saban had personally experienced and had no wish to. Then, of course, there were all the years banged-up in prison. The thought of it filled him with dread and he seriously doubted he would cope – even with his deep-rooted religious beliefs.

The follow-up conversation in the bakery would be different: business-like, forensically focused and wide-ranging in scope. Guzim was into detail. Always had been. He would examine the accounts. It was about results and there would be no fobbing-off. As Erjon well knew, those who failed to perform to his big brother's expectations – or missed deadlines – had cause to be anxious.

Reassuringly, Erjon knew the overall balance sheet was strong: taxes were always paid on time; the property portfolio was expansive; growth had risen exponentially year-on-year – emerging threats were invariably identified early and promptly addressed. Furthermore, the portfolio of illegal activities was also in a healthy state and, importantly, their many alliances and networks remained strong. *"Better together"* continued to serve them well as the prevailing business strategy. The Albanian footprint in the UK – always under threat from the Russians – was slowly expanding. No, all things considered, Erjon was confident he could put a positive spin on everything. The big message was emphatically that there was scope for optimism. Although a forlorn hope, he would continue to encourage his brothers to diversify but not into the really lucrative people-related stuff. In parallel, he would plan their deaths.

During conversation over lunch, Erjon had picked up the undisguised enthusiasm for a break in the sun and volunteered to make the necessary arrangements.

"I'd like to catch my breath," Guzim said when the

subject of the cruise arose. "This civilian thing is still a novelty. Maybe we could go in a week or two – being a free man is exhausting me," he said laughing.

"I'm sure that won't be a problem," Erjon responded.

"Will we be able to see some of our people in Albania?"

"Absolutely."

Erjon could tell that Saban was angling to be on the trip and, grudgingly, accepted that he, too, would have to be involved – not least to ensure that none of his undeclared activities in the region were inadvertently compromised... which would be disastrous.

****

Mary called Finlay to say that the *"Watchers"* had successfully *"housed"* the brothers at the town house and handed over responsibility to their colleagues in the covert observation post overlooking the property. A separate team tailed Erjon back to what was assumed to be his own house in Chelsea and, from there, to the family office in Limehouse. She said she was deferring any decision on covert building entry to the Shala properties or fitting devices to their private vehicles. It was too risky.

****

In his fifth-floor flat, Vinny was working away on his computer and overdue a break. It had been a long night. This sort of punishing routine was not unusual and, once engaged, the hours became meaningless. It was the same when he was writing code – totally absorbing. Always up for a challenge, cracking this particular nut was proving a major test of his skill and patience. *Fair play*, he thought to himself, *someone's spent a lot of money making it difficult for guys like me to mess with them*. However, the puzzle was slowly beginning to unravel and, he felt, within his grasp. Two hours later he was proved right.

****

The GCHQ Team continued monitoring the repeated

attempts *"by person or persons unknown"* to access the Prison Records Database and, unfazed by the unsociable hours, had kept pace. Just after four in the morning, one of the operators spotted a small mistake by their unseen adversary. Yet again it served to illustrate that people, not computers, are invariably the point of weakness. Triggering a pre-loaded contingency response and separate programme, they were able to make copies of the hacker's software – in effect potentially exposing his or her *"computer identity"*. This was a game-changer and a report was immediately fired off to Mary Stewart and Brian Finlay – who agreed to meet first thing in the morning.

****

"It actually doesn't change anything in the short-term, Brian," Mary said as they walked through St James' Park the next day. "Yes, of course identifying the hacker is helpful, but all we wanted at this stage is confirmation that he or she had got hold of Bremner's prison record which, as our Cheltenham pals have confirmed, has now happened." Brian was struggling to understand her thinking but chose not to comment. "The big question," she continued, "is whether the Shalas actually believe what our hacker friend gives them. I'm convinced the legend is strong and, as you know, we've added further detail to cover what happened to Bremner immediately following the shooting."

"You're referring to the decision to send the ambulance directly to the Queen Elizabeth Hospital in Birmingham rather than Stoke?" Brian asked.

"Yes, I am," she replied. "Mainly because of their experience in treating military casualties from Iraq and Afghanistan. The record now includes that move and, don't forget, for the express purpose of simulating emergency surgery for a bullet wound to his lower left side. It also includes recuperating under protective custody and early release, with a discharge date and so forth."

"Is that where it ends?" asked Finlay.

"It does," she said. "The final piece to be inserted into what we might term the *"credibility jigsaw"* which, you will also recall, was to arrange for a cosmetic surgeon to perform his art on Bremner and replicate the scar of a bullet hole. I might add that when we first floated the idea of surgery our man was – how shall we say – less than wholly enthusiastic."

Feeling in need of an espresso, Brian suggested stopping at a nearby favourite café opposite the Institute of Directors on Pall Mall. Once seated at the window, he said, "Presumably, the record we're discussing omits any forwarding or contact address for our man?"

"Exactly," said Mary – scanning the breakfast menu. "We can't make it too easy for them, can we. I'll have the poached eggs and smashed avocado, please."

****

Back in the office, Finlay popped up to see his chief on the eighth floor. Satisfied with the overall situation, Everard made a note to write a personal letter of thanks to the Director General at Cheltenham. He planned to write separately to the Director of the Security Service to say, amongst other things, how impressed he was by Mary Stewart. Copies of both notes would go to his future fishing pal in Downing Street.

Listening to Finlay talking, Everard once again found himself assessing the man's suitability for the still vacant Director of Operations position. The trouble with Brian Finlay was that he could sometimes be a bit too quick off the mark; he took things personally. Although an acknowledged intelligence practitioner, the Director's job might prove a bit of a stretch. Besides, at no stage since becoming vacant had Brian indicated any ambition for it.

****

Suitably refreshed after a café lunch and good kip, Vinny returned to duty at the computer. Then, with a loud *"yes"*, he was in. The full prison records lay before him: all listed alphabetically by year of conviction. The volume of files was vast. It would have helped to have had the year he'd gone down or, if not, at least Bremner's initials, date of birth or Social Security Number. He had bugger-all except a surname. Undaunted, he typed *"Bremner"* in the search box and hit the *"Enter"* key. Then, as an afterthought, added *"Scottish"*. The list shrunk dramatically but was still too long. He next entered *"HMP Maxwell"* and the year. Bingo. "*Bremner, C; DOB: 23 April 1978; Offence: Fraud; Date of Conviction: 8 March 2015.*" The last entry stated, "*Released on medical grounds...*" and gave the relevant date. For the next twenty minutes he worked his way through the file. It was gold dust.

On the principle that one never took things at face value, he decided to run some additional checks. His first action, informed by the date of conviction, was to hack the Formal Record of Proceedings of the Central Criminal Court in Aberdeen. Next, he looked at open-source records of local newspapers. Finally, as indicated in the file, he tried to get corroboration of admission to hospital in Birmingham. It would be another long night.

Accessing the Queen Elizabeth Hospital database proved much harder. But it was all there; "*admitted for emergency gunshot wound, protective custody*" with, some weeks later, the eventual date of release – irritatingly without any contact address and nobody listed as Next of Kin. So much for the first part of the exam question set by the client. The next stage would be much harder – namely, finding out where the hell he was. Time for more biscuits.

****

Bremner's ferry crossing to Santander was invigorating. The weather stayed friendly and the notorious Bay of

Biscay behaved and stayed calm. Sleep had come easily. When not in his cabin dozing or looking at the Spanish road atlas, much of the time was spent on deck or over-indulging in the canteen. Although his ultimate destination was Mallorca, there was no rush and he would take his time getting to the next ferry departure in Barcelona. A road trip – nice and gentle.

Spain was familiar territory to him. It had so much to offer and he had always felt welcome. Proud of their history and culture, being able to speak the language was a distinct advantage. The weather was warming up nicely. So many places to stay: spoilt for choice.

As briefed, he planned to use cash rather than credit cards. The iPhone would remain off until Mallorca. Not entirely a novelty, the idea of being *"off grid"* for a while was hugely appealing. As his controller had said, there was no point making it too easy. The emergency telephone number in Monaco had been committed to memory.

Although off route, he had always wanted to visit Madrid and was excited at the thought of the so-called *"Golden Triangle"* of art museums – the Prado, Reina Sofia and Thyssen-Bornemisza. Yes, he reminded himself, there's no rush whatsoever. The Discovery was proving the perfect vehicle to travel the toll-free backroads. Thirsty but happy to tick along, it seemed to be enjoying the trip as much as he was. Before leaving Plymouth, he had found a specialist outdoors store and bought some basic camping equipment – thereby giving himself loads of flexibility for accommodation: the thought of sleeping under the stars was particularly appealing. Memories of his prison cell were beginning to fade. Things were definitely looking up and reinforced his determination to make the most of the next week or so.

****

In London, John Pelham obligingly played his part in

warming-up the Israeli Ambassador – evidenced by the gracious reception Everard was accorded on arrival at the Embassy where, after a courtesy call, he was shown to a separate office by a man he assumed to be Mossad's Head of Station. New to post, Alon Carlebach's name was known to him although they had never met. Touted as a future head of the organisation, Everard was keen to build a relationship. They chatted across a broad range of subjects before getting down to specifics about the Shala Family.

Small in stature with a receding hairline and wearing a cotton suit, the Israeli displayed an easy-going manner. Slightly professorial in appearance, largely as a consequence of his wire-rimmed glasses, Everard saw that, like himself, the man dispensed with notetaking. Not that it mattered, the characterless room with minimal furnishings would be wired for audio recording. Listening attentively to what was said, Carlebach agreed to consult with colleagues in Tel Aviv. Clearly sizing each other up, Everard formed the distinct impression that the name *"Shala"* had triggered a definite reaction. Exchanging business cards and choosing not to prolong the meeting, he took his leave. The ball having been placed squarely in the Israeli's court, it was now a question of waiting upon events. Something was telling him it would not be long before Carlebach was back in touch.

And so it proved when, two days later, they met again – this time on a bench by the river close to Chelsea Bridge. It was late morning; the weather holding to the forecast – warm and dry. The Israeli lost no time confirming the Shalas were indeed subjects of interest to Mossad and, specifically, the youngest of the brothers. Carlebach knew all about Erjon's conversion to Islam – believed to be Sunni. He went on to infer there was possibly some sort of financial relationship with terrorist groups. But, as he sought to stress, it was largely conjecture and they had no firm evidence on which to base the assertion. Insofar as it was known, Erjon Shala had never visited the Middle East, although there was evidence of business associations in the region, possibly with a connection to Cyprus. Never having been formally put on Mossad's *"Watch List"*, Carlebach said his name would now be added. He also gave an assurance that anything of substance would be passed on. Their meeting concluded, they shook hands and agreed to stay in touch.

****

Randell was parked at the pre-arranged point close to Carriage Drive North on the South Bank and had kept his boss in sight throughout the meeting. Once back in the car, Everard suggested, "Let's pop into Farlow's… I hear they've got a new selection of dry flies." Arguably one of his favourite fishing stores anywhere in the country, he was a regular visitor to the Pall Mall emporium. A guilty pleasure, Penny would be surprised if she knew what he spent on fishing tackle. One of his few vices, a bit like smoking good cigars – hard to put a price on such things.

****

Mary Stewart called him on the secure phone at his flat that evening. "There was a long meeting of the brothers at the office in Limehouse this morning," she began. "The younger two are regular visitors and, as we now know, the family name is openly displayed in the lobby. One of my people posed as a delivery man and happened to notice a private lift. I think the next few days are going to be really instructive, especially in regard to Erjon who, they tell me, is acutely surveillance conscious."

"That's a good result."

"Just so you know," she continued, "we're holding fire on any search ops: that includes the office and their individual residences."

"Fair enough," Everard said. "There will be time for

that in due course."

It had been a long week; he was more than ready to go home to Penny and the dogs in Norfolk. Marjorie was encouraging him to *"beat the traffic"*. Randell sat reading in the outer office.

****

Feeling increasingly at home in his new flat, Vinny was grappling with what he chose to call his insurance policy. As he saw it, the biggest risk was handing over Bremner's file to the client in person and then ending up in concrete shoes somewhere in the river. Or, worse, on a one-way trip to a crematorium. Too horrible to contemplate. Safer to pass the file electronically to the man he now knew to be Saban Shala – a name which routinely featured on dark web chat sites with accompanying notes: *"to avoid at all costs – these are seriously not nice people, have long memories, low tolerance thresholds and do not appreciate being messed with."*

Vinny was missing his mother's cooking but not much else. She had become far too inquisitive. In point of fact, London was not essential for his line of work and, if things got too stressful, he would simply find somewhere abroad. His weakness – which he had long recognised – was being slave to his natural curiosity. It invited unnecessary risk and had landed him in trouble more than once. The deeper one explored, the more interesting things inevitably became. Instinct was cautioning that this client would be no different. Everyone has something to hide and, he reminded himself: his insurance policy depended on unpacking their secrets – the stuff they preferred not to disclose – especially to those charged with upholding the rule of law.

It was out of curiosity that he ran the name *"Shala"* through the Justice Ministry's database and, surprisingly, only one name surfaced – Guzim Shala. The file revealed all the now familiar details including family and, critically, the date of his recent release. Companies House proved equally informative on *"Shala Holdings"* and gave an address for the company in Limehouse. Everything was telling him that his client, or clients, were seriously minted and, given what was stated on the dark web chat sites, he was even more determined to find out not only how they made their money, but where they stashed it. Nasty people, he reasoned, do not just do charitable works, run betting shops and bakeries and purport to be pillars of the community. Deeper and deeper – into the darkness and away from the light. What a spooky and yet thoroughly intriguing world he inhabited.

Thinking back to his meeting in the bakery and, in particular, his impression that the first-floor office had a *"lived-in"* feel, it might be an obvious place to take a closer look at. Accepting there would be protective security in place, he decided to test its resilience. Sending Bremer's file electronically created an opportunity to introduce some high-grade *"malware"* – the effect of which would be to make everything fully transparent. The clever bit was that it could be done without their knowledge – at least until they upgraded or installed new software. The difficulty he faced was trying to talk the client out of any face-to-face meetings.

Having rehearsed what he was going to say, he rang Saban on the burner mobile. "I've got something for you," he said. "The good news is that, from the checks I've run, it's genuine."

Saban stood up and started to pace the office. "Excellent. I want it as soon as possible."

Anticipating this, Vinny said, "There's a complication …a technical problem."

"What technical problem?"

"The system they employ will automatically alarm if I extract the file to make us a copy. It's built into the software programme because they employ a sophisticated numbering system specifically to prevent paper copies and inappropriate use."

"How do we get round it?"

Fairly certain that this dialogue was way over the man's head, Vinny continued, "What I will have to do is create a work-around simulating another department requesting sight of the file. In simple terms, the only way to pass you the file is electronically and for that, as you appreciate, I need an email address."

Saban's delight at the news overcame any natural instinct for caution and he promptly read out the address. Vinny repeated it back and undertook to send across the document within the next couple of hours.

Having ended the call, he began integrating the malware into the Bremner file which, as intended, would activate and infect the Shala's computer as soon as it was opened. Having written the code himself, he was confident it had every chance of defeating existing countermeasures – something feedback loops would confirm. With no time to waste, he double-checked the bundle and sent it to the address. "Now that's interesting," he said leaning back in his chair. "It's a different email address." Everything suggested a dead-end, probably an old computer serving no other purpose. It was a sensible thing to do and, most likely, someone else's idea. Be that as it may, he needed to keep up the pretence and role-play the *"authenticator"* – thereby providing some form of supporting reassurance. This he did with a short message to the effect that *"Hacker Number One"* had indeed run checks to validate the man Bremner's record, and everything seemed legitimate.

Conscious of time, Vinny resumed his efforts to unpick the Shalas' business empire. As a picture slowly emerged, he was genuinely impressed. Two things struck him: first, the scale and diversity of their operations in the UK and second, having quickly scanned several of the referenced financial accounts, the annual revenue generated. The property portfolio was huge and by far the biggest earner. What interested him most, however, was the way it was wired together – especially given the fact of the oldest brother's long stint in prison, not to mention the apparent technical shortcomings of Saban. The obvious conclusion was that, as they say in the movies, Erjon Shala was the brains behind the mob. That made him the biggest threat.

Lack of sleep eventually caught up with Vinny and he voted himself a weekend off. As the prodigal son, he would check on his mother and wangle an invite to Sunday lunch. Maybe even take his dirty washing along on the off chance. The screens could wait until he returned to the chase on Monday.

****

Mary Stewart and Brian Finlay sat around a conference room table in GCHQ. The meeting had been called at short notice. "If I interpret last night's report correctly," she said, "there's been a break-through of some sort. Is that right?"

Mike, quickly glancing at his two colleagues said, "Yes, we think the target made a mistake. Assuming there's just one of them, probably as a result of all the frenetic activity undertaken over the last three days."

"So what exactly happened?" Mary asked.

"In short, they dropped their guard and, using programmes designed for just this purpose, we have managed to identify a good electronic signature."

"You'll need to explain."

"Sorry… right… everyone has idiosyncrasies when it comes to writing codes or for software programmes: try to imagine it as a thumbprint. Our target is no different and, like most of those who operate in this field, certainly within the UK, he or she is probably unaware of it for the simple reason they tend to operate alone."

"Without anyone marking their homework?" Brian asked.

"Precisely."

"So," Mary said, "you know who we're dealing with?"

"Yes and no…" Mike replied. "We have a fair idea of their capability from historical matches but it doesn't give us the full answer. However, my people at the Justice Ministry, who are very familiar with your man's prison file, ran some of their own checks. For example, as you suggested, they looked for patterns of activity in several places other than the ministry's computer database: local newspaper websites in Aberdeen and the Queen Elizabeth Hospital in Birmingham. It was those matches which gave us the breakthrough."

Mary and Brian Finlay looked at one another and then across the table. "How do we exploit this?" she asked.

The answer involved another long technical explanation, culminating in Mike saying, "In essence, we *'hack back'* the hacker. We can now effectively monitor some but not all of what they do and have done – his or her lines of enquiry. It becomes a source of evidence to support a prosecution under the Computer Fraud and Abuse Act. Title 18, Section 1030."

"Quite possibly," Mary said, again looking across at Brian. "Shame to let such talent go to waste. How good is this person?"

"Very," Mike replied. "A serious player."

Then, getting up to leave, she thanked their hosts and, as a final thought asked, "Can we presume you have already started – what did you call it *'hack back'*?"

To which Mike said, "Yes, Mary, you can."

14

SUMMONING HIS brothers to an urgent conference at the bakery, Saban tried hard to conceal his delight as he handed out the individual hard copies of Bremner's prison record. All three took their time reading it before Guzim made the first statement.

"Are we sure this is genuine?" he asked.

"Yes," Saban responded.

"How do we know that?" asked Guzim, stirring his coffee.

"Because it's been independently verified."

Erjon let the conversation run without interrupting. All three of them were in suits. It was raining outside.

"So," asked Guzim, now fully rested and feeling more confident after the visit to Harley Street, "you're telling me that this man Bremner is who he says he is?"

Both brothers nodded.

"In which case," said Guzim, reaching for a cup cake, "there's only one conclusion: I was the target, not him. Do you agree?"

Again, both brothers nodded and said, "Yes."

"Okay, since he clearly took a bullet meant for me, I am in his debt." He then got up and refilled his coffee mug. Saban and Erjon had a good idea where this was leading. After a long pause, "We repay our debts… I want him found."

Erjon seemed troubled. Speaking for the first time, he said, "Saban, was the file handed to you personally by the hacker?"

Knowing full well that his younger brother only asked questions for a reason and, like any good lawyer, almost certainly already knew the answer, Saban replied, "On the advice of our young friend – for technical reasons – it was sent to me electronically."

Erjon, pausing before speaking said, "That was most unfortunate, Saban. I'm no expert in these things, but it potentially exposes our computer to the risk of being hacked. We need to close down all systems immediately."

Unable to fault the logic, Saban nodded. "Oh… right… an oversight on my part… I apologise. I will see to it immediately… we'll shut everything down."

Guzim, having nothing to add and already thinking back to the desperate business in the prison allotment, got up to refill his coffee a second time. He then turned to his brothers. "Once our young hacker friend – as you call him – has found Bremner, I see no further use for him," he said looking directly at Saban.

"Just to be clear," he said, "are we talking about the Hacker, Bremner or both?" After the laughter stopped Guzim said, "We're talking about the Hacker. Have you got that?" Which sparked another round of laughter.

"Yes… but which hacker? We've got two of them." More laughter followed and to such an extent that Guzim broke into a coughing fit.

A pity, thought Erjon to himself whilst Saban produced a glass of water for the now red-faced Guzim, such obvious talent could always be put to good use. "If as I suspect we have not yet paid him," he said, "I suggest the eventual settlement is handled face-to-face – no ifs or buts." To which the other two nodded. Erjon then said, "Leave it with me."

Guzim and Saban looked at one another and both said that it was fine with them.

"As you have inferred, Saban, we shall at some point

128

also have to deal with our friend, Hacker Number Two," Erjon added, almost as an afterthought.

****

Back on the other side of the river, after a rushed hamburger and chips at the local café, Vinny returned to his screens and tapped-in the Shala email address used earlier. For some reason, there was no response and, despite repeated attempts, he still couldn't gain access. The only logical explanation was that it was either offline for routine maintenance or, undergoing a security upgrade. There was nothing he could do and would have to revisit it later. Trying to stay positive, at least he still had a link to the Client through either the burner mobile or the second email address.

****

On the eight floor of Vauxhall Cross, Brian Finlay was updating *"C"* on the conversation in Cheltenham. As he ran through the main *"So whats?"* Everard reflected on the technical wizardry of GCHQ's remarkably clever men and women. "It appears they use an alternative place to meet," Brian said, "one of the bakeries they own in Streatham. The three brothers were there this morning, all arriving and departing in separate cars. Snappy dressers, too, I'm told."

Another useful piece of the Shala jigsaw, Everard thought. "Does Mary think the bakery merits a closer look?"

"That," said Brian, "is precisely her thinking and she's already submitted the relevant legal request. The risky bit is access because the bakery operates on a shift system. In other words, it's permanently occupied and operating on a 24/7 basis. However, I'm sure her people will come up with a cunning plan."

A soft knock on the door announced Marjorie's arrival. "The Foreign Secretary has asked if you're available for dinner this evening – just you and him – at his Club – seven thirty for eight."

129

Everard said that would be fine and continued the conversation with Finlay. "What timeframe is Mary thinking about for the bakery?" he asked.

"As soon as possible, maybe over a weekend depending on the shift pattern. The technical boys are giving it a thorough looking at."

It all made obvious sense and they were both well versed in the technical sophistication of the experts in question. There were far too many missing pieces in the jigsaw.

****

That evening, after agreeing timings, Randell delivered Everard to John Pelham's Club on Pall Mall, close to St James's Square. Pelham greeted his guest in the bar and, after a quick gin and tonic, they walked through to a table in the far corner of the dining room. Grand though it was, Everard's initial impression of the room was that being stared down at by long dead grandees in gilt-edged picture frames on the walls was mildly disconcerting. Not his call, but if he'd was in charge the place would be given a facelift – no pun intended!

With no immediate neighbouring diners, discussion was unconstrained. Everard reassured Pelham that everything was proceeding to plan with Mildred. The routine report two days earlier had set out the salient points.

The conversation then shifted to significant forthcoming events; Pelham mentioning a G8 Foreign Ministers' conference he was going to in Italy. Everard had always been very fond of that particular country and liked Italians. He and Penny spent their honeymoon in Capri, and he had very special memories of the place. There was a time when they thought about buying a bolthole in Umbria – a *"chimney with rooms around it and a bit of land"*. That was the general idea, but external influences intervened and Penny was talked out of it by her parents:

"lovely people but a bit lawless and probably not your sort of place, darling". That decisive intervention had killed it stone dead and, sadly, blown any idea of a fishing boat on Lake Trasimeno right out of the water.

"Have you lined anyone up to take over the Director of Operations job?" Pelham asked as he scanned the wine list for a second time.

"Still working on it," Everard replied, "but I've got someone in mind and will be asking for your endorsement if they sign up."

After a superb meal, they took coffee and brandy in the anteroom and, mindful that his host was a non-smoker, Everard dismissed the idea of a cigar.

All in all, it was a most agreeable dinner. John Pelham was a generous host and, unusually for a politician, actually listened and thought before offering an opinion. Also, refreshingly, unlike so many of his contemporaries, he did not have the intensely irritating habit of asking a question and then providing the answer. Precisely the sort of individual needed in Downing Street although, if Marjorie's sources were to be believed, the odds were against. He was still thinking about all of this as Randell turned into Pimlico.

****

An established once a week habit, the following morning Everard walked the corridors of his headquarters, occasionally sticking his head into different offices. Marjorie kept track and normally suggested a plan for where he might want to go, together with a gentle reminder of names he may have forgotten and any current topics of interest. It was not an exercise in trying to catch people out. Leaders, as he had been taught at the Military Academy, needed to be *"seen"* rather than stuck in ivory towers. Sitting on the edge of a desk listening to whatever anyone wanted to tell him was always time well spent. The in-tray could be dealt with in his own time.

What he found particularly interesting was which of his senior managers got unsettled by his impromptu visits, and which welcomed them. Brian Finlay was a good example of the latter and, to such an extent, he never bothered accompanying him.

His walkabout completed, Everard relaxed into a faded armchair in Brian's office and accepted the offer of – it had to be said – a pretty ordinary coffee. "They've had another look at the bakery," Brian said, scanning a briefing paper on his desk. "We also know, which might surprise you – it certainly did Mary – there are no native Albanian speakers in the Security Service, which puts the mockers on any idea of infiltrating the workforce. However,…" he said, looking up, "the technical guys reckon an adjacent building might offer a reasonably good position for a directional microphone – maybe more than one – with remote rebroadcast facility."

Everard was paying close attention.

"Apparently," Brian continued, "it's always been a bakery and, fortunately, happens to be Grade 2 Listed."

"Why's that relevant?"

"Ah… well… as I've just learnt, amongst other things, it prevents the owners from modifying windows and doors. In theory it should not, therefore, be double-glazed."

Hugh Everard knew all about listed buildings from his home in Norfolk. He completely got the point about heritage and custodianship but those involved could be a pain in the arse, bordering on evangelical. "Anyway," Brian continued, "Mary's agreed to the indirect approach and a team is lined up to have a crack at it tomorrow. It will be interesting to see how effective the suite of microphones are."

Everard finished his coffee and returned to the eighth

floor.

****

On receipt of the email from Erjon Shala, Jed Crosby – Fleet Manager for Worldwide Yacht Charters (WYC) in Monaco – tapped his keyboard and recovered the previous charter contract for *"E Shala"*. Everything had been in order, with no significant issues reported during the two-week Mediterranean charter. Centred on Cyprus, the trip report mentioned visits to Turkey, Egypt and Greece. The invoice had been settled promptly and without question. In accordance with established practice, a generous gratuity was paid to be shared amongst the crew.

As a Brit ex-pat, in his twenty years with WYC Crosby had built up a solid international network across the yacht charter industry. On leaving the Royal Navy he'd pursued a commercial qualification – eventually captaining superyachts. Now mainly shore-based, he was responsible for all the yachts on WYC's books – motor and sail – and was directly answerable to individual owners or their representatives.

It was accepted practice for owners to put their yachts under management companies like his which, for reasons of tax efficiency, they would be obliged to pay a charter fee for their use. Some, but not all, were content for their yachts to be made available for others to charter; thereby offsetting some of the operating costs. The routine on many of the larger boats was to engage key staff *"on rotation"*; in other words, key positions would rotate – two months on, two months off.

Crosby was alone at the desk in his spacious, well-appointed office on the second floor of an old building overlooking the busy waterfront. Beneath him, in long orderly rows sat gleaming yachts; deck crew busily polishing brightwork, wiping away the dew or hosing down decks. The marina hummed.

Re-reading the charter agreement on his screen, he picked up the phone and dialled a number in Miami. After two further calls to colleagues in other Monaco-based agencies, he rang a longstanding friend and former naval pal in London. Brian Finlay took the call in his office and, after a brief pause, spoke to Marjorie to get approval for a return flight to Nice at the earliest opportunity – paperwork to follow. Verbal agreement came back to him within the hour – signed-off by Head of Admin and endorsed by *"C"*.

Crosby and Finlay met in a bar outside Nice Airport the next day. Firm friends from their time in the Navy, Jed Crosby had a shrewd idea about his friend's subsequent career in SIS and they had often met up in foreign countries. Finlay was godfather to his eldest daughter, Katherine.

"Thanks for the heads-up, Jed," Finlay said. "Bit of a longshot, but I thought it was worth running the name by you. You'll have worked out that the individual in question is of particular interest to us. I really appreciated your call."

Crosby looked at his friend. "That's a relief, Brian." The fact that Finlay had reacted so quickly was clearly indicative of the importance attached to the name *"E Shala"*. The call to Miami had failed to come up with anything – confirming that the man had not chartered yachts in Florida or the Caribbean.

Crosby handed Brian a copy of Erjon's email without comment, which Brian quickly scanned and pocketed. Some aspects of the subsequent chat surprised Jed and he knew he was being given privileged – not to say highly classified – information. Moving on to family matters, Brian was keen to hear about his goddaughter – with whom he had always tried to stay in touch. Business concluded, they shook hands and Finlay walked back into the airport to await his return flight. In normal circumstances he would have stayed the night with the Crosbys at their delightful farmhouse just outside Antibes.

On return to London, Finlay wrote up his post trip report and emailed it to Everard – certain that a summons to the eighth floor would follow in short order. It came in the form of a phone call from Marjorie. "'*C*' would appreciate a word at your convenience." Sipping what was unlikely to be the last espresso of the day, Everard rose from his chair as Finlay entered. "That was very nicely done, Brian: sounding out your chum in Monaco was inspired. We owe him one."

Taking a seat Brian replied, "Top man, Jed. We've seen a lot of each other over the years and it's been useful having someone with his knowledge and contacts keeping an eye on that increasingly popular industry."

"Perhaps you might introduce us if he ever comes to London?" Everard said.

"Easily fixed," Brian replied. "By the way, Mary called me first thing: the operation to put microphones opposite the bakery in Streatham was successful and, much to the tech guy's relief, the recording quality is pretty good. She said Saban and Erjon met there again yesterday: we'll get a transcript within the next couple of hours. The breaking news, however, is that they are definitely going ahead with the yacht charter." At which point Finlay handed over the email from Crosby.

"In that case," Everard said, "talk to Mary as soon as possible about the option you and I discussed the other day. We need to stay ahead of the game. I would also welcome her thoughts on our hacker friend and, in particular, when the boffins in Cheltenham think they've nailed his or her identity."

"You see the hacker as a potential asset, don't you?" Finlay asked.

"Absolutely," said Everard. "Pound to a penny Mary's

had the same thought. Persuading the individual in question to serve Queen and Country will be a challenge: it'll be a *'stick and carrot'* approach I'll wager. What form the carrot takes will be the complicated part, but it could make a difference. As regards to the stick, why don't you talk to Mike in Cheltenham and see whether they've got sufficient information on our hacker friend to put the frighteners on him. The worst outcome is that he or she shuts everything down and disappears – which we can't allow to happen."

Back at his desk, Finlay dialled Mary's number and, switching to fully secure means, gave her the substance of his conversation with Everard. She was indeed on exactly the same thought train and agreed to talk to Mike. He told her to expect a copy of the note he gave to *"C"* and also the email Crosby had given him, both with the *"for your eyes only and no further dissemination"* caveat.

"Leave it with me; I'll get back to you before lunch," she said.

Before hanging up, Brian said, "There is one other thing, Mary, perhaps best face-to-face if it's convenient to meet – preferably today if possible."

Mary smiled. "I'm free for lunch as it happens – my treat – we can go to that Italian place I mentioned to you, just off the King's Road."

Just after one o'clock she and Brian sat opposite one another in the small but bustling restaurant working their way through overly generous bowls of seafood pasta, complemented by an unpretentious white wine.

"So," he said. "Don't get cross but, having met her at the cottage the other day, I took the liberty of checking out Jo's background. Did you know she'd worked in the yachting industry?"

Christ, Mary thought to herself, *you cheeky bastard*, but it was exactly the sort of thing she would do. "You naughty boy," she said, "and yes – I did know."

"Well," Brian continued, "thing is, Mary, we think she's uniquely qualified for a sensitive placement we're considering for Mildred."

"Okay, I'm listening," she said, taking a sip of her wine and, at the same time, looking with more than passing interest at the not unattractive fifty-something-year-old sitting across the table. He had kept himself in good physical shape and, if one ignored the flecks of grey around the ears could be taken for someone a lot younger. She liked his smile: they shared a similar sense of humour; he made her laugh… quite often unintentionally. "You're talking about Jo Williams?"

"Yes, well…" he said, clearly flustered. "Is she available?"

"I'd have to run it past my boss, but I don't envisage a problem. Would you like pudding?"

✳✳✳✳

Jo Williams was not accustomed to being asked to "*pop up for a chat*" with a grown-up like Mary Stewart. It lasted thirty minutes and, although the specifics of the assignment were not disclosed, Jo said she was up for it. "Okay, I'll get HR to make all the arrangements – there will be the usual paperwork to sign," Mary said.

"Assuming it's abroad, do you have any idea how long I'll be gone?" Jo asked.

"Not exactly but you'd be wise to think in terms of months rather than weeks," Mary replied. "If not in-date with your firearms certification, you'll need to requalify just in case SIS wants you to be armed – something you can ask your new controller, Brian Finlay. He was the man you met at the cottage."

The next day Jo received a text from Finlay, giving a time to meet at a house in Mayfair. Marjorie arranged for Randell to drive him over to the house in question, one of several used by SIS when they didn't want people coming to the headquarters. The house was set on a side street and had nothing to differentiate it from others in the smart Regency row. A polished nameplate on the door gave the house number and two hanging baskets and a weed-free path added a nice touch of colour and sense of occupancy. The house manager and his wife were retired civil servants, most of their careers spent with SIS at overseas stations. Meetings were conducted in a spacious room at the back of the house overlooking the tidy but uninspiring garden and, like the cottage in Kent, it was wired for sound. Maps and photographs had been arranged on a pin board at the end of a large conference table. Jo was invited to sign several bits of paper.

Minded to get things moving, and having poured coffee for them both, they sat down at the table and Finlay began with a quick summary of the operational context and then the current situation. "Any questions so far, Jo?"

"No, thank you."

"Okay, let's move on to your part in the operation. The basic idea is that we want you to go undercover on a Monaco-based yacht being chartered by the Shala brothers for a cruise in the Mediterranean."

She had trouble masking her surprise. "What will my position be?"

"Chief Stewardess."

"It's been a long time since I was on boats," she said. "They probably speak a different language now."

"Not a problem," Brian replied. "A full legend is being worked-up to support your cover, including all relevant documentation – Seafarer's Discharge Book, B1B2 visa and suchlike. In the meantime, coming to your point, we've arranged for you to attend a refresher course in Miami… essentially to renew your yacht crew certifications – medical, firefighting and sea survival."

"Will it include what I need to know as a chief

stewardess?"

"Yes," he said, grinning.

"That's a relief."

"Once you've finished you'll fly to Nice and, carried on the books of World Yacht Charters, await to be assigned to the yacht."

"Does anyone know I'm undercover?" she asked.

"No," he said. "Only the boss of the charter company… a guy called Jed Crosby."

"Do you see me being armed?"

"No, but we've made arrangements for a weapon to be concealed aboard – a Sig Sauer 38. If you get the chance you might want to put in some practice on a local shooting range in Florida."

Handing her a bundle of papers he said, "This gives you everything you need to mug up on for the course. It includes contact details for your fictitious aunt in Bristol – which is how we'll keep in touch. You will also be issued with a new iPhone."

"So you can track me?"

"Correct. Now, Jo, the other thing I need to tell you is that you're probably going to become reacquainted with Callum Bremner."

"Oh… he's going to be with the Shalas is he?"

"That's what we're hoping, yes."

Finlay registered the slight look of surprise on Jo's face. So Mrs Grant's observations were correct.

"Not an issue for you is it, Jo?"

"No, not at all. He's a nice guy but there's nothing beyond a professional relationship."

Having answered her questions, Finlay stood up. "Unless you have any other questions, I think we're done, Jo. A car is waiting outside to take you back to your flat.

The tickets for Miami will be delivered later this evening, together with your initial draft legend – which, of course, you will shred before leaving the UK. Finally, just so you know, the course in Miami is being run by an affiliate of World Yacht Charter. Good luck," he said as they shook hands. "Let me show you out."

Once outside, Jo climbed into the passenger seat of the car beside Randell, who was pleasantly surprised and trying hard not to show it. "Hello," said Randell. "I'm Steve, where are we going?"

"Hackney please," came the reply.

Finlay watched them leave and smiled. "That's one you owe me, Randell," he said to himself. He then grabbed a taxi back to the office and typed out a summary of the meeting and sent it up to *"C"*.

****

"Fine to drop me here, thank you," Jo said to Randell. Having chatted amicably during the drive, he'd quickly established that, not only did she possess a delightful sense of humour but was also completely at ease.

"What time tomorrow?" he asked.

"Not sure I know what you're talking about," she said.

"I'm taking you to Heathrow," came the reply.

"In that case you can drop me a bit closer, I live in that apartment block over there."

Handing her his business card, he said, "Call me when you have your flight timings and we'll sort it from there."

Jo noted from a window reflection that he did not leave until after he had seen her enter her building. *What a nice guy*, she thought to herself.

****

He was back at the agreed time the next morning and drove her to Terminal 5. During the journey she asked him about his life before Vauxhall Cross – keen to know more about his military service. Randell, aware from Finlay that she was on secondment from the Security Service, chose not to ask about her own background or what was going on in Miami. He did, however, raise the question of her apartment and whether, if she was likely to be away for a while, someone was organised to keep an eye on it. Jo had said it was taken care of but thanked him anyway.

Dropping her inside the Short Stay Car Park on the same level as the Passenger Terminal, he retrieved her case from the boot and handed it to her. "Have a nice trip," he said, "and mind how you go."

Giving him a lovely smile in response, she said, "Thank you, it would be great to meet up when I come back to London."

To which Randell replied, "I should like that very much indeed."

Jo grinned and walked away in the direction of the terminal.

****

In the comfort of his flat, Vinny was applying intense mental effort to the perplexing challenge of finding Bremner. Where on earth did one start? The man had been banged-up in prison; not unreasonable, therefore, to suggest he might be looking for somewhere to chill. Since Scotland failed to tick the relevant boxes at this time of year weather-wise, logically it must be somewhere abroad. This assumption was supported by reference in the prison record to him having worked as a former geologist in the oil and gas sector. Pausing to make a mug of tea, and assuming he was correct about Bremner being abroad, or headed there, it dawned on him that there might be merit in taking a look at agencies and organisations involved in travel and tourism.

So, returning to the computer, he entered "*UK Border Agency*" and, an hour later, "*UK Border Force*". Failing to reveal anything of interest, in the early hours of the following morning he started on budget airlines and, from there, to the Channel Tunnel rail option – again without getting a result. Now completely frazzled, he was in dire need of sleep. Before calling it a day, he hacked into two of the main UK-based ferry companies but, exhausted, decided to follow up later.

Sleeping longer than intended and grabbing a late breakfast in the café, Vinny picked up where he'd left off earlier. To his immense satisfaction, within a matter of minutes the name *"Bremner"* appeared on the booking record of the company operating the ferry service from Plymouth to Santander. "Yes!" he cried. "Nowhere to hide these days, is there Mr Bremner?" establishing when he'd made the crossing, also picking up from the reservation that the man was using a long wheelbase vehicle. The next obvious question was how long he planned on staying in mainland Spain or, for that matter, if the idea was to transit to somewhere else like France, Portugal or North Africa.

Vinny brought up a map of ferry routes operated from Spain. Unhelpfully, there were loads of them. Another option was to try and get into the Spanish equivalent of the UK Border Force. Which, after a strong black coffee, is what he decided to do.

In the early hours of the following morning, his logic and persistence were rewarded when he discovered that a Brit by the name of Bremner was booked on a ferry from Barcelona to Palma, Mallorca. Glancing at a calendar he realised that the date of the crossing was for that very day. If the timings were correct, it had already taken place.

****

No strangers to working long hours, Mike and his team at GCHQ were impressed by the technical sophistication unfolding on their screens. No question about it, they were dealing with a clever and technically formidably sharp opponent. In the daily report sent to Stewart and Finlay, he asked for a meeting as soon as practicable, proposing the expedient of secure video tele-conferencing.

In the subsequent 3-way VTC between GCHQ, SIS and the Security Service later that morning, it was agreed that the case against the hacker was irrefutable; at the very least inviting a long prison sentence. Legal officers had reviewed the evidence and concurred. The risk, however, which everyone appreciated, was in convincing the hacker that he'd been nabbed and had nowhere to hide. It was therefore agreed that, if necessary, a demonstration might be required to reveal to their adversary just some of what was known about him, or her.

****

Two days later, Mary Stewart met with Finlay and Everard at the safe house in Mayfair. Rain clouds were gathering and unprepared tourists looking anxious were picking up the pace and searching for contingency boltholes. Everything moved up a gear as the first drops fell.

Everard opened the discussion to a loud clap of thunder. At another time and in different circumstances, it would have been quite theatrical, but nobody appeared to notice. "As I understand it," he said, "we are now in a position to *'turn'* the hacker. Is that right?"

"Yes it is," Mary said. "The evidence is overwhelming – *'bang to rights'*– as our Met chums would say."

"So what's the plan?"

Getting a nod from Finlay, "We agree with GCHQ," she said. "The only realistic option is to handle this electronically. To do otherwise risks them taking fright and doing a runner. Besides, we have no way of knowing where they physically are on the planet."

"How would it work?" Everard asked.

"What we're thinking is something seriously scary magically appears on the hacker's screen; credible, irrefutable and leaving no room for negotiation or manoeuvre; firmly on the hook with nowhere to go," Mary replied.

"That's the stick," Brian added, "but we also have to have a sufficiently tempting *'carrot'*."

"These *'swingers'* or *'Grey Hats'* need extremely sensitive handling," Mary said. "Fortunately, there's precedent. We'll have to see how they react and what their conditions are."

"By *'precedent'*, do I understand you to mean your Service already employs these sorts of people?"

"Yes."

"And we're comfortable with this idea of *'conditions'* are we?" Everard asked.

"That's the advice," she said. "I'll talk to my boss and make sure he's fully signed up."

15

HAZEL PELHAM was sitting in the kitchen of her farmhouse near Warminster. Drinks poured in anticipation, she had cooked a special dinner for their wedding anniversary and, calling in a favour with one of her riding mates, her two teenage sons were away with school pals for the weekend. Tonight was about having fun.

She had met John at university, quickly discovering a mutual interest in horse riding. To be precise, three-day eventing. They kept a number of horses and, although no longer competing, she ran a riding school specialising in two of the three disciplines – dressage and show jumping. Hazel still rode with the local hunt, but her husband had given it up on becoming a Member of Parliament. Too contentious, he had been advised. Constituency business kept them both busy and, since John was one of the big players in national politics, there was no lack of social opportunities in London and abroad.

She adored her husband. All anniversaries were special. Making the final preparations for dinner, she remembered John talking about a forthcoming conference in Rome. Perhaps there was an opportunity to have some fun in the sun? Thinking more about it, her mind went to their Italian friends who, although they hadn't seen them for ages, might be worth calling. Her immediate challenge was trying to remember exactly where they lived.

John emerged from the study after working through his very full ministerial red box. "I've had an idea," he said. "Why don't you come with me to the conference in Rome?

I'm sure your sister would help out with the horses if we asked her."

"That's a great idea: I'll ask her… she owes me more than a few favours," Hazel replied. "Maybe we could go and see the Moretti's, they live near Rome, don't they?"

John Pelham smiled affectionately.

"No, darling, Alberto and Francesca live on the opposite coast: about three hours away by car – south of Ancona; you know, halfway up on the right-hand side." Sensing her disappointment, he added, "But yes, if they'll have us we can certainly fit in a few days before or after the conference. Why don't you give Francesca a call?"

****

In the darkened room of his flat, Vinny had just finished a pizza and was weighing up his next move against the Shalas. No sooner had he powered up the computer, a message flashed up on all three screens in bold, uppercase print. Quickly scanning the text, the effect was instantaneous. He froze. *"Whaaaat?"* he cried and, jumping up from his chair and close to panic immediately began shutting everything down. *"Code Red"* – an often-practiced drill but never done for real. He knew he'd been hacked. The message on the screen was chilling.

"YOU ARE IN VERY SERIOUS TROUBLE. WE HAVE IRREFUTABLE EVIDENCE OF YOUR ILLEGAL ACTIVITIES, SUFFICIENT TO BRING ABOUT A CIVIL PROSECUTION WHICH, BE IN NO DOUBT, WILL LEAD TO A CONVICTION CARRYING A SENTENCE OF NOT LESS THAN 14 YEARS IMPRISONMENT.

HOWEVER, THERE IS ROOM FOR NEGOTIATION WHICH, POTENTIALLY, MIGHT ADVANCE YOUR INTERESTS AS WELL AS OURS. THE DECISION IS YOURS. YOU HAVE TWELVE HOURS TO REPLY TO THE ADDRESS STATED AT THE BOTTOM OF THIS MESSAGE. IF NOTHING IS RECEIVED BY THAT TIME, WE WILL INITIATE FORMAL

CRIMINAL PROCEEDINGS AGAINST YOU."

Vinny was shattered. The ultimate nightmare: a professional humiliation. Always believing in his own invincibility, he was at a loss to know what to do. The sense of being alone was overwhelming; no one had ever gotten remotely close to threatening him before. This message, which was patently not a joke had a frighteningly real feel about it. How on earth had they found him? Who could possibly have the wherewithal to conduct such an attack? It was outrageous – he was now a victim – the sublime irony of it all and so unfair.

Feeling in urgent need of fresh air, he shot down the stairs to the lobby and went onto the street. Already dark and lightly drizzling, he walked for the next two hours … mind in overdrive and, like a computer program, running one option after another. On returning to the flat – soaked but calmer – he rebooted the computer and, to his dismay, the same message reappeared, only this time with an additional paragraph, also in red.

"YES, THIS IS REALLY HAPPENING TO YOU AND, IF IN ANY DOUBT, WE WOULD BE HAPPY TO SHARE WHAT WE KNOW WITH SOME OF YOUR KNOWN ASSOCIATES – INCLUDING YOUR CURRENT CLIENTS IN THE BAKING BUSINESS."

That did it. They – whoever *"they"* were – meant what they said. This was now damage limitation. People had told him in graphic detail what happened to young men in prison. It terrified him. He would not survive. After a further hour trying to decide what to do, he arrived at an uncomfortable but inescapable conclusion: he would have to negotiate; try to salvage what he had worked so hard to create. Reluctantly, he typed a short message. "Okay … I'm ready to hear what you have to offer," and hit the *"Send"* key.

****

The Duty Controller in Cheltenham was called to a console in one of the Operation Rooms. "Good!" she said. "Let London know right away and ask how they want us to play it: specifically, whether or not to push for a face-to-face meeting." Mary and Everard reckoned this was a long shot still worth a go. Three hours later, a message appeared on Vinny's screen.

"EXPECT TO HEAR FURTHER FROM US – ON THIS MEANS – AT 1200 GMT TOMORROW. DO NOT DISCUSS THIS MATTER WITH ANYONE."

The screen went dead.

Vinny, now more in control, sat in the local café working his way through a large plate of fish and chips. The message hinted at room for compromise; he needed to be ready with his terms and conditions, including non-negotiable *"red lines"*. Mindful of the risk of trying to be too clever, and without knowing what *"they"* knew about him, he grudgingly accepted that he would have to play with a straight bat – more or less – and share what he had found out about the Shalas – more or less. Yes, he was prepared to work for *"them"* but not without certain undertakings: guaranteed immunity against any current and future prosecution; all charges dropped with immediate effect. Then there was the money side of things and, as part of the deal, he would definitely try to negotiate a financial retainer, payable to an overseas account – the details of which he would supply.

His biggest worry, by far, was safeguarding his identity. He would therefore insist on a single point of contact, which he accepted might prove a stumbling block, and absolutely no face-to-face meetings with anyone, anywhere at any stage.

Vinny studied the outline proposition crafted by Mary Stewart and Brian Finlay, the principles of which had been agreed by Mary's boss and shared with GCHQ. In essence, the Hacker – himself – was to become a *"government asset"*, for which precedent existed. As the lawyers cautiously sought to remind everyone, this moved things into a legal *"grey zone"*. From Mary's standpoint, in this instance the ends more than justified the means. Cyber-crime was a young person's game: one needed young people to play; individuals who understood and could write and interpret code; clever, disciplined and curious young people with a taste for risk.

As she had discussed with Mike – previous experience gave them a good idea of what to expect when it came to the hacker's conditions: none of which had proved insurmountable in previous cases. Both appreciated that for individuals like this, protecting their anonymity was sacrosanct; they may never know their true identity or physical location. To make it work, the relationship would have to include some basic level of trust which, of itself, suggested that choice of the hacker's controller needed special consideration.

At precisely 1200 hours Greenwich Mean Time, Vinny's screen lit up with an invitation to state his *"conditions"*. Quickly replying and hitting the *"send"* key, the response came back within minutes.

"THIS WILL BE FORWARDED TO INTERESTED PARTIES AND YOU CAN EXPECT TO HEAR FURTHER FROM US WITHIN 24 HOURS. IN THE MEANTIME, UNDER NO CIRCUMSTANCES COMMUNICATE WITH YOUR FRIENDS IN THE BAKERY BUSINESS OTHER THAN TO INFORM THEM OF YOUR LATEST DISCOVERY RELATING TO THE MAN THEY ARE KEEN TO FIND."

The screen then went blank. "Christ," he said to himself, "this is seriously spooky." As instructed by the client, he then picked up the burner mobile and pressed the pre-set number.

"Yes?" came the terse response.

"Your man is in Spain," Vinny said. "Somewhere on the island of Mallorca in the Balearics – I don't know precisely where but I'm working on it. He got there yesterday and has a vehicle... some sort of long wheelbase... possibly a van or four by four."

The information was abruptly acknowledged and he was told to *"get it sorted"*.

There was no getting away from it, Vinny had formed an intense dislike of Saban Shala; there would be, without question, a day of reckoning. Bloody man. He deserved what was coming to him.

****

Hazel Pelham, fighting a persistent headache after the late-night anniversary celebration, rang her husband at the office overlooking Horse Guards Parade on Great Charles Street. "Darling, I've had a chat with Francesca, they'd love to have us to stay... for as long as we like... ideally after – rather than before – your conference. And yes, she says... pack our riding gear. Isn't that great?"

John Pelham smiled. He loved Hazel and, despite their differences, they always managed to agree on the big issues. She was a superb mum and devoted to him and the boys. Emphatically her own woman, unpredictable and very lively company in any social setting, she adored parties and it was a constant struggle keeping up.

****

That evening, at their rather grand house with a fabulous view of the Adriatic south east of Anacona in the Italian region of Marche, Francesca and Alberto Moretti were having dinner.

Speaking in Italian...

"Alberto, I have invited the Pelhams to stay with us for a few days next month. John's doing something in Rome," she said as Sophia their maid brought through the main course.

"That'll be nice, we haven't seen them in ages," he said. "Quite an honour to have the British Foreign Secretary staying with us. Our friends will be fighting one another to meet them."

Back in the kitchen, the housekeeper was busying herself cleaning the stove while Sophia ate her supper. Once everything was cleared away from the dining room and after saying goodnight, Sophia changed into her jeans and a tee shirt and, jumping onto her battered but still functioning motor scooter, strapped on her helmet and shot off. Ten minutes later, she pulled up at a local bar and parked – joining a lone figure at an outside table.

Chatting away happily and very proud of her good-looking boyfriend of nearly two months, she recounted the highs and lows of her day – casually remarking that she would soon be even busier than normal with English guests coming to stay; as she understood it, quite important guests… something about Foreign Secretary… whatever that was. Pleading an early start in the morning, the dark-haired twenty-something year old kissed her goodnight and watched as she drove off. He then walked a short distance to a phone kiosk and dialled a number in his home city of Split – across the sea in Croatia.

****

Jed Crosby, back in the bar adjacent to Nice International Airport, gratefully accepted the beer from his friend. "Cheers Brian," he said, raising his glass. "I had a feeling we'd be seeing you again."

Grinning, Finlay then asked, "Where are you with the charter?"

"Your man wants the same yacht as last time; we'll have to juggle a few things – including hastening a scheduled refit for the boat in question – but it can be done."

"Excellent. Is the yacht still in Toulon?"

"Yes," Jed replied.

"How do you see it working?" Brian asked.

"Well, the client says he's happy to embark in Malta, which might be of interest, and has asked for the first destination to be Mallorca." Jed then got up, walked to the bar and returned with more beers.

"How well do you know the captain, Jed? I'm asking for a reason."

"What reason?"

"Well," said Brian, "would there be a problem if we wanted to provide a qualified chief stewardess?"

"One of your people, I assume."

"Yes. She used to work in your industry and we're getting her requalified. Her name's Jo Williams."

"Should be okay: appointing crew is management business these days – much to the irritation of some of our captains. Pretty sure there won't be a problem with Henry Constance."

"What's he like?"

"Well... he's forty-three years old, a seasoned operator and widely respected. Runs a tight ship and is renowned for being unflappable. All that said, he expects high standards, above and below decks." Anticipating the next question, Jed continued, "He's new to the yacht and won't have met the client."

They went on to discuss some related details until, looking at his watch, Finlay said he had to scoot if he wanted to catch the return flight to London. "I owe you for this, Jed," Finlay said as they shook hands. To which his friend smiled and replied, "No doubt we'll get to that in due course – stay safe."

****

Mary Stewart met Brian the following day to discuss recent developments. "We've received the hacker's demands and none of them are show-stoppers," she said. "We understand that Bremner's location has already been passed to the Shala brothers?"

"By the hacker?"

"Correct."

"They plan to join the yacht – *Cygnus* – in Malta: Valletta to be precise and from there head directly to Mallorca," Brian said.

"What about Jo Williams?" Mary asked.

"Jed's happy: she'll join as chief stewardess. I had to reassure him that she was in all respects fully qualified."

"Good," Mary said.

"On a separate but related point, who do you have in mind as our new hacker friend's controller?"

"Assuming," she said, "we're correct that he or she plays in the first division, then we'll need to find someone similar."

Brian suspected she already had someone in mind and probably on the Security Service books. "Got a candidate, have you?"

"I do, as it happens. He's been with us quite a while now. Class act."

"How do you see the command-and-control arrangements working?" he asked.

"Given that we're effectively your supporting agency, we think that you get *'primacy'*. In short, our guys all work directly to you – including our young hackers. However, I would ask to be kept in touch because there's bound to be information of specific interest to my firm."

"Fair enough," Brian said.

****

Callum Bremner sat on the balcony of his rental apartment in Sóller on Mallorca's west coast. Linked to Palma by a scenic railway, it's a favourite tourist destination and equally popular with locals.

The road trip from Santander more than matched his expectations. Frequently detouring, he went wherever caught his interest. The highlight was unquestionably the three-day stopover in Madrid. Remembering from his youth that Museo Nacional del Prado possessed a fabulous collection of works by the great masters – El Greco, Titian, Rubens, Rembrandt and Goya to name but a few – the treasures inside the nearly two-hundred-year-old building held him captive for hours. He had always liked Barcelona's distinct personality – lively, stylish and creative. Much of his time was spent strolling the tree-lined streets and bustling covered markets.

Once aboard the ferry to Palma, he had switched on the iPhone, thereby instantaneously revealing his location to folk watching screens in London. They would also register his first use of the credit card. Regrettably, the holiday was over. It was time to concentrate exclusively on the mission: he would need all his wits about him.

After contacting the rental company stipulated by Finlay, and having checked out several of their listed properties, he had settled on the modest apartment with its own pool and, which is what had clinched it, a fabulous view of the sea and evening sunsets.

Conscious of his expanding waistline – not having spared himself on the food stakes during the road trip – he resumed his exercise routine of a daily run. When not pounding the roads and tracks, he headed off in the Discovery to explore the countryside. What the immediate future held was far from certain; the big question remained what would happen when, as they would, the Shalas eventually tracked him down. Plainly something outside his control, until such time as they made contact, he had little choice but to continue playing the role of a Brit holidaymaker. Finlay had mentioned that at some point he would be contacted by an SIS operative already on the island.

****

Emma was new to the property rental company in Sóller, but not the island – which she loved. It was only her third day. "Definitely worse jobs," she said to herself every morning. In fact she was delighted to have landed such a plumb assignment, only the second in her SIS career. It was proving a welcome respite from Madrid where she was entering her third year at the Embassy under the cover of *"Deputy Cultural Attaché"*.

Scrolling through recent rental contracts, it didn't take long to find the name *"Bremner"* and, calling-up on screen the specification for the apartment in question, she immediately saw its appeal. Not overlooked, breath-taking views and nicely placed for restaurants and stores, it met all the essential criteria. Sóller was delightful. She had already been thinking about how best to connect with him and, ideally, meet face-to-face.

Her brief was pretty straightforward; if and when the Shalas turned up on the Island, she was to report back everything seen and heard but without risking compromise to either Bremner or herself. Intriguingly, which added a minor complication, neither she nor Bremer knew what the other looked like.

For some reason assessing him to be a morning person, Emma rose bright and early and drove to a cul-de-sac within sight of his apartment, a flask of coffee close at hand. When he failed to show after an hour, she called it quits and returned to the office. Repeating the exercise the following day yielded the same result. Undeterred, on the third morning she was rewarded by the sight of him jogging briskly down the road. "About bloody time," she said to herself. "Nice stride pattern, you've done that before." The next day being a Sunday, and assuming he was a creature of habit, she, too, would be going for an early morning jog.

And so it was that, rising at the ungodly hour of 5am and donning her running kit – complete with headphones and appropriate music – she returned to the familiar cul-de-sac, parked-up and duly commenced her run. It was going to be another lovely day and, by the look of things, rather warm. Working up a sweat climbing towards Bremner's place, if the timing was right she would see him on his way down and then follow at a distance.

And so it played out; studiously avoiding eye contact as they passed one another – despite him looking directly at her – it became a struggle keeping up on the descent. "The sod's got ridiculously long legs," she muttered – trying to increase her stride pattern; not easy being a little over five feet four inches in height. Fortunately, fate intervened when he stopped at a public water fountain.

Gasping, she almost knocked him aside to get at the water. "Lovely morning," she said, slurring her words.

"What? Oh… yes… certainly is," came the reply, and after the briefest of pauses, "do this every morning do you?"

"Try to," she said, "but the office keeps me busy and I have loads of properties to keep an eye on… along with other things."

Bremner looked at her and smiling said, "What else do you keep an eye on then?"

Emma, still clawing at the water fountain, said without looking at him, "You, mainly."

Showing no facial reaction whatsoever, he said, "Okay, how do we do this?"

Adjusting the laces on her trainers and avoiding eye contact, she replied, "When and if they make contact, you are to call the rental office and ask for Emma… me. Say something along the lines of an appliance isn't working and ask to have it fixed or replaced. If out of hours, leave a message by phone. We're closed on Sundays so leave a message on the answerphone – stipulating it's for Emma. Is that clear?"

"Yes," he said, rubbing his left calf muscle.

"The day after they make contact you can expect to see me at this water fountain at exactly this time." Still not looking at him, "Happy?" she asked.

After a pausing, he replied, "Yes, Emma."

With the slightest hint of a grin, she adjusted her music system and jogged off. The whole exchange took less than a minute. Bremner watched her: "More a sprinter than a distance person by the look of it," he said aloud. "Nice surprise, though."

****

As was all too often the case, despite being a Sunday, Mary Stewart – dressed in jeans and trainers – was sitting at the computer in her office. More homely than most, she'd made an effort to acquire some decent furniture and, proud of her prowess with plants, the room included a variety of exotic species. She found the fragrance calming. Inheriting green fingers from her mother, when not at work she derived inordinate pleasure messing about in the garden of her detached house in Hammersmith. It had been the family home when her parents were alive and she still occasionally found the memories emotionally difficult. But it was ideally positioned for now and any plans to find somewhere else had been put on hold.

A short list of candidate *"controllers"* for the new hacker associate had been compiled by the Technical Department in consultation with HR. It was now her job to make the selection. These people led fascinating, albeit quite narrow, lonely existences and were well paid for their services within what was by any measure a highly sophisticated and specialised field. Having read the file of all five names on the list, she settled on Tom *"Tommy"* Manners. English, and one of the earliest hackers to be recruited by her Service, he was still in his early thirties. An acknowledged expert in what he did, the thirty year old had repeatedly proven himself to be a priceless asset. As was the way of things, there was no home address for him: no country either for that matter. All financial transactions were handled through an overseas bank account.

Annotating her decision electronically on the file, she sent it on its way. Then, turning off her computer, she grabbed her jacket and set off to meet Brian Finlay who, at some stage soon, she would interrogate about gardening. It was time to discover what interests they had in common, although she doubted gardening would be one of them.

****

Having just finished a call with Jed Crosby in Monaco to agree terms and conditions for the charter of Motor Yacht *Cygnus*, Erjon was excited about the prospect of being reunited with the elegant, sixty-five metre, three-decked beauty. The portfolio sent by Crosby included new photographic coverage of the refurbishment: stunning white paintwork, gleaming brightwork and replaced teak decking. Guzim was going to be blown away when he saw it and especially his personal stateroom. There were two VIP cabins for Erjon and Saban and, as required, four additional guest cabins on the lower deck – two singles and two doubles – all with private bathrooms.

Crosby had reaffirmed that the chief stewardess and her team would cater for all guest needs – irrespective of the time of day. Nothing would be too difficult; anything not readily to hand could be delivered by helicopter. Down below, unless fetching drinks or serving food, the established modus operandi for stewardesses would be to try and stay out of sight of guests; a bit of a stately dance at times, each guest being assigned a code name for use by the below decks team on their personal secure radio net. With a crew of fourteen, plus two specialist nurses arranged by WYC and the additional Albanian chef found by Erjon, *Cygnus* was fully configured and in all respects ready for extended cruising.

As Erjon remembered from his previous experience, this sort of luxury didn't come cheap. They would be expected to pay for food, booze and fuel costs in addition to the daily charter fee – plus a gratuity on completion. *Cygnus* had the standard toys; jet skis and all manner of water slides, diving equipment and assorted tackle to chase fish. An elegant *"tender"* would handle runs to shore or exploring shallow bays. Yes, his brothers were in for a real treat. "Worth every penny," he tried to convince himself.

On the eve of their departure for Malta, Erjon told the other two that something had cropped up needing his immediate attention… a business matter. He would see them in Valetta in a couple of days, adding (which raised a laugh), "Please don't go without me."

Twenty-four hours later, having hastily arranged a flight to Cyprus, he was sitting in a hotel just round the corner from Paphos International Airport. The man he was there to meet had also flown in that morning and would, on completion of their conversation, return to Islamabad in Pakistan, via Dubai. After a discussion lasting less than two hours, the two men prayed together before going their separate ways.

Immediately on return to London, having doubled-checked that his brothers were physically on their way to Malta, Erjon flashed up his computer. Using a complicated routing pathway, he typed a short message to an address in Croatia and pressed *"Send".*

****

Across the Atlantic in Miami, Jo was deep into her training course. When not getting drenched on sea survival, struggling to extinguish fires in claustrophobic metal containers dressed in a far too big fire-retardant suit under breathing apparatus, she was deeply engrossed in the intricacies of *"silver service"*: decanting wine, supervising all manner of settings and seating plans for lunch and dinner parties. The syllabus even included sessions arranging exotic flowers.

Standards were uncompromising and non-negotiable; *"seven-star service"* in every sense of the expression. On completion of evening exercises – designed to get the team used to coping with guest demands such as buffet suppers for ten at short notice – whilst her fellow students would collapse in their rooms, she would slip away to a local gun club to spend a couple of hours on the range. Nobody batted an eye at her request to borrow a Sig Sauer 38.

Course completed, and after a brief pause to catch her breath, she flew to Nice prior to joining the yacht. Captain Henry Constance had met her off the plane and chatted away on the drive to *Cygnus's* berth in La Seyne-sur-Mer. He explained that timings were tight; coming out of refit early meant confirmatory sea trials would have to be completed whilst in transit to Malta. He would take it on risk.

Impressed with the calm, matter-of-fact way he talked her through the list of priorities, Jo had listened closely to the pen pictures he offered of individual crew members – many of whom he knew from other yachts and had personally requested. Confirming the Maltese port of Valetta for guest boarding, he reassured her that there would be ample time to rehearse above and below deck routines. By way of guidance, he made clear that she would be responsible for everything involving the guests; he stood ready to support whenever needed and, of course, was always available. As she already knew, and in accordance with the client's wishes, on completion of embarkation they would proceed directly to Mallorca.

Without being too inquisitive, he asked about her recent appointments which, having spent a lot of time reading up her legend, she fielded without too much difficulty. Using the well-established conversational tactic, she subtly encouraged him to talk about his own career rather than hers. The file told her a lot about Henry Constance: mid-forties, medium height, fair-haired with a slight paunch, a deep tan betraying extended periods at sea, he was married with a home in Grasse – famous within the cosmetics industry. Warming to his understated, matter-of-fact character, she found his grasp of detail very reassuring.

In the hectic days that followed, Jo was all over *Cygnus* like a rash. Reassuringly, Hilary, the second stewardess, knew her stuff, was experienced, took direction and policed standards – in everything. It was agreed they would both be *"client-facing"*; supported by the other stewardesses – Minnie, Lola and Daisy when not *"house-cleaning"*. Less sure about how to handle the two nurses expected to board before departing for Valletta, she didn't have the faintest idea what to expect or what their routines were likely to involve.

The hours and days flew by. It was fun to be back on a yacht. Crew accommodation had substantially improved – more generous and altogether better organised than she remembered. Sharing a cabin with Hilary, the crew galley and recreational space soon became familiar gathering places. Her new charges were young, boisterous, demanding of her time and in need of close supervision – especially, she anticipated, when ashore on nights off. And why not? It was the same for her at that age. The key message she continually sought to remind them all was about the guests; service would be calm, orderly and discreet – nothing would be too difficult; no bitching about long hours, loss of sleep or any of that sort of thing. They could expect to be put through their paces well before arrival in Valletta and she didn't doubt it would be a steep learning curve for them all.

****

Tommy and Vinny set up an exclusive one-to-one communication link through a compartmented *"chat room"* on the dark web. Exchanges were business-like, both preferring to work unencumbered by set schedules. Neither knew the other's location and there were no plans to physically meet. The priority, Tommy emphasised, was finding Bremner in Mallorca. The fact that he and Brian Finlay already knew his location was deliberately not shared with Vinny because they wanted to test not only his discretion and reliability, but also his technical prowess. Tommy explained that, if and when time allowed, their second priority was to discover as much as possible about Erjon Shala. In regard to the division of responsibilities, Tommy made clear that he would take over Vinny's dual-role with immediate effect. He would report separately to Saban Shala as circumstances demanded. That way, he said, there was less chance of a screw-up. The issue of how Vinny, and for that matter Tommy in his new role was paid by the client remained unresolved but, between the two of them, it had been agreed that neither would be going anywhere near the bakery in Streatham, or anywhere else for that matter.

Their introductory chat had been predictably terse. "So…" Tommy had typed, "I'm Tommy and I guess you must be… Vinny?"

"Yep."

"And is there anything you think I should know before we get started… Vinny?"

"Nope."

"Right… any questions for me?"

"Can't think of anything right now. What do you want

me to do?"

****

In between sips of a superb espresso provided by the ever more creative Marjorie – doyen of the Vauxhall Cross fraternity of coffee baristas – Hugh Everard was reading Mary's latest report. It was fascinating. Erjon Shala had flown to Cyprus twenty-four hours earlier. His *"Watchers"* were nearly caught out when, without warning, he drove to Heathrow and jumped on a plane just prior to gate closure. Fortunately, quick-thinking saved the day when one of the operatives called in a favour with a former colleague now retired on the island. A photograph enabled a hastily assembled trio of former Special Branch officers to place Erjon under surveillance on landing – subsequently following him to an airport hotel where it subsequently transpired a room had been pre-booked under a different name.

Not long after arriving at the hotel, Erjon had a visitor – whom the team covertly photographed. As luck would have it, the individual in question was already on the FBI watch list: *"A Pakistani male known to be associated with fundraising for a particular terrorist group – the Islamic State of Iraq and the Levant (ISIL), also known as the Islamic State of Iraq and Syria (ISIS)."* Pure gold, priceless.

Hugh Everard knew all about ISIS. Less easy to understand was how Erjon Shala was involved. It had to do with money, he concluded; there was no other rational explanation. Reading it a second time, he was intrigued to note that the meeting in the hotel had been quite short with, on completion, both men going their separate ways – the Albanian to London and the Pakistani to Dubai – connecting with a flight to Islamabad.

Reaching for the intercom, he asked Marjorie to arrange an office call with the Foreign Secretary – at his earliest convenience – and, before then, to have Brian Finlay come up. Five minutes later, reading the report, Brian said, "Well, well – now isn't that interesting; two obvious conclusions. First, the limited time they had together rather suggests it wasn't their first meeting. Second, it provides irrefutable evidence that Erjon Shala is somehow involved with seriously dangerous people."

Everard, looking out of his window, replied, "It does, Brian – in fact, if anything, my guess is that it was a confirmatory meeting; you know – checking that everything was in order. Question is: is this solely about money, or does it go deeper?"

"Meaning what?"

"Not sure: maybe it's got something to do with the religious connection?"

"Could be," Brian said. "Bit of a stretch though… don't you think?"

"Maybe… anyway… park that for now: I'm seeing John Pelham later and will mention what our Washington friends have come up with. You can bet your life he'll give me a hard time about the gaps in our knowledge. I'll be emphasising that we're cranking up the tempo and that, with immediate effect, Erjon is our principal focus."

Finlay was nodding. "Understood. He's at the Limehouse office. His brothers having already left Luton Airport for Malta. I'm assuming that's where he'll join them."

"Okay," said Everard, now pacing the floor. "Let's take stock. We have two of our people on the ground: Emma in Mallorca keeping an eye on Bremner; Jo on the yacht. If we're right, the next significant event ought to be the Shalas contacting Bremner. Is that the way you see it?"

"I do," Brian replied.

"Tell me about the Hackers."

"Hacker Number One is a young man called Vinny –

he was required to give his name when he electronically signed the Official Secrets Act and a separate Non-Disclosure Agreement."

"Vinny what?" Everard asked.

"Just Vinny as far as I know," said Finlay. "So, just to be clear, he's now a fully signed-up member of SIS. He'll work in partnership with an existing Security Service asset – Tommy Manners. The GCHQ assessment is that they are technically well-matched, both at the top of their game."

"And they don't know one another?"

"According to Tommy …apparently not."

"And do we know where they're working from?"

"No idea… as Mike at GCHQ says, they could be on Planet Zarg for all he knows."

"Right," said Everard, taking a while to process the information. "Is Mary planning anything for any of the Shala offices or individual homes?"

"Not at this stage but I'm told planning for covert entry is well advanced; it can be done quickly if needed."

Everard was now staring out of the window, it was a gorgeous day. "Maybe I should have another chat with our Israeli friends."

"Yes… there are still an awful lot of unanswered questions," Brian said.

"Such as?"

"Well, for a start, we don't know what Guzim has in mind for Bremner. Maybe he'll invite him to join some part of the cruise: he might dump a load of cash on him."

"Certainly possible outcomes: what else are we missing?"

"The biggest known unknown for me is how Erjon's going to react if and when Bremner reconnects with Guzim."

"At some stage," Everard said, returning to his desk and almost as if talking to himself, "we might have to chuck a big rock into the Shalas' cosy pond."

****

Alon Carlebach was already waiting for Everard at their agreed meeting point in Regent's Park – his personal security team indistinguishable amongst office workers milling around thinking about where to spend their lunchbreak. It was a gorgeous day, parks bursting with sun worshippers desperately trying to get their faces into the rays. Keen to build trust and noting dark shadows under the Israeli's eyes, Everard chose to speak first. "Thanks for coming at such short notice, Alon, there are some developments concerning our mutual acquaintances with the bakery business." He then proceeded to give an expurgated version of the meeting in Cyprus.

Having listened attentively, a pensive Carlebach said, "That squares with our understanding. I was recalled to Tel Aviv for a conference and got back late last night. It was actually quite timely. Anyway, the Pakistani gentlemen to whom you refer is indeed involved in financing terrorist groups and, just in case anyone asks," he said with a grin, "he's not on our payroll. Is there anything specific you want me to try and find out?"

Considering this for a moment or two and choosing his words carefully because he didn't want to appear too pushy, Everard said, "No, not at the moment, thank you – but I'd appreciate hearing from you if anything comes up."

The Israeli, with the hint of a smile, said, "My friend, of course... you have but to ask. What I should tell you is that we are now going to pay much closer attention to the gentleman in Islamabad." And with that he got up and left.

Everard sat for a while. It was nice being outdoors and, after slipping off his suit jacket, he lit a cigar. Such opportunities were not to be squandered. Reflecting on the conversation, his instincts were telling him that the Israeli knew considerably more about Erjon Shala than he was choosing to impart; what was it they weren't seeing?"

****

Back in his office Everard made a short file note recording the meeting and the main issues discussed. He then went down to see Brian Finlay and gave him the gist of what had been said. Trying to ignore how cluttered and cramped the office was, he sat in one of the faded armchairs. "I've sent advisory notes to our representatives in Washington, Tel Aviv and Islamabad," Brian said. "Once we know all three brothers are aboard the yacht in Malta, we'll be set up nicely for our next move."

"Remind me?" Everard asked – distracted by the photographs of sailors and warships on the walls.

"Vinny steers them towards the property rental office in Sóller. Or, he simply passes them the address of Bremner's apartment – purportedly having hacked into the rental office's computer system. I personally favour the latter. Are you happy for me to set the wheels in motion?"

"Yes, I quite like the second option. Go ahead. While I'm here, we might usefully discuss that metaphorical rock we intend chucking into the Shala pond: what, when and how?"

"I've been thinking about that," Finlay said. "The nuclear option would be to drop Erjon in deep shit; make it known that he's involved in trafficking – has been for several years. In passing, we could also throw in that he's ditched his Christian faith and converted to Islam. That should do it."

"Evil, Brian… positively evil. Bound to trigger a punch-up – maybe resulting in Erjon being thrown off the yacht – maybe worse." They went on to discuss the details – agreeing that the *"revelation"* would reach Guzim via email from an anonymous source in Albania – engineered and delivered by Vinny on Brian's say so. As an afterthought, they agreed that Jo should be warned off in advance. Bremner likewise. In this scenario the potential for things to turn ugly on *Cygnus* was very real.

16

TOMMY AND Vinny were bouncing ideas off one another in the chat room – fingers flying over keys at spectacular speed. By his own admission, Vinny was struggling to find Bremner. It was testing not just his technical skill, but also his patience. "This is bollocks," Vinny said expressing his frustration. "The effing lack of bank details doesn't help," he added irritably. "According to the company's records, the ferry crossing to Santander was paid for in cash – likewise the leg from Barcelona to Palma."

"Very old fashioned," Tommy said.

"He has to be staying somewhere," Vinny said, "but working through all the property agencies will take bloody years."

"Why don't we divvy them up and start cold-calling," Tommy said. "It'll be much quicker."

Subsequently outlining the plan to Finlay, Tommy was told, "I suggest you play along for a couple of days and then tell Vinny you've nailed the rental office in the small west coast town of Sóller."

On completion of the call, pretending to be a relation, using the pretext of a death in the family, Tommy rang the office in question asking for Mr Bremner's address and telephone number. After reluctantly agreeing to provide it, Tommy forwarded the information to Vinny who, forty-eight hours later, sent the details to Saban. Emma reported the exchange back to Finlay.

****

For his part, Brian Finlay was relatively comfortable with

Tommy and Vinny's developing relationship but, which Mary Stewart agreed, they couldn't drop their guard. An eye would need to be kept on Vinny. The risk he might pursue a private agenda was always a possibility. As he kept reminding himself, Official Secrets Act or not, they were both criminals by instinct. The technical sophistication of these two *"Grey Hatters"* was, by any measure, quite remarkable. Deeply unsettling, too. No question about it, he reflected, they were seriously dangerous young men who – if so minded – could be formidable adversaries and wreak havoc. In the margins of penning a quick update to *"C"*, he made a mental note to change the passwords on his home computer.

****

Valletta justifiably lays claim to being one of the most picturesque yacht marinas in the Mediterranean, if not the world. Grand Harbour, a UNESCO World Heritage site, with a backdrop of five-hundred-year-old architecture crammed with expensive boutiques, restaurants, yacht brokerages and chandleries is a popular tourist destination in its own right and rarely disappoints. Home to many of the finest privately owned yachts money can buy, Guzim and Saban were simply overawed by it all. Literally billions of dollars-worth of gleaming hulls, dazzling metalwork and sumptuous interiors. Row upon row; some sail but mostly power, the multi-decked and occasionally towering vessels sat contentedly at berth – in the background the ever-present sound of sail halyards beating rhythmically against masts.

Sitting in the front of the Range Rover hired to collect them from the airport, Jo had given a running commentary as they drove the narrow streets into the marina where, on arrival, Henry Constance stood waiting to greet them on the quayside by *Cygnus's* gangway. After quickly introducing himself, he led the way on board. Guzim and

Saban exchanged a smile and followed. Shown to his stateroom by Jo, Guzim stared in wonder at the sheer size of the space. Spanning the width of the yacht, it even had its own private patio deck and Jacuzzi. He couldn't help smiling when he thought back to various prison cells. Daisy and Lola would unpack, iron and stow his clothes later.

Joining them for evening drinks, the captain asked his guests if they were amenable to departing after lunch the following day; by which time their brother was expected to have joined. As he explained, Mallorca was approximately 600 nautical miles away which, cruising at an efficient speed of 15 knots, would see them reach the island in just over a day and a half. The weather was forecast to be sunny and calm. Should they wish to take a time-out during the passage, he knew some delightfully secluded coves – ideal for swimming and picnics. Guzim, clearly enchanted by his new surroundings, was becoming increasingly relaxed – as was Saban – helped by the never-ending supply of vintage champagne, two shapely female Italian nurses and a bevvy of busy stewardesses.

Next morning, collected by Jo from the airport, Erjon was delighted but not surprised to hear that the yacht lived up to its billing and, if anything, surpassed his brother's expectations. Effusive in their praise, everything had got off to a perfect start and, for the first time in four days, he managed a proper night's sleep.

After a superb buffet lunch under sunshades, *Cygnus's* deck crew let go of her mooring lines, recovered the large blue protective fenders and the yacht slipped gracefully out of Grand Harbour. All three brothers, clutching binoculars supplied by Jo, were transfixed by the scene. It felt very grand and, somewhat out of character; they revelled in the unadulterated luxury of it all as tourists watched on with envy.

****

Across the sea in Italy, Hazel Pelham was feeling mildly short-changed that the G8 Foreign Minister's Conference failed to include the traditional *"Partner's Programme"*. Finding solace in the ever-reliable *"retail therapy"*, the central location of their assigned five-star hotel was perfectly positioned. John did his conference thing and she did hers – mainly on Via del Corso, reputedly the most famous shopping street in Rome. Other than a drinks reception on the first night, her time was her own. The itinerary she'd put together took in the Colosseum, St Peter's Basilica and, which she had read so much about, the Trevi Fountain. Packing her husband off after breakfast each morning in the protective custody of his security team, she was free to plan her day. All was reported to be well in Wiltshire with sons and horses and, after checking the weather forecast and putting on her recently acquired designer sunglasses, she stepped out into the busy street. Perfect: no time to waste.

****

Opting to stay an extra night after the conference ended, the four-hour drive to the East Coast went in a flash. The Foreign Office security team of three had already liaised with the Morettis and carried out a discreet recce of their property and surrounding grounds close to Portonovo, south east of the provincial capital Ancona. They had also touched base with local Carabinieri – the national gendarmerie of Italy responsible for domestic policing duties.

The Pelhams were warmly received by their hosts. Once introduced to Marina the housekeeper and Sophia the maid, they settled into their quarters before a light lunch and tour of the extensive grounds. The Moretti family home for over three hundred years, the farmhouse sat perched near the top of a hill surrounded by woods and lush Marche countryside. Envious of the extensive stable complex and its six four-legged occupants – all thoroughbreds – Hazel's eyes lit up at the large infinity pool. Delightful aromas from Marina's herb garden drifted on the breeze: basil, oregano, rosemary, sage and thyme. It had been a long time since she had felt so completely relaxed.

There were eight bedrooms: two assigned as guest quarters, complete with separate sea-facing patio, bathroom, kitchen and covered observatory. Older than the Pelham's children, the Moretti offspring were all away at university. "Fantastic," Hazel said as she stood on their patio being cooled by a gentle onshore wind. "It's absolutely ideal." Leaving John to check his email, she lost no time accompanying Francesca and Alberto to the stables.

The security team were housed separately in a small, self-contained building beyond the stables; even though the fridge was fully stocked, they would be treated to regular feasts by Marina and the delectable Sophia who, it appeared, was rather struck by the tallest of the *"three men from London"*.

Later that evening, after a relaxed supper and generous supply of superior white wine, the Pelhams said good night and retired to their quarters for a nightcap on the patio. Having rained earlier, the scent of mimosa and damp pine – tempered by lavender – served to remind them where they were. The unmistakeable smell of the Mediterranean. "Perfect," said Hazel. "Just perfect."

17

BRIAN FINLAY sat opposite Hugh Everard in a corner of an old pub on the cobbled streets of Greenwich's Ballast Quay. A special place and familiar haunt, it held a strong sentimental attachment from his days on various courses at what was then the Royal Naval College – just round the corner. They took a table by the window with a good view of the river. Both in suits, it had been a long day. Randell sat by the door.

"Definitely edgier in the old days," Brian said to Everard, "and popular with visiting merchant seamen from the Continent."

"Bit rough but a good pint," Everard said smiling. "Where are we with the bakery boys?"

Brian, temporarily distracted by an old chap in the corner – clearly the worst for wear and becoming increasingly vocal – said, "Last reported position according to Jo's iPhone put them due south of Sardinia; probably stopped for a swim off San Pedro Island."

Taking a sip of his pint, "Nice," said Everard. "I could use a bit of that myself. Can you imagine; everything on tap – your every need anticipated and catered for. Penny would love it. Costs a fortune I should imagine."

Still with his eye on the old man in the corner, now being assisted out by senior management, "You wouldn't get much change out of eighty thousand a day, plus food, fuel and booze," he replied.

"Goodness… I had no idea," said Everard. "Weren't you tempted to go the commercial route after leaving the Navy?"

Lifting his glass Brian replied, "In all honesty, it never crossed my mind. Probably missed a trick; those who did make a good living from it. The big disadvantage, much like the Merchant Navy, is the separation. High divorce rate I hear."

"Are we expecting to get anything from Jo?" Everard asked.

"Only if there's a problem. The arrangement is that, using an agreed code, she will periodically email a fictitious aunt in Bristol. It will automatically be forwarded to us and our representative on the island – who can route messages through the same portal."

Like Randell, Everard was also now looking at the old man who was putting up stubborn resistance and turning the air blue with some choice language. "Emma, isn't it?"

"Yes, she's been borrowed from our team in Madrid; bit of a fitness fanatic I'm told. Doesn't take prisoners apparently."

"Fancy something to eat?" Everard said, scanning the menu card.

"The pies here are outstanding, but I'm seeing Mary for supper later," Brian replied, rather to Hugh's disappointment.

Back in his flat in Pimlico, Everard was preparing an omelette. A man of fixed routines, he always included a green chilli to accompany the bacon, peppers, red onion and garlic. A bottle of his favourite Rioja – "Roda-1" – was uncorked and awaiting attention. Whilst reassured that Mildred was proceeding to plan, the associated risks were not lost on him. There was no hiding the fact that both Bremner and Jo Williams stood in danger in any fight between the brothers. That said, it was precisely the operational environment for which they were trained. The wild card was undoubtedly Erjon Shala. There was too much they didn't know.

176

Thinking about his people, it ultimately came down to trust. He'd given them the cards and it was up to them to play them as their instincts and judgement dictated. It had been the same for him; often operating alone in a foreign country and obliged to keep company with unsavoury and dangerous people. Emphatically not the sort to sit at Penny's dining room table.

****

Cygnus sat quietly at anchor in a sheltered cove on San Pietro Island within sight of the Sardinian Coast. The tender was launched – Erjon and Saban eager to swim. Guzim declined, preferring a lounger on his sun deck. The warm, crystal-clear water was invigorating; the brothers chatting contentedly as they trod water.

"You've done us proud," Saban said, barely able to take his eyes off the younger of the nurses towelling herself off on the beach, "This is the perfect holiday for Guzim and, I have to say, me, too."

Erjon, also distracted by the changing act taking place on the beach, said, "What do you think he's got in mind for Bremner?"

Saban had been giving this some thought ever since arriving in Malta. "To be honest, I don't know; we haven't discussed it. However, I'm pretty sure he'll invite him to join us for some or all of the cruise. How would you feel about that?"

"Fine by me: an entirely reasonable gesture for a man who saved your life," Erjon replied. "That said, perhaps we might raise it with him at dinner this evening?"

Saban nodded. "Okay, we can do that. No question he feels seriously indebted to the man; you've seen how emotional he becomes when he talks about it. Showing his age: it wouldn't have been like that a few years ago."

Later, at the end of another sumptuous evening meal – this time inside in the dining saloon – Jo and Hilary were gently dismissed and the conversation turned to Mallorca. Asking his brother directly, Saban said, "What's the plan for Bremner?"

"I want to ask him," Guzim said after a long pause, "to join us on the yacht. He and I have much to talk about. I want him to come with us to the Adriatic; I'd like him to meet our family. Do either of you have a problem with that?"

Saban, who by tradition spoke before his younger brother, said, "No, not at all: we owe the man a debt which we shall struggle to repay."

Erjon added, "I agree. We must make him feel welcome. I'll warn the captain to expect a fourth guest." And with that the conversation shifted to Albania.

****

Emma was growing into the new job in the property rental office. The staff were friendly: Sóller was a lovely town and she'd already done the train run to Palma. The funicular tram down to the harbour was another oddity in which she, like the tourists and locals, took great pleasure. More sail yachts were arriving by the day, restaurants busily gearing up for the tourist season to begin in earnest. There being no shortage of inexpensive places to eat, she was out and about most evenings.

Bored with her hotel room, she had jumped at the Office Manager's offer of a vacant rental property. Affordable and fully furnished, albeit a bit on the small size, the amazing view over the harbour more than compensated.

Emma was very comfortable in Spain. Fluency in the language had done wonders for her social life in Madrid. The climate and culture suited her. There was never a lack of interesting things to do, places to go and people to meet. Thriving on human interaction, she was rarely bored and, apart from the worsening status of her personal relationship in London, life was fun.

The boyfriend, however, was definitely an issue; unsurprisingly, the long periods of separation was straining things and it couldn't continue much longer. Her partner of nearly two years, the time was fast approaching to throw in the towel. His occasional weekend forays to Madrid, and hers to London, increasingly ended in acrimony and tears. What was the point of continuing once the fun had gone? It wasn't meant to be a prison sentence. She thrived on spontaneity and, over the last few months, it was gently being snuffed out. No point reinforcing failure. Besides, there was no shortage of potential suitors in Spain, at which point her mind came back to Callum Bremner. Thinking about her duty of care, she should probably check in on him. *Yes*, she thought, *this assignment is beginning to get seriously interesting.*

****

Just after weighing anchor at San Pietro Island and resuming the transit to Mallorca, Henry Constance found Erjon in the saloon and asked if there was anywhere in particular he wanted them to berth or anchor on the Island. Experience told him that, if Palma remained the preferred destination, being early season there would be no difficulty securing a berth. Erjon agreed that Palma would work well and the decision was made. Constance then went looking for Jo and gave her the estimated time of arrival. The intention was for the guests to eat ashore that evening: a reservation had been made at a restaurant known to Erjon. Returning to her cabin, Jo fired off a quick email to her aunt in Bristol: *"Having a lovely cruise; guests are super-easy; everyone is looking forward to visiting Mallorca, where we expect to arrive this afternoon and will be berthing in Palma."*

After reading the email, Emma knew she ought to give Bremner a heads-up. There would be a brief conversation at the water fountain the following morning. Arriving just ahead of him, drenched in sweat and without looking at him directly, she said, "They're in a marina in Palma and have got your address and apartment phone number. My guess is you'll hear from them sometime after ten o'clock this morning." Pausing for another mouthful of water, she added, "No idea exactly when or what form that will take, or for that matter what they intend to do. Just so you know, I've borrowed the keys to the vacant apartment next to yours up the hill. I'll be there throughout today and this evening. For the record, I won't be armed. Got it?" She then jogged off.

"Nice turn of phrase," he said to himself, "*'Got it.'* She's not big on chat – that's for sure," he murmured – smiling to himself and accepting he'd be staying by the pool for the next few days.

Back in her apartment, Emma left a message for her boss on the office phone to say she was feeling sick and wouldn't be coming in.

****

At precisely ten o'clock the burner phone lit up and Saban received the answer to the question put to Vinny the day before.

"He's taken a four-week contract on the apartment," Vinny said.

"Excellent my friend," Saban replied. "You have done well; there will be a bonus when I come back to London."

On concluding the call, Saban rejoined his brothers on the aft deck – sharing with them that he'd successfully found Bremner and had an address and phone number. "Sóller," he said, holding up a map and pointing at it. "On the west coast. How do you want to do it?" he asked, looking at Guzim.

"Good work. I think you or Erjon should call him rather than do the gangster thing and knock on the door with a bulging back pocket." After the laughter subsided, he continued, "We don't want to frighten him. How about seeing if he fancies joining us for dinner this evening. We can arrange a car." Then, looking at his younger brother, "You're the smoothie in the family, I think this is one for you. You can say that we'll get him home whenever we finish dinner."

Saban, clearly a bit put out but choosing not to react, said, "I'll speak to Jo and sort out transport."

"Good," said Guzim, "I've waited a long time to be properly introduced to Mr Callum Bremner; Saban, please inform Miss Jo that we might be four for dinner."

****

Bremner heard the car as Emma pulled up and parked outside the adjoining apartment shortly after ten o'clock. Just before midday the phone rang in his kitchen.

"Good morning, am I speaking to Mr Bremner... Mr Callum Bremner?"

Pausing to gather himself, he replied, "You are, who is this?"

Erjon, standing on the aft deck and admiring the striking lines of Palma Cathedral in the distance said, "Mr Bremner, my name is Erjon; we haven't met – I'm Guzim Shala's brother. Does that name mean anything to you?"

"Yes, it does."

"Good," Erjon continued, "my brother extends his warmest greetings and asks if you might be available to join him for an informal dinner this evening on his yacht here in Palma. He's been trying to find you ever since that unfortunate business at Maxwell. By the way, I do hope you've recovered from your injuries."

"I have – thank you."

"If you are free for dinner, we'll put a car at your disposal."

"I don't know what to say," Bremner began. "To be

honest, I never really knew your brother that well, but it would be good to meet up again."

"Excellent," said Erjon, "you'll also get to meet myself and my brother, Saban who, I should say, has done most of the work trying to track you down. Shall we say six o'clock for the car to collect you?"

"I take it from that you know where I'm staying?"

"We do. See you later."

Replacing the receiver, Bremner walked out onto the patio. A fisherman was recovering his pots in the bay below. "Heard the phone," a female voice said, "anything you want to share with me? Come round and I'll put the kettle on."

Struggling to supress a laugh he turned and looked up to see his occasional blonde jogging pal hanging out of an adjacent upstairs window. "How nice," he said, "can I bring anything?"

"Not unless you've got any cake or biscuits."

"Funny you should say that, as it happens I do."

Five minutes later, dressed in shorts, tee-shirt and deck shoes, he entered her apartment and, happily accepting the offer of tea, handed over a packet of biscuits.

Also in shorts, sandals and wearing a loose pink, short-sleeved cotton top, Emma parked herself on the sofa and tucked up her legs. "And...?" she said.

Reminding himself that he knew nothing about her other than she was an MI6 employee, this was the first time he'd really looked at her: the defining feature was unquestionably her green eyes. They were striking. Tanned, trim and with shoulder length blonde hair, she looked a picture of good health. She seemed completely at ease and was clearly hanging on his every word. Trying hard not to get distracted by the unsettlingly tanned body, he was curious to see whether his first impressions were correct about her being a woman of few words.

Emma sipped her tea as he repeated the substance of the telephone conversation, never taking her eyes of him and deciding not to interrupt. She had been looking forward to meeting him properly and was not in the least disappointed by the tall, good-looking man sipping his tea and sizing up a biscuit. "I reckon there could be a cruise in the offing if you play your cards right this evening," she said with a smile. "It'll be a cracking dinner, too. I don't suppose you asked if partners were invited?"

Bremner laughed. "No, the thought hadn't crossed my mind, and sadly he didn't leave a number."

Also laughing, she said, "Probably just as well; I don't have anything to wear. Pity though. Anyway, don't be unsettled if you see me loitering in the vicinity. More seriously, don't be thrown off your guard if you recognise someone else on board tonight. The chief stewardess is one of ours."

"Is she now."

"Yep. I haven't met up with her yet but she knows you could be heading her way."

"Am I allowed to ask where you're currently based, Emma?"

"Madrid," she said. "Due a move soon… quite fancy London."

"Somebody special there I imagine?" he asked, reaching for another biscuit.

"Nope," she replied, amazed how easily she could keep a straight face.

Knowing he ought not to stay too long, even though he was loving the chat, he thanked her for the tea and left via the side door. Emma sat for a while. "He'd be a keeper, that one," she said to herself. "It's so unfair." Then, gathering her things, she secured the apartment and drove off. She was about to make a miraculous recovery and return to the office.

****

At home in Norfolk, Hugh Everard had company on his bench under the majestic cedar tree beside the lake. Recently stocked, fish were showing all over the place. Penny had invited James Wadsworth and his wife for the weekend. Her parents were coming for Sunday lunch: lovely people albeit Hugh thought his lordship was overly fond of provoking political argument. He could also be uncomfortably inquisitive.

Closely monitoring developments with the imminent arrival of their grandchild, Penny was still giving Hugh a hard time for not being able to accompany her to France – for which a bag was permanently packed in readiness.

Hugh and James had spent most of Saturday afternoon afloat in the boat of which he was so proud. There was serious sport to be had and, across the lake, Randell was enjoying considerable success. A bottle of his better-than-average red wine at their feet, Everard was feeling completely relaxed. Overcast but without as yet any rain, the conditions for fishing were perfect.

Clearly an accomplished angler, Wadsworth cast a tidy line. As the afternoon progressed, he, too, became increasingly relaxed – helped, it could be supposed, by red wine and Cohiba cigars.

"Hugh," he said. "This is great: I can't tell you how much I'm enjoying it."

Everard, watching admiringly as Randell's line went taut replied, "Our pleasure James. I'm glad you're getting the chance to fish with all the stuff happening in the office these days."

Wadsworth, also watching the fish being deftly played by Randell as he reached for the landing net said, "Yes, things are a bit hectic at the moment, Hugh. John Pelham reported back favourably on the conference in Rome – the arrangements for which I understand were delivered with customary Italian aplomb. He and his wife Hazel are staying on for a few days: they've got pals on the East Coast – due back at the end of next week."

Taking a sip of wine, Everard said, "Yes, I was aware of that. He's been chasing me to nominate someone for the vacant Director of Operations post: wants a name by the time he gets back to the office. I've got a candidate in mind: exceptionally well qualified I might add – but probably in the minds of some an unorthodox choice."

Drawing deeply on his cigar, Wadsworth said, "Do say if you want me to put in a word, I'd be very happy to help."

"Thank you. Best we get back to it before the rain comes."

After packing away the lunch hamper and polishing off their wine, they returned to the boat – Everard gently positioning it upwind of some rising fish. An hour later, two fish taken, both by Wadsworth, they broke for a coffee from the flask. "By the way, Hugh, the PM read your note about that Shala chap's meeting in Cyprus. Interestingly, it came up in conversation the other evening at a private supper with the American Ambassador. He'd mentioned something about colleagues in Washington discussing it with Israeli friends."

Did they indeed? Everard thought. He would be having a word with Elon Carlebach about that next time they met. If true, it was distinctly unhelpful.

****

On a warm early evening in Mallorca, Callum Bremner – casually dressed in chinos, a long-sleeved open necked blue cotton shirt and deck shoes – was feeling apprehensive as the car approached the security entrance to Palma Marina. Swiftly waved through, he was forcibly struck by the serried ranks of multi-masted yachts. This was a different world – a manifestation of wealth almost bordering on the obscene. He reminded himself to play the role of star-struck tourist with all the conviction he could muster.

Regrettably, because he knew it was included in his prison record, he had decided to stick to the line of being teetotal. Living a lie for so long didn't make things easier. He needed his wits about him, and downing copious glasses of alcohol wouldn't help.

If anything, seeing Jo in uniform at the bottom of the gangway did nothing to allay his anxiety. Hair tied back, dressed in a white blouse with three gold stripes on the epaulettes and a short black skirt, she was clearly the surprise to which Emma had hinted. Consciously taking a deep breath to compose himself, he stepped out of the car.

"Good evening, Sir," she said – reaching out to shake his hand, "I'm Jo, the chief stewardess, welcome to *Cygnus*. Let me show you aboard and introduce Captain Henry Constance; your hosts await you on the aft deck." Following her up the gangway and remembering to avert his gaze from the well apportioned bottom in front of him, a man with even more gold bars on the epaulettes of a heavily starched white shirt stepped forward and shook hands.

"How do you do, Mr Bremner. I'm Henry, it's lovely to meet you; allow me to take you along to your hosts. Please come this way."

Walking aft to where three men stood around a table with drinks in their hand, all bare-footed and casually dressed, Bremner noticed the subtle deck lighting and soft music playing in the background. A stewardess was placing trays of canapes on a teak table. Guzim turned to face his approaching guest.

"Ah, here he is… how good to see you. It's been a long time my friend and I am truly delighted you could join us. May I introduce my brothers; Saban and, who you spoke to on the phone earlier, Erjon." Both men stepped forward and, like Guzim, warmly grasped Bremner's hand.

"Thank you, sir, Bremner said. "It is very kind of you to invite me." But before he could continue, Guzim interrupted.

"No, please, I insist you call me by my name – Guzim – and, if acceptable, I believe yours to be Callum?"

The ice having been broken, Bremner – gently explaining that he had not drunk alcohol for many years – accepted a non-alcoholic beer. He couldn't help noticing Erjon was drinking the same thing.

Jo, busying herself with checking the table setting in the dining saloon had been nervous at the thought of seeing Bremner and, not for the first time, realised he definitely had an effect on her. He looked so well: tanned, fit and predictably focused. The impression was of someone totally in control whilst, at the same time, showing the right amount of awe at his surroundings. The tan definitely suited him. The next few weeks were going to be tricky and she had already decided that the safest way to play it was to steer well clear of him. It wouldn't be easy, though. She, too, had to concentrate. He had the same relaxed smile and, for a fleeting moment she got the sense that he was not altogether a stranger to posh surroundings.

Guzim and Bremner had walked across to the capping rail, overlooking the Marina. Palma was gearing up for the evening action in bars, restaurants, casinos and clubs. The presence of three enormous cruise ships boosting crowd numbers; there was already a distinct party atmosphere to the place… street vendors with trays of cheap goods hassling passers-by.

"I was very concerned for you," Guzim said. "They refused to tell me anything after you were taken away to hospital. Are you fully recovered from your wounds?"

"Only the one, thank goodness. But, yes – I am thank

you. To be absolutely honestly, I don't remember much about what happened other than waking up in hospital. They kept me there quite a long time."

"In Birmingham?"

"Yes," Bremner replied, the old man had obviously read the file.

"And they let you out of prison early?"

Bremner took the question as further evidence that he was being checked out. It was odds on they had studied his file. "Yes, they did, and I've been drifting about quite a bit ever since – eventually deciding I needed a proper holiday. As a Spanish speaker, it wasn't a difficult decision to come to Mallorca."

"How did you get here?"

Suspecting he was being gently tested, "I bought a land rover in the UK and crossed on the ferry to Santander." Bremner saw Guzim was watching him closely. So, too, although some distance away, was Erjon. Saban seemed pleasantly distracted by Jo and Hilary.

"Callum," Guzim said in whispered tones, "I think we both know the bullet you took was meant for me. Why, and on whose authority, I'm still trying to discover. I swear to you that whoever arranged the contract will have cause to regret it."

Choosing not to interrupt, Bremner took a sip from his glass.

"Let me speak plainly," Guzim continued. "You saved my life. I owe you a debt; one that will be difficult for me to repay, but I am determined to try. Therefore, as a starter, I want you to join my brothers and me as our guest on this cruise. Stay as long as you like. No need to answer straight away, I quite understand you'll want to sleep on it. But, please know that I am sincere and would be truly delighted if you felt able to come with us. I can promise it won't be boring."

After pausing for a moment Bremner said, "Mr Shala… sorry, Guzim… – I'm touched by your generosity. I can think of nothing I'd like more and so yes, thank you, I should love to join you and your brothers on this magnificent vessel."

"Excellent," Guzim said and, turning to the others "He's accepted the invitation and will join us as soon as he's put his affairs in order." Looking back at Bremner he said, "We will arrange for you to be collected."

And with that Jo announced, "Gentlemen, dinner is served."

Much as expected, it proved to be a superb meal, Bremner half regretting not being able to sample the selection of fine wines accompanying the different courses. Jo stood in the background: studiously averting her gaze as Hilary and her team worked their magic with the service.

Bremner and Guzim chatted between themselves, reliving their shared experience of Her Majesty's Prisons – even managing to laugh. The atmosphere became increasingly relaxed as the evening progressed and the wine flowed. Discussion moved to the family business run from the Limehouse Office but without any mention of a bakery in Streatham. Saban, clearly not holding back with the wine, was becoming increasingly loud and patently enamoured of his wit and repartee – not to mention sly glances at Hilary and Minnie as they cleared away plates and refilled glasses. Bremer got the impression that Erjon was playing along; laughing at the appropriate moments whilst, at the same time, trying to keep half an ear on his conversation with Guzim.

Bremner left the yacht just before midnight, thanking his hosts profusely for their hospitality and restating his excitement at joining them the following day. Guzim had mentioned that, after circumnavigating the island, they would head east towards the Adriatic. There would be stops at interesting places on the way – Sicily being high on his personal list, closely followed by Capri. Jo had disappeared but the captain was in attendance to walk him to his car, repeating how pleased he was that he would be joining as a guest. Passing through the security gate, Bremner convinced himself he spotted a diminutive blonde in a bulky jacket loitering on the waterfront. She definitely looked familiar.

Down below in her cabin, Jo typed a brief email to her aunt in Bristol. The text made reference to *"One more guest expected from tomorrow"*.

Sitting on her balcony in Sóller, Emma received the message and, despite the obvious attraction, resisted the urge to call Bremner at his apartment. She would, however, pause at the water fountain on her run in the morning in the off chance of seeing him. It would almost certainly be the last time they would meet before his departure and her return to Madrid.

Early next morning, after packing a bag, Bremner donned his running kit and headed out for a jog. With plenty of time before the car was due to pick him up, the only loose end he could think of was the Discovery to which, unsurprisingly, he had become rather attached. "I wonder…?" he said, smiling.

Emma was panting harder than usual at the water fountain when he arrived unannounced. "That worked out pretty well," she said between gulps, "you jammy sod."

Sitting down on a wall and pretending to take off his shoe to remove a stone, he said, "You do know you do a passable impression of a hooker, don't you?"

Which prompted a bout of coughing as water went down the wrong way.

Seeing she was temporarily unable to speak, he said, "I don't suppose you could look after my Discovery while I'm gone, could you? It's insured for any driver."

Lost for words at the cheek of the man and having regathered her composure, Emma said quietly, "Okay, but only on condition that you come and collect it from Madrid."

Tightening up his laces and without looking up he said, "That's great. I'll leave the key under the mat outside the front door. Please treat her gently."

Watching him disappear up the hill she couldn't resist grinning at the idea of seeing him again. "You take care of yourself Callum Bremner, or whatever your name is," she said. "You and I have unfinished business."

That evening, after discreetly watching him board *Cygnus*, she dumped her things in the Discovery and drove onto the Barcelona Ferry. Her last two acts before leaving the island were to quit her job and email the boyfriend in London – essentially calling an end to their relationship and wishing him every happiness and a long life.

18

THE PELHAMS were loving every minute of their time in Italy – especially the long rides on meandering tracks through the woods and, occasionally, along deserted beaches. The Morettis were exceedingly generous hosts; no expense spared. Marina and Sophia had catered to their every need – attentive but unobtrusive. Francesca and Alberto hosted several informal drinks parties and buffet suppers – no doubt, Hazel thought, showing off their smart English friends. Why not? She'd do exactly the same.

It had been idyllic. John was sleeping soundly at night, rising early each day to deal with email and making a big effort to ignore the phone unless his PA called on the other mobile and said it was important. They laughed, talked and, now and then, wondered what it might be like to buy a place in Italy when the boys were grown up – maybe even before. She recalled a conversation about Umbria with Hugh Everard. Nice man, Hugh, although her jury was still out on Lady Penny.

Alberto announced at breakfast that the Pelhams last night was to be spent at a local beach restaurant – which he had conveniently been allowed to reserve for their exclusive use. Sophia, having cleared away the plates, put in a call to her boyfriend, "They're all going to the beach restaurant tomorrow night so I'm free – where are you taking me?"

Back in their room, Hazel said, "That man thinks of everything, what a gem – always has been – aren't they a brilliant couple? Must help being minted though." She looked forward to the day when John got a *"proper"* job or, better still, loads of them; directorships, specialist adviser to hedge funds and big banks. It would be good if he could make some decent money for a change and, deciding to interrupt his study of a map, said, "Have you ever thought about the House of Lords, John?"

"Not really," he said grinning, "Quite happy as I am, thank you."

"You surprise me," she said. "You'd look good in the fancy cloak."

"Do you know what they're trimmed with?" he asked.

"Fur," she said.

"Ermine; white – usually from stoats or weasels. Imagine the flak you'd get for being associated with someone who wore real fur. Do you hanker after becoming a lady or something?" he said, teasing her.

"You always said I was a lady," she shot back. "No, I was just thinking that a peerage would open up all sorts of opportunities. You'd make some decent money, too."

On seeing him turn and begin advancing towards her with lust written all over his face, she roared with laughter and bolted for the bathroom.

****

The little beach restaurant stood alone at the bottom of a winding track fifty yards from the sea. Unashamedly *"rustic"*, the single-story building had subdued exterior lighting and a covered veranda. The four of them were warmly greeted on arrival and treated like royalty. A favourite with the Morettis, the traditional menu fare was spread over five courses. Exquisitely cooked and presented, the food was accompanied by copious glasses of exciting things to drink. The owner, a family friend, took personal charge. After dessert, he accepted the invitation to join them for a calvados and coffee. Candles flickered in the dimly lit dining room and the sound of the sea drowned out by taped music.

The sea was like glass, the star-filled sky lit by a new moon. Sensing that the dinner was reaching its conclusion, the security team vehicles were parked with engines running facing up the track, at the top of which was positioned a stationary vehicle manned by four, armed carabiniere. The Pelhams had driven to the restaurant with the Morettis in one of the security team's Range Rovers. Exchanging fond farewells with the owner, Alberto climbed into the front passenger seat next to the security team driver.

Everyone was feeling very relaxed, slightly the worse for all the drinks and laughing at the slightest provocation; one amusing anecdote followed another. John Pelham sat in the back with the giggling ladies and, after a brief exchange on a hand-held radio, the Range Rover's engine powered up and moved to take position behind the lead vehicle already threading its way up the hill through the woods.

Two things happened within a matter of seconds. An explosion detonated underneath the first vehicle, shattering the windows and sending it flying into the air – falling back down to effectively block the track. The sound of tearing metal and exploding tyres echoed across the hillside. Birds screeched in alarm. In what must have been a millisecond later, a rocket-propelled grenade from a Russian made RPG decimated the stationary carabiniere vehicle at the top of the track, setting the fuel tank ablaze. The resulting fireball lit up the night sky. Although out of sight, the scene further down the hill was equally dramatic – smoke pouring from the security team's saloon and flames threatening to ignite petrol spilling onto the track. One of the front doors was missing, the other hanging from its hinges. Beyond the shattered windscreen, a contorted body lay inert across the bonnet; the other in the shrubs at the side of the track ten feet away. A man was groaning, the other silent and still.

Around the Range Rover – choreographed with surgical precision – a gloved hand snatched open the driver's side door and, clutching a silenced handgun, put two bullets into the driver's head and a further two into Alberto Moretti – one in the shoulder and the other into his chest. At the same time, a rear passenger door opened and John Pelham was dragged out. Hazel and Francesca, both screaming hysterically, were pulled sideways through the opposite door and thrown to the ground; mouths taped and hands shackled to the vehicle's bumper. Kicking and screaming, Hazel was laid unconscious with a glancing blow from a pistol and fell forward. Further sounds were heard from the restaurant and, trying to make sense of what was going on, Pelham assumed something awful had happened to the owner and his two helpers. Clearly visible in the front seat, Alberto was slumped forward and bleeding profusely.

Now gagged and hooded, Pelham was lifted under his arms by two figures and half carried across the beach to the water line and bundled into one of two stationary rigid inflatable boats. Once aboard, he was pulled to the rear and tied to a strong point. The men pushed off and jumped in while the coxswain started the twin 200hp outboards. Several minutes later, four armed figures came jogging across the beach, also dressed in black from head to toe with ski masks covering their faces. Without a word spoken, they clambered onto the second craft. Once aboard, both boats reversed off the beach and sped away into the darkness. The only sound on the beach was Francesca crying and low groaning from Alberto. Returning to consciousness, Hazel started to scream hysterically.

At the top of the hill, a second carabiniere vehicle parked further along the road at a separate junction reacted swiftly to the sound of the explosion, failing to notice two figures speed past in a blue saloon estate car heading for

196

town. On reaching their colleague's burning vehicle, they discovered four grotesquely charred bodies. Immediately putting out an urgent call for reinforcements, including a coastguard helicopter equipped with a searchlight and infra-red. It would be twenty-five minutes before local emergency services began arriving at the scene. Not long after, the first helicopter was overhead and sweeping the countryside with an intensely bright light. As reinforcements closed up, officers began moving cautiously down the hill – weapons drawn and flashlights in hand. A muzzled police dog was straining at its leash.

Further reports followed as they came across the carnage and casualties surrounding the security team vehicle slewed across the track – a small black crater clearly visible together with the remnants of what looked like firing cable. Bullet holes had peppered the contorted wreck. It was over an hour before ambulances and police reached the restaurant car park and recovered Hazel, Francesca and the still heavily bleeding Alberto. The driver was dead but thankfully the restaurant owner and his staff were found alive – tied up but unhurt in a storeroom.

****

First reports reached the Foreign Office Resident Clerk in London shortly after ten o'clock that night. Once validated, appropriate contingency plans were set in motion and phones started ringing in Rome and the offices of duty personnel in Whitehall. Alerted by pager, Everard, Finlay and James Wadsworth received the situation report within minutes of each other. So, too, did officials in the Home Office, Metropolitan Police and Ministry of Defence. Cabinet and Foreign Office staff began drafting a holding statement for the Press. As a matter of routine, calls also went out to mobilise national specialist counter-terrorist organisations – civil and military. A Foreign Office team was dispatched to support Hazel's sister at the farm in Wiltshire; police patrol cars having already established perimeter security and positioned an armed presence at the house.

Brian Finlay spoke personally to the SIS representative in Rome – who was in close touch with the major Italian National Crime Agencies, including the Carabiniere. He then briefed *"C"* in his office. More lights were going on by the minute across Whitehall, as sleepy staff began to arrive.

"The situation as I understand it," Finlay began, "is that John Pelham has been abducted by persons unknown – believed to be armed – from a beach near Portonovo, south east of Ancona on Italy's Adriatic Coast – here," he said pointing at a map on his iPad. "It happened around ten o'clock this evening – Central European Time – at the conclusion of dinner with Italian friends at a local beach restaurant. Early indicators suggest he was taken away by boat.

"On his own …without his wife?"

"Yes."

"What's the status of the casualties?"

"Four carabiniere officers died at the scene. Their vehicle was struck with some sort of rocket propelled grenade – presumed to have been an RPG 7. Two Foreign Office security personnel also died in a related but separate attack. The other team member driving the Pelhams and their hosts tragically died of gunshot wounds."

"What about Hazel Pelham?"

"Bruised but otherwise reported to be okay," Brian said, "as was her Italian female friend. Alberto Moretti, the host, is in hospital receiving treatment for gunshot wounds – his situation is assessed to be critical."

Finlay went on to say that all the right things were happening, including support being provided to Hazel by consulate staff in Rome. Anticipating the question, he said, "Nothing has been heard from the kidnappers and the whereabouts of the Foreign Secretary is unknown,"

"Do we know if Pelham was carrying any form of concealed personal tracking device?" Everard asked.

"We don't know – probably unlikely but the Foreign Office is checking. What we do know is that both his phones have been turned off and neither of them has so far been found at the scene. Probably chucked into the sea."

"What are you getting out of the Cabinet Office?"

"I've just heard the PM has convened a meeting in the Cabinet Office Briefing Room for ten o'clock. You should be aware that the No 2 at the Foreign Office, whose name I can't remember, has already assumed the duties of Foreign Secretary.

"Have we informed our guys in Washington?" Everard asked.

"Yes." Brian replied, "And all embassies in the region."

"Definitely no demands so far?"

"No."

"Okay," Everard said. "I'll give James Wadsworth a call to make sure he's fully up-to-speed. Ask someone to get me the personal file on the interim Foreign Secretary would you."

"Will do. Just so you know, I've called-in the Jedi Knights," Brian said. "They've already begun *'optioneering'*. I've told them I'll be along to hear their initial ideas in two hours' time."

Everard knew all about the group of individuals to which Finlay was referring. Amongst some of the brightest minds SIS could muster: all unorthodox thinkers able to formulate creative solutions and, which was a definite strength, not slave to personal biases. "Good," he said, "please call Marjorie and ask her to come in, although I'll bet she's already on her way. I want a secure VTC with our various Embassy Liaison staffs as soon as we can arrange it. What else should we be doing?"

"I think that about covers it for the time being. Regarding the VTC, I'm assuming Italy, Croatia, Montenegro, Albania and Greece?"

"Yes, and we should include Kosovo, Serbia and Turkey."

"Got it."

"Brian, just so we're all clear, the SIS's strategic objective, using all means available, is to acquire information for the purpose of expediting the safe recovery of the Foreign Secretary. Please include that in the warning order ahead of the VTC."

Jotting it down as Everard had been speaking, "Understood," he said.

****

James Wadsworth was quick to answer his phone. "Morning, Hugh, what an awful business, PM's all over it. I'm trying to rein him in."

Everard talked the Chief of Staff through the event's chronology; suitably caveating any dubious or unsubstantiated information. Both men knew that rumours always ran rife in such situations. Pedlars of fake news would have a field day. Wadsworth said that his main effort was to ensure any external messaging to media platforms was coherent, credible and not creating any potential hostages to fortune.

Reuters already had the story. He said he was in touch with the Queen's Private Secretary at the Palace and his people were getting ready to brief the Speaker and Leader of the Opposition. "The approach," Wadsworth said, "is to under promise and over deliver. We will stick to the facts and try to deter speculation – a message the duty minister will be reiterating on the early morning talk shows."

Thanking Everard for the call, Wadsworth hung up, leaving him to reflecting on what a hell of a start to the day it had been. Marjorie walked in with an expresso. It was just after two o'clock in the morning.

****

Cygnus left Palma soon after Bremner boarded. Shown to his guest cabin by Hilary and stowing his ample things in the generous wardrobes and drawers, he quickly worked out that the chief stewardess was making a point of keeping busy elsewhere and deliberately avoiding him. Joining Guzim on deck, they watched together in silent fascination as the lines were let go and Marley – the Chief Officer – eased the yacht from her berth under the close supervision of his captain.

Guzim shared the planned itinerary with Bremner; Sicily first, then Capri. "After that, Callum, I am keen to carry on to the Adriatic," he said whilst watching Palma recede into the distance. "We will head west from here and follow the coast north east past Sóller. Rounding the top of the island, we'll turn east and proceed towards Menorca from where – I'm told – it is something like four hundred and twenty nautical miles to Palermo in Sicily. All these nautical terms I seem to be acquiring. Impressive, eh?"

"Absolutely," Bremer replied.

There was no mistaking the old man's enthusiasm for his first cruising experience. Bremner immediately saw the attraction and was also getting into the swing of it, quite deliberately choosing to wear shorts without a top to ensure his host caught sight of the ugly and remarkably lifelike scar on the lower left side of his stomach.

"I hear there's been a kidnapping in Italy," Guzim said, putting down his binoculars. "No lesser person than the Foreign Secretary, would you believe."

"Who, John Pelham?"

"Yes. Pretty stupid thing to do if you ask me. A wife or son for ransom perhaps, but why such a prominent politician? They must be mad."

This was the first Bremner had heard about it and could well imagine the pandemonium in Whitehall. Seen from any perspective, it was a very big deal. The full machinery of government and its global diplomatic network would, he knew, be swinging into full operational mode.

Erjon was reading the same breaking story on the BBC News website over a leisurely snack in his cabin. Finishing his coffee, he went up to the saloon and switched on the big plasma TV which, with the yacht's fully integrated Wi-Fi system, gave instant access to the internet. CNN News showed the British Prime Minister standing behind a lectern in Downing Street facing a hostile media scrum jostling for the coverage and looking for choice soundbites. Pelham's curriculum vitae was already in the public domain receiving close scrutiny – back catalogues being trawled for photos or footage of him. Already privately aware of the kidnapping, Erjon had no need to turn up the volume. He resisted the urge to smile. Joining him in the saloon, Bremner watched the silent images on screen. As he had on deck with Guzim, he made a point of positioning himself where Erjon would see the scarring on his stomach. Which he did, but without making any comment.

****

Back in a second-floor conference room at Vauxhall Cross, Brian Finlay was paying close attention as the appointed leader of the Jedi Knights summarised the team's initial thinking. "Logically," he began, "this has to be politically rather than criminally motivated. Why? Because the perpetrators took the Foreign Secretary rather than his wife. It is reasonable to assume that they expected him to have security and were ruthless in neutralising it. They are no strangers to violence and our Foreign Secretary looks to have been taken alive. Our next deduction, therefore, is that he is of no value to them dead."

"What about the abductors?" Finlay asked.

"From what we've been told, it appears to have been a professionally executed job. As I say, they were patently not deterred at the prospect of confronting armed security. In our opinion, the perpetrators knew precisely what they were doing. Weapons and equipment were top notch. If the timeline is even broadly accurate, they must have done some sort of recce. There has to be a suggestion of prior knowledge. Italian law enforcement agencies are reviewing coastal radar tapes in the firm belief that Pelham was transferred to a mothership – something like a fishing boat or tramp steamer."

"What do you think about that?"

"It's a reasonable deduction but we see it differently. In our view, using a parent vessel of some sort would be too risky. We think a more likely scenario is that he crossed the Adriatic by the shortest route – a distance of approximately 90 nautical miles – which, at 40 knots, would take just over two hours. If that assumption is correct, it would put him somewhere amongst the island complex off the Croatian coast… in this area," he said, pointing to a map.

Unable to fault the reasoning, Brian watched and listened with increasing dismay. This was a bloody nightmare. Looking around the room, he couldn't help noticing how young they were. All unsettlingly sharp people and, amongst them, the Service's future leadership. "Have we shared this with our people in Rome, and does it align with their thinking?" he asked.

"We have, and it does," came the reply.

"What proactive steps should we be considering; specifically in Croatia and possibly Montenegro?" he asked.

"Yes, we've started to look at that," the team leader said. "The first priority should be to step up our presence in Croatia. We've heard that UK military specialists will probably elect to forward base either at sea in readiness for any recovery operation or, alternatively, at an airhead in Italy or somewhere else in the Region."

"What are the Italians doing?"

"All the right things as far as we can tell. They're naturally very embarrassed and, although only a rumour, colleagues in Rome are picking up that a substantial six figure reward is being offered for information."

"Okay… good work… thank you. Give me a shout in an hour or two and don't be surprised if 'C' pops in."

****

Finlay and Everard met for an early breakfast in the Canteen which, despite the ungodly hour, was doing brisk trade. Recounting the Jedi Knight's early analysis, Brian said, "They're not saying it, but I got the sense they're convinced it was an inside job; someone must have tipped-off the abductors."

"That's a bit of a stretch, isn't it?"

"Possibly," said Brian, "but I get the thought process: it was far too slick – too efficient – almost military precision by all accounts."

"Maybe," said Everard. "But I'll reserve my position on that."

"On detail," Brian continued, "once the SF guys decide where to base themselves, I think we should collocate our own liaison cell. In fact, thinking about it, we should probably do that right away."

Everard, thoroughly spoiled by *"Barista Marjorie"*, was struggling with the canteen coffee and, grimacing, said, "God that's awful… I'm talking about the coffee, Brian."

"It doesn't improve that's for sure," said Finlay, smiling.

"I want you to go to the Cabinet Office briefing at ten o'clock. If asked why I'm not there, just say I'm pursuing enquiries with international colleagues. On a related issue, do you think there's merit in you personally going forward – maybe to Zagreb, Sarajevo or Podgorica?"

Considering it for a moment, Finlay replied, "Possibly, but my instinct is to let the dust settle first. There's not much value I can add at the moment unless, of course, our people start encountering resistance."

"From where?"

"Oh, you know, the usual suspects in a crisis – well-intentioned but risk-averse bureaucrats."

"Fair enough, but can we keep it under review please. If you decide to go over there, just do it – maybe taking a communications team with you and someone with the requisite languages."

Finlay, glad he had opted for tea, said, "Understood. On a separate matter, mindful that Bremner is now on *Cygnus*; have you had any more thoughts about when to chuck the rock we discussed?"

Contemplating a second bacon sandwich, Everard said, "Within the next three days. Does that make sense?"

"Yes, that'll be about right," Finlay said. Then after a pause added, "If you have the time, you might like to stick your head into the conference room where the Jedi Knights are doing their thing. They'd appreciate hearing any feedback?"

****

Back at his desk, Brian Finlay was scrolling through names on his computer, listing all the language capabilities of serving SIS operatives. The focus, in priority order, being Croatian, Bosnian, Albanian and Serbian. One in particular stood out and Finlay called up the individual's file.

Surprised by what he was seeing, he asked his personal assistant for the name and secure phone number of the SIS Head of Station in Madrid. Put straight through, he said, "First of all, thank you for lending us Emma to support Mildred, she did a great job. I see from her file that not only does she speak fluent Spanish but also Croatian and Albanian, with conversational Bosnian. Is that correct?"

"Yes, it is, Brian. Her surname, as you know, is Asllani and, although born in England, her parents were originally from Kosovo.

"Now you mention it, I remember reading that in the file. She was christened *'Era'* but thought *'Emma'* might be less confusing for people."

"Correct."

"In which case," Finlay asked, "is there any chance she could be made available to join a small communications team we're putting into the Region?"

"You're talking about Pelham's abduction, I presume?"

"Yes… I'd need her in London for briefing as soon as it can be arranged."

"I'm sure that won't be a problem, leave it with me."

****

Two days later, Emma Asllani knocked on Finlay's door and was introduced to Mike, leader of the GCHQ supporting communications team. The briefing lasted over an hour. The intention, Brian said, was that she and Mike's team were to immediately assume twelve hours' notice to move to RAF Northolt, just outside London, where a HS 125 jet stood ready to fly them to wherever required. He said he planned to deploy separately, linking up at the eventual destination. He asked them to talk to HR and sort out accommodation and visas. Pagers would be provided within the next hour or so.

That night, Emma was amused to find herself in a very

smart hotel in Knightsbridge. Seeing no reason whatsoever to call her former boyfriend, in between mouthfuls of a particularly good seafood pasta she found herself thinking about Bremner. What she wouldn't give to be on that cruise.

****

Now within 100 nautical miles of Sicily's north coast, *Cygnus* was steaming at a sedate 15 knots. Continuing in the manner to which they were now becoming accustomed, the four guests basked in sunshine and delighted in their luxurious surroundings. Meals were usually taken together but Erjon often chose to spend the morning hours working on a laptop in his cabin which, as Jo had deduced soon after they first embarked, meant he was using the yacht's Wi-Fi – an observation she passed in code to her auntie in Bristol.

Once alerted to this timely snippet of information, Tommy tasked Vinny to take a closer look and probe the resilience of the yacht's systems. For his part, even though Tommy was as they say in American football speak, *"running protection for him"*, Vinny was fully seized of the need for caution. It was already apparent that the brother they called Erjon was demonstrably sharper than the rest and therefore the biggest threat. Furthermore, it was reasonable to assume that it was he who had suggested closing down their system and thus thwarting any hack of the system at the bakery. The man was a dangerous, well informed and technically savvy opponent.

The idea was that, once penetrated, the yacht's Wi-Fi servers would reveal all communication sent or received over the internet. Rejecting the idea of simply getting hold of the access code because they didn't want to signpost involvement, the skill came in not only defeating the yacht's sophisticated cybersecurity protection software, but also whatever individuals had in place on their personal laptops.

Alternative potential entry points, which Tommy had suggested – *"Not teaching you to suck eggs, Vinny"* – were the iPhones used by the two older brothers which, it was reasonable to assume, would also at some stage hook into the onboard Wi-Fi, either for social media, or email. Game on.

****

Six hours later, *Cygnus* manoeuvred deftly into her assigned berth in the most central of Palermo's half dozen marinas. Conveniently surrounded by waterfront restaurants, the position was ideal from Guzim's point of view. He had already requested a drinks reception aboard for local friends that evening before they all went ashore for dinner. Preparations were set in hand and Jo was told to expect no more than eight or so guests for *"cocktails and fancy small eats"*.

In the event, the number was closer to eighteen and, worryingly, once things got underway, no one seemed in any rush to leave. The drinks locker took a hammering and Hilary's team worked flat out. Guzim made a conscious effort of introducing Bremner to his Sicilian associates, all of whom spoke passable English.

The party was a roaring success and, not without difficulty, the brothers managed to shepherd their increasingly lively flock down the gangway and off to the restaurant. Observing from a flank as her stewardesses constantly replenished glasses and handed out food prepared by the celebrity Albanian chef, Jo was in little doubt that the guests were significant figures within Palermo society. In hindsight, she regretted not trying to get photographs – maybe one of the Marina's security cameras could oblige.

Guzim left Bremner in no doubt about his status as a member of the home team. He was expected to join them for dinner. Accepting the inevitable, he made every effort to get into the swing of things and decided to chat up the ladies, all expensively dressed and glamorous. It proved an inspired tactic and they seemed happy to be flirting with the handsome and charming Brit who had an unmistakeable twinkle in his eye. Fortunately, only a few of the party made it back to the yacht for a nightcap, the last of whom left just after three o'clock next morning. Nobody other than the second officer, duty deck crew and stewardess was up early.

Just after midday, all three Shalas went ashore to meet more *'old friends'* and returned in time for dinner. Jumping at the chance of spending some time on his own, Bremner grabbed a taxi and disappeared in the direction of Mount Etna with the intention of going for a long run. Jo watched him leave. Her auntie had already been advised of the next destination.

Cygnus departed Palermo the following day, bound for the enchanting Isola di Capri. In keeping with his new regime, Guzim was on station on the yacht's bridge. He liked the calm and relative tranquillity of the place and, ever curious, was learning the rudiments of navigation from the Chief Officer. Computing approximate speed and distance on the electronic charts was absorbing. This leg, he had deduced, was one hundred and sixty nautical miles which, at their customary fifteen knots, translated into approximately ten hours passage time.

The plan was for *Cygnus* to anchor on the south side of the island rather than look for a marina berth. All a part of the cruising experience they had been told. The yacht's tender was on hand to ferry guests to beaches, restaurants or shops as required. A more sporting option was to use one of the two jet skis.

Guzim had read about Capri but, never having been there, was determined to lunch at a particular restaurant popular with locals. Erjon, who spoke Italian, duly made a reservation for the next day. That evening, with the yacht at anchor half a mile from shore, the four guests sat down to another sumptuous dinner on the aft deck. By now relaxed in Bremner's company, Erjon was speaking knowledgeably about Capri's history. "The early Greeks were here," he said. "Then the debauched Roman Emperor Tiberius decamped from Rome in fear of assassination." Nobody appeared to get the joke.

"Smart move," commented Saban.

"Very popular with pirates in later centuries," Erjon continued, "the English under Sidney Smith defeated the forces of Napoleon Bonaparte the year after the Battle of Trafalgar and took possession of it."

"That'll be 1806," said Bremner.

"Correct."

"It was very popular with movie stars," Guzim said, reaching for his glass, "Audrey Hepburn and Grace Kelly both kept homes here."

Listening to this historical dissertation with more than passing interest, Bremner noticed that Jo had been looking at him while Hilary and Lola served the meal. For a fleeting moment, he caught her eye. No question about it, he decided: not only was she thoroughly convincing undercover, but also a gorgeous looking woman – exceptionally well-suited to a tan. Worryingly, he was getting the distinct impression that Erjon had reached the same conclusion. Quickly turning away, Jo replenished their glasses before disappearing into the adjacent saloon.

19

I T WAS RAINING in London. Umbrellas were up. Sitting in front of his computer screens, Vinny was putting the final touches to an email drafted by Tommy. Contrary to expectations, gaining access to *Cygnus's* Wi-Fi proved easier than it should have been. Once in, it was comparatively straightforward identifying which email address belonged to who.

****

After an exciting day touring the island, partaking of a thoroughly good lunch in the process, the Shalas and Bremner were sitting on deck under the stars being treated to yet another sensational dinner. The conversation was relaxed and, for two of them, pleasantly accompanied by some spectacular red wine. Bremner and Erjon remained steadfastly abstemious – something Bremner was seriously regretting. Fascinated by the history of the island, even Saban was holding forth on what he could remember from the tour guide. He somehow managed to confuse everyone including himself but it didn't seem to matter. They all found it hilarious.

A ping on Guzim's iPhone announced an incoming email just before the cheese board appeared. Lifting it from his shirt pocket and quickly scanning the text, he went very still. Saban, always sensitive to his brother's mood swings, asked in a slightly slurred voice, "Is everything okay?"

"It is, thank you. I'm feeling a little tired. I'm going to call it a day." The others stood as he got up to leave and, after saying goodnight and thanking Hilary and Lola, he retired to his suite.

"What was that all about?" Saban asked looking at his brother.

"Like he says, probably feeling knackered. Too much sun: it's been a long day. I'm sure there's nothing to worry about and," said with a big smile, "we can always ask one of the nurses to check on him later."

Back in his stateroom, bringing up the email message again on his iPhone and re-reading the short text, Guzim slumped into an armchair. The next hour saw a flurry of phone calls, all deliberately short and without reference to names, places or events. Struggling with conflicting emotions – incredulity and disbelief – for the first time since boarding *Cygnus* and much as it was in the aftermath of the shooting – he found himself unable to sleep. But, he reasoned, there was nothing more to be done for the present and he would make further calls before breakfast.

****

Copied on the anonymous email Vinny had sent Guzim, Tommy fired off a short text to Brian Finlay: *"Your rock just landed in the pond."*

Vinny and Tommy were closely monitoring email traffic aboard the yacht and, in an exchange in their chat room, Vinny expressed surprise that nothing had been seen in response from Guzim. The only conclusion was he must be communicating by phone; in itself unfortunate because they hadn't yet managed to gain access to it. That apart, it was entirely likely he would be using a messaging app with end-to-end encryption.

Earlier that evening, Jo had received an email from her aunt – essentially warning that *"stormy weather"* was forecast for central Italy *"things might turn ugly and to take care"*.

****

After further phone calls at daybreak, Guzim was the first in to breakfast in the saloon. The weather promised another gorgeous day, but the old man had more pressing things on his mind. The high cliffs in the distance made him think of Tiberius who, as he had discovered at dinner, was fond of chucking people off the top. An efficient way to assert one's authority. Trying to keep his composure, he thanked the young stewardess as she set down a cappuccino next to a plate of croissants and local pastries brought aboard before first light. Saban appeared and, by the look of him, was again nursing a hangover.

Waiting for him to take a seat, "We have a problem," Guzim said, still looking at the clifftops and having evil thoughts. "It involves Erjon. There needs to be a conversation. I will deal with it and you will not say or do anything. Understood?"

Clearly confused, his mind still addled, Saban nodded and reached for a croissant without uttering a word. On seeing Bremner approaching, Guzim said, "Callum, would you be so kind as to allow me a conversation with my brothers, there are some sensitive family matters to be dealt with."

"Of course. I'll take breakfast on the aft deck and leave you in peace."

Erjon, feeling suitably refreshed after an early morning swim and still in a towelling robe, approached his brothers. Bidding them good morning, he reached for the orange juice. But, reading Guzim's body language and seeing Saban pretending to ignore him and staring fixedly at his coffee cup, he asked, "Is there a problem?" At that moment, a stewardess appeared with a pot of tea.

"Leave us Daisy, please," said Guzim, "I don't want to be disturbed."

Now on edge, and doing his best to conceal it, Erjon looked at his older brother.

"Erjon," Guzim said without any trace of emotion – his hands flat on the table, "I have to ask you some questions. Important questions, and I want you to think very carefully how you answer them." At this point Saban looked even more confused. "It has been brought to my attention," Guzim continued, "that, against my express wishes, our family name is associated with human trafficking and has been for the past four years. What do you know of this?"

Erjon was stunned and momentarily at a loss to respond. "Who has fed you this ridiculous story?" he asked. "It's nonsense."

Eyes never leaving his youngest brother, Guzim spoke in a quiet and controlled voice, "I have spoken to some people who have at my request pursued discreet enquiries. Guess what? Your name came up." Guzim rose from the table, his face beginning to colour. "I ask you again, are you involved in trafficking?"

"No, I am not."

After a long silence Guzim said, "I don't believe you and, which I also find disappointing, I understand there are other secrets you have also chosen not to share with us."

"Such as what?"

"Such as the fact that you renounced our faith some years ago and converted to Sunni Islam."

Saban, also now on his feet, started moving towards his younger brother.

"Leave him alone," Guzim said and, turning again to Erjon, "You have broken a bond of trust. Your choice of religion is your own business, but I am deeply troubled you felt unable to speak about it. If, as I am led to believe, you have accrued earnings from human trafficking as a separate and private enterprise – which I am sure is the case but will make further enquiries – there can be no place for you in this family. If the information proves conclusive, you and I will talk further. In the meantime, you will leave this yacht immediately and return to London and await my call. Do you understand me?"

Erjon was staring at his untouched glass.

214

"I asked you if you understand me," Guzim repeated angrily – now also standing with both fists balled. Nodding slowly, Erjon stood up and, unable to hold his brother's eye and visibly shaking, walked back to his cabin. Half an hour later – clutching a suitcase – he climbed into the tender and was taken directly to the old fishing quay on Naples waterfront. Still in shock and having stood by the harbour wall for nearly an hour staring out across the bay, he felt in need of a strong coffee.

Ten minutes later, seated outside at a street café, he began a series of international calls – the first being to reserve a seat on the next available flight to Germany. He needed time to think; two words sprang to mind – damage limitation.

****

Bremner had watched Erjon's unscheduled departure from the side of *Cygnus's* bridge. Unclear about what had happened, it was obviously serious. Judging by the facial expression as he passed him, Saban was barely managing to contain his anger. Guzim had not left the table and seemed fixated on the distant high cliffs.

An hour later the tender returned and, once hoisted aboard, the yacht weighed anchor. Bremner passed Jo in the corridor where, touching his arm, she whispered, "We're going to Albania." They looked at one another for a few seconds. He could smell her perfume. She was still touching his arm. Without saying anything, he slowly nodded and held his gaze before smiling and continuing along the passageway.

Recovering her composure back in her cabin, she quickly dispatched an email to Bristol: "Weather worsening so we're heading east to the Adriatic, now only three guests to worry about because one's returning to London."

Aware that there had been some sort of scene over

breakfast, Bremner thought it best to keep out of the way and spent the rest of the morning reading in his cabin. Just before one o'clock, Daisy knocked on his door: "Mr Guzim is having lunch and hopes you'll join him."

Five minutes later he walked up to the aft deck where Guzim sat alone. "Ah Callum, come and sit down."

"As you may have heard," he began, "Erjon has unfortunately had to return to London on urgent business. However, we shall not let that spoil our fun and, as I mentioned several days ago, the plan is to sail directly to Albania where, as I also said, I want you to meet members of my family. Saban has decided to rest and won't be joining us for lunch."

****

The weather was still atrocious in London, the rain torrential. Brian Finlay and Hugh Everard were in *"C's"* office having a sandwich lunch. "Well," said Everard. "That email stirred the pot, didn't it? Good that no blood got spilt on the new teak decks. It will be fascinating to see what happens when Erjon comes back to London."

Finlay, still carrying the image of rocks and ponds said, "Assuming he does come back here, I have to say, were I in his shoes, I'd be seriously thinking about going elsewhere. I'll bet you he doesn't stick around long."

"We'll see. Still nothing heard about the Foreign Secretary?" Everard asked.

"Not a thing which, in itself, is surprising when you think about the money being offered. Hazel Pelham has been flown home and so have the bodies of the security team."

"How are the Italian couple doing?"

"Alberto Morelli is reported to be on the mend and, together with his housekeeper and maid, is being interviewed at length by the authorities who, I'm told, also think the kidnappers had inside information. What's

216

particularly worrying is the absence of any demands."

"It'll only be a matter of time before someone gets tempted by the cash. When are you thinking about going over there?"

"I'm sending the Communications team tomorrow," Brian replied. "They'll use a house arranged by our guy at the embassy – Ben. It's near the Albanian coast, Durres – I believe. One of the team members is an Albanian speaker." Everard remembered his time in the Balkans and had fond memories of the beaches in Albania – unquestionably amongst the best anywhere in the Mediterranean.

"We have, as you suggested," Brian continued, "co-located a liaison team with the nominated special forces unit currently providing the Standby Squadron. I understand they're likely to move forward to a holding position in Kosovo within the next 24 hours. However, the preferred option is a ship of some sort. MoD are seeing what can be arranged."

"That all sounds very sensible," Everard said. "Not interested in getting some sea time, then?"

****

John Pelham lay on the damp, stinking floor of what was some sort of cellar. Chained to the wall but no longer hooded or gagged, at least he was receiving food and water and had use of an old bucket when nature called. Already unsure of how long he'd been held captive, his abductors had given no clue as to their identity. Desperately worried about Hazel and their friends, his memory of what took place outside the beach restaurant was at best sketchy. It all happened so quickly and, perversely, reminded him of exercises he'd been required to undergo with specialist firms skilled in *"surviving capture"* techniques: most were former SF people from Hereford.

In hindsight, although emphatically not at the time, he

was grateful for the experience; forced to endure the physically and mentally harsh training, the key lessons had stayed with him. Unsure of his captor's nationality, it seemed probable that their motive was political rather than criminal. This wasn't about money. He'd been chosen for a reason. Thank God they'd taken him and not Hazel. If he was right, it was reasonable to assume they would want to keep him alive. Important, therefore, not to be confrontational or do anything rash.

Self-evidently, they knew their business; not a word had been spoken at any stage, including during the bumpy ride in the boat. His iPhones had been taken from him on the beach and chucked overboard once underway. He remembered a methodical body search which, he was surprised by, included being electronically scanned from head to toe.

Estimating the boat ride to have been at least a couple of hours, he was racking his brains to visualise the Adriatic: trying to work out where he might have been brought ashore. The trouble was, without any reference to direction or speed, he could be anywhere. The absence of motor transport after the boat ride suggested he was close to water – a thought reinforced by the lingering smell of fish. The most important thing, he rehearsed in his mind, was to remain calm; eat and drink whatever he was given and to bank as much sleep as possible. The other lessons he remembered were to keep his mind busy during waking hours and never, ever, look his captors in the eye. Subservience was the order of the day.

Later, overwhelmed by the feeling of helplessness as he lay alone in the dark, he started to pray: for Hazel, their boys and himself. Bruised but with no significant injuries, this was going to be an ordeal. To survive, he must discipline his emotions. The focus was now inwards – on him – rather than others. He recalled being advised to avoid *"bankrupting yourself emotionally"* and to *"find and hang onto the positives"*. His body gave an involuntary shudder as he heard something scratching beneath the floor.

****

On receipt of the call, Emma had quickly packed a bag before being collected by car and taken to the departure airfield on the outskirts of London to meet up with Mike and the communications team. The compact jet was ideal for their purposes and the considerable number of aluminium boxes full of equipment were efficiently stowed in the hold.

It was a comfortable flight and, after a brief stop to refuel at a United States Air Force Base in Germany, they touched down at Tirana International Airport and disembarked inside a hangar. Met by the local SIS representative, Ben, the freight and personal baggage were quickly loaded into two vans. There was no immigration process and they were soon heading west towards the coastal town of Durres.

Climbing up to the high ground overlooking the sea, the vehicles followed a narrow road to an isolated single-storey building. "Home," Ben said, "It's recently been bought by a German couple, but they don't plan to start renovations until later in the year. You get to keep one of the vans and I'll drop off a second vehicle tomorrow. We've checked the electricity and utilities and they're all working. There's stuff in the fridge and you'll find camp beds, sleeping bags and mosquito nets in the back rooms. Phone coverage is a bit hit and miss, but I imagine you'll be on satellite phone anyway. There are some rat traps and bait in the cupboard in the pack porch – you'll be needing them. Here's my contact details and do shout if you need anything."

"That's great," Emma said, "and thanks for all the arrangements. This place looks perfect, don't you think,

Mike?"

"Couldn't be better… we'll start setting up."

"I'll drop by tomorrow with the extra car you wanted," Ben said. "It's not exactly top end but should do the job."

Emma and Mike walked through the building and agreed where to establish the operations room. She took the bedroom with what she hoped would have a sea view, leaving the others to fight over their spaces. Without anything else immediately needing her attention, she strolled into the kitchen, found a broom and started sweeping. The place was a tip. When that was done she mopped the floor and disinfected and wiped down the surfaces. An hour later she started preparing something for them all to eat.

A regular visitor to Albania during her childhood and teenage years, usually accompanying her parents and younger brother, Emma knew her way around the country, had cousins in the south and was comfortable with the culture. Conscious of not having spoken the language for a while, she was keen to get in some early practice. So, the next morning she drove the van into town and spent time listening to the chat in the cafes and marketplace.

Growing in confidence, she struck up a conversation with two fishermen repairing their nets and was delighted when, after a couple of minutes, they asked where she lived in Kosovo. Blonde hair and green eyes were an Albanian characteristic and, as her mother had explained when she was young, in due course her hair colour would change from brown to blonde and then gold. It was all the Greek's fault.

Back at the house, she called Brian Finlay to give him a quick update and ask if there was any further tasking. Her ears pricked up when he said that *Cygnus* was heading her way. "So, Mr Bremner's coming here is he?" she said to herself thinking how best to prepare the fish she's bought for their lunch.

****

Mary Stewart was not having a good day in the office and her surveillance people an even worse one. For whatever reason, they had somehow managed to miss Erjon's arrival at Heathrow Airport. All incoming flights from Naples had been checked and he wasn't on any of them. If that wasn't bad enough, the UK Border Authority had searched all passenger manifests in their database and couldn't find any record of him entering the country.

Alarm bells were ringing. Further checks with the Italian authorities also proved negative. Mary worked through possible explanations; either he was returning to London by some other means – which would in theory still require him to show his passport at whichever entry point he used – or, he was still in Italy or some other EU country. It might also be the case that he was travelling under an assumed name on a different passport – which meant he could be anywhere and the least helpful scenario.

Brian Finlay tried hard to hide his disappointment when she gave him the news but, as he sought to remind her, they were dealing with someone known to be living a double life. It was entirely reasonable, he suggested, that Erjon would have rehearsed a range of contingencies including when he needed to disappear. "In all probability," Brian said, "he'll have ditched all his phones."

"I'm not stupid, Brian."

"What about scanning departure gate camera footage as a means to identify the flight?" he suggested.

"Brian," she said, trying hard to control her impatience, "We're on it, but don't hold your breath. In winter, let alone the high summer season, Naples processes something like 4,600 flights every day to 27 countries flying over 120 routes."

Resisting the urge to ask if that number was a total of

inbound and outbound flights, "Oh, right," he said, "but what about facial recognition software?"

"Unfortunately," she said, still trying to sound calm, "our European friends are not quite there yet with the technology. And, before you ask, yes… I have issued an Identify and Report request through the UK Border Authority, but it's irrelevant if he's travelling under an assumed name."

"We don't know that, do we?"

"No, Brian."

****

Which, needless to say, was precisely what Erjon had done. Travelling on a Canadian passport under a pre-planned alias in the name of Eric Semple, he had with him supporting documentation confirming his status as a resident of Toronto; there were credit cards to back it up, as well as a bill of sale for a recently acquired property in the city.

Following a seven-and-a-half-hour drive from Naples, *"E. Semple"* had taken a direct Lufthansa evening flight from Milan to Strasburg, overnighted and then connected with a transatlantic flight to Ottawa. From there he had driven a hire car to Toronto and caught a direct flight to Bermuda where, more than ready for some peace and quiet, he booked into an exclusive golf resort just down the coast from Hamilton.

Armed with an inexpensive pay-as-you-go *"burner"* mobile phone bought in Strasburg Duty Free, and having replaced his laptop at the same time, he was to all intent and purpose now *"off grid"*. That evening, after prayers, he took a taxi to a local restaurant and enjoyed a splendid dinner and, in the margins, tried to take stock.

Long recognising the risks associated with Guzim's release from prison, his mistake, he now realised, was in underestimating the extent of his brother's grip on the various criminal networks. Membership of the Albanian mafia was for life and, which was enshrined within the culture, trust could not be bought. He had broken that trust and would have to somehow manage the consequences. Meanwhile, it pleased him that the British Foreign Secretary had disappeared without trace and equally that, within a matter of weeks, he would magically reappear for the world to watch in horror when his fate was decided.

****

Wandering around the Durres house, Emma was amazed at the array of computer screens and electronic paraphernalia arrayed in the team Ops Room. As Mike had explained, their role extended considerably beyond merely providing a secure rear link to London.

"So, what exactly are you doing?" she asked.

"In a word," he said, "hacking; eavesdropping and trying to access and exploit anything we think is or might be of interest."

"Is this where I come in… as a translator?" she asked.

"No," he replied, "Between us we have all the local languages covered. What we need from you, Emma, is guidance on priorities for targeting our efforts." He went on to explain that they also had the technical wherewithal to employ covert tracking or listening devices within set range limitations, which is why the van was being converted for a mobile role.

That evening she got a message from Brian Finlay; he was tied up with operational commitments in London and couldn't see himself joining her for at least the next four or five days. He did, however, give her the name and contact details of what was reputedly a trusted source in Tirana. He said that, having cleared lines with Ben, she was authorised to set up a meet – providing, that was, Ben accompanied her. The contact was described as a middle-ranked player in one of the local crime syndicates, almost certainly linked to the mafia: *"Caution is advised"*.

****

Vinny, still struggling to make progress in the hunt for Erjon Shala, was not giving up without a fight. He and Tommy were spending a lot of time in their personal chat room scoping options, bouncing ideas and – which came naturally – thinking outside the box. "If he's away on business a lot – which is what we're hearing from the surveillance guys – there must be a way to find out where he goes, how often and why," Tommy said.

"Yep."

"If I were him I'd be travelling under an assumed name. No point making it easy for anyone who might be trying to find you. And no point hanging around in Italy."

"Unless he's got interests there," said Vinny. "We're buggered if he's using fake ID."

"Well, there's a choice; either follow the money or try to identify and follow the passport."

"Or both," Vinny remarked. "True."

"Maybe you should tell the Controller to start looking at the UK Border Authority – or I can," Vinny wrote, with *"joke"* in brackets.

"Okay, I'll feed it in. Meanwhile, we'll keep monitoring the yacht in case either of the other brothers inadvertently compromises their accounts."

"Okay. It's chucking it down here."

"Where's that, then?"

"Having a laugh are you?"

"Worth a try," Tommy wrote, adding a smiling emoji.

"As a matter of interest, are you thinking we might make a bob or two on the side from these nasty people?" Vinny wrote. "It's not as though they're short, are they?"

"You read my mind," Tommy replied.

****

Mary subsequently confirmed to Finlay that her team was already working on the passport tracking line and were also talking to UK-based international airlines – especially the long-haul operators. She said that the name *"E. Shala"* was being run through a series of different databases but, in the knowledge that he almost certainly had access to other passports, a separate programme was being run for the purpose of establishing patterns amongst frequent fliers – particularly those with a preference for travelling Business or First Class from and to London Heathrow – a reasonable assumption given the emerging profile of Erjon Shala.

****

Everything was going well aboard *Cygnus*. Bremner found himself spending a lot of time talking to Guzim as they made their way towards the Adriatic and was regularly invited to join him for coffee on his private sun deck. Transiting the narrow Straits of Messina had been the highlight of the trip so far and, now clear of the toe of Italy, their course was north easterly for the two hundred mile run to the tiny port of Ypsos on the sheltered east side of the Greek island of Corfu – just off Albania's southern international border with Greece.

The captain had told them that the island was a good place to spend time; loads of reliable and sheltered anchorages protected by land on two sides. He confirmed the expected time of arrival as six o'clock that evening.

****

Tracking their progress through Jo's iPhone and knowing the yacht's normal cruising speed, Brian Finlay had already calculated their likely destination and date of arrival – later confirmed to an auntie in Bristol by her devoted niece.

****

When Emma learned of the yacht's destination, she

225

checked a map and saw that the port of Ypsos was something like a hundred and twenty miles south of where she was in Durres and, expecting to take custody of a car from Ben, she was keen to meet the source Finlay had given her.

"Oh… really… what do you call that?" she said later that morning on seeing the battered old saloon that had enjoyed better days.

"Inconspicuous," Ben replied. "Perfect. She's a runner and the plates are from this area."

Regretting her decision not to bring Bremner's Discovery, she said, "Have we got a place and time for the meeting?"

"We're on for five o'clock this afternoon," Ben replied. "By an inland lake near Sarande. He'll be fishing."

Examining the map, she said, "I reckon that's got to be at least a three-hour drive. There's another place I wouldn't mind having a look at when we're down there."

Ben explained that he'd met the source a number of times and that he had provided useful but relatively low-grade information on criminal activity. As yet, there had been nothing beyond smuggling and protection rackets. The man was not interested in being paid which Ben could only assume related to a longstanding grudge. "I'll have my fishing kit with me. Do you know anything about fishing?"

"Bugger all," she replied, "but I'm prepared to learn – it's all about chucking flies, isn't it?"

"Not the sort of fishing they do out here," he said.

At which point she uttered a stream of Albanian profanities prompting him to say, "I reckon that just settled who'll be doing the talking."

****

They arrived early at the lake, immediately spotting what they took to be their man on the far bank. He was fishing.

Once they got close, Ben began baiting his hook with sweetcorn while Emma sauntered over to the huddled figure sitting on a box dangling a rod. Dressed in agricultural worker's clothes and a straw cap, she put him in his mid-sixties, but the sun ages people prematurely and his grizzled face suggested he spent most of his time outdoors. Cigarette smoke was keeping the flies at bay. Clearly surprised to be chatting to an attractive young woman who apparently wanted to learn to fish, it was not long before the conversation turned to more substantial matters.

"Do you know anything about the kidnapping of that English politician: the one who got nabbed in Italy?" she asked.

"Not really," he replied, "Saw it on the news. Nobody understands who'd be crazy enough to do such a thing. Barking: it's asking for trouble."

"Where do you think he's being held?

"Up north somewhere: most people think Croatia or possibly Montenegro. It's only speculation," he said. "If he's being moved it will be along stablished smuggling routes."

"Which, presumably you'd get to hear about?"

"Perhaps."

"Would you expect to be told if the Englishman was brought into this country?

"Possibly," he replied, "but it depends on who's involved. People who tell tales in these parts usually end up dead." Looking at his watch, the man began packing up his kit. "If I hear anything I'll be in touch through your boyfriend over there."

"Thank you," she said. "We're interested in anything you can find out, even rumours. And, for the record, he's not my boyfriend."

"Bet he wishes he was," the man said with a chuckle.

After watching him walk back to his van, and unable to help smiling, Emma played back the conversation she'd recorded on a concealed microphone.

"Good result," Ben said, "but I'll be amazed if it comes to anything. Great line about the boyfriend – at least he's got a sense of humour."

Emma was thinking about an appropriate response when, looking across the lake, Ben said, "Are you really interested in learning to fish?"

To which she replied, "Not in the slightest, I'd rather stick pins in my eyes… let's go for a drive."

Half an hour later they watched *Cygnus* drop its anchor just off Ypsos which she told Ben she would be visiting the following day – crossing by the twice-hourly ferry. Back at the house that evening – after stopping for a bite to eat on the way and having written up and dispatched her agent contact report to London – in hindsight she regretted not putting a tracking or listening device on fisherman's van. Tricky but it could have been done.

She was getting to appreciate Ben's company; of similar age, nice sense of humour and clearly very bright, they were discovering a lot in common. For example, he was unattached and had ended a relationship shortly before taking up the position of assistant cultural attaché. He was an attractive bloke who, as she discovered, had gone to Cambridge after attending a prestigious public school in Surrey. Everything suggested a privileged upbringing and, which was already apparent, an aptitude for languages. It led her to wonder how her ex was managing in London without her. Bit like a fish, she said to herself: "Gutted."

****

Next day she drove on her own to the car ferry opposite Corfu. It was a beautiful morning; she wished she'd brought her running stuff. There was little traffic other than agricultural vehicles lumbering along under excessively heavy loads of hay. Fruit sellers were plying their trade at the roadside. Making good time, she was soon tucking into a plate of cakes and sipping a weapons grade expresso at a small harbour front café in Ypsos. What happened next took her completely by surprise.

"Don't look round," a familiar voice with a Scottish brogue said, "where's my Discovery?"

Emma, straight-faced, replied, "Tucked up in Madrid although I was sorely tempted to drive it here. They've assigned me a crap vehicle. Any news?"

Ordering a cappuccino from the waiter in pigeon Greek, Bremer said, "Apparently, we're here for at least a week."

"Plenty of time to sharpen up your Greek… which could use some work by the way."

"I'll give that some thought," he said with a beaming smile that she couldn't see. "Where are you basing yourself and has anything been heard of the younger brother?"

Emma, still attacking the cakes said, "I've got a team near Durres and no, the trail's gone cold. The assumption is he's travelling under an assumed name."

With that he finished his coffee and, before walking away, said "Okay, thanks – I'll no doubt see you around… I seem to remember you like hanging around waterfronts."

"You…." She was about to say but suspected he'd already left. And she was right. Not long after she heard the sound of a powerful engine and caught sight of what she assumed to be the yacht's tender heading back to the gleaming, white-hulled yacht sitting at anchor less than half a mile away. *Wasn't expecting that*, she thought to herself and, after paying her bill, drove off to the ferry.

When she got back to the house, she had a long chat with Mike and they walked out to the black van – now full of technical wizardry and complete with an improvised desk, set of chairs and two small fans bolted to the ceiling. The side windows were all fitted with one-way glass and there was even a socket for a kettle.

****

The next day the same van made the crossing to Ypsos and, within a short space of time, had *Cygnus's* Wi-Fi network displayed on one of the screens. Another showed live shipping movements in the southern Adriatic and a third, the computer network serving the Albanian National Police Service's Central Operations Room. All sound was muted, both support team guys in the back wore headphones. Mike, leaning on the bonnet, was reading a local paper and in radio contact with the third team member back at the house.

****

Cygnus's tender was kept busy over the next three days. Guzim and Saban – sometimes with Bremner if meeting members of the extended Shala family – were transported to the mainland where they would jump into parked, dark-windowed limousines and roar off. Often away for hours, lunches and occasionally dinners were taken ashore. Bremner struggled to remember the names of all the cousins, great nephews and nieces he'd met and was becoming very taken with the warmth of the people. It was a close-knit group; Guzim unquestionably the titular head. The Albanian language remained a major limitation for him, but those he met showed understanding and a generosity of spirit. Being *"paraded"* was rather humbling and he struggled to see where it was all leading.

****

For his part, Saban appeared to enjoy having Bremner around and, like his older brother, had never once mentioned Erjon's name. Largely a change of scene, after the second day at anchor the yacht relocated to a different spot a few miles to the south. The water proved even more inviting for those minded to swim or explore local beaches.

Cygnus's toys were in constant use – including recreational diving gear by the two nurses as well as the ever-popular jet skis. Fresh provisions were brought out from the town every morning by tender, usually under the supervision of the chef, Hilary or Jo – all of whom welcomed the chance to peruse the local fish market, buy fresh fruit, vegetables and sample the island's famed local bread and pastries. Now well into the tourist season, beaches, streets and the harbour front teemed with people of all nationalities. Cafés and bars were doing a roaring trade, extending well into the early hours. The weather was sublime.

Just before noon on the fourth day at anchor, the tender was on its way back to *Cygnus* after the daily provisioning run. It was scheduled to collect Saban from the mainland where he had overnighted in Tirana. Being unwell, Guzim had elected to stay on board and was rather enjoying the close attention of one of the nurses.

Bremner, snorkelling alone amongst rocks a short distance away was also expecting to be picked up by the tender which, in addition to Saban and the duty coxswain, carried Jo, the chef, the other nurse and a junior deckhand. Perching on a rock, he basked happily in the morning sunshine after what had been a thoroughly invigorating swim. The visibility was remarkable with sufficient sea life to keep him amused for hours. Watching the tender crossing the bay and collecting Saban, he saw it turn in his direction and increase speed.

He could get used to this lifestyle: the privacy, no real sense of time other than meals. And what meals: the preparation and service was exemplary. In fact, the whole experience aboard had been surreal; unseen fairies meticulously cleaning his cabin every day, spiriting away his washing and returning it within a few hours immaculately pressed and hanging in the wardrobe. Sleeping better than he had in years, his skin was slowly darkening. It felt as though he was being purged of the after-effects of prison. *Cygnus* increasingly felt like home, at least for now. In private moments he often found himself thinking about Jo, with whom there had been no direct conversation apart from the one fleeting encounter in the aftermath of Erjon's unscheduled departure. The only thing he knew for certain was that she wore Chanel: if he wasn't mistaken 'Mademoiselle' although, thinking about it, possibly 'CoCo'. He knew he was grinning. She'd bewitched him, and he loved it.

Reflecting on his spoilt existence, and still looking at the approaching craft – now only a few hundred metres away and beginning to slow down – there was suddenly a blinding flash and loud bang as the rear end of the tender exploded in flames – throwing up a huge fireball and sending splinters and bodies flying in every direction. Instinctively ducking, and falling off the rock into the water, the sound was deafening. The pressure wave followed a nano second later. As he watched open-mouthed in horror, he felt the shock wave from a secondary explosion that obliterated the cabin and foredeck.

In only a matter of seconds, the once beautiful craft was gone. No movement, no noise – only smoke drifting slowly away in the wind. Everything had fallen silent. Gathering his wits about him he dived into the water and started swimming frantically towards the wreckage. In the background, the sawtooth siren of *Cygnus's* general alarm was sounding.

The explosion had brought every member of the yacht on deck. An inflatable craft and jet ski were quickly launched and powered towards the carnage. Guzim, awoken by the noise, ran from his stateroom to the Bridge, silently surveying the floating debris and knowing instantly he would never see his brother again. Bremner's search effort proved futile and he was dragged into the inflatable. Distress calls had already gone out to emergency services but they would inevitably take time to arrive. Several local boats set forth from the Ypsos Marina and similarly from other small settlements in the area. Two passing yachts offered to help but there was nothing to be done.

It took thirty-six hours to recover the bodies. Only the junior deckhand was in any recognisable state. *Cygnus* was directed to a berth in the marina, cordoned-off and everyone subjected to exhaustive police questioning. Guzim was sedated. The crew were in shock and Captain Henry Constance, Hilary and Marley were doing all they could to console grieving crewmates.

Bremner was trying hard to manage his emotions and experiencing a burning sense of outrage. Unable to think about Jo, he felt nauseous and completely numb. The sense of loss was profound when, later in his cabin, he thought about their all-too-brief time together. There was something incredibly special about her. He would never get to experience it again. But he knew that any private grieving would have to wait and, remembering the task at hand, reminded himself of the importance of staying in control. Now more than ever, he needed to focus. The immediate priority was all about exploiting the situation with Guzim and, specifically, searching for ways to get even closer to him. Before that, he sent a text to the emergency number in Monaco.

****

Emma received the news from Ben with disbelief. "Do we know who died?" she asked.

"First reports are of six fatalities including the Chief

Stewardess Jo Williams and the middle Shala brother… Saban."

"Oh God," she said, visibly distraught.

"We're monitoring the police net and they're already talking about a bomb, possibly two," he said. "We also know from the yacht's Wi-Fi net that the charter company are informing next of kin. Our people in Athens will arrange repatriation once all enquiries are completed."

"I know it's early but, assuming it was a bomb, who do we think they were after, and who might have planted it?" she asked.

"London believes that whoever set it up was after both Shala brothers. The only reason they didn't get Guzim was because he was not feeling well and remained on the yacht."

"Where was Bremner?" she asked.

"Off on his own, swimming," came the reply.

****

Brian Finlay walked upstairs to Everard's office. The tragic loss of an operator was a game-changer. It made everything very personal. Jo's parents had been informed and a liaison officer assigned to provide whatever support they needed. There would be a memorial service in due course. Repatriation of Jo's remains was in hand.

Randell sat in the outer office reading the incident report handed to him by Marjorie. Thinking about the lovely young woman he'd taken to Heathrow, he felt desperately sad for her family. They would be devastated. In due course, her name would be added to those on the Wall of Remembrance at the headquarters.

****

"Hard to disagree with Ben's assessment that it was a bomb," Finlay said as Everard sat down at the small conference table. "It would have been relatively easy for someone to slip a couple of devices into the boxes of provisions. According to Emma, they picked up on the police network that things changed markedly when the name of S. Shala was listed amongst the fatalities. The focus of their investigation has become criminal."

Everard was listening intently. "Bremner was the first to report the incident, wasn't he?"

"He was," said Finlay. "I've already had a very difficult conversation with Jed Crosby. He is, to put it mildly, seriously pissed-off and feels I should have made him more aware of the risks. He told me the charter has been terminated and that Guzim plans to move ashore once the police have finished with him. What we do not know is what if anything he has in mind for Bremner."

"Okay," said Everard, "who do we think did it?"

Choosing his words carefully, Finlay replied, "I'm bound to say I think it bears the hallmark of Erjon Shala; reasonable to assume he had both motive and, through local surrogates, opportunity. Proving it of course is entirely another matter."

Everard pressed his intercom and asked Marjorie for two coffees. "As we both appreciate, what matters, Brian, is what Guzim Shala believes. If he can somehow be persuaded that it was Erjon's doing, true or not, it might offer leverage."

"For what?"

"For getting him to help us find our Foreign Secretary. The question is, how do we influence that outcome and tie it to the younger brother?"

Considering carefully what *"C"* was suggesting, Finlay replied, "And what if we're unable to prove Erjon was responsible?"

To which Everard looked at him and said, "Then we'll have to get creative, won't we."

20

JOHN PELHAM was unquestionably losing track of time and definitely hallucinating. The absence of windows and irritating presence of the permanent electric light were playing tricks with his mind, making it impossible to differentiate night from day. For all he knew, meals were being deliberately served at irregular times to exacerbate his disorientation.

They came for him after forty-eight hours in the cellar. It was becoming a horribly familiar routine; first he had his mouth taped, then hooded and finally unshackled. His next sensation was being jostled into some sort of boat – a rubber boat with a solid floor and engines that sounded familiar. It had to be the same boat.

Four hours later, the boat grounded on shingle and, once the engines had been silenced, the process was reversed. His instincts were suggesting it was night but, being sealed at the neck, the thick hood offered no clues. Logically, it had to be night-time, if only to minimise the risk of detection. Fairly sure only one boat was involved, he didn't know whether he was shivering from fear or cold. The cover they'd thrown over him made no difference but probably kept the spray off.

On landing, he was again dragged ashore and manhandled into a building. Once unhooded, he was roughly reattached to a strong point on the floor and the tape ripped off his mouth. A different but equally horrible bucket was placed within reach. This space, like its predecessor, was also devoid of windows and, which was a particular frustration, also had a permanent electric light.

Constantly telling himself that everything possible was being done to find him, he stuck resolutely to the fervent belief that his release was only a matter of time. His faith provided comfort but, try as he might, nagging doubts were eating into his resolve. His abductors were professionals; disciplined, organised and, on the face of things, leaving little to chance.

****

What Pelham did not know was that, still embarrassed by the outrage committed on their sovereign territory, the Italian Government was sparing no effort or expense in the search for him. Maritime forces, overt and covert, were on the ground. Maritime Patrol Aircraft, augmented by several other NATO nations – including Britain – were running multiple round the clock sorties over the Adriatic. The east coast was depicted on a huge array of screens in different countries for the express purpose of tracking, logging and analysing everything that moved. No stones left unturned: data repeatedly tested, evaluated, compared and shared.

The eventual break-through came from human surveillance teams deployed to covert observation posts discreetly positioned along the coasts of Croatia and Montenegro. The two rigid inflatable boats used for Pelham's second move had been detected as they headed south during the hours of darkness. Integrated air-based surveillance radar of a maritime patrol aircraft was able to lock-on and give coordinates for what was assumed to be the final destination in Montenegro. The area of the *"box"* search was then put under space-based satellite surveillance but, at Italian insistence, the information was not immediately passed across to Montenegro's security agencies.

Trying to snatch some sleep in the early hours of the morning, Pelham was woken abruptly by two masked individuals – no longer wearing black. He got the sense there was some urgency as they quickly unchained him, taped his mouth and roughly placed a hood over his head before half carrying him into the fresh air and lifting him into the back of a truck. Chains were locked to his wrists, the engine started and he felt the vehicle get under way.

****

Hugh Everard sat alongside his Mossad contact on a bench in Regents Park. Alon Carlebach had asked for the meeting and, already aware that Everard was unamused by the substance of their last exchange having found its way to the intelligence community in Washington, was feeling a degree of discomfort – not helped by Everard's stiff body posture. "There are some developments," the Israeli began. "My people, as I undertook to do, have been busy trying to discover more about the Pakistani who met with the subject of your interest."

"We're talking about the meeting in Cyprus I presume?" Everard said, fixated on the ducks to their immediate front and subconsciously struggling to name them.

"We are, at the airport hotel. Anyway, his name is Syed Sher Usmani.

"What do you know about him?" Everard said, turning to the man beside him who was lighting a small cigar.

"Usmani might once have been a member of Pakistan's Inter-Services Intelligence.

Everard was very familiar with ISI which, it was well known, had global reach and enjoyed formidable influence with various groups – including the Taliban. "Now that is interesting," he said.

Continuing after relighting the cigar, Carlebach said, "Yes, it is, and it gets better. Usmani is definitely connected to a number of Sunni radical groups: both within Pakistan and further afield. Possibly a broker... you know...

middleman of some sort. He allegedly keeps homes in Peshawar and across the border in Afghanistan."

"Do we know where?"

"Jalalabad."

Everard got the feeling there was even better news coming.

"However," the Israeli said, "our friend is also a regular traveller to Dubai from where, it would seem he pursues interests in Iraq and a number of other countries who share one thing in common."

"Let me guess," Everard said, "a hatred of the West and profound disapproval of the relationship Israel enjoys with the United States."

"Correct."

"Is that the substance of it?"

"Not quite, Hugh," Carlebach said without looking at him. "I am authorised to tell you that, as of yesterday, Usmani is assisting my government with their enquiries."

Choosing not to ask how this had been achieved, Everard said, "Is there any chance one of my people might get to question Usmani… I'm talking about the kidnapping. Anything at all would help and also the related matter of Erjon Shala's involvement?"

Also absorbed by the ducks and other pond birds creating mayhem on the lake immediately in front of them, Carlebach replied, "Alas, arrangements have already been agreed with our friends at Langley."

"Oh, right…" said Everard. "If the CIA's involved there's every chance we'll get sight of the product. Bound to become political. No matter. My government is most grateful and, presumably, there won't be a problem if I discuss this directly with my own contacts in Washington?"

"No, that's not an issue," said Carlebach, who stubbed

out his cigar. "What's that one," he asked, pointing.

"Great-crested grebe: amazing courtship displays. Not strictly a duck."

"What about that clumsy one?"

"Ah, if I'm not mistaken, that's a Ruddy shelduck: they hardly ever leave the water – which explains why they stumble about on land."

The Israeli smiled. "Hugh, I'm sorry my people over-shared with others: you have my assurance it won't happen again."

"Thank you," Everard said, watching Carlebach walk away as he lit up one of his own cigars – his attention drawn to a motionless and aristocratic-looking Grey heron. A lesson in patience. While still absorbing the activity in front of him, Randell walked up and sat down.

"Had to park on a meter," he said.

"Know anything about Grey herons?" Everard asked.

"You're referring to '*Ardea cinerea*'."

"Now that's impressive," Everard said, turning to look at him. "You never cease to amaze me."

"Not really... I just read it on that board over there."

****

Back in his office, still thinking about the heron – and smiling – Everard typed up the conversation and sent an amended version to his Head of Station in Washington with direction to follow-up with Langley at the earliest opportunity. Having forwarded the full transcript to Brian Finlay, he then asked Marjorie to get him an appointment with the Prime Minister at his earliest convenience and, in advance of the meeting, to book a call with James Wadsworth or, better still, see if he fancied a chat over lunch. Not long after, Marjorie stuck her head round the door and told him that he was booked to see the PM at four o'clock that afternoon and yes, the PM's Chief of Staff would love to have lunch but on condition he paid. A restaurant on Jermyn Street had been proposed.

Shortly before one o'clock, Everard and Wadsworth sat down to lunch. Without going into names or nationalities, Everard summarised the information gleaned from his conversation in Regent's Park and said that he would be giving the PM the same information, *"more or less"*. It was, they agreed, a significant breakthrough and might well expedite the recovery of John Pelham. "We must not allow our political masters to get their hopes up, James," he said, casting an eye over the menu.

"Indeed, as you can imagine, the PM is calling his Italian counterpart at least twice a day. I've said there's a danger of overdoing it, but he won't listen."

"I can well imagine," Everard said, passing across the menu.

"It would be helpful to give him some positive news if you've got anything."

Both men knew that a British Special Forces Task Force was embarked in a helicopter-capable Royal Naval support ship that had been hastily diverted from a NATO exercise and would soon be entering the Adriatic. Later that afternoon the PM – heartened by what he'd heard from Everard, fully took the point that it was still early days and accepted the need to avoid inflating expectations. He told Everard that he'd been down to Wiltshire to see Hazel Pelham in person and was impressed by her unwavering conviction that Pelham would be found and returned to his family.

****

When the time came to leave *Cygnus* in Ypsos, Bremner accepted Guzim's offer to accompany him to Tirana; a car was arranged and a hotel booked. A second vehicle accompanied them which, he was told, contained *"trusted friends concerned for my safety"*. There had been no real discussion between them in the aftermath of the bombing. The Albanian was grieving. Sullen, stooped and markedly older, he had lost the sparkle so prevalent during their time at sea. *"Broken"* would be too strong a word, but the sense of strain was unmistakeable. Bremner, who was also grieving but refusing to allow it to dominate his thoughts, got the distinct impression that the old man's life had changed irreparably; one brother dead and not a word heard from the other. The Albanian was exposed, vulnerable and angry. Not good omens but ideal from an exploitation standpoint.

Several times during the drive to Tirana, Guzim talked about Erjon and, in particular, his dismay that he hadn't called. "Surely he must know of Saban's murder," he said repeatedly, "this is his brother we're talking about for God's sake." Bremner chose not to say anything. To his mind, Erjon headed the list of suspects. But, as yet, there was no collateral to support the assertion.

The nature of his relationship with Guzim had noticeably strengthened in the aftermath of the bombing. Without any suggestion of moving into Saban's now vacant shoes, the scope of their conversations was broadening. All meals were taken together and they would often chat long into the night. His ill-defined status was patently of little consequence for the old man who, as a matter of course, flatly refused to let him to pay for anything. The hotel in Tirana proved to be no different and, as they had told him on checking in, he was on an *"open tab"*, with all *"charges being handled by Mr Shala"*.

Popping out for fresh air, and reasonably confident that cybersecurity would be the last thing on Guzim's mind, he sent a brief text to Monaco giving the hotel's address. An hour later it was forwarded to Emma who, on receipt, mentioned to Mike that she was off to Tirana and might be gone for a while. Before leaving, she asked him to install a concealed GPS tracker in her car as a back-up to her iPhone – the sim card which at his prompting she had replaced.

****

Early next day, after a night in a very ordinary city centre hotel, and on the assumption that he was still a creature of habit, Emma went jogging in the vicinity of Bremner's hotel. Appearing just after six o'clock, she watched him go through his familiar stretching routine before jogging off. Quickly crossing the road and intercepting him she said, "Follow me." Fifteen minutes later they were in the Memorial Cemetery situated in a large central park. Joining her on a bench, he dismissed the idea that the old lady replacing flowers on a nearby grave was hostile. They had the place to themselves. It was going to be a very warm day.

"How's Shala coping?" she asked.

"Not well, but he isn't ready to go back to London just yet."

Looking at the woman by the grave, she said "How do you think he'll react if he ever gets proof of Erjon's involvement in the bombing?"

Bremner, thinking about the question for a few seconds said, "The short answer is I honestly don't know. He's a difficult man to read at the best of times but, if the evidence is irrefutable, I think he'll feel obligated to respond. In fact, I'd put money on it."

"Why?"

"Several reasons. First and foremost, he's an inordinately proud man. For him, it's all about personal reputation and family honour."

"Presumably," she said, "it also raises another uncomfortable question?"

"Such as what?"

"Such as whether he's beginning to suspect his own brother might have arranged the shooting at Maxwell?"

"Possibly, although he hasn't said anything to that effect... at least not to me. You have to remember that, had he not been ill, that bomb would have killed him, too. If I were him I'd be a worried man."

"Where do you think Erjon is?"

"No idea," came the reply, "but he'll surface at some stage and I'd be amazed if the mafia networks aren't turning over every stone."

"I was so sorry to hear about Jo's death," she said. "Sadly, I never got to meet her."

"One of a kind," he said.

Suddenly conscious that she had stumbled into sensitive emotional territory and noticing he was staring into the distance at nothing in particular, she got up and began stretching. Bremner remained silent. "Assuming we turn up hard evidence of Erjon's guilt and the decision's taken to share it with the old man, presumably it would be better coming from someone other than you?" She asked.

"Why, so I'm not compromised?" he said, having seemingly returned to the present and feeling obliged to avert his gaze as she continued to limber-up."

"Yes," she said. "I'll talk to London and see how they want to handle it. Why don't we meet here tomorrow morning – same time. If for any reason I don't show, or you don't, we can roll it forward to the next day." She then reset the timer on her watch, gave the slightest suggestion of a grin and headed off into the park.

****

Emma called Finlay when she got back to Durres. After listening patiently, he tried to reassure her that Bremner knew very well the risks he was taking and no, he was not in a relationship with Jo Williams. In regard to her suggestion, he agreed that any bad news for Guzim should be routed through other channels rather than Bremner. Reminding her that they already had the Albanian's email address – already used to good effect. Assuming it hadn't been changed since leaving *Cygnus* – it was probably the most expeditious way to reach the old man and at least risk of compromising Bremner. Before ending the call, he said that new leads were being pursued which, if successful, might well deliver the evidence to link Erjon with the kidnapping and, maybe, also the separate business of the bombing.

****

The weather in Albania was markedly hotting up. In the continued absence of rain, dust was thrown up by traffic whilst, overhead, vapour trails criss-crossed the sky as tourists came and went. Guzim had been summoned to a meeting – *"with colleagues"* – in the port of Vlore.

Eight men sat around a table above a restaurant in the old part of the town. All in suits, representing the heads of the principal families sworn to serve the Albanian mafia, the gathering had been convened for the express purpose of discussing the kidnapping of the British politician. Guzim was effectively third in seniority of those present, both in age and status. The collective mood was sombre. They all knew the form: proceedings would be disciplined, with no long speeches, superfluous oratory or anyone out to score points.

The men had known one another since childhood. With the exception of Guzim when detained at Her Majesty's pleasure for so many years, they were all regularly in each other's company – without necessarily being close friends. This was business, a single item on the agenda.

In his opening remarks, the Chairman expressed the Council's deep regret at the murder of Saban Shala, which Guzim acknowledged by nodding slowly. Discussion then began in earnest and a consensus quickly reached that the kidnapping was an unmitigated disaster and directly threatened their collective interests. It was causing all sorts of difficulties and impacting business. The last thing they needed was someone shining an unhelpful spotlight on things that happened in ungoverned spaces – all, as the Chairman reminded everyone, bought with cash to guarantee no interference from the law. Everything had changed. Public interest in the kidnapping had intensified: politicians and law enforcement were obliged to follow suit. It was spreading inexorably southwards down the coast from Croatia.

As the Chairman sought to remind everyone, business associates in neighbouring countries were also feeling the heat. Certain lines of commercial activity were currently unsustainable with, of necessity, operations being put on hold. None of them had experienced anything like it and there was deep resentment at the intrusion on their territory of what they chose to call, *"outsiders"*. It was, they all agreed, totally unacceptable and something had to be done.

Guzim listened carefully to the discussion and, when invited to give his opinion, asked, "Do we have any idea at all where the Englishman is being held, and by whom?"

"Croatia, we heard," said the man on his right, "but that was some time ago and, if true, he's bound to have moved by now."

Another hand went up to catch the Chairman's eye, "My sources tell me the authorities think he is, or was, further down the coast in Montenegro. The police are conducting searches in places they've always previously ignored."

The Chairman, a distinguished looking man well into his eighties who until now had kept his own counsel then said, "He must be found: those responsible shown the error of their ways: you will instruct your people accordingly. Someone out there will know where the man is being held. Find them."

And with that, they retired downstairs for a lunch of roast beef in fermented milk sauce and cabbage rolls, accompanied by an indefinite number of bottles of wine – the ever popular *"Vera Shqiptare"*. There were no other diners and Guzim slept most of the way back to Tirana.

****

Everard and Finlay were deep into strategy in the back bar of the Cabbage and Faggot pub near Borough Market. Randell sat by the door debating whether to order another orange juice. Returning from the bar clutching two pints and resuming his seat by the fire, Finlay said, "I had a long catch-up with Emma earlier. She met our man this morning – in a cemetery apparently. She suggests, and I tend to agree, that if and when we get evidence directly implicating the youngest brother, it ought to be shared with the old man as soon as possible."

Everard, thinking for a moment, said, "What, by her you mean? "

"Yes, safer that way and doesn't compromise our asset."

"I can see that. Okay, yes, let's play it that way when we have the necessary evidence."

Finlay looked up from his pint and said, "Have we heard anything back from anyone on that score?"

"No – not as yet but I'm due to meet a contact tomorrow. Are we absolutely certain Emma can handle this, Brian? She's still quite inexperienced," he asked looking at Finlay very deliberately.

Appreciating that, like them all, *"C"* was still affected by the loss of Jo Williams, Finlay replied, "Yes, I am." They were then both distracted as an older woman clutching a large gin and tonic plonked herself down next to Randell.

****

The next day, just after eleven o'clock on a blustery morning, Everard walked into a small café on Pall Mall. Carlebach arrived five minutes later and, catching the waitress's attention and remembering his guest had a liking for it, ordered a pot of tea.

"How's it going?" Everard asked whilst reaching for the menu and thinking about a sandwich.

"Slowly. I'm told by Tel Aviv that a deal has been struck with our friends in Washington. Basically, Usmani is to be handed over to them because he's linked to some other interests they have. It dates back to when he was employed by his country's national intelligence agency."

Everard, stirring his tea, said, "That's a result. What about the business I'm interested in?"

Carlebach, in between tasting his tea, said, "I'm told you will shortly receive a signed statement solicited from Usmani. My understanding is that it will give you precisely what you're after. Our friends in Washington are of course equally determined to secure the release of your Foreign Secretary and, I'm told, see this as significant step forward."

"It certainly is," Everard said. "To be clear… is your understanding that this statement directly implicates the man he met in Cyprus… Erjon Shala?"

Alon Carlebach – looking into the street – said, "Yes, that's correct."

****

The statement, forwarded by SIS Head of Station in Washington arrived the following morning. A covering note said that Syed Sher Usmani had accepted a plea deal rather than face formal charges relating to his involvement with bad people trying hard to kill Americans.

What colleagues at Langley proposed to do with Usmani in the longer term was of no interest to Everard.

The legality of the one-page statement by the Pakistani , *"given freely of his own volition"* confirmed that Erjon Shala, whom he had met on three separate occasions, the last being in Cyprus, had come up with the original idea of kidnapping a senior British politician. It went on to state that, through him as interlocutor, Islamic State had been successfully persuaded to support the idea since it would send a powerful message to the West. Moreover, the statement said, Erjon Shala arranged for funds to be transferred through a third party to help with costs of the operation. The fact that John Pelham happened to have been the in the wrong place at the wrong time was purely coincidental.

"That's it!" Everard said to Finlay when they met to discuss the fax. "Let's talk about timing and sequencing for our next move." At which precise moment he received a text from Penny in the South of France informing him that they'd had a new granddaughter: *"name to follow and still a matter of debate. Don't forget to tell the organisers I won't be available to judge anything at the village fete next weekend."*

****

In the rented apartment in Bermuda – still living under the assumed name of Eric Semple – Erjon was just back from an encouraging round of golf. The money invested in lessons with the resident professional was beginning to pay off.

There had been no great sense of loss at the death of his brother. They had never felt especially close. It stemmed from their childhood. Saban was a bully: always had been. He'd grown up in fear of him – not helped by the frequent, unprovoked and gratuitous thrashings. Being candid, the man was also incredibly stupid. The immediate question was how Guzim was likely to react. It was a sublime irony that, as the primary target, he had somehow managed to escape. As a statement of fact, it wouldn't take

Guzim long to find the culprit – him.

The separate business of the Foreign Secretary's kidnapping was now beyond his control. In theory, if the plan succeeded, Pelham would reappear at some point – most likely blindfolded in a cage – dressed in orange overalls in some unrecognisable desert somewhere, with a man in black standing over him brandishing a sword. The subsequent beheading would send a seismic shock through the West whilst, in parallel, reinvigorating jihad; the message inescapable – no one is beyond reach.

Closer to home, he was becoming increasingly worried that the Albanian mafia snake he'd poked would already be manoeuvring in preparation to bite back: a deeply unsettling prospect. The question, therefore – hope, as they say, not being a course of action – was whether he ought sensibly to put out another contract. It invited risk but he was running short of options.

****

Brian Finlay flew to Tirana two days later, met by Emma on arrival. As he reminded himself on the flight over, some things are best done in person and it was important that the next stage of the operation was handled with inordinate care. He had explained to her it would be a brief meeting; he was needed back in London to cover for *"C"* who had routinely been playing truant from Cabinet Office gatherings – no matter who was chairing them. The so-called COBRA meetings were largely a myth spun by the media – the name quite simply derived from the venue. The circumstances of the crisis in question dictated who took the Chair – usually a Home or Foreign Office minister, although the PM would become involved if the situation in question was sufficiently grave or, more likely, political expediency so demanded.

Emma drove Finlay to a café in a local park on the outskirts of the city. Feeling the heat and starting to sweat, he judged it best not to remark on the car's lack of air conditioning or, for that matter, its distinctly dilapidated appearance. Sitting outside in the shade, he talked her through the current assessment in London and handed over a copy of Syed Sher Usmani's statement.

"Wow," she said whilst still reading, "this nails it doesn't it?"

Contemplating a second cold drink, Brian said "Pretty conclusively we think."

Looking across at him she asked, "What deal have our cousins struck with Usmani?"

Adjusting his sunglasses Brian replied, "None of our business, Emma. First and foremost, he's a businessman and maybe not quite ready to surrender a very good lifestyle. Who knows, perhaps martyrdom or a long prison sentence didn't appeal. Anyway, our intention is to send Guzim another anonymous email: from the same fictious address as before saying that the sender has sensitive information about his younger brother and would prefer to discuss it face-to-face. If he takes the bait, you are to then arrange to meet him and hand over a copy of Usmani's statement."

"Will I be on my own?"

"No, Ben will be with you, but you'll be doing the talking."

"Okay," she said. "Will we be armed?

"That's your call, but I'd advise against it." Finlay let her assimilate what he'd said before continuing, "It would be good if Bremner was present, but there's no way of knowing whether or not Guzim would want him there. Our objective – to be absolutely clear – is to co-opt Shala's support in finding John Pelham."

Emma was nodding slowly.

"As far as we're concerned," he continued, "the fate of

his younger brother is, frankly, second order business and can be dealt with in slower time.

"When do you see this happening?" she asked.

"We will send the email within the next twenty-four to forty-eight hours. At the risk of stating the obvious, Emma, do not misjudge this man. I want you to have adequate back-up close at hand when you meet him. Ben can provide whatever additional assets you need and has been warned-off. Lastly, just to repeat, we do not want to compromise Bremner. Any questions?"

Emma shook her head.

"Okay," he said smiling, "don't cock it up."

Their meeting concluded; she drove him back to the airport. "Don't bloody cock it up," she said out loud on the way back to the Durres house having, before leaving, asked Ben to meet her for a chat later that evening. "Don't bloody cock it up…!"

****

Further north on the Montenegro/Albania Border, John Pelham was being thrown around in the back of the truck. Gears crashed, the engine whined and brakes squealed as it negotiated sharp descents and tight corners. This was a mountain track judging by the constant bumps and buffeting, but where and in what country was anyone's guess. He was trying hard to keep his mind occupied by mentally drawing the Adriatic's coastline – starting in Greece and going north. The challenge was trying to visualise the topography away from the coastal plain. He and Hazel had once taken a holiday in Corfu and he vividly recalled the gorgeous water and, to the east, high mountains in the far distance. Recently married, it was a stunningly brilliant two weeks and Hazel had loved every minute.

The thought of her sent a shiver through him; fighting to stay on top of unceasing waves of emotion threatening to drag him below, he saw her face. She was talking to him but without sound. Resisting the urge to submit to fear, he stiffened and went back to his imaginary drawing.

The truck stopped abruptly – the tailgate dropping with a loud clang. Once again he was unchained and pulled out, landing hard on the ground and uttering a muffled cry. Next, he was dragged down a steep set of steps and pushed roughly through a doorway. Feeling another metal clasp being attached to his wrists and padlocked, the hood and tape over his mouth were removed. Another cellar-like room: he was fixed to an eyebolt in the wall. The only fixtures and fittings was a foul-smelling bucket. Before disappearing, his masked captors threw down bottles of water, a chunk of stale bread and meagre assortment of fruit. This space, on closer examination looked more like some sort of storeroom – blankets pinned over two windows. A single lamp on a low wooden box provided the only light.

Thankfully dry, judging by the smell, animals were the most recent occupants. Eyes adjusting to the gloom, he began to see images on the walls. They were drawings; crude marks scratched with a small sharp object. It then dawned on him that children had been held captive in the place – by the look of it, lots of them.

****

Hugh Everard and James Wadsworth sat in the Old Coffee Shop in Montrose Place. Linda had refilled their mugs of coffee and, unprecedented for a Friday morning, the place was empty. Out of habit, Everard was facing the window and could see Randell parked on the corner.

"What do you think?" he asked his guest after the first mouthful.

"Superb," said Wadsworth, "I have to say I'm not usually a fan of brown sauce. It reminds me too much of school."

Glancing across the table Everard said, "Our cousins in Washington have played a blinder. We now have a sworn statement by a third party, directly implicating the youngest Shala brother in Pelham's kidnapping."

"And it's genuine, is it?"

"Absolutely. It confirms the whole thing was his idea and, although not personally involved, he made a significant contribution to the costs."

"What are you going to do with it?" Wadsworth asked.

"We'll use it as leverage. The last thing the oldest brother wants is his family's reputation trashed."

Having settled the bill and moved outside, Wadsworth asked, "When will this happen?"

"In the next day or two." Everard said.

As they walked towards the car he went on to explain that the bombing in Corfu was, at least for the time being, a secondary consideration. Further, that they still didn't know the whereabouts of Erjon although everyone seemed to think he was lying low abroad. "Of course, what we still don't know," he said, "is whether Guzim will cooperate. Should he refuse, we'll be no further forward in finding Pelham."

"Why are you telling me this, Hugh?" Wadsworth asked.

"Because, if things go pear-shaped it might get very nasty. If that happens, I want you to be ahead of the pack and better positioned to manage the political fallout."

"Presumably, I'm to keep this to myself?"

"Yes, you are, please."

****

Brian Finlay was chatting to Marjorie when Everard came back and followed him into his office. For the next half hour, they discussed the trip to Tirana and Finlay restated his opinion that Emma was unquestionably the right person for the job. Moreover, he was absolutely convinced that she understood the imperative not to do anything that risked compromising Bremner. He then handed over a draft of the email being sent to Guzim, to which *"C"* nodded without further comment.

Back in his own office, Finlay fired a message off to Tommy instructing him to send the email without delay. That done, he sent a note to Emma saying the email was on its way and attached a copy – *"for yours and Mike's eyes only".*

****

Guzim sat alone in his hotel suite in Tirana. Continued lack of sleep was beginning to take its toll. He looked and felt genuinely exhausted. The direction of the Council left little room for misinterpretation and, like the others, he was honour-bound to comply. Reaching for his laptop, he began scrolling through his email. Inexplicably, even before opening the solitary new message he began to feel apprehensive. The sender's address looked familiar. Having read the message twice, he picked up the phone and asked Bremner to come up to his suite as soon as possible.

Sensing the urgency, Bremner went straight up and, sitting in a chair by the window started to read the email while Guzim paced the room. "What can this possibly be about?" the old man said. "What the hell does *'sensitive information about Erjon'* mean?"

Bremner looked up from the laptop and said, "The only way you're going to find out is to agree to a meeting and, by the sound of it, somewhere here in Tirana."

Guzim was silent for several minutes. "Suppose it's a set-up. What if someone has placed another contract on me? I can't believe it's any of my people." Bremner watched the Albanian trying to think his way through the problem. "What would you do?" Guzim asked.

"Crudely put, whoever sent you this completely understands the value of what they've got. Otherwise, they wouldn't be offering to meet. They will have worked out that you won't accept anything they say without proof of its authenticity. Maybe they want money."

"So, what do you advise?"

"I don't think you have a choice: you'll have to meet them, but I suggest it should be on your terms."

Guzim continued to stare out of the window. Lack of sleep was definitely numbing his brain and he was struggling to process the information. "Yes," he said eventually. "Better this so-called *'sensitive information'* comes to me rather than anyone else. The phone number is here in Albania. I want you with me when I do this." And with that he reached for his mobile.

****

Emma took the call in the operations room. Mike and Ben were with her and had it put on broadcast. "You want to speak to me?" Guzim asked.

"That would be good Mr Shala," Emma replied in Albanian. "Will you prefer to say when and where, or shall I make a proposal?"

Guzim, weighing the risk for a second or two said, "Do you have any idea who you're dealing with?"

"I do."

"Okay, I will meet you at twelve noon tomorrow, here in Tirana, in an open space. I will have one other with me," he said.

Quickly looking at a map and receiving a nod from Ben and Mike, Emma said, "In that case, I propose we meet at the fountain in the centre of Park Rinia, north of the River Lana. I, too, will have an associate with me. If for any reason you don't show, I will assume you have no interest in what I have to show you… although be in no doubt that others will, Mr Shala."

Things went quiet. Bremner winced as the Albanian kicked over the coffee table, shattering the ornate glass top and breaking a ceramic bowl full of fruit. Having gathered himself, Guzim's tone became even more menacing. "You would be unwise to threaten me," he said.

"This is not a threat, Mr Shala: it's a statement of fact. Do you want to meet or not?"

Slumping into a chair Guzim said, "I will be where you have said at noon tomorrow."

Pausing for effect she said, "Very good Mr Shala, but if I see anything suspicious in the Park – anything at all – you won't hear from me again. I hope that's clear." She hung up and Guzim gave Bremner a short version of the conversation.

On completion of the call it went temporarily silent in the Durres Operations Room as Emma, Ben and Mike exchanged looks. "You definitely succeeded in pissing him off," Ben said, attempting humour but not quite achieving it.

"It sure sounded like it. At least he's agreed to meet," she said, noticing her hand was trembling slightly. "It's the result we wanted. I will be fascinated to see if he brings Bremner. We need to walk through the plan again. No room for a cock-up with this one. Anyone else like coffee?"

****

Things were a little calmer in the hotel room. Guzim turned to Bremner. "Who are these people… how can they possibly be Albanian?" Then, his whole manner changed. "I don't like the feel of it. I hope you know how to use a gun, Callum, because you'll be carrying one tomorrow, as will I. Please find me a street map."

Back in his room Bremner sent a short text to the number in Monaco: *"Attending meeting tomorrow and am told I'll be carrying."*

21

NEXT DAY, Emma and Ben entered the park five minutes before noon. It was ridiculously warm and even the ducks were seeking shade. The ambient noise of a lively city could be heard in the distance. Acutely wary of snipers, the venue for the meeting had been carefully chosen. There were few trees and the nearest buildings were over five hundred metres away. The fountain sat at the hub of what was, in effect, a wheel: gravelled pathways, its spokes. The tall jet of water was giving off a fine mist. Ben and Emma were both unarmed but wired for sound.

As they approached the fountain, two figures could be seen walking towards them from the opposite direction, the old man and Bremner both in in a loose-fitting jackets. Everyone wore sunglasses, Emma in a baseball cap, trainers and a green cotton jump suit with her hair pinned up. Ben was in a linen suit and open-necked shirt. Mike's team was parked by the river monitoring the police radio nets with, as yet, nothing to report.

Taking position by the fountain slightly upwind and avoiding the spray, Ben kept a distance between himself and Emma. Both had their backs to the sun, leaving the others no choice but to face it.

Bremner glanced at Emma and then Ben without any sign of recognition. Speaking in Albanian, Emma said, "Thank you for coming. I'm the person you spoke too yesterday. This is my associate. Our names don't matter and we mean you no harm. What does matter is what I have to tell you and, more important, show you."

Guzim looked at the young woman with undisguised

hostility.

"I should tell you, Mr Shala," she continued, "we are not carrying weapons. We have no need to because our colleagues are covering every entrance to the Park.

Guzim continued to stare at her, physically struggling to contain his anger.

"I must also mention," she said, "that highly skilled marksmen are positioned out there and, right now, you are in the sights of at least three of them. If you don't believe me look down at your feet."

Guzim glanced down and saw red laser dots dancing on the concrete and then abruptly stop.

"Should you not choose to believe what you're seeing Mr Shala, a demonstration can very easily be arranged."

"That won't be necessary," the old man said.

Realising she now had his full attention, Emma continued. "What I'm here to tell you, Mr Shala, is that we have irrefutable proof that your brother, Erjon, was complicit in the kidnapping of the British Foreign Secretary. Moreover, not only was it his idea, which we can substantiate, but he also made a significant contribution to the costs."

On hearing what she said his expression changed dramatically and, for a moment, it looked like he might stumble.

"Mr Shala," she said, "I'm going to reach into my pocket and take out a piece of paper which, as you will see, backs up everything I've said. Are you happy for me to do that?"

Guzim nodded and she stepped forward and passed him the paper. "You'll note its authenticity from the formal notepaper and the stamp of the US State Department," she added.

Guzim grasped the paper and slowly started to read.

Had he not worn sunglasses his eyes would have betrayed his emotions and, once more, he became unsteady on his feet. Bremner took a pace forward just in case of a fall and Guzim passed him the note to read.

"Mr Shala," she said, "you will wish to reflect on what I've given you. I'm sure you'll have questions. May I therefore suggest we conclude our discussion for now and, if convenient to you, arrange to meet again within the next twenty-four hours? You know how to reach me."

Guzim stared at her for several seconds but without really focusing. "Yes," he said, "I will contact you." And with that he abruptly turned round and, Bremner at his side, walked out of the Park. Emma remained for a couple of minutes allowing them to get well clear before she and Ben left in the other direction. Remembering they were still being recorded, neither said a word. Emma could feel the sweat under her armpits and was trying hard to conceal her fear. Once clear of the park gates she sat on a wall and exhaled. Turning off the recording machine, she looked at Ben. "That was pretty tense. I was scared shitless. Hope it wasn't too obvious."

"Emma," Ben said, "you did that really well: the man radiates menace."

"Thank you," she said, accepting a bottle of water from Mike. "We'd have been in trouble if he'd sussed they were only red laser torches. Do you think he'll get back to us?"

Ben looked across at her and said, "I'd put money on it."

"I need a cigarette," she said.

****

Once transcribed into English, the taped conversation was sent to London where, two hours later, it was read by Finlay and Everard.

"So far so good," Brian said. "She handled it very nicely. Those laser torches must have put the fear of God into

Shala."

Everard replied, "Bremner, too, I should imagine. How long is she giving Guzim to get back to her?

"At least 24 hours."

****

The old man hadn't uttered a word on the way back to the car and, from the comfort of his air-conditioned suite at the hotel, asked Bremner if he would ring room service and order some coffee for them.

Staring out of the window until it arrived, he said, "So… let me see that piece of paper again would you." After a further quick read he asked, "What do you think?"

A knock on the door halted the conversation and, having taken the tray and tipped the waiter, he poured them both a cup.

"I think," Bremner began, "this is a copy of the original statement signed by this man Syed Sher Usmani. I'm no expert but it looks genuine to me."

"I agree," said the old man.

"Only you can know whether Erjon had the opportunity to meet Usmani in Cyprus on the date stated."

Sitting in an armchair sipping his coffee Guzim replied, "I remember him being late joining Saban and me in Malta – something about a business commitment. So yes, he could have been in Cyprus as they claim." After a very long pause he continued, emotion barely disguised in his voice. "I confess I'm at a loss to know what to do. My family has been dishonoured. My associates will not condone my brother's actions and my own life may be in danger. That woman wants a second meeting and I cannot see I have any option but to agree. Is that the way you see it?"

Choosing his words very carefully, Bremner said, "I do. You will have to follow up with her but, perhaps dictating the time and place?" Guzim was staring intently at him.

"You have been given the information for a reason: the expectation is that you'll use it. There's going to be conditions attached. You lose nothing by hearing what more she has to say. On reflection, perhaps it might be wise not to share any of this with your family or, more importantly, your associates."

"What about security?"

"Frankly. I think it's too risky – they seem to have that well covered. I didn't like their marksmen's demonstration – that's for sure."

"Me neither," Shala said and, looking at his watch, picked up the telephone.

****

The following day at midday they were all back in the park. Emma had insisted the venue remain the same, Guzim having lost the will to argue. "Thank you for agreeing to this meeting, Mr Shala. Do you have any questions about the document I gave you?"

"No, I do not."

"Do you acknowledge it to be genuine?"

"Yes."

"Do you therefore accept that your brother is indeed implicated in the kidnapping of the British Foreign Secretary – John Pelham?"

After a considerable pause Guzim looked at Emma and said, "It seems that way."

Emma, choosing her words carefully and speaking slowly and deliberately then said, "Mr Shala, our priority is the safe recovery of our minister. What we want from you is help finding him. The fate of your brother is not our concern. It's as simple as that. How you do this is a matter for you. There will be no recriminations. For our part, you have our word that we will not disclose your brother's name, or yours, at any stage – even after the safe return of the Foreign Secretary. Do you understand what I have said?"

"Yes," he replied.

"Just so there is no misunderstanding, Mr Shala, we're leaving you to deal with your brother. Is that clear?"

"Yes."

"Very well, unless you have any questions this conversation is over. You have my telephone number and you can reach me at any time of day or night. Let us hope, Mr Shala, you are successful. We want our man back, alive." She then promptly walked away leaving Ben remaining in place until she'd left the park.

Forsaking the car, Guzim and Bremner walked slowly back to their hotel, the old man translating the conversation on the way. On entering the hotel lobby, he said he had some calls to make and would see Bremner later.

Alone in his suite, Guzim replayed what had happened in the park. Everything was telling him they were government people. But which government? The bitch was impressive, her Albanian faultless. He thought he'd detected a slight accent – maybe from the east of the Country. Despite her companion not uttering a word, his body language suggested that he, too, understood everything being said. Staring out over the city, Guzim's instincts were telling him they were professionals.

He knew he needed to concentrate and was under no misapprehension about how the Council would react if they found out about Erjon. Retribution would be mercilessly swift. His family would never be forgiven. It was as simple as that. Trust had been irreparably broken; the cardinal sin of *"Bese"*. Heads would roll – quite literally – starting with his. As the woman had said, the imperative – which the Council also recognised – was to find the missing politician. Everything else could be dealt with later.

Including of course his brother. If the opportunity arose he would kill her, too: something for the future.

No, all was not lost, he decided and, providing the Englishman was returned alive, he could claim a share of the credit – at no risk to himself or his family. Yes… that was the smart way to handle it. First, though, he needed to have a conversation with Callum Bremner who, although he liked having around, there was no useful role for in the days ahead. His presence would only add an unnecessary complication when it came to the Council. He was not Albanian, could not speak the language and attempting to integrate him into the plethora of illegal networks in the country was a non-starter.

However, he still felt indebted to the man; there might well be a position for him within the family business structure in London. *Yes, that could work*, he thought as he reached for the telephone.

Guzim laid out his thinking as he lunched with Bremner in a local restaurant in the city centre. "Callum, I have greatly enjoyed and valued our time together and have come to appreciate your wise counsel. My debt to you is important to me and remains unpaid."

Bremner tried to say something but the old man raised a hand.

"Finding the English politician," he continued, "will take all my time and energy in the coming days and, to be honest, I see no reason for you to stay on."

Bremner again tried to speak.

"In fact, my wish is that you return to London where, in due course, I want us to become business associates. Perhaps you might like to have a think about it and get back to me. Definitely no more prison time," he said laughing.

Then, reaching into his jacket pocket, he pulled out an envelope and handed it to him. "Don't be embarrassed, but please accept this ticket for tonight's flight to London. I have included with it the address of my town house in Chelsea, which you are most welcome to make use of for as long as you wish. I have forewarned my housekeeper accordingly."

Bremner reached for his glass as he processed what he'd just heard. Unquestionably a significant and unforeseen development but, from where he sat, it did not constitute a showstopper. A complication, setback – call it what one will – but a sensible and pragmatic decision based on sound reasoning. The good folk in London would be upset, but that was their problem. Guzim Shala was mafia, that much was irrefutable. It was reasonable to assume he was at or close to the top of the Albanian hierarchy. He fully accepted that it might be different if he spoke the language, but he didn't. He also acknowledged that there was no useful role for him in the search for John Pelham. The idea of a business relationship in the UK was intriguing. But that was for another day.

"Thank you," he said, "I completely see where you're coming from and of course accept your decision. The last thing I want to do is get in the way but, if I can help, you know how to reach me. Your offer of a business opportunity is very generous and I will, as you ask, give it some serious thought."

On arrival back in the hotel foyer, he offered his hand but Guzim chose to embrace him instead. "Stay safe my friend, I will see you in London," the old man said and walked to the lift. Bremner wandered over to the front desk, only to be informed that his bill had already been settled in full. Back in his suite having packed a bag he sent a short text to the number in Monaco: *"Returning to London this evening at host's suggestion."* Gazing out across Tirana's business district, he experienced mixed emotions and somehow felt that the job wasn't finished. He was also reluctant to leave Emma on the Albanian mafia's home ground. In fact, he was reluctant to leave her, full stop.

****

On receipt of Bremner's message, Finlay replied saying he was to make contact on arrival in London – suggesting he found a hotel under his own arrangements just in case – although judged unlikely – he was being watched. Finlay next called Emma. She had not caught up the news about Bremner going home which, thinking about it, was an entirely sensible move on the part of Guzim Shala. She was quietly relieved that he would no longer be in the firing line.

Bremner landed in London just before nine o'clock that evening, found a hotel on the Cromwell Road and walked out for fish and chips. Troubled by images of Emma Asllani, sleep proved elusive. Shortly after breakfast, and having had a brief conversation with Brian Finlay, he watched as a Mercedes saloon with two occupants drew up in front of the hotel – a rear door was held open with the obvious invitation to get in.

It wasn't until they were clear of the city that he recognised the woman in the front passenger seat whom he had last seen in the back of an ambulance in Shropshire dressed in the uniform of a paramedic. Turning round she said, "Good to see you again – and nice tan by the way. We weren't properly introduced last time we met: I'm Hannah and this is Pete. We're going to your country retreat in Kent and likely to be there for a few days. I understand people are queuing-up to talk to you."

Two hours later he was standing in the familiar gatehouse cottage garden with a mug of tea in his hand having on arrival, received a prolonged hug from Mrs Grant and accepted the offer of lunch. They talked about Jo Williams and he could see that her death continued to cause distress.

****

Vinny was rarely away from his computer screens these days. Still preoccupied with trying to find Erjon Shala, he received a message from Tommy to say that the UK Border Force had come up trumps. Clever application of sophisticated software, cross-referenced to two of the major airlines' frequent flyer programmes had established a pattern of movement for Mr E. Shala. Principal destinations were listed as Cyprus, the Cayman Islands, Canada and Barbados. Of the four, Barbados was the most frequently visited.

Vinny and Tommy immediately started bouncing scenarios off one another, concluding that the first place to put under the lens was Barbados. "If, as they say," Tommy began typing, "he goes there as often as he does, it's reasonable to assume he owns property on the island – a house, apartment, a time-share or maybe a boat."

"In which case," Vinny replied, "there will be some sort of record or listing."

"Correct. Maybe a rental agreement if he doesn't own it. There will be property tax to pay and, unless he's using an assumed name, he could well be on their equivalent of our Electoral Roll. So," Tommy continued, "why don't you have a dig into Barbadian Government records and I'll start checking rental agencies in the capital – Bridgetown isn't it? The next step will be to look at phone companies."

****

Brian Finlay and Mary Stewart were having breakfast in one of her favourite places not far from Trafalgar Square. Cheap and cheerful, she loved their *"All American"* and never refused the pancakes. "Unexpected development, our boy coming back at short notice," she said in between mouthfuls.

"Yes, hadn't envisaged that happening but I imagine you see all sorts of opportunities should he be persuaded to accept the offer of a business relationship?"

"It could work out very nicely," she said.

"Which reminds me," he said, "thank you for allowing us the use of the place in Kent – I'm going down there tomorrow; fancy joining me?"

"Love to, Brian. I could use some fresh air. At some point, I guess we need to discuss his contract termination?"

He replied with a nod. "How are Jo's family coping?"

"Badly," she said. "We're helping with the arrangements. Her parents didn't have the slightest idea what she did for a living and had always assumed she was a fulltime employee of a translation company. Bloody tragic, she had such a bright future."

"Who's minding Bremner in Kent?"

"Someone we've got on loan from Special Branch – Hannah. No reason why you would remember, but she was the one who role-played the paramedic when he was taken out of Maxwell. How long do you see him being at the cottage?" she asked.

"Until such time as we both consider him fully debriefed," he replied. "I also want a psychiatric assessment done before we formally hand him back to you."

Beginning to struggle with the size of her breakfast, she said, "Okay, I need to start thinking about the whole exploitation piece if it's decided he's to retain his cover and accept the business offer from Shala. As an aside, with him having been offered use of the town house in Shala's absence, I expect our tech guys will want to pay a visit."

Standing by the door, Mary watched Finlay settle the bill. *Yes*, she thought to herself, *she might have to start taking charge of their developing relationship*.

****

The COBRA meeting chaired by the PM that morning had

been predictably tense. Exasperated at the lack of progress with the kidnapping, the atmosphere was turning hostile – not helped by the media postulating all manner of theories and an endless queue of ex-military *"experts"* and retired diplomats eager to voice their opinion. Speculation on the whereabouts of John Pelham was rife and, as ever, uninformed. Conspiracy theorists were allowing their imagination free rein although, unusually, visitors from outer space were not thought to be responsible.

Wadsworth had watched the PM single out several attendees for special treatment – both of whom were accused of failing to *"grip the bloody media"* – in itself a forlorn hope. Hugh Everard had remained silent. Doing his best to sound positive, the interim Foreign Secretary mentioned *"new reasons for optimism"* and *"Italian colleagues being hopeful of a breakthrough"*. He did not sound at all convincing. Nobody actually went so far as to say they thought Pelham was in Albania, despite it being the opinion of the British Ambassador in Rome.

The MoD representative used some fancy graphics to summarise current military dispositions in the Adriatic, in the air and at sea. Director Special Forces reaffirmed the high state of readiness of the SF Task Force currently embarked in Royal Naval shipping but did not disclose that the PM had already delegated authority to proceed in the event a rescue opportunity arising at short notice.

It had been decided several days earlier that a small two-man SF liaison team would co-locate with Emma in Durres. Meanwhile, back in London, satellite imagery was being updated and made accessible electronically to those forward deployed in the Adriatic. US military authorities had made available further intelligence-gathering platforms and deployed a small liaison team to co-locate with the UK SF Task Force Commander.

****

John Pelham, oblivious to all but his immediate surroundings, was determined to remain positive and kept telling himself that everything was being done to secure his release. Steadfastly refusing to take the counsel of his fears, in his darkest moments he continued to find solace in prayer. He would be found, unharmed; it was only a matter of time. Still at a loss as to the identity the nationality of his captors, attempts to engage them when his food was set down and toilet bucket replaced had met with stoney silence. The strong smell of garlic every time one of them entered the room didn't help either – instinct was telling him these were not local people.

Having thought about it some more, the crude scratchings on the walls raised the question of *"trafficking"* and, as he recalled from briefings on the subject, it was prevalent in that part of the world. Sickeningly, there was a thriving market for small children in particular. It was big business and too horrible to contemplate. There and then, he made himself a promise; he would do everything in his power to reinvigorate international collaboration to combat human trafficking. From now on, he would make it a personal crusade. But that was for the future; his priority right now was survival and, once again, he began trying to name all fifty US States and, thereafter, the individual state capitals.

****

Finlay and Mary Stewart began debriefing Bremner at the cottage. Technical staff reactivated all recording devices and Mrs Grant ensured everyone was properly fed. Hannah did not attend the sessions which, she noted, often continued outside in the surrounding grounds. Debriefing followed established practice: Bremner recounting the narrative and the others frequently pressing him on matters of detail. As his *"inquisitors"* concluded at the end of the first day, not only was he a keen observer, but also blessed with a formidable memory. They had been genuinely struck by the *"ordinariness"* of the man: an anomaly; not freakish in any way – quite the opposite – but distinctly unorthodox and unsettlingly rational, especially when it came to risk.

Discussion continued over the next three days. Brian and Mary took rooms in a local hotel rather than flogging up and down from London each day. Quite deliberately, there was no talk about their asset's future – unquestionably the *"elephant in the room."*

Hannah, and occasionally Pete, joined Bremner for meals. As she had hinted earlier, she was more than competent on a vegetable patch and, like Jo, seemed happy to roll up her sleeves and get stuck in. No shrinking violet this one, he mused as he watched her spreading a barrow load of manure. The weather was cooperating and Kent was showing off its seasonal palette of ever-changing colours. The days were warm and, once again, he felt able to relax. Conversation with Hannah was effortless but for some reason different to that he had enjoyed with Jo who, he now realised, had inadvertently led him into completely new emotional territory. Her death had marked him – no question about it – and her image was rarely far away. "There will be a reckoning," he was increasingly telling himself. No question about that whatsoever.

****

Vinny worked patiently to unpick the Barbadian government's protective software designed to keep their secrets secret. "Where are you hiding, Mr Shala?" he hummed, having got precisely nowhere with Land Registry or voter registration. No joy on the first pass, it was time to try something different and he entered *"Security Companies in Barbados".* Almost at the same time a note came up on the screen from Tommy asking how he was getting on, to which Vinny replied, "Bloody impossible, how are you doing?"

"I'm struggling."

"What with?"

"Their equivalent of Customs & Immigration?"

"What's the problem?"

"It's all paper based. And don't ask about car rental companies, there's nothing on record with any of the big ones for "E. Shala.""

"If money wasn't an issue, where would you want to live in Barbados?" Vinny asked.

"Ideally, within easy reach of the airport outside Bridgetown," Tommy replied, "I'd want good security and everything close at hand, so there was no need to go out and shop; top end, in amongst the rich folk who drive flash motors."

"Flash motors – now there's a thought – I'll take a look at car dealerships. Something like a four by four maybe, known brand – top end."

Tommy, bored with scrolling through estate agents and property rental companies said, "I'll have another go at Inland Revenue and, after that, the major banks on the island."

****

Guzim Shala was back at the restaurant in Vlore. Huddled round the table were the same eight members of the Council – all summoned at short notice. Only two of them weren't smoking. Opening proceedings, the Chairman asked for any developments in the search for the missing Englishman. A hand went up and everyone turned to listen.

"There's a rumour he is, or was, being held in a farm close to Koplik – near Lake Scutari, next to the border with Montenegro."

"That," someone else volunteered, "is on one of several

routes favoured by smugglers."

"Smuggling what?" the Chairman asked.

"Everything," came the reply, prompting a ripple of subdued laughter.

"How did this come to your notice?" the Chairman asked.

"From an acquaintance in Montenegro: he's short of money and looking to retire."

"If this is correct," the Chairman said, "we have a decision to make. Either we rescue and release the Englishman for the authorities to find or, we arrange for someone else to do it. We need closure: who gets the credit is immaterial."

Guzim put up his hand. "I have a proposal on how we might want to handle it, Chairman."

"I'm guessing you'd prefer not to fully disclose details?"

"Preferably not, if that's acceptable. I will take full responsibility."

"Are you confident of success?"

"As much as I can be. Do I have permission to make the arrangements?"

The room went quiet before the Chairman spoke. "In which case," he said without troubling to call for a vote, "the Council agrees that you have six days to resolve this problem. We will meet back here, at the same time, one week from today."

Everyone looked at Guzim who had started smoking again. Business concluded they walked downstairs to lunch. Several tapped him on the shoulder and others shook his hand. An hour into the drive back to Tirana, he asked his driver to pull into a layby. Walking away from the car he sat on an old stone wall, surveying the countryside. It was glorious and, for a few moments, he forgot his problems. This place suited him. Less frenetic than

London and – in normal circumstance – infinitely less stressful. After lighting a cigarette and deeply inhaling, he took out his mobile phone and dialled the number given by the woman. Answering in Albanian, "Yes, Mr Shala – how can I help?"

Collecting his thoughts and speaking with as much control as he could manage, "I have the information you want."

"That's excellent news."

"After extensive enquiries conducted by my people, I'm given to believe the individual you seek is being held at a farmhouse near Koplik, north east of Lake Scutari – close to the border with Montenegro."

She repeated what he said whilst at the same time studying a map. "Can you be any more specific?" she asked.

"No," he said irritably.

"Is there any information about the kidnappers, numbers, nationality – anything at all?"

"No."

"Very well," she replied. "Let us hope we are successful and, if so, you will not be hearing from me again."

"Bitch," he said after hanging up, "you'd better pray we don't meet again."

As if by magic, the SF team leader appeared at her shoulder. "Our man is – or was – being held at a farm, in that area, there," she said, pointing at the map.

"Got it," came the reply. "Anything on numbers, weapons?"

"I'm afraid not," she replied.

"Okay," he said, looking at his watch. "We'll put some guys in after dark tomorrow and have a look. I imagine they'll choose to enter from Montenegro but that's for the Squadron Commander to decide.

"What, in helicopters?"

"Too risky for the insertion," he said. "Unless you tell me otherwise, I'm guessing we aren't asking host country permission for this?"

"Correct."

"Right, so that definitely rules out using drones and we can't risk flooding the area with teams. If by chance we do manage to nail the location and they chose to move him before we have time to get him out, it would be good to have some form of technical tracking on any vehicles in the farm complex. The other thing we might want to consider is ensuring we don't get inadvertently screwed by the national police and, as you say, this isn't going to be a joint operation so we need them distracted."

"Why?" she asked.

"Because we don't want a dead Foreign Secretary," he said." Let's hope he isn't moved."

Emma nodded and started typing a short report to Brian Finlay.

****

"C" and Finlay were on the eighth floor studying a large-scale map of Albania and, for good measure, had also brought up Google Earth on the computer.

"If," said Everard, "the SF boys are able to positively confirm Pelham's location, I imagine they'll keep it under surveillance until such time as a main assault goes in, for which I happen to know the PM has already delegated authority to DSF."

"I guess so but, as an insurance policy, they'll tag any vehicles they find."

"If we pull this thing off," Everard said, "the Albanians are going to be very upset that we didn't consult them."

"True, but we can't risk a leak."

Everard agreed. "I'll talk to the PM," he said and picked

up the phone to dial James Wadsworth's private number.

****

Vinny leaned back in his black leather chair increasingly stressed from spending hours trawling through various Auction Rooms on the dark web. The search for anything relating to data for sale on the good Barbadian citizens and nefarious institutions on the island was proving fruitless. There had to be another way. Barbados was too difficult. Time to switch effort to Canada, Cyprus and the Caymans. The latter he knew to be a popular place of registration for offshore companies and it was well known that money flowed in and out of the place with comparative ease. If, he reasoned, they processed financial data electronically, it was a fair bet that the government's system would be the same.

Calling up a map to remind himself where the Cayman Islands were, he searched for border control and immigration procedures. Three hours later he had the answer. "Okay people," he said aloud, "Let's see just how good your government's cyber-security is." The answer to his rhetorical question took a further four hours and, having hacked the Immigration Office database on Grand Cayman, he began trawling for "Shala, E."

His patience and industry were eventually rewarded when he found the record summarising – by date – all visits by *"Shala, E.".* There were eight in total and, in each case, the Port of Final Destination was listed as Barbados. Fortunately, although no address was given, the record gave the name and address of a hotel on Grand Cayman where *"Shala, E."* routinely stayed… or purported to.

Switching target, he then proceeded to hack the hotel and, once into the system and having entered dates of known visits, he found the name he was looking for. "At bloody last!" he said throwing his hands into the air staring at the screen. *"Address of Residence"* was listed as a resort complex close to Bridgetown, Barbados. "Got you," he cried and promptly invited Tommy into their Chat Room.

"Bloody brilliant," Tommy said. "I need to pass this up the line straight away." Twenty minutes later, a message was handed to Brian Finlay at the cottage.

****

Sitting with Bremner and Mary Stewart in the drawing room and having quickly read the note, Finlay remarked, "That's a result. Our tech guys have found one of Erjon Shala's boltholes – an exclusive resort close to Bridgetown in Barbados.

"Impressive," Mary said.

"Yes, but it doesn't mean that's where he is."

"It's a bloody good start though, isn't it?"

"Sure, and what's really helpful, they've established that he's also regular visitor to the Cayman Islands – always to Grand Cayman."

Bremner showed no reaction whatsoever but, back in his room, made a note.

****

After the fourth day of debriefing at the cottage, Finlay decided that the process had run its course and told Bremner he was free to leave – mentioning he would now revert to the Security Service as soon as the paperwork was squared away. The technicians on the floor above began the unenviable task of transcribing all conversations and Bremner dutifully handed over credit cards issued by SIS, and also his iPhone but kept the passport. Mary immediately replaced both the cards and phone and thanked him for his part in the operation. She suggested that he ought to take extended leave, on completion of which they would talk about his future. When she asked for a contact address he gently reminded her that his last known address in the UK was HMP Maxwell.

"Ah, yes – sorry," she said. "We'll sort out a place – where would you like to take your leave?"

"That's very kind but I'll make my own arrangements if that's okay."

"Fine," she said, "you've got my number and don't hesitate to call if you feel a need." She then rang Hannah and asked her and Pete to drop him at whichever airport or railway station worked best.

Sipping tea in the vegetable patch, Bremner had several immediate thoughts: first, at some point he ought to reclaim his Discovery from Madrid; second, there was the question of Erjon Shala and third, he would send Mrs Grant some flowers… maybe even a bottle of perfume – Chanel most likely.

22

DISCREET MILITARY deployments were well advanced in the eastern Adriatic. Four UK special forces teams were on the ground in Albania: two in covert observation posts covering roads leading to Koplik and the other two tasked to find the farm where Pelham was thought to be held. If feasible, vehicles would be electronically tagged because the main concern was Pelham being moved – hence the decision to go with what were in effect, *"cut-offs"*. All four teams were inserted into Montenegro by sea at night and crossed the border on foot. A fifth team was held in reserve at short notice afloat – to be deployed by helicopter if needed for any additional cut off *"in depth"*. To ensure the area didn't suddenly fill up with national police digging around, Emma had anonymously leaked a story to the National Headquarters about a possible sighting in the east of the country.

The weather in the vicinity of Koplik was ideal: no moon, a stiff offshore breeze and thunderstorms. As ever, apart from humans, the biggest worry to the teams on the ground was dogs and, just as likely, geese. Fortunately, any sensible person would be indoors on such a foul night. The teams tasked with finding the farm worked in pairs. Every man was equipped with night vision goggles and a small but efficient handheld thermal imaging devices. Having laid up during daylight and observed the two candidate farms, the teams agreed their respective targets – splitting into pairs to handle their *"close target recce"*. No dogs had been seen or heard at either location during the day but that didn't mean they weren't chained-up within the complex.

The first team completed its task but without seeing any positive signs and went to ground. The second team chose to further split into two pairs, one operator from each going in for a really close look. Systematically scanning outbuildings with the thermal imager and deliberately staying downwind in case dogs picked up his scent, one operator clocked what looked like a serviceable albeit rusty truck. Passing the information to the team leader, they agreed to fix a covert tracking device. That done, one of them began systematically scanning the farm building whilst the other took the outbuildings – one of which had vehicle tracks leading up to it. On closer inspection with the thermal imager, the heat outline of a figure sitting on the floor against a wall was unmistakeable.

Immediately retracing his steps and reuniting with his partner, they regrouped with the rest of the team. A huddled council of war ensued. This exact scenario had been rehearsed and the original brief was that further support was to be requested rather than go it alone.

"Okay, said, the team leader who, like the others, was soaked. "It's coming up to 0300, this rain will be with us for at least the next two hours and, as far as we know, there are no dogs. What do we think?"

"The weather could prove difficult for aviation but makes our job easier because the bad guys will be trying to stay dry. Suppose they move him?"

"I agree and, although the vehicle's tagged, it's the biggest risk."

"You haven't forgotten we were told to call in other teams if this situation arose, have you?"

"No, I haven't. We've got the advantage of surprise and, as you say, the bad guys will be at their least vigilant. I propose we go for it." The others looked at each other and then nodded.

The team leader sent an encrypted message to the ship giving the confirmed position and his intentions. He also asked for emergency evacuation by helicopter to be put on standby. A time for the assault, *"H Hour"*, was agreed – by when the helicopters would be in the air in a holding pattern less than five minutes flying time to the west in Montenegrin air space. Additional helicopters would recover the other three teams at landing site locations already confirmed.

Sketching the layout of the farm, he assigned individual responsibilities and walked them through the plan. "Just to repeat," he said as they huddled against the rain, "we've only clocked three men, all in the farmhouse, and we have to assume armed – but that doesn't mean there aren't others. We deal with them first… then we get our man. So much the better if we can take one of them alive, but it's a second priority. Any questions?"

There were none and, at the appointed time and having thoroughly checked that nothing was left in the undergrowth at the observation post, they synchronised watches and did a final check on their individual equipment and weapons. Receiving three thumbs-up, the leader moved forward and his men, all on night vision goggles, followed – each ensuring they were well spread out and covering one another as they moved very slowly and silently towards the farm. Periodically stopping to scan the building and immediate surroundings, one man went directly to a position by the outbuilding and the other three to the main house: two at the front, one at the back.

The rain was coming down in stair rods. On full night vision, everything looked very green. At that precise moment, a dog started barking and things happened very quickly. The first partially clothed figure to run out of the house was clutching an assault rifle and received five bullets fired on automatic from a suppressed machine gun.

He died before hitting the ground. A second figure came flying out of a side door, no doubt momentarily terrified as red dots appeared on his chest and was also put down. The only noise was torrential rain battering tin roofs. Even the dog stopped barking.

Another man in shorts and a tee shirt suddenly sprinted out of the back of the house and was hit full in the face with the butt of an assault machine gun, dropping instantly. Still unconscious, his hands were bound with plastic ties, mouth taped and a hood put over his head. Two of the team then entered the building and systematically cleared every room and space. Meanwhile, when instructed to do so over his personal radio, the fourth team member entered the outbuilding through a side window and, sitting before him in the dark, found a very disorientated, clearly terrified but alive and intact British Foreign Secretary.

The information was immediately passed to the Team Leader who, on receipt, reported mission success to the Task Force Headquarters at sea and requested immediate evacuation by helicopter of all sub units. The last act by the house clearance operatives was to release a very confused dog and bag up and remove two laptops, three phones and a marked map. The dead bodies were photographed, fingerprinted and had DNA swabs taken. The unconscious kidnapper was revived and taken to the adjacent landing site. In due course he would be turned over to the Albanian authorities.

John Pelham would later recall thinking it was all a dream. Woken by the dog barking and only picking up the sound of someone crashing about, he was completely unaware of shots having been fired and that two kidnappers were dead. Once the chains were removed by bolt-cutter and he had been helped to his feet by his rescuer, he had started sobbing with relief.

"It's okay, sir," a voice said quietly. "We'll have you

away from here within the next few minutes – helicopters are coming to get us."

Pelham, clearly having lost the use of his legs, was caught as he fell forward, given water and assisted outside. The helicopters, showing no lights and, flown on night vision goggles, landed as directed and within a minute or so lifted off again with their human cargo. Once airborne, the crewman double-checked Pelham's seat belt whilst a medic made a cursory examination, deciding to put his charge on oxygen.

****

Word of the operation's success was received in London and Durres within a matter of minutes after the helicopter's safe return to the ship and all participants accounted for. The surviving kidnapper – now hooded and clothed in a green flying suit – was taken below deck. The laptops and iPhones were removed for analysis. Pelham was stretchered to the Sick Bay but showed no sign of injury beyond bruising and dehydration. All his clothes were checked for forensics and subsequently taken away and burned, the ship's captain providing a fresh set and a pair of shoes and socks. Lice were removed from the Foreign Secretary's scalp, armpits and crotch. All SF team members were extensively debriefed and statements recorded from those who had fired live rounds. Once fully secured, the mothership proceeded to the Italian port of Brindisi.

****

After an early start in Downing Street, James Wadsworth was busily drafting a press statement with the communications team and, separately, a script for the PM to use – weather permitting – at a press conference outside 10 Downing Street later in the morning. The PM personally shared the news with Hazel Pelham who, understandably, broke down and wept. She would later ring Alberto and Francesca Moretti.

John Pelham was flown to London by a pre-positioned RAF HS 125 accompanied by a small medical team. Just before leaving Italy, he was handed a phone to make a very emotional call to his wife and, separately, had asked to speak privately to the remarkable men who had risked their lives to rescue him – all of whom were at the airport to say goodbye and one of whom gave him a shackle cut from the chain.

****

Choosing to forego the circus of the press conference, Hugh Everard and Brian Finlay took Mary for a late breakfast. Finlay had rung Emma to congratulate her and the Team on the superb way they had managed the operation. Brian told her that Everard would be speaking to the British Ambassador in Tirana – mainly to ensure he had the full facts – and that the interim Foreign Secretary was lined up to speak to his Albanian opposite number and, if required, also in Montenegro. There would be a long conversation with the British Ambassador in Rome and, separately, a letter sent to US colleagues in Washington with the *"thanks of a grateful nation"* for their technical support.

****

After an affectionate and very memorable fleeting hug from Hannah outside London's King's Cross Railway Station, Bremner waited until her car drove off before going to find his reserved seat on the train to Inverness. He had booked a hire car on arrival and arranged to stay overnight before driving up to Ullapool on Scotland's west coast.

This was his home territory where, for many years he had owned a small, isolated croft beside an inland loch. The approach track was in need of urgent attention and likely to test the suspension of most vehicles. No other dwelling in sight, the only immediate company was grazing sheep. Sea eagles and red kites patrolled above, sharing the sky with screeching gulls. This was deer country, too, although outside the culling season he no longer saw killing them as sport.

The croft, along with other property in the Borders, had been left to him by a distant relative. A kindly neighbour kept an eye on things when he was away. Containing the more valued of his personal possessions, the only other tangible assets were a fibreglass fishing boat and a rusting short wheelbase land rover kept in one of the outbuildings. It was bound to be raining and he hoped Mrs Morrison had picked up the message about lighting the stove.

The drive to the croft never failed to uplift his spirits and, in keeping with habit, there were frequent stops to breathe the air and absorb the remarkable scenery. It was the feeling of unspoiled space he liked most and, if one ignored the occasional telephone poles, there were few clues to the century let alone decade. The yellows, blues and purples of the hillsides were striking and sharply contrasted with a darkening sky. Approaching the turn off to the croft, he crested a hill and, stretched out before him, caught sight of the loch. His loch. And, padlocked on the foreshore, his boat.

God bless Mrs Morrison – the place was lovely, warm and, as usual, spotless. Dropping his bag on the table, he popped upstairs to the converted loft, removed a rug and lifted a floorboard. Beneath the wooden boards there was a long narrow recess in which sat a steel box – in effect a safe – where he kept a number of documents, including a passport and driving licence in his real name together with a number of credit cards. Extracting the box, he dialled in the combination and was relieved to see that everything was as he had left it. Critically, the passport was still in date. Substituting all documents in the name of *"Bremner"*, he locked and replaced the box, returning the rug to its original position.

A chicken pie had been left in the larder, together with a bottle of fresh milk, loaf of bread and tub of butter. There was a pot of soup on the stove and logs in the basket. That night he ate and slept well. Waking late, he decided the Land Rover should probably be turned over which, after many attempts and a lot of smoke, it eventually agreed to.

Whilst desperately keen to fish, there were more pressing matters needing his attention. Unlocking his rifle from its illegal storage box in an outbuilding, he walked back to the croft to collect a box of ammunition before climbing up to higher ground. There, against a rock, he positioned a wooden crate on which was marked a series of concentric circles in black paint. Satisfied with its placement, he turned around and counted out two hundred paces. Settling into a prone position amongst the heather, he checked the wind direction before adjusting the telescopic sight. Steadying his breathing, he slowly squeezed the trigger and released the first round at his improvised target – missing wide to the right. A second round clipped the edge of the crate and, after further adjustments to the scope, results started to improve until he was consistently placing rounds inside the outer ring.

After an hour he was satisfied and returned to the croft, cleaned and oiled the rifle and placed it back in its box. Now it was time to get serious about catching some trout. Turning the boat over and wiping off the seat, he placed his fly rod and tackle bag on the floor and pushed off. Ducks were observing him from a distance. This was their home, too.

Sitting in front of the log fire that evening his thoughts went back to Jo, Emma and, most recently, Hannah. All strong women; gifted, understated, their own people and not in the slightest way self-obsessed. Women of substance – the missing piece in his life. He had learned from all of them – including about his own inadequacy as a communicator: inhibited and for some reason unable to voice or share his personal feelings. There was, he now admitted, a need to change; to accept more risk in his relationships. Jo was unquestionably the catalyst, an indelible mark and a rare opportunity he had singularly failed to grasp.

The abruptness with which she had entered and subsequently departed his life had inflicted an acute psychological wound. The scar less visible than that he already bore on his stomach. The anger simmered: there had to be some form of atonement, retribution. He owed her that much. It would start the next day when, having returned the hire car at Inverness Airport, he planned to catch a flight to Gatwick. From there, he was booked on a direct flight to Bridgetown, Barbados.

****

Things were getting lively in the first-floor restaurant in Vlores. Bottles of wine close at hand and glasses full, the Council was engaged in lively debate. Basking in the reflected glory of the English politician's rescue – which continued to dominate world news – Guzim was revelling in the accolades. Nobody had pressed him for explanations, and none were offered. A triumph with no losers, only winners – especially the increasingly animated associates surrounding him at the table. Life could get back to normal: business as usual.

Not slow to recognise a political opportunity, the Albanian Government was effusive in its praise of the security agencies. Leaked photographic coverage of the dead kidnappers' bodies – together with their weapons – received wide press coverage. Neighbouring Montenegro wisely decided to turn a blind eye about the unauthorised intrusion of its airspace… rather suggesting some sort of high-level deal had been struck.

23

J OHN PELHAM'S release from captivity was a bitter disappointment to Erjon Shala. There would be consequences; fingers pointed and scapegoats sought, but he doubted his contacts in the Middle East would sever all ties. Money counted and he had deep pockets. The failed operation was attributable to the incompetence of those directly involved. An example would be made but he was blameless.

The pressing issue for him was how best to protect his wider business interests which, of itself, meant restructuring and, for openers, cutting all links to Cyprus and wiping clean electronic footprints. His property investments were realising significant returns and there was a good case for expanding the portfolio. He saw no reason to alter current management arrangements in the Caymans.

Of greater concern was his surviving brother. Guzim was not stupid, and, in hindsight, it had been a mistake not to make contact after Saban's death. He could have professed his innocence and offered to lead any retaliation. As he now realised, if anything, the prolonged silence arguably telegraphed his involvement. Ever the pragmatist, "what's done is done," he mused and, attack being the best form of defence, he knew there was only one sensible course of action. Guzim had to be neutralised as a threat: as quickly as possible. Apart from anything else, he had no intention of spending the rest of his life looking in the rear-view mirror. "Albanians don't forget," he kept telling himself. It was only a matter of time before Guzim, or someone, came after him and, despite its many attractions,

Bermuda felt too exposed.

With Cyprus now out of the question, Canada was definitely an attractive option but probably for the longer term. Right now, he reasoned, Barbados represented the safest bet. It had everything he needed and, crucially, efficient global internet connectivity and reach. Picking up the phone, he began making the necessary arrangements. On a positive note, his recently established golf handicap could only improve.

****

At the end of a long day, Bremner grabbed an early supper in the ground floor restaurant of the Gatwick Hilton and turned in. The direct flight to Bridgetown next morning – on which he deliberately booked a less conspicuous seat on the aisle in Economy rather than Business Class – would put him onto the island around four o'clock that afternoon – local time. A car had been reserved for collection on arrival and, for no other reason than geographic convenience, he had pre-booked a hotel adjacent to Grantley Adams International Airport.

It was still pleasantly warm when he landed. The hotel had everything he needed and he quickly settled in. Without any sort of objective beyond finding Erjon, he took a leisurely swim and ate supper in his room. Next day he rose early and, after breakfast, headed out to familiarise himself with the island.

****

Everard and Finlay sat together on a bench in London's Green Park, vaguely registering successive waves of commuters emerging from the nearby Underground. The bright early morning sun was making many of them blink. Jubilation at the rescue of the Foreign Secretary had largely melted away and no longer dominated the news. Last reported, John Pelham was taking extended leave in Wiltshire whilst, on a daily basis, receiving specialist counselling. Unusually for a politician, he had sensibly declined all media requests for interviews but gave a brief statement thanking all those who facilitated his recue – especially the *"professionalism of the Albanian security services who had been instrumental in securing his release"*. Everard was far from convinced that the man would return to office. "Not if Hazel has anything to do with it," Penny had said on the phone from Provence that morning. "A peerage and a proper job, that's what Daddy thinks," she had said, quoting the noble Lord Brigstock. "He intends having a word with the PM."

Never much of a gossip, Finlay was focused on more urgent issues. "Any thoughts on what to do about our friend Erjon?" he asked, watching a dog yapping at a contemptuous squirrel perched ten feet up a tree with a mouthful of nuts.

"I've been thinking about that," Everard said, "and I'll bet his older brother has, too. Not sure I'd want to cross Shala Senior and it wouldn't surprise me if Erjon hasn't concluded the same thing. Do you believe in natural justice, Brian?"

Still watching the dog, "To a point," he replied, "but sometimes we have to help it along. He'll surface in due course and we're bound to hear about it, or the cousins will."

Everard looked at his colleague. "I need to talk to you about the vacant Director of Operations job, Brian. I've got a candidate in mind but I want to run it by you first."

Finlay turned towards Everard and said with a degree of concern, "Not me I hope? I'm very happy with my present position and, to be honest, I have zero interest in all the political stuff: not cut out for it."

Wishing he had a coffee Everard said, "Fair enough. Suppose I said I'm thinking about an outsider?"

Clearly relieved, Finlay said, "Like who?"

Recognising that what he was about to say next might not play well, Everard paused. "Like Mary Stewart," he said.

Finlay began to nod slowly, "I could see that, Hugh," he said. "She's bloody good – no question about that. It'll piss off a lot of the flat-earth brigade but I'm sure she'd win them over. It would also send a strong message about the increasing need for even closer ties to our sister Service. I'm all for this new joint approach doctrine. It makes sound operational sense and, frankly, the less friction the better. Mary has thick skin. She doesn't bruise easily and, I think, is the intellectual match of most of the senior folk in Vauxhall Cross, with the field experience to back it up."

Everard listened without interruption. It was going better than he'd hoped.

Finlay paused for a moment before continuing, "She's done the hard yards. I think it could work, although I'm not sure how it would affect our personal relationship. Have to find out, I guess. And, before you ask, yes – we are an item… at least that's how I'm seeing it."

"That's great. Penny will be delighted. A proper relationship, eh?"

Finlay smiled, "Not sure what *'proper'* means in that context but, yes – I think it's fair to say we're now in a relationship."

Everard also smiled and said, "She'll have you gardening next."

"I've already signed-up."

"On the appointment business, we need to keep this to ourselves until I've got my ducks lined-up," Everard said, thinking back to the patient Grey heron.

****

Erjon was sitting alone on his patio in Barbados. It was

nice to be back and the decision to foreshorten the Bermuda stay unquestionably the right call. His only immediate concern was a report from Cyprus that *"unusual activity"* had been detected in two of the financial accounts. Specialist forensic audit investigators had been brought in – at exorbitant cost – and would need a few days to look at the books. The issue related to a pattern of cash transfers dating back at least two weeks. He had been told that the sums in question were relatively small, but there were a lot of them – ostensibly all having been personally authorised by him. Attributing it to an accounting error of some sort, he asked to be informed as soon as the audit was complete. With nothing else to occupy him for the rest of the day, and watching a tidy golf shot on the seventh hole immediately in front of him, he went looking for his clubs.

****

Bremner was parked at the side of a narrow coast road studying a tourist guidebook. All he had on Erjon's whereabouts was what he'd overheard in the cottage. *"An upmarket resort near Bridgetown,"* Finlay had said. Recalling him mentioning it during their time on board the yacht, Erjon had expressed an interest in golf. If true, it was therefore not beyond the bounds of possibility that he would want to be close to, or within easy reach of, a course. If so, it narrowed the search considerably and, on further consulting the guidebook, there were only three serious contenders: one on the south coast, another on the east side of the island and one in the west. All exclusive, expensive and self-contained, especially the Hampton Grange Country Club.

Rather than driving straight to it, he went back to the hotel and did some research on the internet – including Google Earth. It was time well spent. Arguably the most exclusive resort on the island, with property eye-wateringly expensive according to several articles about it, the complex was separated from the coast by a lateral road. Spacious, single-storey houses were set in their own grounds, all with large swimming pools, facing the sea and overlooking one of the two golf courses. Protective security arrangements were impressive, camera coverage by day and night and tightly controlled access. A *"gated"* community in every sense of the word, the Club had *"only for the exceedingly rich"* stamped all over it.

Just before sunset, he drove out to the complex and walked up a path he'd spotted on Google Earth – the raised ground commanding good views of the northern end of the resort. It confirmed his suspicions: the place was a veritable fortress. Picking up his mobile phone, he dialled the number listed in the Guidebook. "Hampton Grange Country Club, this is Monty – how may I help you?"

Bremner had rehearsed his lines: "Yes, good afternoon, I'm visiting the Island for a few days looking at property to buy and wondered if there was someone I might speak to."

After a brief pause, "Absolutely sir, that would be Marsha. She'll be back in office from eight tomorrow morning. Why not give her a call on Extension 4215."

"Thank you," he said. "I'll do that, Monty."

Next day he called the extension: "Good morning, this is Marsha, how may I help you?"

Loving the husky sound of her voice he said, "Marsha, good morning, I was given your number by Monty at reception last night when I rang enquiring about potential property purchase. A friend in London recommended the resort. I believe he's been resident here for quite some time."

The sultry voice then said, "And to whom would you be referring, sir?"

Caught slightly on the hop, he heard himself say, "Shala – Mr Erjon Shala." Guessing that Marsha was checking her computer screen.

"Oh yes, Mr Shala has been with us for quite a few years now and owns a lovely property overlooking the North Course. I believe he intends to play more often when he's here."

"Oh, okay, that's helpful, I didn't know he was in town and I'll try to get in touch. Marsha, I was wondering if it might be possible to look at one of the properties you have for sale, I'll be on the island for a week or so?"

"That's very easy to arrange. All you have to do is give me a call before you want a viewing. You know there's a property for sale very close to Mr Shala's – number 31?"

"Marsha, it's stupid of me but I've forgotten the number of Mr Shala's property."

"That'll be Number 34, sir."

He then drove into Bridgetown and went to see several estate agents. Declaring a specific interest in Hampton Grange Country Club, he asked for particulars of any properties on the market – preferably as a golfer – on one of the courses. Back at his hotel he opened the packet of documents and quickly identified Number 34. The next issue, which was always going to be the tricky part, was sourcing a weapon: checking out internet listings for gun shops was a start.

The following morning Bremner rang the club's golf shop and spoke to an assistant professional, explaining that he was looking to buy a property at the resort and had arranged with Marsha to go and see some in the next few days. "I was wondering," he said, "whether there is any possibility I might be able to play the North Course while I'm here? The house I'm interested in overlooks it."

"As a general rule we aren't open to the public, Sir, but in the circumstances I'm sure we can make an exception. Do you have your clubs with you?"

"No, I'm afraid not."

"That's not as problem: we can provide everything you need. Will you want a caddy?"

"No, that won't be necessary – thank you – but I'd like a buggy and I'll buy some shoes when I come in."

"Could you tell me what your current handicap is, sir?"

"I haven't swung a club in a while but I used to play off eight."

Suitably impressed, the assistant said, "That's great, I can get you onto the course any time after the morning rush – so, how about sometime after ten o'clock?"

"If there was anything a bit later I might bump into a work colleague," Bremner said, "Shala… Mr Erjon Shala… lives at Number 34 if I recall correctly."

This struck a chord with the assistant, "Ah yes… Mr Shala is playing pretty much every day. He prefers the North Course – usually after lunch and tees-off around two o'clock. Just like clockwork."

"Unfortunately, that's a bit late for me, could you please reserve me a tee time for one o'clock?" Bremner asked.

"No problem at all, sir – we'll have everything ready when you come in tomorrow. Have a good day."

****

There was no easy solution to procuring a weapon: mugging a member of the police or a security guard were non-starters. Unable to purchase a handgun over the counter on the island, he did not have time to explore more creative solutions such as bringing one in by boat. Attempting the same thing by commercial airline was also a no-go unless, possibly, by executive jet. In practical terms that, too, was unworkable. There was a solution out there somewhere but it was proving incredibly elusive. What mattered was the objective; namely, getting Erjon Shala to confess to the murders of his brother, Jo Williams and the others on the tender. Saying it was the easy part: making it happen was going to involve a healthy dose of improvisation. Even though Barbados had one of the lowest crime rates in the Caribbean, experience had taught him that when drugs, alcohol and poverty co-exist, violence was rarely far below the surface. The likelihood was that Erjon would be armed.

Presenting himself at the golf shop next day, he bought some shoes and was measured-up for the correct size of clubs. Green fee paid, and, clutching the map of the course, he walked outside to his assigned buggy. The weather was glorious. After strapping the bag of clubs on the back, he put on his sunglasses and baseball cap and drove to the first tee.

Millionaire's golf – he had the place to himself and nobody was playing ahead. Acres of lush grass stretched before him – fairways all immaculately sculpted with criss-cross patterns, interspersed with intimidating sand bunkers raked smooth as if with a comb. Distant greens beckoned with fluttering flags above the target. It looked like a tourist brochure; azalea bushes flanking the course, small lakes thronged with wildlife and, traversed by stone bridges, small streams threaded their way to the sea.

Parking up and dismounting at the first tee, he saw the seven-foot-high security fence next to the coast road and, beyond it, scattered shacks along white beaches then the azure blue sea. A concrete pathway marked the route for buggies. The place was utterly gobsmacking: no other word could adequately describe it. Placing the ball on a short wooden tee, Bremner stepped back and breathed deeply to settle his nerves. A couple of practice swings later he moved forward to the ball, gathered himself and, after aligning with the distant green, to his genuine amazement fired it over two hundred and forty yards. "Nice shot, sir," the assistant professional said behind him as he picked up his tee, put the club back in the bag and drove off trying not to feel smug.

Just before two o'clock, Erjon parked his golf cart next to the North Course's first tee and, after a cursory wave to the folks in the shop, selected a club. Without undue hesitation or apparent signs of nerves, he quickly checked his alignment, adjusted his feet and slowed his breathing. Pleasingly, a firm strike arched the ball in a perfect trajectory down the fairway. The absence of other golfers was the reason he preferred playing in the afternoon when, with time zone difference, London and Cyprus had both closed for the day.

Bremner was deliberately playing slowly and, with the place to himself, occasionally put down a second ball to practice a particular tricky shot. He wanted to be caught by the golfer behind him who, with any luck, would be Erjon. To his left, the sea stretched to the horizon and, as he drove down the fairway, he saw scattered palm trees flanking the lateral road. Grateful for the cooling onshore breeze, it was warm but not oppressively so. Scattered vehicles were parked beside the road, adjacent to the fence – their owners most likely swimming or sitting amongst the palm trees in the shade of one of the wooden rum shacks at the back of the beach.

Sitting on higher ground to his right were the opulent properties he had read about in various brochures – all facing west with uninterrupted views to seaward. Periodically checking behind him, he caught sight of another buggy some four hundred yards back down the course and closing quickly. It was too far away to identify the sole occupant.

Researching the course layout, he had already decided that a low bridge carrying the buggy path over a small stream by the seventh hole was the preferred spot for the intended confrontation. The hole was immediately in front of Erjon's single storey house – Number 34 – which, like all of them, had direct buggy access onto the course, via a gate. Closer inspection on the pretence of looking for a lost ball suggested the gates were operated by remote control – most likely hand-held and for exclusive use by the property owners. Being able to access the electronic gate was a crucial part of his plan.

24

THE HEAT in the back of the stationary white van was becoming insufferable for the figure lying prone on the floor. Constantly wiping away beads of sweat threatening to mist-up the lens of the rifle's telescopic sight, time was passing uncomfortably slowly. Technically, the intended shot was comparatively straightforward and, at a distance of only two hundred metres, and providing it had been properly *"zeroed"* – which it had – accuracy was guaranteed. The wind was of little consequence and neither was the sun since it was high and any shadows cast in the direction of the target. The *"off the shelf"* weapon rested on two sandbags. The only accessory was a suppressor – which, by its length, dictated the shooting position and slightly protruded through the eighteen-inch square hole he had cut into the rear boot panel beneath the number plate, hinged to allow it to be swung up from inside and clipped to the roof with shock cord. The full-length mattress was proving a godsend. His expectation was that only two rounds of the 30-06 subsonic ammunition would be required, but spares were available in the five round internal magazine. Not long now.

****

Bremner's drive off the seventh tee was probably better than he deserved given the increasing anxiety he was experiencing at the prospect of the imminent confrontation with the man he had come a long way to find. Calculating his next shot, he was reminded that the thing about streams and bunkers on golf courses was that one either took the risk of trying to hit the ball over them or, if in doubt, deliberately play the safer option and hit short. The decision was made for him by his increasing heart rate. Stealing a quick look behind, he was relieved to see Erjon sitting in the shade of his buggy waiting for him to play his second shot. Adjusting the peak of his baseball cap and thankful for choosing to bring dark sunglasses, he took out a metal club and struck the ball solidly into the air, rolling it to a halt just short and right of the green. Replacing the club, he climbed back into the buggy, drove over the small bridge and abruptly stopped, effectively out of Erjon's sight and blocking the buggy pathway. The electronic gate to Number 34 was three yards ahead of him.

After completing his second shot to the green, Erjon needed a further three putts to get the ball down the hole. Also wearing a hat and sunglasses, he returned his putter to the golf bag and drove towards the small bridge, jamming hard on the brakes at the top to avoid hitting the stationary buggy. "Is there a problem?" he called to the figure sitting behind the wheel. Bremner climbed out and turning around – removed his baseball hat and sunglasses.

The effect was instantaneous. Erjon froze. Bremner started to walk the short distance toward him, at the same time registering that the man was staying close to his buggy. "Well, well, you're full of surprises aren't you, Callum? And increasingly, it would seem, a problem. I have underestimated you and can only assume you aren't here by accident or for a reunion."

Bremner stared at the man who had dominated his thoughts since Corfu; there was a brief flashback to the slow-motion fireball and the blast hitting him milliseconds later and then the second explosion. In his mind he saw the billowing smoke, distressed sea birds flying in all directions. Lives callously ended and loved ones denied the chance to say goodbye. Despicable and utterly unforgiveable. Removing his own sunglasses, and without Bremner having spoken a word but with contempt written all over his face, Erjon said, "You are an irrelevance. You might have fooled my brother, but you don't fool me. You're a chancer – a grifter – insignificant, a nobody. I owe you nothing and had rather expected you to die with the others."

"So, you did kill them?"

"That is no longer a matter of concern for you," he said, reaching into a bag inside the buggy and pulling out a small, snub-nosed pistol, turning back and raising the weapon. No trace of emotion; his eyes firmly on Bremner and intensely focused on what he was about to do. "Saban was a bully – had been all his life. Having been on the receiving end for most of my youth, I can vouch for that. It was unfortunate that Guzim wasn't with him at the end, but no matter."

"You murdered innocent people."

"Collateral damage... I have always–" The sentence was abruptly ended as a bullet smashed into his head – a second right behind it, this time into Erjon's chest – spinning him round before hitting the ground. As if in slow motion, Bremner was transported to a vegetable allotment in Shropshire. This time a spectator: upright, motionless, hands by his side, trying to comprehend the horror unfolding before him.

Everything went quiet: even the green parrots looking down from palm trees and azalea bushes were temporarily silenced. Bremner stared down at the inert figure. Had he heard a confession? It certainly sounded like it. Erjon's face, or what was left of it, stared back at him – eyes open, set in a mask of disbelief. Trying to think about what to do next, Bremner's body was steadfastly refusing to move, anchoring him to the spot. Somewhere off to his right he heard the sound of an engine starting up. Looking again at the lifeless body, the man had expressed no remorse whatsoever and, checking for any sign of a pulse but finding none, the sense of justice was overwhelming. Retribution.

It took him several minutes to order his thoughts before slowly taking out a mobile from his bag and calling the golf shop. "A man has been shot – by the seventh hole, North Course – he's dead. Call the police. I'll remain here until they arrive." A window blind twitched in Number 34 but went still again and the parrots resumed their chorus.

****

The police and emergency services were annoyingly slow to respond and it took two days for the interviewing of key witnesses – the primary ones being himself and Erjon's housekeeper who, as the police established, had seen Erjon fall to the ground but could not recall him ever possessing a gun. Security cameras covering the electronic gate only captured images of the back of Bremner standing talking to someone: hands at his side and calmly looking straight ahead. Perimeter cameras picked up a departing white van with an indecipherable number plate. It was later found burned-out in a disused quarry and, Bremner having removed it and stuffed it into his golf bag, no weapon was recovered from the scene. His subsequent statement omitted any reference to Shala being armed and the weapon was summarily ditched in a swamp.

Three days later – travelling as he had done since leaving Ullapool the previous week under his real name – Bremner boarded a plane for Miami. From there, he flew direct to Glasgow, collected a hire car and drove home to his croft. One of the first things he did on arrival was to recover the metal box from under the floorboards in his bedroom and reclaim all documents relating to Callum Bremner. The hire car was returned to the airport. He took a train back to Ullapool and, from there, an expensive taxi ride to the croft. As far as the world was concerned Callum Bremner had never left Scotland.

There had been plenty of time to think about the manner of Erjon Shala's death during the flight home. Clearly bearing all the hallmarks of a professional killing, a bit of him felt cheated at not having pulled the trigger. But at least he could now draw comfort from the fact that Jo's death had been avenged. He would leave it to others to pursue the killer and whoever had placed the contract. The important thing, he reminded himself, was that a chapter had closed. There was a tremendous sense of release. One day he would try to get a photograph of Jo and mount it in a frame at the croft – maybe on the mantelpiece over the fireplace. A permanent reminder of one of the best things that had ever happened to him.

Yes, he was now ready to move on. A good start would be to collect his Discovery from the diminutive blonde with green eyes who fancied herself as a runner.

****

Everard and Finlay sat beneath the cedar by the lake in Norfolk, he and Mary were guests for the weekend. Penny was giving Mary a tour of the gardens. The house was full of grandchildren and Everard loved the pandemonium; being repeatedly ambushed by little people intent in putting the fear of God into him in corridors, bedrooms and dark passages – invariably compromising themselves by giggling in anticipation. Mealtimes were the most fun and he enjoyed following the banter around the table: impromptu concerts; excruciating sounds from the piano and, in her element, Penny resolved to maintain order but never quite doing so. Bread rolls thrown but rarely at him and spaniels constantly on the prowl in eager anticipation as scraps rained down from above.

Randell was not far away, attempting to teach Number One Grandson the art of fly-casting. There had been an extended lunch. "How's Mr Bremner doing?" asked Everard – watching his grandson thrash the water like someone swatting wasps and laughing loudly.

"Went to ground in the wilds of Scotland I believe," replied Finlay, "Mary will call him for a chat in a week or two. No talk of Shala Senior coming back to London just yet."

Everard, resisting the urge to tell his grandson to keep his wrist straight on the back-cast, said "You'll have seen the report from our people in Bridgetown about the fatal shooting of Erjon Shala the other week."

Finlay, now also fascinated by the lesson going on in front of him said, "Yes, I did – no loss to humanity, is he? Maybe there is such a thing as natural justice after all."

"A bit odd though, don't you think?"

"It depends on your perspective. The mafia have their own simple way of dealing with complicated issues, don't they."

****

Vinny and Tommy were also discussing Erjon's death in their private chat room on the web.

"That's interesting," Vinny typed, "Looks like I won't be getting paid for the work I did after all."

"Having a laugh are you? What about the money you've already helped yourself to in Cyprus? Oh I think you'll do alright – in fact, we both will."

Vinny scratched his head. "Oh, you know about that then?"

"Bloody right I do, and I imagine you were going to mention it at some stage?"

"Of course, what do you mean about *'doing alright'*? Not sure I follow you," he typed.

"It's simple, as far as the property company in the Caymans is concerned, you and I just became E. Shala. We need to act quickly before they hear about his death and, as him, we should move whatever cash there is somewhere else – into an account we set up."

Vinny then wrote, "That's very naughty – we'll be rich."

"Quite; as soon as that's done, we'll start instructing them to sell some of the properties. They'll cotton on eventually, but that's okay, we'll be long gone."

****

In Vauxhall Cross, Marjorie stuck her head round Everard's door and asked him to call James Wadsworth at his earliest convenience. They subsequently agreed to meet for a stroll in St James's Park. It was a beautiful morning – crisp under a blue sky. Gardeners were busy at their work and being watched by inquisitive tourists. Joggers cursed at cyclists contesting space and ducks carried on doing whatever ducks do.

"I heard on the grapevine," Wadsworth began, "that you're going ahead with proposing someone from outside your Service for a senior position. I recall you mentioning to me you had a candidate in mind. Is that right?"

Everard, distracted by all the planting activity going on and wondering whether Penny was on the case in Norfolk replied, "Yes, James – not sure whether you've met her but I'm keen to run someone from the Security Service. It's a bit radical but the person I'm thinking about is a class act."

Wadsworth, his eye fixed on the lake, said, "There's a bit of concern about the timing, Hugh. The PM is keen to avoid any big fallouts. My understanding is that it's about the principle – an outsider and all that. Not everyone's likely to sign-up."

Everard went quiet, finding it hard to conceal his profound disappointment. "You're suggesting I drop the idea of an outsider altogether, James?"

Wadsworth, clearly embarrassed, said "Probably the wise move Hugh – your business, of course, but you know what people are like, they see threats everywhere. Let's go and find a coffee." Everard suddenly got the sense that a heron was staring at him.

****

Standing by the window in his office, Everard reflected on the conversation in the park. Thank goodness he hadn't discussed it with Mary Stewart. Which prompted a thought, "Marjorie, ask Brian Finlay to come up would you."

Fifteen minutes later Finlay knocked on the door and walked in. "Brian, you remember I told you about the Director of Operations job, you didn't mention it to Mary, did you?"

Finlay, clearly a bit miffed, said "No *'C'* – you said not to."

"Had to ask, Brian, sorry, but I've had the word it might not be the right time. As far as I'm concerned, it's a postponement, not a cancellation: I'm going to continue gapping the post."

Finlay's face betrayed his disappointment. "That's a real shame," he said, "not entirely surprising, though, is it? One day we'll have folk who can see beyond the walls of their fiefdoms."

"While you're here Brian," Everard said, "my Israeli contact has asked for a meeting – something about mutual interests. I'll lay odds it's about our Pakistani friend Usmani." Then, almost as an afterthought, "I imagine you read the after-action report on John Pelham's rescue; did anything strike you as unusual about the surviving kidnapper?"

Finlay had studied the report at length and, in particular, the accompanying very thin transcription of the kidnapper's interrogation. "If I remember correctly," he said, "he didn't say anything, not a word. You can be sure the Albanians will do better: they've had him in custody for quite a while now – although we've had no feedback from our people in Tirana."

Everard nodded. "Let's press them a bit harder please. If the Albanians choose to be unhelpful, maybe you could talk to the Cheltenham guys who were with Emma at the Durres house – they should still be able to access the National Police database."

****

That afternoon Everard was proved correct. Alon Carlebach did indeed want to talk about the Pakistani when they met in Regent's Park. "Interesting developments in Washington," the Israeli began, "much to the surprise of US colleagues, our man has apparently agreed to swap sides rather than face a long jail sentence. I understand a substantial sum of money is also part of the deal."

"Yes, I received a note about this from my people in Washington. It was a bit thin on detail, though."

"Colleagues in Tel Aviv are being pragmatic and, as far as they're concerned, the end justifies the means. The Americans will handle the strategy and we'll manage the man."

"Where is Usmani at the moment?" Everard asked.

"He returned to the Middle East three days ago."

"Can I be assured we'll be kept informed of any significant developments?"

Carlebach, turning to look at him, said "You have my personal guarantee, Hugh, but perhaps it would be wise to keep it between the two of us."

"Agreed."

As Everard later said to Brian Finlay, he would be fascinated to see what the Pakistani actually managed to come up with or, more likely, whether he did a runner and disappeared into the tribal areas bordering Afghanistan, never to be seen again. It was an obvious risk and he felt sure the Americans or Israelis would have it covered. There was bound to be a contingency plan against just such an eventuality.

Everard did not envy Usmani, or, for that matter, rate his chance of surviving for long in the hugely dangerous, duplicitous and inordinately violent world to which he was returning. Then again, everything he had read about US Federal prisons was equally horrible and with palpably fewer places to hide. Talk about the lesser of two evils.

****

Although toying with the idea of going back to London, Guzim decided to extend his time in Albania. The climate suited him and his Albanian family were delighted to have him *"home"*. It was, he confessed privately, beginning to feel where he belonged, and he was becoming increasingly more comfortable as the weeks went by. However, it remained a comparatively poor country and he was sufficiently realistic to accept that his years growing up in London had spoiled him. It was also an uncomfortable truth that personal wealth in Albania invited envy and, by association, risk. That aside, having served his dues in prison, England no longer held much attraction. Moreover, he wasn't getting any younger and, with his best years behind him, the Adriatic offered everything he needed – good food, acceptable wine, stimulating company and adequate private health clinics.

He particularly valued the slower pace of life and, of course, the weather. Perhaps it was time to think about a more permanent arrangement: somewhere he could feel secure and not worry too much – about anything – and yet be close enough to continue working with the Council and its many and varied interests. That, he reminded himself, was the beauty of the Internet – geographic location was irrelevant. It had dawned on him whilst researching property that an attractive solution might be the island of

Corfu. With its international airport and efficient ferry connections to the Albanian and Greek mainland, it ticked all the right boxes.

Being honest with himself, he had done his grieving and of no longer of any relevance that Saban had died there. What's done, is done: we move on.

Further investigation identified a selection of interesting places for sale and, with money not an issue, he focused on the upper end of the market. Personal security considerations dictated it would have to offer sufficient space to house permanent domestic and security staff; privacy guaranteed and not overlooked. After his time on *Cygnus* he had grown rather fond of the sights and sound of the sea and, not for the first time, toyed with the idea of buying a yacht. It would be a great way to visit pals in Sicily.

But that was something for the future and, having decided that Corfu met his requirements, two weeks later he popped over on the ferry to view a couple of properties, eventually deciding on a cliff top villa near Kassiopi, on the north east coast. His initial idea had been to rent the fully furnished property but, so taken was he with the poolside terrace and magnificent panoramic views, he bought it outright. An exquisite location, one of its many selling points was sight of the Albanian coastline and mountains beyond. But, what really clinched it for him, was the smell of cypress, eucalyptus, pine and the captivating fragrance of wildflowers. Despite being a popular travel destination – especially with Brits – he had bought himself privacy. This was a hideaway in which to relax. A place to audit thought. In due course, he would ship over some of some possessions from London – especially his favourite paintings.

Contacts in Tirana helped to source domestic staff and, through his family, he was able to arrange a permanent team of three security guards. The villa received a full security survey, including a technical sweep and the installation of a new Wi-Fi setup. Completing the package, he agreed to buy the previous owner's white Toyota Land Cruiser four by four with darkened rear windows. It would suffice until the armoured version he had ordered arrived from Italy – all nine tons of it. No point making it easy, he reasoned.

****

Brian Finlay went to see Everard two days later in order to update him on the surviving kidnapper in Albanian police custody.

"You were right," he said, "Cheltenham tells me the Albanians eventually established that the kidnapper speaks an East European language – Chechen."

"Does he indeed. I didn't think he'd hold out for ever."

"I'm not sure what it tells us other than it's surprising they screwed up." Formerly Chechnya – now the Republic of Dagestan – predominantly Sunni Muslim and with a long history of conflict, they both knew that Chechens were renowned fighters and often to be found supporting nationalistic causes. A bit like Afghans, they loved fighting, were inordinately good at it and not averse to availing themselves to the highest bidder. Neither was it lost on them that Chechens enjoyed almost unfettered access to modern weaponry and equipment from earlier conflicts and the breakup of the Warsaw Pact and demise of the former Soviet Union. In sum, they were to be taken seriously.

"What possible reason could Chechens have for kidnapping a senior British politician?" Everard asked.

"Because someone was paying them, I imagine," said Brian.

"I agree: it's the only feasible explanation," Everard said. "Presumably acting as surrogates on behalf of fellow Sunnis?"

"Well, it might explain the connection between Usmani and Erjon Shala."

"I agree," said Everard. "The involvement of Chechens will seriously worry the Albanians, and not just the National authorities, I imagine the mafia will be wondering what it all means for them. Why don't you talk to Ben and see if he's picking up anything locally – I assume we're still monitoring the Albanian police nets."

"Yes, we are," Brian replied.

"I'd be really interested to know what if anything came out of Pelham's release. The national police were bloody quick off the mark taking credit," Everard said. "If they're smart," he continued, "someone will eventually cotton on to the fact that Pelham's rescue had third party thumbprints all over it."

Finlay was struggling to see where this was heading. "I suppose this could lead us back to the surviving Shala, couldn't it?"

Everard nodded. "Where is Emma Asllani at the moment?"

"Back in Madrid as far as I know, but I'll check."

****

Unbeknown to anyone but Callum Bremner, Emma was technically on leave in the UK having agreed to drive Bremner's four by four back to Scotland. The phone call three days earlier caught her completely off guard. "How's my Discovery?" the familiar but unexpected voice had asked.

"More dents than when you left it but otherwise firing on all cylinders," she replied, "I suppose you want it back?"

After a pause and trying to suppress a laugh, Bremner said, "That would be nice. What are your plans?"

By now he had her absolute attention. "As it happens," she said, "I'm owed some leave and was toying with the idea of coming home. Let me guess, you want me to bring it with me?"

Bremner smiled. "I'd pay your petrol," he said.

"What about the ferry?" she asked – all sorts of thoughts beginning to surface.

"Okay, have you ever been to Scotland?"

***

Three days later Bremner was sitting on a gate watching the Discovery make easy work of the muddy track along the shoreline. Having carefully weighed up the pros and cons, he'd decided it was best to keep his own croft a secret – at least for now – and had therefore rented a similar place on the north coast – an equally isolated and stunning location. The breath-taking landscape, complemented by steep cliffs, sheltered coves and sandy beaches, reminded him why he loved the country so much. Emma had not said how long she would be staying. In fact, she hadn't said much at all beyond giving him an approximate time of arrival. This was a new experience, and he would be lying if he said he didn't feel apprehensive.

"Bloody hell it's a long way," she said climbing down from the Discovery and then, smiling, "What a lovely place – is it yours?"

Bremner stepped forward and kissed her on both cheeks. "Hello," he said. "No, I just got it for somewhere to chill. I hope you're going to stay for a while so I can show you around."

Emma gave him a big beaming smile, "Can't think of anything I'd like more. Are there any rules we ought to discuss?"

Half expecting the question – she was after all a trained SIS intelligence officer – he replied, "I think we should stay off any work-related stuff and, for all the reasons you understand, perhaps it might be better if we keep your visit to ourselves; wouldn't want to distress the good folk in London would we. Is your phone switched off?"

"Yes, it is."

"Did you bring your running kit?"

"I did," she said, "and my hiking boots, wellies, thick socks, rain gear and winter woollies. I even chucked in a couple of bottles of Spanish plonk."

"Brilliant," he said and helped unload her gear, affectionately stroking the Discovery in the process. "The fire's lit and I've got coffee on the go. Let me show you your room."

****

Emma was transfixed by the incredible seascape from her first-floor bedroom. The adjoining bathroom had underfloor heating: the long, deep bath fitted with old fashioned brass taps and a hand-shower. Thick towels were stacked by the sink and a bathrobe hung off the door. She smiled at the small bunch of fresh wildflowers by the double bed, the eclectic selection of books in the wooden bookcase and numerous sets of neatly folded Ordnance Survey maps. No phone, radio, television or kettle. Just a wind-up alarm clock and set of expensive-looking Swiss binoculars. Quickly unpacking her bag and dispensing with shoes she went down to join him for coffee. "Were you serious about the offer to stay for a while?" she asked.

"Absolutely. By the way, I don't suppose you fish, do you?"

Emma grinned, "No, but I'm desperate to learn."

"Great."

"Funny thing to ask," she said, "but what should I call you?"

Now it was his turn to smile. "Callum will do fine," he said.

25

SYED SHER Usmani sat at a table in a shaded corner of the walled courtyard in his house on the outskirts of Jalalabad. The heat was fearsome and the air uncomfortably still. He had owned it for many years and always felt secure in Nangahar Province. Eastern Afghanistan had long suited his purposes – close enough to Kabul and yet also conveniently linked by a modern highway to his other home across the border in Peshawar. The two houses had afforded him considerable flexibility during the years of the Taliban and subsequent Soviet occupations.

His guest was sipping yellow tea. They both wore the traditional shalwar kameez and waistcoats. Conversation focused on recent events many hundreds of miles to the west. "A most unfortunate outcome," the guest said.

"Indeed."

"Unusual for our Chechen brothers to mess up. Word reaches me they are embarrassed and wish to atone."

"Is that appropriate?" Usmani asked.

"Yes – they were paid handsomely. Their offer has been accepted and they're being encouraged to get on with it. We shall take out an insurance policy this time," he said, without elaborating. "The message will be unambiguous: lessons need to be taught and people reminded of their place in life. We will have our revenge and our brothers will see to it. Retribution."

"What sort of timing are we talking about?"

"Soon – while memories are still fresh."

****

Usmani mulled over the conversation after his rather intimidating guest departed. He always envisaged some sort of after-shock following the debacle of the Englishman's rescue, not helped by the excessive hyperbole so favoured by western politicians. Unsurprisingly, since their meeting in Cyprus, there had been a deafening silence from the Albanian. Never a believer in coincidence, he was convinced his own detainment by the Americans was in some way related. At least now there was no longer any prospect of spending the rest of his days behind bars – not American ones anyway.

The financial package he'd been offered was generous but, as ever, there were strings attached and he was under no misapprehension about the consequences of failing to deliver his part of the bargain. One did not mess with these people. They wanted information – timely, accurate and relevant information. On the other side of the equation, compromise was guaranteed to result in a painful death. It was a perilous balancing act. Alas, he had regrettably sold his soul to the Devil and would have to live with his conscience. What mattered, was not jeopardising his own or the lives of his family. The risks were enormous – almost beyond comprehension. Mulling over what his visitor had said, the immediate priority was to find out more information on what his visitor had termed, *"retribution"* – which he took to mean reprisals. The answers would necessitate an intense programme of travel, but so be it. A coded initial report would be sent to his assigned contact in Tel Aviv.

****

Forty-eight hours later, Everard was back alongside Alon Carlebach on the bench in Regent's Park. It was late morning: sun with scattered cloud – possibly showers later according to the forecast. "We're hearing that there are to be reprisals for the failed kidnapping of your Foreign Secretary," the Israeli said. "It seems our Chechen friends, strongly encouraged by Muslim brothers, have decided lessons are needed."

"Reprisals?"

"Yes. The word being used is '*retribution*'."

"Don't like the sound of that. Do we have any idea what they have in mind?" Everard asked, his mind racing and trying not to appear flustered.

"No, not yet. Our assessment is that something will happen in Albania."

"What makes you say that?"

"For the simple reason it's where the kidnappers screwed-up."

"Presumably the Chechens will be looking to salvage their reputation?"

"That's our assessment. There's a commercial slant: they are mercenaries. It's as much about money as prestige. You can bet your life the outcome will be different this time."

"What is our Pakistani friend doing about it?"

"Trying to get more information. Whatever they have planned is going to happen soon. That's all I know."

Everard thanked the Israeli for the heads-up and agreed to stay in touch. Walking back to his car he mentally reviewed the immediate priorities, the first of which was to inform the relevant government departments – recommending stepping up security alert states in London and all overseas embassies. The complicated part would be how best to forewarn the Albanian authorities – something for the Foreign Office to think about. Then, there was the question of whether or not to alert Guzim Shala – a key decision he would discuss with Brian Finlay and Mary

Stewart. His instincts were telling him there might well be opportunity in this turn of events, but he was unsure how to exploit it.

****

Back in the office, Everard replayed the conversation to Brian Finlay. Action to upgrade the security threat assessment was already in hand and various messages had been issued by the Joint Intelligence Committee to that effect. A brief and suitably bland explanatory note was circulated by the Cabinet Office to Number Ten, Foreign Office, Home Office, Ministry of Defence and the Commissioner of London's Metropolitan Police Force. Finlay said he had spoken to Ben in Tirana.

"By the way," Everard asked, "did you manage to track down Emma Asllani?"

"Not yet," he replied, "all I know is that she's home on leave from Madrid and must be off grid somewhere. Can't say I blame her. Why do you ask?"

"I was thinking we might send her back to Tirana but, on reflection, maybe she would be more useful here in London. Could you float that past Mary?"

"I can."

After a pause, Everard said, "As a matter of interest, what are our hacker colleagues doing to keep out of trouble at the moment?"

"Trying to unpick the complex financial web spun by the late Erjon Shala."

Reflecting on it, Everard said, "Depending on how we decide to proceed with Guzim, we might have need of their services again… if they're not too busy with their fingers in somebody's till somewhere."

****

The secure one-to-one VTC with his Head of Station in Washington proved timely. Everard was told that senior people at Langley were equally concerned about the rumoured involvement of Chechens. It significantly changed the risk calculus. The intention was to increase human and technical surveillance whilst, at the same time, raising alert states in US embassies. Importantly, he learnt that intelligence analysts also leaned to the view that the most likely reprisals would be directed against Albanians. However, Langley did not dismiss the risk of something being targeted against UK interests – which put embassy and diplomatic staff firmly in the frame.

The other significant point of note for Everard was hearing that, according to US sources, large sums of money were being offered for information in Croatia, Montenegro, Albania and Greece. Whoever was bank-rolling the Chechens had deep pockets. He then asked Marjorie to see if Brian was available for a chat.

"Okay," he said after Finlay sat down, "If someone's splashing the cash it won't be long before the likes of Guzim Shala gets to hear about it."

"Which could raise all sorts of delicate issues for him?"

"Correct," said Everard. "Not only will he profoundly resent being manipulated – blackmailed is probably more accurate – he will feel compelled to react. It's the unpredictability – not to say volatility – that makes the man so dangerous. We're going to have to be really careful how we handle him."

"But he won't know it's us he's dealing with, will he?"

"That's where the finesse comes in."

"You find the Chechen threat credible, don't you?" Finlay asked.

"I do, Brian. If someone's minded to have a go at British interests – anywhere – never mind Albania – all bets are off."

"Which means what?" asked Brian.

"Which means we need to re-engage with our mafia chum."

****

Emma made the most of her five days with Bremner in Scotland. Sitting alone in Departures at Inverness Airport, it was very obvious during the drive from the croft that neither of them wanted to break the spell. She had loved every minute of it: being brought a mug of tea in bed every morning, their long runs together and the leisurely breakfasts he cooked. To her surprise, she had even enjoyed the hilarious fishing lessons in the rain. He was an accomplished cook and, she noticed, had remained teetotal throughout but encouraged her to enjoy the wine.

Against all expectation, she had slept right the way through every night – occasionally reading herself to sleep. Happy, secure and untroubled. The radio had never been turned on and neither, albeit for different reasons, had her iPhone. Their conversation was effortless and avoided straying into their respective pasts or private lives beyond confirming that neither was in a relationship. Bremner had only kissed her twice, on arrival and when saying goodbye at the airport. She was curious but not unduly bothered by his lack of physical affection and concluded that he was an inherently shy man – probably emotionally burnt at some time in the past. She chose not to take the initiative. Self-effacing, soft-spoken, articulate and with a wry sense of humour, he allowed – indeed encouraged – her to be herself. There was a refreshing honesty about it and, although the circumstances in which they found themselves were far from straightforward, it didn't seem to bother either of them at all. How the future would play out was the big question but, as far as she was concerned, she wanted hers to be inextricably bound up with Callum Bremner – or whatever his name was.

****

For his part, after dropping Emma at the airport, Bremner was left experiencing a similar amount of emotional turmoil. She was such uncomplicated and stimulating company. They had discovered so much in common, prominent amongst which was a shared sense of humour and the ability not to take themselves or each other too seriously. Very much as he had imagined, she was strong as well as feisty; opinionated, hard-edged and physically tough. In every sense of the expression, a handful. But she had a delightfully softer side and could be incredibly undemanding and affectionate. He was happy just listening to her talk and, with minimal provocation and just an innocent prod, go off on a rant about something on which she held strong views.

Refreshingly unaware of her beauty, she didn't fuss with makeup and was impervious to whatever the Scottish weather threw at them. She looked at peace when curled up on the sofa with a book in front of the fire – occasionally glancing at him and smiling. He carried a similar image of her from the apartment in Mallorca. Much as Jo had done, she made him feel valued and appreciated. In hindsight he hoped his lack of physical attention hadn't put her off but, also like Jo, he couldn't risk mortgaging his emotions – not yet… not with the life he led. It would be selfish and he was reasonably sure that Emma understood. There had been no signalling of any expectation.

Winding his way north in the Discovery with the windscreen wipers barely managing to cope with the remorseless rain, he couldn't stop grinning. The very thought of her gave him a warm feeling. Maybe those green eyes had put a spell on him – time would tell.

****

Guzim Shala quickly settled into his new villa and was comfortable with the domestic and security routines. Out of courtesy, he informed the Chairman of the Council about his new living arrangements but chose not to divulge the address. A meeting had been called for two days' time at the usual venue in Vlore – something he intended having a word about because it was becoming far too predictable and dangerous. The reason given for the short notice was vague: the message about attendance unequivocal. There had been a development of some sort. All would be explained. He would have to wait to learn more. Nothing to be done. The infinity pool beckoned.

Gazing out across the bay, he knew his brothers would have adored the place. The ultimate party house, it was right up their street. Leaning on the lip of the pool scanning the horizon, he was seized with the image of Erjon. An enigma: what you saw was not necessarily what you got. The quintessential chameleon. Always wary and slightly suspicious of his little brother, more out of curiosity than anything else – several years previously he commissioned a discreet investigation. Saban was deliberately kept out of it other than to transfer funds to a specific account for an unspecified purpose. The investigation unearthed a property company Erjon ran from the Cayman Islands and also that he owned a place in Barbados. It did not, however, uncover his involvement in trafficking and, nor, for that matter, that he had relinquished his Christian faith in favour of Islam.

In the end, Guzim had reached the inevitable conclusion that his young brother posed far too great a risk: to the family reputation and to him personally. Although unproven, he was pretty sure Erjon was behind Saban's death and, which was not lost on him, he, too, should have died in the explosion. Then, there was his involvement in the botched kidnapping of the British politician – not to mention engaging in trafficking. His death in Barbados was a matter of honour. He had no regrets. Arranging it through associates in America was easy enough. There would be no comebacks.

Despite his many attractive qualities, Erjon's loyalty, priorities and values had become confused. From a family perspective, he was a liability. It was as simple as that. His death reduced the risk to himself but there was no room for complacency and he did not dismiss the idea that further contracts might have already been put out. Appreciating his remarkable good fortune at Maxwell, next time the outcome might be different. On the positive side, however, he was satisfied that the family audit trail now held fewer potential hostages to fortune and, importantly – at least for now – the Shala name was safe. The only loose end, which was still keeping him awake at night, was the most unsavoury deal he'd been forced to strike with, as he now termed her, *"the blonde bitch in the park"*. The question was what, if anything, could be done about it.

****

The Council meeting in Vlore took its usual form as the Chairman welcomed those present.

"We have only one thing to discuss," he began. "Word has reached me that there are foreigners in our country trying to buy information. I've been told that similar enquiries are being made in Montenegro and Croatia."

"Information about what?" someone asked.

"About the failed kidnapping of the British politician. I'm also hearing that the money on offer is substantial." He let this information sink in before continuing, "What troubles me is that, in time, these enquiries are bound to lead to our acquaintance in Montenegro. As you will recall, we did business with him on this very matter and Guzim paid handsomely for valuable information on the then whereabouts of the Englishman."

The Chairman had his colleagues' absolute attention. Guzim was hanging on his every word. "The problem of the kidnapping was not of our making," he continued, "and we are indebted to Guzim for its satisfactory resolution. However, these outsiders are clearly not prepared to let matters rest and I fear we will be forced to act. What do you think?"

Guzim spent much of the ensuing discussion collecting his thoughts. This was exactly the scenario he most feared. "Mr Chairman," he began, "as we all know, money talks. As I see it, there are two people at risk: our colleague in Montenegro, and myself. If substantial amounts of cash are being offered, it can indeed only be a question of time before the trail leads to us. My concern," he said, looking at each of his associates in turn, "is that enquiries will inevitably expose this Council."

"What are you proposing?" the Chairman asked.

Deliberately pausing for a moment or two, Guzim continued, "I suggest we do two things: first, unpalatable though it may be, we must reduce our exposure by eliminating our associate in Montenegro; second, we must mobilize our resources and confront these so-called *"outsiders"* and thereby eliminate the threat to ourselves and our interests. Apart from anything else, it would send a very powerful message."

The room went quiet. Cigarettes were lit, coffee drunk and looks exchanged. Eventually the Chairman said, "Thank you all for your opinions. I share Guzim's analysis: we must be pragmatic. I therefore endorse his proposed course of action. Does anyone want to say anything?" Nobody did. "In which case," he said, "I will deal with our colleague in Montenegro and each of you will muster all the resources at your disposal. We will activate our networks and, if necessary, pay for information. Let me be clear. The objective is to find and confront these outsiders as soon as possible. I want us to take the fight to them before they realise they are even in one. Are we agreed?"

"Yes," each man said in turn and, in the absence of any dissenting voices, they adjourned to lunch, at which the mood was initially subdued but predictably improved once the wine was uncorked.

****

Bremner was recalled to London by Mary Stewart and they met at a house in Battersea. Needing reassurance, she again asked if he was happy to continue undercover and he repeated that he was. "In that case," she said, "we want you to re-establish contact with Shala. Our understanding is that he's still in Albania. Timing is rather important, so the sooner the better."

"Okay… what approach do you suggest I use?"

"That you have given a lot of thought to his generous offer of a potential business partnership and are keen to discuss it with him, preferably – which is the point – face-to-face."

"Understood," he said.

"There are a few related points I need to mention," Mary continued. "First, under no circumstances are you authorised to use lethal force except in self-defence. Second, you are to tell him that you will only engage in legitimate, by which I mean lawful, activity – saying that you have no wish to go back to prison. Third, you will make clear that your preference is to stay in the UK."

"I understand."

"You will be reporting directly to me through the conduit in Monaco." She then updated him on developments in Albania and the strong possibility that the Chechens were planning to return. "Having poked the snake," she said, "it looks like it's minded to strike back. These people are utterly ruthless and Guzim Shala is in the thick of it."

****

The old man took Bremner's call just before lunch and, expressing his delight that his offer was accepted, suggested they meet without delay. It was agreed that he would fly to Corfu as soon as practicable and that he should plan on staying at least a week. He was told that he would be met on arrival and was asked to forward flight times when convenient. Bremner duly informed Mary Stewart, who in turn told Brian Finlay. Two days later he landed in Corfu having, after much consideration, decided not to contact Emma whilst in London.

****

Alon Carlebach and Hugh Everard sat drinking tea in a café just up from Embankment Underground Station. They were the only customers. "Our Pakistani friend has been busy," the Israeli said. "It appears there's confusion in certain circles about whether it was your people who rescued Pelham or your US counterparts."

"Where does the confusion come from?"

"Washington thinks it stems from the operation: you'll recall him being taken to Brindisi where, as we know, there's a permanent US military presence."

"Why does it matter?" asked Everard.

"It matters within the context of retribution and prioritising targets. Washington intends hedging their bets."

"In what way?"

"The issue has apparently been overtaken by events and, being unable to attribute blame, the bad guys intend sending a message to both governments and, at the same time, teach the Albanians a lesson."

Everard was watching people in the street making their way to the Tube. Rain was imminent. "That's unhelpful. Do we have any idea who the intended targets will be?" he asked.

"Our Pakistani friend says they will be in Tirana itself."

"Which suggests embassies or diplomatic staff?"

Everard said.

Carlebach nodded. "Yes, that's our assessment, too. What form the retaliation takes against the host nation is unspecified. The other thing you need to know, Hugh, is that whatever is being planned will happen soon." After the Israeli had gone, Everard watched the arrival of the first drops of rain. He needed time to think.

****

On return to office, Brian Finlay was briefed on the conversation and asked to put out a summary report to all key stakeholders. A separate briefing paper would be sent to the PM's Chief of Staff in Number Ten. Everard also asked him to speak to his opposite number at the US Embassy. Everard said he would update Ben in Tirana and SIS Head of Station in Washington.

On receipt of the SIS report, the interim Foreign Secretary formally requested military assistance from the MoD to beef up security at the Embassy in Tirana. Receiving Number Ten approval, a special forces contingent flew to Kosovo's Pristina Airport by RAF transport aircraft. Under the cover of darkness a small command element and five, four-man teams moved by road to the Embassy compound in Tirana. Separately, a two-man team – in civilian clothes and driving an Albanian-registered four by four acquired for them by the Defence Attaché checked into a hotel in the city.

Mary Stewart joined Everard and Finlay for a catch up in *"C's"* office. Bringing her up to date on everything he knew and had already discussed with Brian, he asked whether she saw any merit in Emma Asllani returning to Albania because she knew the country so well and spoke the language. He said he felt there was also a strong argument, as before, to include Mike and his team. Everyone knew Bremner was in Corfu but, having kept his iPhone switched off, not precisely where – presumably collocated with Guzim and likely to remain so for at least the next seven days.

"Bremner works for my lot," she said, "and Shala is of direct interest to my Service."

"What's your point?" Asked Everard.

"I think I should go out there, and I'd be happy to have Emma with me."

"Are you sure about this Mary?" Everard asked, sensing it was news to Brian Finlay, too. "Our thinking is that whoever deploys would reoccupy the safe house we used previously in Durres. Better than crowding out the Embassy."

"I'm okay with that," she said, will you formally approach my Director General?"

"I'll go and see him." Everard said, "Are you sure about Emma?"

"Yes, even though Shala has seen her up close, I want her on the team."

****

A warning order went out to Mike in Cheltenham and Emma Asllani. Ben had cleverly renegotiated use of the Durres house and, as before, sorted out ground transport – including the *"customized"* van used previously. The Security Service Director General approved Everard's request concerning Mary Stewart, asking to be included on the distribution of all future reports. Technically, she would remain on Security Service books rather than become formally transferred to SIS and report to Brian Finlay which, when it was first suggested, brought a smile to his face but not hers.

Three days later, Emma was showing Mary round the house in Durres, the operations room of which was already up and running under Mike's direction. Out of deference, Emma grudgingly surrendered the room with a view to her new boss.

****

It was Friday in London and there was widespread relief at the arrival of the weekend. Everard and Randell beat the rush-hour traffic and had a good run to Norfolk. A dinner party was planned for that evening and Penny had invited her parents, John and Hazel Pelham and James and Judy Wadsworth – all of whom had accepted the invitation to stay overnight. Randell was on duty to receive and brief personal protection teams as usual and couldn't help noticing the attractive blonde stepping out to open the rear passenger door for James Wadsworth – whose wife was travelling separately with the Brigstocks.

Once the Everards had greeted their guests and shown them to their rooms, Randell took charge of the protection officers, delivered the standard security briefing and walked them through the house and grounds. Introducing himself to the blonde, he said, "Hello, you aren't the Chief of Staff's regular driver are you?"

"It's Hannah," she replied. "I'm on loan from the Branch and will be with him until the security alert state reverts. Nice place. How long have you been with 'C'?"

Randall smiled, "Coming up eight years," he said. "Do you live in Town or commute?"

Hannah, still taking in the big house and lovely gardens said, "I've got a place in Battersea, what about you?"

"I live further up the river – Wandsworth. Crazy hours so I find living on my own works best.

She then turned to look at him directly, "Me too," she said, "perhaps we should meet up some time."

Randell, holding her gaze, said, "Give me your phone number, Hannah and I'll make sure we do."

She reached into her pocket and handed over a business card. "That'll be good then," she said, grinning.

****

Hugh Everard always enjoyed having guests to stay and liked nothing better than sitting at dinner in the company of interesting people. Hazel Pelham was in lively form and, as he remembered, possessed a wicked sense of humour. Even his mother-in-law was getting into the swing of things as the claret flowed. Penny was engrossed in conversation with John Pelham who, earlier that day – which James Wadsworth already knew – had resigned as Foreign Secretary. It had been mentioned quietly to Everard before they went in to dinner. Interestingly, Penny's father was already aware and tipped Penny off when he arrived.

As Hazel sought to explain to Everard, her husband was far from fully recovered – not physically but mentally and emotionally, "John resigned this morning," she said to him in whispered tones, "and I couldn't be more pleased. He needs his life back. It hasn't been easy, Hugh. At times it's like having a different man in the house."

Everard, professing not to know about the resignation said, "Not really a surprise Hazel, I cannot begin to imagine the ordeal he went through."

Penny's radar was in full *"lock-on"* mode to the conversation at the other end of the table. She still wasn't sure about Hazel; far too attractive, vivacious and not shy in sharing her opinion. "So John," she said turning to her right, "do you plan to remain a Member of Parliament or are you thinking of leaving politics altogether?"

Admiring the silver military figurine lit by candlelight on the polished oak table in front of him he replied, "Not sure to be honest, Penny: I need time to think. What I will tell you is that whatever I end up doing, I intend to add whatever support I can to those combatting human trafficking." Penny noticed her father and James Wadsworth were following the conversation very closely. There was no mistaking his *"thousand-yard stare"*.

26

O N THE IDYLLIC island of Corfu, Guzim and Bremner were relaxing on the patio under an expansive sun awning fashioned to replicate a sail. A cooling breeze rustled through the stand of pines. The view was absorbing: a major distraction for both of them. Privately, being uncomfortably close to the site of the bombing, Bremner was finding it difficult not telegraphing his emotions.

On arrival at the villa and receiving an effusive greeting and prolonged hug from his host, his eye had been drawn to the frighteningly large dog staring up at him.

"Ah," said Guzim, "This is Bujar, he came with the house. The previous owner died so I took him on."

Bremner stepped forward, squatted down, and offered his hand for the dog to sniff. "He's a mastiff isn't he?" he said. "I know about these amazing creatures, one of my relations used to breed them; fabulous dogs, amazing history. They allegedly date back to Babylonia in 2000 BC. Phoenician traders are said to have introduced them to Britain in Roman times, but they were, like other breeds, employed for dreadful purposes – mainly put to fighting bears, wolves, badgers and other dogs."

Both men looked down at the hazel brown eyes, fawn colouring and black muzzle, nose and ears. Bujar slumped down on the tiled floor and rested his heavy neck and broad, muscular shoulders. "Loyal, intelligent gentle giants, my aunt used to say, undemanding and incredibly protective."

Reaching down to stroke the dog, Guzim said, "He

335

seems to have accepted me. Matter of fact, he's started sleeping in my bedroom for some reason. Farts quite a lot, but nobody's perfect. Anyway, it's good to see you Callum – my housekeeper will show you to your room."

Ceiling fans turned slowly keeping the air circulating through the villa. Unsure quite what to expect, Bremner was taken aback by the magnificent panoramic view facing him through the floor to ceiling glass. Not for the first time with Guzim Shala, he was experiencing first-hand a degree of luxury of which most could only dream. Spacious, private, quiet and secure, he quickly saw the property's attraction. It offered everything the old man needed and, as far as he could determine, was a fortress.

Guzim did not jumped straight into a conversation about the future business partnership, preferring to listen to Bremner recount his holiday adventures in Scotland – which he did but naturally omitting any mention of a vivacious blonde with green eyes. The setting was conducive to reflection: Guzim gave the impression of having a lot on in his mind. It would be interesting to see whether he was prepared to unburden himself to his new ex-con Scottish business associate.

Fairly certain the emotive subject of Erjon would arise at some point – Guzim having already briefly mentioned his younger brother's unexplained murder in Barbados – Bremner would be fascinated to see whether the subject came up again. Hitherto, it had all seemed a bit matter-of-fact: the old man's conversation indicated no apparent signs of regret or, for that matter, remorse. It was different with Saban: memories too vivid, too recent.

The housekeeper appeared and whispered in Guzim's ear, who then excused himself to take a telephone call – Bujar trotting along behind him. Returning five minutes later, Guzim slumped back into his seat – ashen. "For the love of God…. I despair."

"What's happened?"

"The legacy of my irresponsible brother continues to threaten the good name of my family. I learned some days ago that those responsible for the failed kidnapping of the British politician are back again and seeking revenge. Money is changing hands for information. Big money. That call was to tell me that one of our associates in Montenegro has been tortured and killed."

Bremner watched the old man without interrupting and knew more was about to follow.

"It has to be assumed that he talked," Guzim continued. "And, if so, I and my colleagues are now in considerable danger. These foreigners are ruthless – Chechens most likely, acting on behalf of others. You are safe here for now but should return to London within the next few days. Things are going to turn nasty."

Bremner nodded slowly and said, "Why do you choose to stay?"

Guzim smiled, "Because, Callum, this is now my home; my only family are here. Besides," he said with undisguised menace, "I don't take kindly to being threatened… by anyone." After a pause he continued, "We can discuss my business affairs over dinner."

Before going to bed, Bremner sent a short text to the number in Monaco. It was automatically patched through to Mary Stewart in Durres and, at the same time, Brian Finlay in London. The text simply said: *"Staying with a friend in Corfu – should be home by the end of the week. So glad I didn't go to Montenegro – much quieter here. Trouble with my phone – working again now, thank goodness."* Just after ten o'clock that evening, Guzim also received a coded text – this one from the Chairman requesting his presence at a meeting the next day: *"usual time, usual place."*

****

Mike and his team were monitoring Albanian police and

border control radio networks. US national assets were doing the same and information was being shared over dedicated secure links. An increased threat assessment for the US Embassy in Tirana and neighbouring national capitals hastened a decision to forward base a US special force component at the former NATO facility at Pristina Airport in Kosovo, complete with a tailored air package of specialist fixed and rotary wing aircraft, and drones. Liaison teams were exchanged between the UK and US SF command cells – a well-established arrangement.

As far as Washington was concerned, the operation fell neatly under the *"Global War on Terror"* remit – a proactive strategy which ruthlessly pursued and dealt with threats to the US. Predicated on the notion that it was better to fight on someone else's territory rather than at home, and to strike before being struck, it implicitly assumed a right to act unilaterally and, when necessary, employing lethal force. Technology and precision played a big part. It was all about finding and exploiting information for competitive advantage. The so-called *"ungoverned spaces"* were the modern equivalent of gladiatorial arenas but on a much larger and more sophisticated scale. There were few rules and almost unlimited scope to experiment with new technologies, techniques and tactics. But as always, it ultimately came down to the rather trite but politically expedient phrase, *"boots on the ground"*.

****

Guzim and his security minders left the villa after breakfast for the meeting in Tirana. He and Bremner briefly touched on the issue of future business collaboration at dinner the night before but without reaching any firm conclusions. Very much exploratory, Bremner nonetheless judged it inappropriate to introduce *"conditions"*. They agreed to talk more before he returned to London.

The ferry to the mainland was running late. Guzim was

becoming irritated. His driver checked with the ticket office and reported back that the returning ferry was experiencing a technical problem – hence the delayed departure. The problem was expected to be resolved within forty-five minutes, he said.

On hearing this unwelcome news – he hated being late for anything – Guzim fired off a text to the Chairman, apologising in advance for his delayed arrival. Insofar as he was aware, most of his fellow Council members knew about his place in Corfu but not exactly where it was. For the time being, he intended keeping it that way.

At the Chairman's picturesque residence outside a small village in the hills to the north west of Tirana, a two-vehicle convoy – including four armed bodyguards – was ready for departure and, after a brief radio check, they headed out through the electrified gates. The road leading down the hill was well surfaced but steep, twisty and narrow. Travelling in the back of the rear vehicle, the Chairman was deep in conversation with his principal adviser – what Italians would term, *"consigliere"*. "The killing of our former colleague in Montenegro was not of my doing," he said. "The bastards got to him first."

"And they now have the initiative?"

"Correct. What I don't know is what they got from him before he died. We must revisit our strategy as a matter of urgency: everyone will have to upgrade their personal protection arrangements."

"Understood."

Looking out of the window and pointing he said, "Is that not magnificent? I never tire of the view." His own olive grove was coming along nicely and would soon be ready for harvesting – something he would never live to see.

As the front car slowly exited from a bend it braked hard to avoid hitting a logging truck half blocking the road.

At the same time, it was struck by a shoulder-fired rocket from above. The violent explosion was deafening, stopping it dead in its tracks and skewing it sideways. A second strike twisted it further to the right and ignited the fuel tank, sending tremors through the road. Such was the speed at which it all happened, the driver of the second car was caught off guard and, too hastily, jammed on the brakes.

The heavy vehicle slewed towards the edge of the road, the only token protection being a low concrete wall. A further rocket then ripped into it with such force that it was knocked sideways over the barrier into the void – freefalling to the valley below… bouncing several times on the way before eventually bursting into flames at the base of the cliff. The sole survivor from the front vehicle threw himself onto the road and was promptly shot.

Hooded figures moved cautiously down from the hillside above the road and, tearing open the mangled doors of the wrecked vehicle, put two bullets into each of the inert occupants. A bomb was then attached to the underside of the car and the vacant logging truck. Fifty metres further down the hill, once his companions had jogged past, a hooded figure riding as passenger on one of the three motorbikes turned round and initiated the bombs causing both vehicles to explode.

****

Still some distance from Vlores, Guzim took an anxious phone call from one of his fellow Council members. The Chairman had not arrived and, for whatever reason, was unreachable. Same with his security team. Everyone was naturally concerned. It was highly irregular and distinctly ominous.

Gathering his thoughts, Guzim then said, "We can't take any chances. Tell all those at the restaurant to leave immediately. I will send an alternative location by text within the next thirty minutes." As a precaution, he added, "All vehicles should be double-checked for tracking and explosive devices. Oh, and tell them to turn off all phones and only turn them back on in order to check for messages every hour, on the hour – no more than two minutes."

After making a quick phone call, he sent a text with the new meeting place – a bar in the coastal town of Borsh, further down the coast towards the Greek border and owned by a family friend. It was not long before commercial radio stations broke the news of a serious incident resulting in the death of several people in the hills north of Tirana. The word used was *"carnage"*.

The collective mood amongst Council members was one of intense anger when they met two hours later in a back room of the bar in Borsh. No one needed further proof that their esteemed and much liked Chairman was dead. It was quickly acknowledged that a successor should be appointed without delay and, the only other credible candidate being well into his nineties, Guzim was unanimously voted in. Excusing himself for a moment to get some fresh air and muster his thoughts, he walked outside and sat down at a vacant table. Security staff looked on, plainly distressed and understandably nervous. Word had plainly reached them that Guzim Shala was now the main man and there was a respectful nodding of heads.

Self-evidently, his immediate priority as new Chairman was to re-establish some sort of order and, in so doing, offer reassurance. These were powerful men with, should they so decide, the means and resources to wreak havoc. Maintaining collective discipline was essential – no free-styling. Processing the key factors as he lit a cigarette, the next few hours and days would test him. The promotion was not of his choosing, but so be it.

"My friends," he said, returning to the room and calling the meeting to order. "Like you, this was obviously no accident and I fear that our Chairman has been assassinated. Be in no doubt that we shall avenge his killing and those responsible will regret ever setting foot in our country." After pausing for dramatic effect, he said, "I accept the nomination as Chair until such time as we have restored some semblance of order. Be in no doubt, every one of us and our families are in danger. You will, I'm sure, already be thinking about relocating loved ones to a safe place at the earliest opportunity and, at the same time, make appropriate arrangements for tightening your own security. The immediate priority is unchanged: namely, to mobilize our collective resources, locate those responsible by all means at our disposal and then summarily deal with them."

"How should we communicate?" someone asked.

"I strongly advise you to restrict use of all electronic devices other than burner phones and even then, use them sparingly. I propose we meet again – in this location – at the same time in two days. Are there any questions?"

The mood had demonstrably improved; he was reassured to see there were no sideways glances, shaking of heads or dissenting voices. He was now leader and they the followers. "Are we agreed?" he asked, looking at each of them.

"Yes," they said, in turn.

"Very well – I will see you here in two days. Go with care."

****

Mary and Emma had already heard about the incident north of Tirana, but its significance didn't register until Mike showed them a transcript of some email exchanges within the National Police Force. "The victim," he said, "is a known and prominent figure in the Albanian mafia. Initial investigation at the site bears all the hallmarks of a professional assassination. Expended RPG 7 launchers and a proliferation of 7.62-millimetre bullet strikes – possibly from AK 47 assault rifles – point towards a well organised, well equipped and highly capable group."

"In other words, Chechens." Mary said.

"Yes, it looks that way," Ben replied. "The choice of ambush site was text book: the outcome never in doubt. Scorch marks on the road indicate use of motorbikes. Bodies are being recovered from a wrecked four by four in the valley bottom."

"Presumably they can't rule out some sort of inter-factional motive – a revenge killing?" Emma asked.

"True, but the police are saying it looks suspiciously like Chechens," Mike replied.

"I've heard that more US national space-based intelligence assets are being brought into play and there's talk about use of drones," Ben said, "but that involves a conversation with the Albanians."

****

Mike's team were working flat out monitoring national networks. Mary called Finlay on the secure link and Hugh Everard listened in.

"Not much to add to the report I forwarded earlier," she began, "the military guys here are comparing analysis with US counterparts. The threat assessment still has the US and our embassy as prime targets. Nothing has been heard from Bremner, other than he's in Corfu."

"Do we know where?"

"Yes, he's used his phone. We're looking at contingencies in case we need to pull him out in a hurry."

"Have you got a direct link to him?"

"I have," she replied, "but it's insecure."

Looking across at Everard and receiving a nod, Finlay said, "We think you should go ahead and use that means to contact him, Mary."

"Understood," she replied.

"On other stuff," Finlay continued, "the thinking here is that, if the option arises, any military action should be left to our US friends. It reduces political risk for Number Ten for a start, and also simplifies coordination and execution."

"I quite see that. It certainly makes things easier for a single nation to handle apologies after the event and patch up any bruised international relationships."

"Agreed," said Finlay. "Our SF guys won't like it but the PM has given instructions. It's the most pragmatic way forward."

****

After a thoroughly idle day – much of it spent relaxing in the pool staring out across the bay – Bremner was blissfully unaware of the chaos unleashed further north. Neither, until his host returned to the villa that evening, did he have any idea of Guzim's changed circumstances and elevation to lead the mafia Council. The old man was definitely looking his age but, ever resilient, and despite a long and challenging day, he sounded remarkably upbeat. Bujar lay at his feet and Bremner sensed there was about to be some plain speaking. Several glasses of wine later, Bremner having abandoned his teetotal regime, Guzim started to open up.

"Callum, as I'm sure you have worked out, what I do for a living spans both sides of the law – at home and abroad. It's always been that way and," he said laughing, "is what got me banged up for so long."

"Anyway," he continued, "over the years, my brothers and I developed a broad portfolio of financial interests. Is this a surprise to you?"

"Not really."

"Well, as you also know – and for reasons we shall never fully understand – Erjon elected to embark on a string of illegal activities of which he knew I profoundly disapproved – not to mention his direct involvement in funding terrorist organisations."

"You had no idea what he was doing?"

"No, I did not, and Saban – God bless him – wasn't the sharpest note on the piano. I tell you candidly, Erjon lost my respect, and I'm also fairly sure he was involved in Saban's murder."

Bremner chose not to interrupt.

"I do not mourn him; indeed, his death was, if anything a blessing from the standpoint of my family. He was a disgrace and I disown his memory."

Genuinely surprised by what he was hearing and the dispassionate way it was being said, Bremner noted that Guzim made no mention of arranging his brother's death. "So much for that," the old man said as he reached for his glass and took a long drink. "Now, as you either do or do not know, this morning there was an unprovoked attack on some of my associates, not far from Tirana. A very close friend whom I had arranged to meet was brutally murdered together with five of his fellow countrymen. This, I have reason to believe, relates directly to the failed kidnapping of the English politician. You know all about that."

Bremner was intrigued that the old man was opening up to quite such an extent and wished he'd been able to record it.

"My concern," Guzim continued, stroking Bujar's ear as he spoke, "is that the perpetrators of this outrage are planning further attacks. We believe them to be outsiders – paid assassins. The name *'Chechen'* is being bandied about. My associates think it was they, the Chechens, who abducted Pelham. Having badly messed it up, they're back and bent on revenge.

"Where are they getting this information from?"

"We understand that large sums of money are being offered. Do you see why I'm worried?"

"Yes, I do. What's being done about it?"

"I've been authorised to step in for our departed Council Chairman and will lead the response on behalf of the families." After recharging their glasses, the Albanian continued. "Callum, this is not your fight but, if you're receptive to the idea, I would value your support. That said, I shall quite understand if you prefer to go back to London until such time as this wretched business is resolved."

Bremner, completely wrong-footed, knew an answer was expected. "Guzim," he said, "I stand ready to help in any way you require providing, that is, I do not have to do any killing. I would not survive prison again."

At this Guzim smiled, got up from his chair and hugged Bremner. Bujar stood up, too. "My friend," he said, "I'm grateful and will inform the Council and close associates accordingly. There is precedent for such things. In our language we have a word, "*besa*" – trust. They are sworn to me and I am placing my trust in you. I will do what I can to find a way round the language issue – it's important you are able to follow the discussions. Are you comfortable with that and are we agreed?"

"Yes."

"I ask one thing," Guzim said as he moved to a side cupboard, taking out a polished mahogany box and setting it down on the table. "I want you carry this while we're together here. I assume you know how to use a handgun?"

"I do," Bremner said, looking at the box containing a beautifully crafted snub-nosed .38 calibre revolver with accompanying silencer, soft leather shoulder holster, box of ammunition and cleaning kit. Everything looked brand new.

Before retiring to bed, Bremner said he intended taking Bujar for a long walk in the morning at which, surprisingly, since it didn't understand English, the dog's ears pricked up. Back in his room, he sent a text to Monaco asking whether anyone was *"coming my way"* and, if so, he would love to *"meet-up for a chat."* The enormity of his position had markedly just intensified. Things were getting complicated and he needed to stay focused and alert.

****

Emma and Mary Stewart read the text in the Ops Room. "Bremner's out here, isn't he?" Emma asked, clearly surprised.

"Yes he is, he arrived a few days ago and is staying with Shala in Corfu. We think he's bought a property there."

Emma pulled out a map of the island and stuck her finger on Ypsos. "Just before the bombing I inadvertently bumped into Callum in a café on the waterfront – right there," she said. "Couldn't we propose it as a venue?"

"Yes, Emma, we can certainly do that… good idea," Mary said. "Now, since the Albanian knows your face, you won't be coming. I'll go with Mike."

Masking her disappointment but fully understanding the reasoning, Emma started drafting a text.

****

Just before eleven o'clock next day, Mary was sitting at the café in Ypsos: same table, facing the same direction Emma had used just before the fateful bombing. The fishing quay was noisy – traders haggling animatedly over prices. Tourists watched the fun: as did expectant gulls anticipating a snack. It was a beautiful morning, sensible folk wearing hats to seek protection from the sun. She was glad she'd eventually decided to wear the cotton blouse and loose, full-length skirt. At the agreed time, a voice behind her said, "Nice place, but not as nice as Kent – don't look round."

Pretending to be reading a newspaper, Bremner said, "The Chechens have put the fear of God into Shala's lot.

347

They're mobilizing and determined to take them on. Big money's being offered by both sides for information. It was one of their senior guys who got topped yesterday. My man has been promoted and is calling the shots. Are you following…?"

"Yep."

"I've signed up for his team but, like you said, as a non-combatant. He knows his younger brother was murdered in Barbados but isn't putting his hand up to it. Anything we can share about the bad guys would be welcome. Sorry… got to dash."

Mary had continued to eat the delicious croissant as Bremner talked and didn't look round when he left. Only uttering the one acknowledgement, seen the waiter walk past with a dog bowl full of water, followed shortly after by some loud slurping sounds. On return to the house and having back-briefed Emma – who knew better than to press for details about Bremner – she dispatched a report to Brian Finlay.

****

Everard and Finlay were sitting in the window of a deserted café on London's Pall Mall having enjoyed a substantial breakfast. Randell was three tables away finishing his and facing the door. Watching the commuters march past, heads bowed and faces fixated on tiny screens, Everard reflected on the fact that Penny was back from France and in gastronomic vigilante mode. Friday night interrogations were becoming far-too-frequent. Subtle hints at *"body shaming"* were water off a duck's back to her. He needed to take more exercise, she said, casting a fly-rod and rowing his boat on the lake was not, in her ladyship's opinion, sufficient. "Why can't you go running like Randell?" she'd said. One day he would summon up the courage to reply along the lines that he was a grandfather, on the cusp of retirement and had never served in the

Royal Marines.

Walking through St James's Park, drawing heavily on Mary's report Finlay summarised the situation in Albania.

"I want to make sure I've got this right, Brian. We know where Shala's place is in Corfu as a consequence of Bremner's iPhone. Insofar as we know, the old man isn't putting his hand up to placing the contract on Erjon?"

"That's right. He's not admitting to it but Bremner's convinced that he did."

"Okay," Everard said, thinking about a second expresso. "Not sure we care much… the world is a better place without the wretched man."

"Are we still thinking," Finlay said, "about sharing any information on the Chechens with Shala and his mafia thugs?"

Everard took a long time to answer. "If we subscribe to the *'my enemy's enemy is my friend'* doctrine," he began, "the question answers itself, Brian. There is clear attraction in bad guys knocking chunks out of other bad guys rather than us or our American pals having to do it. If the Chechens miscalculate and target British interests – the rules change; same for our US partners – an attack against one is taken to be an attack against us both and so forth."

Finlay could tell that Everard was warming to his theme and chose not to interrupt.

"I can't see any advantage in us picking a fight with the Chechens. It plays into Russia's hands for a start. No, I think we should let the Albanians sort it out. The interesting question is who would handle it best – Albanian national agencies or Shala and his pals?"

"What about hedging our bets and running on parallel tracks?"

"Yes, that would work. We'll need to ensure the sequencing is right. Which suggests to me that we tip the wink to our mafia chums first – give them a head start and then we warn off the government. What do you think?"

Finlay, now regretting giving up smoking cigars, said, "I definitely don't think it's worth risking the lives of any of our SF guys – although, as you say, they would undoubtedly argue the point. It also circumvents the risk of a leak from the government in Tirana. So, yes – I think there should be discreet information-sharing – if and when Chechen locations and/or intentions become known. My only other thought is that we ought sensibly to clear lines with US colleagues beforehand."

As they approached where Randell was parked, Everard said, "Agreed – I'll speak to the cousins in Washington and perhaps you could explain the plan to Mary. You might also ask for her ideas on how any information-sharing should be handled. I have a view on that, but I want to hear what she thinks first."

Just at that moment Finlay's phone rang. After a couple of minutes chatting, he turned back to Everard. "That was Mary, there's been an explosion at the Koplik police station – up north near the border with Montenegro – four reported dead and the building decimated according to information from Mike. Same policemen who claimed credit for John Pelham's release. Talk about a payback. These Chechens don't hang about, do they."

Everard could visualise the national outrage in Tirana and, by implication, the increased risk to the UK and US diplomatic personnel in the city.

"I said I'd call back in an hour or two," Brian said. "This business is turning nastier by the minute."

Everard went directly to the Foreign Office to brief the newly installed Foreign Secretary and, after that, the Security Service's Director General. His last office call was with James Wadsworth in Downing Street – who suggested he ought to have a word with the PM. Having run it past them, nobody questioned the rationale of leaving the Albanians to manage the problem.

Finlay called Everard when he returned to office. "Mary thinks that if and when reliable information becomes available, we ought to set up another face-to-face meeting with Shala."

"That makes sense."

"However," Brian said, "she insists on handling it personally rather than use Ben or Emma to interpret."

"Can't see Emma being happy with that, but it's the right call."

****

Back in his office, Finlay was looking at a report on his computer screen. It was from the Technical Department and listed the movements of a covert vehicle tracker. What made it especially interesting was that it related to Bremner's Discovery which, mysteriously, had somehow moved from Madrid to the North of Scotland and then, some days later, travelled to Inverness Airport and back north again to a different location.

He then remembered having asked the technical guys to discreetly tag the vehicle before Bremner took it to Spain. An amazingly clever bit of kit, the beacon stayed dormant until activating automatically on a pre-set schedule every forty-eight hours. He had been assured it was impossible to detect electronically unless in activation mode. It was accepted tradecraft that being unaware that one's vehicle had an installed tracking device made it much easier to play it straight if stopped. Although unfashionable, the same logic applied for personal implanted beacons – something most practitioners thought too risky these days. Finlay had a shrewd idea how the vehicle got to Scotland but decided to keep his suspicions to himself.

****

Mike and his team were busily transcribing intercepts from rapidly over-heating national police networks seeking to make sense of the tragedy in Koplik. Media speculation was out of control and, for lack of suspects, fingers were being pointed at organised crime.

Guzim was giving Bremner a running commentary as they watched the news on television at the villa. "I feared it would only be a matter of time," he remarked.

"How will the police react?"

"They'll put the area into immediate lockdown – at least for a couple of days. I'll be surprised if it doesn't extend wider."

"Do they know what caused the explosion?" Bremner asked.

"Conflicting opinions on that. Some are saying gas explosion, others a bomb. This will all be discussed tomorrow at a meeting with my associates – to which, by the way – I would like you to accompany me. Its odds-on the police will already have spoken to several of those you'll be meeting."

****

Marjorie told Everard that a Mr Carlebach was keen to see him – *"usual spot"* she'd added. The Israeli was circling the lake in Regent's Park when Everard caught up with him.

"Our Pakistani friend has been in touch," he said.

"That was quick."

"Yes, but he knows that time is not on our side. Anyway, he says there are two groups involved. One is believed to be exclusively Chechen – hired to carry out action on the ground."

"Who are they working for?"

"Tel Aviv thinks Islamic State."

"Are they already in Albania?"

"Apparently so," Carlebach replied. "Their exact

location is unknown but possibly near Kukes on the road to Kosovo."

"What do we know about the second group?"

"Of similar size and includes representatives of their employers – also Muslim."

"And do we know where they are?" Everard asked.

"Thought to be operating from a basecamp just across the Albania/Kosovo Border – south west of Prizren. The geographic proximity is deliberate in order to simplify logistic support."

"Do we know how they got there?"

"Usmani has said that the Chechens crossed the Black Sea by tanker from Sochi to Istanbul, and then overland by truck through Greece and Macedonia. He has no information on the others. Those financing the operation are reported to be pleased with what has been accomplished to date and eagerly await the final outcome."

Staring out across the park, Everard said, "That is incredibly helpful. I assume it's been fully shared with our American friends?"

The Israeli slowly nodded and said, "It has and, which is really significant, US political approval has already been given for pre-emptive action when the Kosovo-based cell is found but not, as yet, for the other cell inside Albania."

And with that the two men shook hands and went their separate ways.

****

Mary Stewart received a summary of the Israeli's information an hour after Everard got back to the office. Everard gave direction that the intelligence was to be shared with Guzim Shala as soon as soon as possible. She, Emma and Mike immediately started work on a plan.

"Remember," said Emma, "unless he's changed his telephone, I still have Guzim's phone number. Why don't we make it easy for him and suggest another face-to-face meeting – maybe somewhere like the Corfu ferry terminal – mainland side?"

"It would definitely send a message that we know where he's hanging out." Mike said.

"Besides," Emma added, "even though he wants to kill me, he knows I delivered last time."

"Don't forget we've got the directional microphones and long-range camera kit in the van," Mike added.

"Okay," Mary said, "that's what we'll do."

****

Guzim and Bremner were chatting by the pool when Emma's call came through. Bujar sat up as Guzim answered. Speaking in fluent Albanian she said, "Mr Shala, I'm the woman you met in a park some months ago. Do you remember?"

Bremner and Bujar both watched Shala visibly stiffen and then get to his feet and begin pacing. "Yes – I was rather hoping not to hear from you again – in fact, I seem to recall that was the agreement."

Emma, trying to control her voice, said "You are quite right Mr Shala and this will be the exception because what I have to tell you I have no doubt you will wish to hear."

Noticeably regaining control, Guzim said, "What?"

Standing in the Ops Room with one of Mike's team translating for Mary on the extension, she continued, "I'm going to share some information but, because of its sensitivity, I will only do it face-to-face."

Guzim looked across at Bremner before replying. "Okay," he said. "When and where?"

On completion of the call Guzim recounted what had been said – agreeing to meet the blonde woman at eight o'clock the next day at the Mainland Ferry Terminal. It would still allow them sufficient time to make the meeting further up the coast.

It was an early start from Durres. They travelled south in two vehicles, Emma's dilapidated saloon and the team's fully kitted-out, air-conditioned van. Mary had bowed to Emma's insistence that she needed to be there to handle any translating. Arriving in plenty of time to recce the optimum spot for photo and audio coverage, they managed to find coffee and cake in a small café by the ticket office.

The working assumption was that Shala would remember very clearly seeing red dots at his feet in their previous encounter and therefore have no reason to think the security arrangements would be any less thorough. Mike had brought two of the infra-red laser torches just in case he needed convincing. In passing, he drew Mary's attention to the security video cameras mounted randomly on rusting poles around the car park. "There will be recorders for those cameras," he said. "It might be something to think about later."

A white Toyota Land Cruiser with darkened rear windows drove off the ferry ramp just before eight o'clock, stopping short of where Emma and Mary stood at the edge of the car park directly below an area of woodland.

Cars were beginning to queue for the trip across to the island. It was going to be a very warm day and, unhelpfully, a conspicuous absence of wind. The Toyota drew to a halt and Guzim and Bremner climbed out. The driver walked to the rear of the vehicle and let out a very large dog on a lead which, after sniffing the air, cocked its leg and in a large cloud of steam relieved itself over a rear wheel. Stopping ten feet from Emma and Mary, facing the sun, Guzim said in Albanian, "So, what is it you have to tell me?"

"Mr Shala," Mary said in English, "Last time it was you who gave us information. We will now return the favour."

Shala was clearly surprised that it wasn't the blonde bitch speaking, and also that the conversation was in English, "Go on, I'm listening," he said.

"I've come to tell you where you can find those who inflicted the recent atrocities on your fellow countrymen. But, before we get to that, you need to know that more operations are imminent which, unless stopped, will result in further indiscriminate loss of life. Time is of the essence."

Guzim, squinting in the bright light despite wearing sunglasses said, "And where are these people?"

"Our understanding is that they are operating in a six-man group somewhere in the vicinity of Kukes."

"Is that the best you can do?"

Ignoring his rudeness, she said, "I should also tell you that this information will be handed to the Albanian authorities in thirty-six hours' time. Is that clear Mr Shala?"

Struggling to hide his frustration, and having looked at Bremner, Guzim said, "Yes, Kukes," and promptly walked back to the Toyota.

Emma glanced across at Bremner – also wearing sunglasses and keeping his hands by his sides – without any sign of recognition or emotion. He, too, turned and walked back to the vehicle which, after the ridiculously large dog had climbed in, promptly drove away.

"Did you get all that Mike?" Emma asked into her concealed radio.

"We did – thank you."

"We all need another coffee," Mary said and, heading to the café, tapped out a short text to Finlay: *"message passed – transcript follows".*

****

Guzim was on his phone before the Land Cruiser had exited the terminal car park. The only word Bremner understood was *"Kukes".* He made at least five calls, seemingly repeating the same message every time. Eventually relaxing back in his seat. "Brits," he said, "I might have known."

"Not much doubt about that," Bremner said.

"The bit I don't quite get is them not wanting anything in return. Nothing's for free is it?"

"The one doing the talking was sending a very clear message emphasising the urgency, wasn't she?" Bremner said.

"You mean about sharing the information with the Albanian authorities?"

"Yes, it sounded like a veiled threat. You know, get a move on or else." Bremner had anticipated the purpose of the meeting but was not expecting to see Emma and certainly not Mary. It unnerved him; they were dealing with dangerous people and he worried about them being exposed to such risk. He was then brought back to the present by Bujar licking his neck.

It didn't take long to reach the bar on the Borsh waterfront. Guzim led the way through to the backroom. The other Council members were standing around drinking coffee and quietly chatting. The place was already full of cigarette smoke. Greetings, handshakes and hugs were exchanged. Guzim introduced Bremner having seemingly forewarned of his attendance. As Bremner took a seat at the back of the room, another man sat down next to him.

"Hi, I'm Marku… Callum isn't it?" he said in perfect English, "Marku Jashari. Mr Shala has asked me to act as your translator – that's my father at the end of the table," he said pointing towards an elderly and distinguished looking man sitting next to Guzim. They shook hands.

Dressed in an expensive suit, his new companion was of similar age and build. A handsome man with dark hair

357

and piercing blue eyes, he seemed relaxed and keen to make Bremner feel welcome. Marku's whispered translation was immaculate and spoken with a slight American accent which sounded to Bremner like New England: possibly Boston.

Guzim called the meeting to order. "Gentlemen, we were all outraged at the savage killings in Koplic. Albanians killing policemen is one thing but outsiders doing it is wholly unacceptable." After pausing for the ripple of laughter to subside he continued. "I said to you we would avenge the murder of our Chairman and we shall." After looking at each of the men in turn, "It has come to my notice that these Chechen animals are holed-up in the vicinity of Kukes. There are six of them."

"How reliable is your information and where did you get it?

"I judge the information to be reliable and, frankly, I prefer to keep my sources private."

"It shouldn't be difficult to find these dogs," Marku's father said, prompting a lot of nodding around the table.

"I want them dealt with," Guzim continued. "Ideally, we should keep one alive. These animals not only murdered policeman – which is a major inconvenience and complicates our business interests – they almost certainly killed our chairman. Are there any questions?"

Marku's father again spoke. "We have what we need in terms of weapons and, with your agreement, Chairman, my family will coordinate the search. If we need more men, we'll ask."

"That is agreed." Guzim said. "You will have been told that our associate in Montenegro – also murdered by the Chechens – is to be buried within the next day or two. I understand it will be just across the Border near Podgorica. If you all agree, I will attend the funeral to represent the Council."

No one disagreed and, there being no other business, the bar owner was summoned and lunch served – at which point Bremner and Marku – still in the role of personal translator – joined the big table. In keeping with habit, everyone was drinking alcohol. At the end of lunch Marku handed over a business card. "Here's my private number and please don't hesitate to call me if I can help with anything." They shook hands and Bremner walked over to Guzim. Having discussed it before leaving the villa and packed overnight bags in anticipation, they were then driven to a hotel in Tirana.

"Marku Jashari seems like a nice guy," Bremner said as they approached the city outskirts. "Couldn't have been more helpful."

"Yes," said Guzim, "I have no doubt he will succeed to the Chairmanship one day. He has a good reputation."

"For what?" Bremner asked as Bujar started licking his neck again.

"The Jashari's are an old and highly respected family. His grandfather was a previous Chairman. The boy was schooled abroad and retains strong links in Italy and with our people in America where, if I remember, he studied economics and then went to business school. When he was young his father used to bring him to London to stay with me – that of course was before I was detained at Her Majesty's pleasure."

"Was Erjon around at the time?"

Managing a wry smile, Guzim said, "They used to see one another sometimes but never became close friends – I think he was wary of Marku; I actually think he was frightened of him. His father says he's being assigned much broader responsibilities: you know, groomed for higher things."

"Do you think that will happen? Bremer asked.

"What you see is not necessarily what you get with

Marku Jashari. There is a hard edge to him – no question about that – I heard that he is not afraid to impose his will. He commands loyalty. Opinion within the Council is that he can be trusted and, for personal reasons that I'll explain later, I certainly hope so."

****

Emma drove Mary back to Durres, who for much of the time, seemed content gazing at the passing countryside as they sped along the coast road. "I can think of worse places to live," she said, "and it beats London."

They both felt the meeting went okay and were looking forward to seeing and hearing what Mike and his team had captured on tape – the product of which would be forwarded to London digitally before the end of the day. Emma had been nervous about seeing Bremner. Thankfully, Mary appeared not to have noticed her anxiety and taken the meeting in her stride. Emma thought she handled the old man brilliantly and showed no trace of nerves whatsoever.

"He frightens me," Emma said without taking her eyes off the road.

"Yes, the contempt was unmistakable wasn't it – goodness knows how Bremner manages to deal with him. The man is wickedness personified."

"Do you mind if I ask you a sensitive question, Mary?"

"That rather depends on what it is."

"It's about Bremner."

"What about him?"

"Do you know who he is?"

"No, Emma, I don't – that sort of information is above my pay grade, and for good reason. What I will tell you is that he falls within a very small pool of special people – all different. I can't even begin to imagine what it must be like to live under alias so long. Personally," she said looking across at Emma, "I think one would need to exercise a degree of caution before embarking in a relationship with such an individual."

"What makes you say that?"

"Because, Emma, they're invariably complicated; with, how can I put it, '*issues*'."

27

GUZIM'S PHONE rang just before ten o'clock: he answered and walked out of the hotel dining room. It promised to be another scorching day, albeit with rain in the forecast.

It was Marku's father with good news. The Chechen basecamp had been found in woods north west of the town. A shepherd had reported seeing an unfamiliar vehicle accompanied by a motorcyclist on a track heading towards derelict buildings next to a disused sawmill. The word had quickly been put out to the family and the place was now under observation. "Marku has been put in charge and I will keep you informed of developments."

****

The rain arrived soon after midnight. Two hours later, dark silhouettes emerged from both sides of the track and crept towards the sawmill. Owls were calling to one another, barely audible above the downpour. The only sentry posted was found asleep against a tree and Marku cut his throat. A hand grenade was tossed into the building and quickly followed by shotgun blasts and machine gun fire. The Chechens were caught completely off guard. Those in the building died instantly from grenade fragments. Another man was found hiding under a pile of blankets in the back of the van and shot where he lay… his throat cut for good measure.

Unaffected by the driving rain, Marku tasked some of the men to check the dead while others searched the area. The four bodies were dragged into a clearing beneath some trees. Phones, weapons and documents were collected and, at his direction, all four were summarily hung by their necks. He then personally castrated each of them in turn. Photographs were taken, petrol poured over the van and set alight. The same for the motorbike found besides the derelict building. The entire event was filmed on video and, with buildings still smouldering, the attackers each shook Marku's hand and slipped away into the darkness.

Personally making the call to Guzim just before three-thirty in the morning – waking Bujar, whose illegal presence in the hotel had necessitated money changing hands. "Four dead, no casualties to any of my people," Marku said. "We've got it all on video and the bodies were strung up and castrated."

"Are you sure no others were hiding, "Guzim asked. "I'd expected there to be six of the scum?"

The answer was emphatic. "No, we did a thorough search; just four men, a van, one motorbike, prayer mats, Russian weapons – including AK 47s – and what looked like plastic explosive."

"Are you saying they had bomb-making stuff?"

"Yes," Marku replied. "We found detonators, timing devices and coloured wire."

"Tell me about the vehicle."

"The van and motorbike had Kosovo number plates. We found a book of unmarked maps in the van."

"Excellent," Guzim said and, after a brief pause, "How many prayer mats?"

"Eight."

"Are you absolutely sure of that?"

"Yes, there were eight."

"Okay," Guzim continued. "As we discussed, go ahead and make your anonymous call to the police and, after that, send your video clip to the media. Ask your father to put the word out amongst our people that, as a matter of priority, they are to look for the rest of the foreigners… maybe as many as four… possibly on motorbikes with Kosovo plates. If found, I want them alive."

"Understood."

Guzim made himself a cup of the distinctly ordinary hotel coffee and fired-off a text to the small blonde with green eyes. It simply said, *"Eight prayer mats – only four bodies?"* A reply came back soon after sunrise, *"Acknowledged."* He then called Bremner's hotel extension and said he wanted to leave early and that they would attend the funeral in Podgorica before heading back to the villa. He would update him about *"overnight developments"* on the way.

After ending the call, he packed his bag and put on a dark suit, white shirt and black tie. With a final look round the room he slipped the lead over Bujar's head and walked to the lift and, not for the first time, reflected on the wisdom of his decision to buy the place in Corfu. It was a safe choice and, as he said to his increasingly faithful hound sat patiently at his side in the lift, "Armed Chechens intent on revenge are not to be underestimated."

****

Mike's team was quickly onto the breaking story at Kukes. First reports on national police networks said it bore all the signs of a mafia reprisal killing… the castrations a dead giveaway. The area was now saturated with specialist forensic experts combing the site for clues which, on past experience, would be few and far between. Footprints on the rain-sodden ground suggested at least fifteen assailants. Four bodies, all mutilated, had been removed to the morgue in Tirana. In the absence of identity cards, passports or driving licences identification was proving difficult.

Mary had been impressed with the speed of the mafia response and decided there was nothing to be gained by following up with the police – clearly already in possession of the key facts. What troubled her most, though, was the missing Chechens – something Emma had already discussed with Ben at the Embassy where, understandably, the alert state had increased to full lockdown. Concrete blocks were positioned to screen off all entrances against the risk of vehicle-borne improvised explosive devices. The police had arranged a tight defensive perimeter. Ben said that the special forces teams were at high readiness to deploy and, in his words, *"champing at the bit"*.

"Something's not right," Mary said to Finlay on the secure phone. "The numbers don't add up."

"Why do you say that?"

"Because of the eight prayer mats found. Either some of the Chechens have gone back to Kosovo, or they're still at large in Albania."

"I'll talk to our people in Washington," he said.

****

The second important development came in a report from the special forces liaison cell co-located with the US SF Task Force. An operation had been successfully carried out against the group in Kosovo also in the early hours of the morning. The narrative, however, differed from events at the sawmill, mainly because the Americans didn't have the advantage of surprise. A series of running firefights ensued during the systematic clearance of a cellar and cave complex. Unlike their colleagues in Kukes, this group, which included two women, did not surrender their lives cheaply.

"Seven bodies in all," Finlay told Everard, "and one man taken alive."

"Chechen?"

"Well, here's the interesting thing; he was an Arab… there were several of them… he's already been whisked off to a secure US facility somewhere."

"That won't be fun."

"Nope."

"What did they find in the caves?" Everard asked.

"Much the same as at Kukes. Helpfully, they recovered laptops, mapping and two satellite phones. Here's the significant part: the target assessment is correct – the recovered maps have the locations for both the British and US Embassies in Tirana marked on them."

"Anything else I need to know?"

"The Americans found two vans but no motorbikes – probably for logistic resupply. Mary's convinced there are Chechens unaccounted for… in either Kosovo or Albania."

"What makes her think that?"

"She bases it on the numbers not squaring with the prayer mats found at the sawmill."

"Okay, what are the authorities saying in Kosovo?"

"They've agreed to keep the incident under wraps until such time as the US Task Force eventually withdraws which, for obvious reasons, won't be until all Chechens have been found."

"And they will keep their people in Kosovo?"

"That's the plan."

Like Mary and Brian, Everard was confused by the disparity in numbers. Although fairly certain he could guess the nationality of the sole prisoner now in US custody, he would await confirmation from Washington. Marjorie was asked to arrange an office call with Alon Carlebach at the Israeli Embassy who, it transpired, was also confused by the numbers and undertook to pursue it with Tel Aviv.

****

The ball was now firmly in Mary Stewart's court. Everard knew she would be keeping in close touch with Ben and, through him, the British Ambassador and special forces squadron commander co-located at the Embassy. Everyone was pretty much agreed they were confronting four – rather than two – Chechens. The working assumption was that they were holed-up somewhere in Albania rather than Kosovo. He also knew from personal experience that the SF would be lobbying hard to join the hunt. But with Albanian police rushing around the place, not all in uniform, it was not a sensible thing to do. The exception would be the two operators living in the downtown hotel. The main SF focus was on providing close protection and a quick reaction force for the Ambassador when his presence was required at the daily National Government's Crisis Committee meeting.

****

Two men faced one another in a layby at the back of a secluded beach north of Tirana. Grubby, unshaven and tired, words were unnecessary as they embraced. They were fully aware from news reports that their friends were dead. As decreed by their faith, the timing and circumstance of a person's death is known only to God. They could only pray there had been time for the others to profess their beliefs before death, thereby resting in their graves until the Day of Judgement.

It was not intended to be this way. But such is life. They drew comfort from the profound conviction that rewards awaited them in heaven. Embracing again, they mounted their motorbikes – both displaying recently stolen Albanian number plates. One headed north, the other south.

****

Guzim updated Bremner as they drove to the border near Podgorica. "The Jashari's handled it well," he said. "Marku led the attack and, in hindsight, I now understand his reasons for signposting our involvement: the castrations are a clear message." Stroking Bujar as he leaned over from the back seat, he continued, "My biggest worry is what happens next. These Chechen scum have obviously not finished what they're here for. We must be vigilant – which is why it's safer for us to be at the villa."

Approaching the church on the outskirts of the town, already deciding not to attend the over-subscribed indoor service, Guzim directed the driver to park by the cemetery's side entrance. After disembarking and stretching his legs, he and the bodyguard at his side moved forward to join the other mourners. Bremner noticed that many attendees were acknowledging Guzim's presence and showing obvious deference. The turnout was impressively large – literally hundreds of people.

Standing with Bujar and the other bodyguard by the vehicle, Bremner noted the conspicuous absence of police uniforms. Men in dark glasses stood at the perimeter wall. Amongst them, which he had not expected, was the dark-suited figure of Marku Jashari who, on spotting him, gave the briefest of nods. The Albanian was standing next to a man of similar height, busily taking photographs. Sharing remarkably close facial characteristics, they could have been brothers.

After embracing the veiled widow, Guzim was encouraged to take up a prominent position by the grave as the coffin was lowered; when his turn came, dropping-in a handful of soil. On his way back to the vehicle, he paused occasionally for a word with several individuals – some who kissed his hand. Marku waved a brief farewell as they headed back to Albania.

****

On re-joining the main road, a motorbike discreetly took station a hundred metres in rear of the Land Cruiser – tucked in behind a lorry. Remaining there until shortly before Tirana, it pulled into the side – its place taken by another motorbike. This one, also with saddlebags but having a faded red rather than black petrol tank, was ridden by a helmeted figure in blue farm worker's overalls. It followed the Land Cruiser all the way to the ferry terminal where, behind a shed, the rider ditched his overalls and bought a ticket for the next crossing.

****

Ben sat with the British Ambassador in the back of an armoured Mercedes four by four in the embassy compound. Driven by one of the contract security staff – all of whom were ex-Ghurkha soldiers from the Indian Army – his fellow escort in the passenger seat was also from Nepal and a lifelong friend. The occupants of the second vehicle – a Range Rover crewed by SF soldiers in plain clothes – contained the SF squadron commander and the Political Counsellor. On receiving the radio order *"move now"*, the two vehicles under a single police escort vehicle headed out of a side gate. The destination was the National Crisis Management Committee downtown, where a meeting was scheduled with the Minister of Interior.

****

City life in Tirana had reverted to normal after the recent spate of Chechen inspired killings and bombings. It was noisy, hot, humid and dusty. The air was cooking through lack of a breeze and tempers were fraying at the slow-moving traffic. Typical on a working day, there was a lot of shouting, mainly from market traders selling their goods. Streets thronged with people seemingly untroubled by the constant racket of car horns expressing their owner's contempt for the government's abortive efforts to deliver a functioning transport system.

Despite the best of planning intentions, the Ministry of Interior was situated within a maze of one-way streets. From an emergency services perspective, it was distinctly unhelpful when it came to responding to any sort of incident. Parked cars, wedged bumper to bumper, lined both sides of the narrow streets and caused frequent gridlock every time there was an accident, breakdown or commercial lorry unloading produce. Heavy-laden donkeys went about their business as usual, owners studiously ignoring the profanities hurled at them by fellow road users. From a security perspective, it was a nightmare.

In keeping with standard practice, the detached two-man SF team were already on the ground and in discreet radio contact with the convoy commander, weapons concealed under linen jackets. Positioned on opposite sides of the street one block away from the ministry, they looked across at each other as they awaited the convoy. Predictably, traffic was moving at a snail's pace. "Inbound," said one of them over the radio on sighting the approaching convoy.

The first explosion detonated just as the lead police vehicle passed a stationary van which burst into flames – the shock wave hurling it on its side, killing all three occupants instantly and setting off a wailing siren. Customers in a café opposite were thrown backwards amidst upturned tables, chairs and flying shards of glass. Windows were blown out. People screaming. Others threw themselves onto the floor, attempting to shield loved ones. Some instinctively ran, abject terror written all over their faces: others stood rooted to the spot. Frozen in terror.

Without the option to reverse, the driver of the Mercedes reacted instinctively and swung his vehicle violently to the right in an attempt to turn into a side street. Before completing the manoeuvre, a secondary explosive device detonated, ripping apart an empty vehicle at the corner of the junction – partially blocking it off. Having fired the explosive devices remotely, two masked figures in jeans and sweatshirts carrying AK47s climbed out of a van twenty metres beyond the shattered and burning wreck of the lead police car and started calmly walking towards the ambassador's stationary Mercedes. Firing aimed volleys on semi-automatic and casually changing magazines as they went, witnesses later reported that both men had been smiling.

Smoke from the two burning vehicles refused to disperse, now screening out the sun. In accordance with their training, the driver and escort made no attempt to get out of the locked Mercedes and prayed that its armour would defeat the pummelling it was receiving from 7.62-millimetre bullets fired at disturbingly close range. Instantly dismounting from the second vehicle and sheltering behind the front doors of the unprotected Range Rover, the SF driver and escort crouched down and returned fire, deliberately drawing attention to themselves. One of the soldiers was struck twice and fell to the ground. Seconds later, his partner – the driver – took a round in the throat.

In the front vehicle, repeatedly hit by bullets, the Ambassador had thrown himself onto the floor – Ben instinctively piling on top to offer added protection. The reinforced windscreen mercifully did its job and refused to shatter. On seeing the police car explode, both members of the covert SF team sprinted down the street towards the flames. The first to arrive dropped to one knee and fired two rounds at the shooter to his front, knocking him off his feet. His partner, talking calmly into his concealed radio as he did so, then moved out from behind a grocery truck and put two bullets into the head of the other assailant, and a further two rounds into his chest.

All firing stopped. It went momentarily quiet until the throaty sound of a motorbike was heard approaching up the side street; its masked and helmeted rider steering the machine with one hand, the other clutching a hand grenade. As he reached the junction, two red dots appeared on his chest. The accompanying short bursts of controlled fire knocked him backwards off the motorbike, sending it crashing on to its side. The grenade rolled free and, its pin already removed, exploded under a parked car. The rider lay lifeless on the road.

As smoke began to disperse, the screams of injured pedestrians intensified and more police sirens joined the chorus. The wounded SF soldiers were given emergency medical treatment where they lay but one was beyond help. Unharmed but clearly in shock, the Ambassador was helped out of the back of the bullet-ridden vehicle and, for reasons of security, bundled into an office doorway by two of the soldiers, later joined by Ben and the Political Counsellor.

****

The squadron commander announced the imminent arrival of the Quick Reaction Force which had rapidly left the Embassy on receipt of the first *"contact – wait out"* over the radio. National policemen were doing their best to remove bodies from the burnt police vehicle and generally reassert their authority. The dead Chechens were carefully searched and photographed, their weapons made safe, bagged and handed over to the police. Fire engines eventually arrived to put out burning vehicles and medical teams set up triage points to assess priorities for casualty evacuation. It would be several hours before some semblance of order was restored. The squadron commander stayed by the Ambassador while his squadron sergeant major supervised the removal of their wounded colleagues. Ben called Mary and gave her a brief account of the incident.

****

Word of the attempted assassination reached London within the hour – just ahead of Sky News and CNN. Thankfully, all bodies had been removed before photographers arrived, but graphic images somehow found their way onto social media. Everard called Mary and, in the presence of Brian Finlay, asked for her assessment.

"We think there's still one unaccounted for," she said, "He, or maybe she, is either going to call it a day and go home: or, which on the evidence thus far seems more likely, attempt a final act of defiance. As to likely targets – I'm afraid your guess is as good as mine."

Looking over at Brian, Everard said, "Thank goodness for armoured vehicles. Where's Bremner?"

"Corfu as far as I know," she said – Emma listening intently.

****

She was right. Guzim and Bremner were sitting outside at the villa enjoying a pre-dinner drink on the patio. Bujar was devouring his food in the kitchen. It had been a frenetic thirty-six hours and, for his part, the old man was once again showing his age and slumped in a chair, fixated at the twinkling lights on the mainland across the bay. His reception at the funeral in Montenegro had surprised him. *"Humbled"* was the word he used to Bremer on the way home. Unable to put a name to most of those he'd met, the significance of his position at the very top of the organisation was only now beginning to sink in.

Strangely, his elevation to the Chairmanship, albeit by default, felt almost pre-ordained: as though it was his destiny. Having given it some thought, he felt comfortable with the decisions he'd taken and, although in no sense of the word a proper *"consiglieri"*, it had unquestionably helped having Bremner alongside. The man had good instincts: didn't seem to get flustered and weighed his advice carefully before proffering it. There was, Guzim decided, definitely more to the man than appearances might suggest. "Pity he isn't Albanian," he mused, "probably not nasty enough."

Looking across at his guest, "Callum," he said, "as you have seen first-hand in recent days, violence is never far below the surface in my world and, as we are fond of saying here, *"wise men sleep with a sword in their hand"*. Frankly, I'm not sure this sort of life is to be recommended and, to be honest, any motive I have for involving you is purely selfish."

Bremner was unsure where the conversation was heading but chose not to interrupt.

"It's complicated," Guzim continued. "I say that because there's no black and white in my business affairs – only grey. My reason for trying to tempt you into some form of business partnership has everything to do with the debt I owe you."

Bremner was about to say something but reached for his glass instead. They were both drinking tequila.

"I like and respect you: you give wise counsel. It has been invaluable." Guzim paused for a sip from his glass. "I have therefore decided, Callum," he said, "that I shall try and repay my debt another way and, in doing so, honour will be satisfied. In brief, I have arranged that, on my death, you will inherit this villa. Hopefully later rather than sooner," he said laughing.

Bremner's laughter was masking a loss for words. "Guzim," he said eventually. "As far as I'm concerned – which I have said to you many times – there's no debt to repay. I nonetheless thank you for the friendship and generous hospitality you have extended to me in recent weeks. You are right when you say I'm unsuited to your world. Prison marked me. I have no wish to return behind bars. And, for that reason, I agree it makes sense for us to go our separate ways."

Guzim, taking another long drink said, "Callum, please listen carefully to what I have to say. The arrangements have been made. As an insurance policy in the unlikely event that anyone should seek to contest my Will, I have shared my intentions with Marku Jashari and his father. What you should also know is that, for lack of an heir, it is now written into my Will that Marku will inherit all my business interests. I have stipulated that, as a condition, thirty per cent of the annual profit goes to my distant relations in Albania. There will be no dispersal of assets. The son of one of my second cousins is at college in London – Hashim Shala – for whom I have set up a trust fund. Who knows, maybe one day he'll take over."

Bremner concealed his surprise, now realising he had profoundly underestimated the regard in which Guzim held Marku Jashari. "So," Guzim continued, "as regards you… my Will stipulates that, on my death, this villa and all fixtures and fittings will come to you. What you choose to do thereafter is your business. My solicitors in London have been given your contact phone number. The matter is settled but, since I don't plan on dying anytime soon, we will remain friends. I have arranged a flight back to London for you tomorrow."

Bremner smiled. "Thank you," he said, still trying to get his head round the remarkable turn of events and the old man's extraordinary generosity. The fact that he didn't actually need the legacy was completely immaterial. Both men stood up, embraced and walked into dinner.

Just as they did so, a lone figure began climbing the steep cliff leading up from the cove, directly below the villa. Although well off being vertical, at over eighty metres in height and comprising loose rock interspersed with thin scrub, it was still a daunting undertaking in darkness. The sound of the sea could be heard below and the scent of mimosa and lavender contrived to make it an almost mystical setting beneath twinkling stars and a First Quarter moon.

Lightly dressed in dark chinos, a black tee shirt and trainers, the perspiring figure was thankful for the headscarf to absorb his sweat. Slung across his back was a small sack containing a Russian pistol with silencer, hand grenade, small knife, gaffer tape, plastic ties and a water bottle. All his pockets were empty apart from a bracelet – his *"Tasbih"* with thirty-three hand-crafted prayer beads.

He had spent the previous twenty-four hours familiarising himself with the area, concluding that climbing up from the cove was the only viable way to the villa which, he was sure would have all manner of sophisticated alarms, armed guards and electronic security. Less likely on the seaward side he had reasoned. Having observed evening prayers, albeit without his prayer mat, he doubted he would see another sunrise. Curiously, he didn't feel alone and neither was he frightened. He profoundly believed God had guided him to this place and that He alone would decide his fate.

The patio was empty as he slid silently over the low wall and slipped into the shadow of the pine trees. Reassuringly, no movement-activated alarm systems sounded. Panting hard, he knew the priority was to recover his composure – not to mention his breath. But, in his favour, there was no time constraint. He was in control of the agenda and the biggest challenge he would face was not succumbing to sleep as seductive music surrounded the patio lit by small oil lamps on bamboo rods. The house was also illuminated by cleverly positioned up-lighting from the flower beds. Steam was coming off the bubbling Jacuzzi which, like the infinity pool, had built-in spotlights.

The vibrant sound of cicadas masked his movements as he squatted down, removed the sack, took a long drink from the water bottle and then lifted out the revolver and screwed on the silencer. Placing his Tasbih on his wrist he began to adjust his night vision to the patio lighting.

377

The old man suddenly appeared clutching what looked like a glass of wine and sat down by the side of the pool. He was accompanied by a tall, thin man. They were laughing at something, but the conversation was unintelligible from his place in the bushes – not that it mattered because he only spoke Chechen and Russian. After ten minutes or so, the tall man stood up and went into the house, leaving the old man on his own. Emerging from the bushes with his revolver pointed at the seated man's head, he silently signalled for him to stand up. Guzim, unarmed and temporarily alone, suddenly felt extremely vulnerable. This intruder appeared in total control and without the slightest tremor in the hand holding the pistol pointing at him.

Motioning he wanted Guzim to turn around, which was steadfastly refused, he walked over and, roughly grabbing him, quickly began trying to secure his wrists with a plastic tie. Eventually succeeding, and with the Albanian screaming profanities, he started pulling him towards the low wall overlooking the cliff. At that moment, a man came running out of the building onto the patio and, stopping in his tracks, began reaching behind his back. Two muffled shots from the Chechen hit their mark and the security guard collapsed abruptly onto the tiled floor, oozing blood and still clutching his unfired pistol.

Guzim, now realising what his assailant was trying to do continued to struggle but was being dragged inexorably towards the low wall. Bremner then returned and saw the inert body of the security guard. Peering round a stone pillar, he watched the old man frantically wrestling with a man in black. Quickly turning round, he raced down to his room to get his own pistol, quickly loading it as he ran back up to the patio. He then heard the old man cry out and realised that the intruder was obviously trying to throw him off the cliff. The risk of firing and hitting Guzim was, he knew, very real. His view was then partially blocked as a blurred shape shot past him and flew directly towards the furious struggle going on by the wall.

Snarling and moving incredibly fast, Bujar launched himself at the man and his master, hitting the Chechen in the back with such force he toppled forward over the wall and, still clutching Guzim, disappeared with him into the darkness. Remarkably, there were no screams. Everything went ominously quiet, including, temporarily, the cicadas.

Bujar stood with his paws on the wall facing outwards and began howling mournfully. Bremner, hardly believing what he'd seen, repeatedly called the dog's name as he walked slowly forward in an attempt to calm him. Checking the security guard for any signs of life – of which there were none – he went back to his room and put on a thin pair of latex gloves stowed in the inside pocket of his bag. Then, having unloaded and wiped the handgun and replaced it in its box, he walked into Guzim's room and put it in a cupboard. Returning to the patio, he slipped a lead over Bujar and led him inside to the kitchen which, being the housekeeper's night off, was empty. After giving the dog a biscuit and settling him into his basket, he closed the door.

Back in Guzim's bedroom, he removed the sim card from the old man's iPhone and, using the burner, fired off a text to Monaco: *"Unforeseen development at this location – host and unexpected guest both departed – assumed dead; blue lights summoned and expected shortly. Might need consular support. Staying on this phone. Acknowledge."* The reply came back almost immediately, *"Acknowledged."*

"What else," he asked himself, "needs doing?" There was no desktop in the villa and he knew that Guzim was fastidious about not keeping email or a contact list on his laptop. It would be clean. Most of his messaging was by phone. Pulling out his own phone and before initiating *"Factory Settings"*, he fired off a quick text to Marku telling him what had happened and that the arrival of the police was imminent. The reply was instantaneous: first to express sadness and then thanking him for the heads-up and saying he would make sure the Council were informed immediately. That done, Bremner removed the sim card and put the phone in a drawer in Guzim's study. After a last quick look around, he hit the security alarm button on the wall triggering a loud wailing noise, flashing exterior lights and, most importantly, summoning the police. Walking back to the kitchen he ditched the latex gloves and, looking down at him, gave Bujar a second biscuit.

28

CALLUM BREMNER sat alone in his boat drifting slowly across the loch – his loch. Hearing a familiar cry above him, his eye was drawn to a joust between two raptors competing for a fish. A motionless Grey heron stood observing from the shallows. Several trout had already fallen prey to the tantalizing team of three wet flies cast effortlessly across the boat's wake and, with the sky darkening and the expected appearance of rain, there was more sport to be had.

The croft had been painstakingly repainted: the white colour suited it. The place was looking halfway respectable and his next task was to paint the outbuildings and make a start on the small allotment in which, until now, he had never shown much interest.

Three months had passed since he came back from Corfu, an obligatory two weeks of debriefing at the cottage in Kent accorded top priority. Mrs Grant had declared him *"far too skinny"* and took it upon herself to put matters right – drawing heavily on produce harvested from what he still regarded as his vegetable patch. There was to be no female company this time, just a team of unfamiliar, intense and not very interesting *"suits"*. The exception was a visit from Mary Stewart, whom he had last seen at the ferry terminal – on that memorable occasion with Emma at her side staring expressionless behind dark glasses. His lasting impression from that hot day was of two consummate professionals. No betrayal of emotion. Alert and taking it all in. He had neither seen nor heard from Emma since coming home and, for reasons he didn't fully understand, had made no effort to call her.

Thanks to Mary's prompt action, as soon as the Greek police investigation in Corfu was completed – greatly assisted by the consular staff representative from Athens having attested to him and Guzim Shala being fellow cons in the UK and conveniently producing an extract from his prison record – he had been spirited away to London by private charter jet. After a protracted search, the body of the dead Chechen was recovered from the sea, together with his bag and its incriminating contents. Guzim Shala's corpse was found two days later and he was officially declared dead by a local judge. Ironically, the tidal current had carried it into Albanian waters, within sight of where Saban, Jo and the others had died in the waters off Ypsos.

On completion of his debriefing, Mary rang to say she would be in touch after he'd had some time off. *"Things to talk about,"* she'd said. Next day, the last thing he did before leaving the cottage – receiving a farewell hug from Mrs Grant and checking his green beans for the last time – was to hand a letter to one of the minders. It contained his resignation.

The decision was uncomplicated. He knew it was time to move on; retake ownership of his life and, critically, no longer have to keep looking over his shoulder. A fresh start which, thanks to the generosity of Mr Guzim Shala, and other assets owned in his real name, meant he was financially independent – albeit, in the case of the villa, tied up with his alias as *"Callum Bremner"*. He did not see the name thing being a problem since, for reasons of security, it had been agreed as a condition of his retirement from the Security Service that he would be allowed to keep all key aspects of the Bremner legend for a period of two years – *"just in case someone comes looking"*. He planned on discreetly selling the villa within in six months and had no plans to visit. Anyway, he reasoned, there was little point making it too easy for anyone looking to find him. His croft and the other properties were a different matter. It, and they, had been in his family for generations.

The only other loose end, which he eventually decided to ignore since it was no longer his concern, was responding to a brief text message he had received from Marku Jashari asking him to get in touch. He assessed the likelihood of a chance encounter with the man to be minimal. In fact, he no longer saw any reason to venture south of the Border. Scotland had everything he needed. Well, almost.

****

Now late afternoon, a prone figure lay in the heather on the higher ground: an uninterrupted view of the loch and approaches. The weather was conducive to being outdoors. The usual squadrons of winged midges were mysteriously absent, no doubt on manoeuvres mercilessly tormenting innocent folk elsewhere. There was a chill in the air; he was starting to feel cold. The telescopic scope on the rifle was precisely calibrated to the required distance which, he accepted, would test his marksmanship. The fading sun was behind him and a strengthening breeze moving from right to left. Making a further small adjustment to the sight, he chambered a round and began the process of controlling his breathing. *Relax, nice and calm, slowly squeeze the trigger.*

In the distance a vehicle was making its way slowly up the track but, not in his eye-line, the driver was hidden in shadow. The car stopped in front of the building. Unloading the rifle and pocketing the round, he slowly stood up. The wooden crate with the black target rings two hundred metres away would have to wait for another day.

A figure climbed out of the vehicle and opened the boot, at which point a four-legged, fawn coloured giant with black muzzle, nose and ears leapt out. Cocking a leg and contemptuously peeing on the rear wheel, it sniffed the air, turned to the approaching figure with the rifle and raced up the hill towards him. The driver, laughing as Bujar barrelled into Bremner – knocking him over and rolling on top – removed the hat and shook out her blonde hair – sparkling green eyes fixed on the man she had come a long way to find. "Thank God for Brian Finlay and his tracking devices," she said – a beaming smile on her face as she walked towards the brawl going on in front of her.

To be continued…

Acknowledgements

One of my better decisions was to share an early draft of the manuscript with a select group of family and close friends, many of whom will find characterisations of themselves in the book. Their counsel was invaluable: often uncomfortably frank but unfailingly constructive. RF's advice was incredibly helpful at the outset of the project and I will always be indebted to CT for her instincts, judgement and forbearance. Her guidance through the labyrinthine process to publication was a godsend. In similar vein, I feel incredibly fortunate to have entered into collaboration with my publishers at the Endless Bookcase, Carl French and Morgana Evans, both of whom have shown, quite literally, 'endless' patience.

As my mentor, RB's encouragement persuaded me to complete the series. His and JR's forensic editing and feedback on the initial draft were well received. So, too, the insightful feedback of MR, TR, DL and, most especially, IG. I am also enormously grateful to CB for his assistance in Scotland tramping through bogs when helping me to acquire imagery for the book cover, not to mention applying his sharp eye to painstakingly reviewing the penultimate draft. I would also like to place on record my sincere appreciation to all those who so kindly took the trouble to review my book.

Finally, I want to thank my wife and family for their love, encouragement and unending practical advice and support. As will be seen in the next book, the principal character, Callum Bremner, moves ever deeper into a duplicitous world in which little is as it appears and where wise men do indeed sleep with a sword in their hand.